Never Go There

Rebecca Tinnelly lives amongst the twisted sessile oaks of the Somerset coast with her two children and two cats. No doubt fuelled by the stories she was told by her stepmother, a consultant pathologist, Rebecca is most interested in writing about the darker side of society and family life. After a successful career in sales, most recently selling wicker coffins, she waved goodbye to the office to pursue a career in writing. And, when not writing, enjoys baking the odd cake or two.

REBECCA TINNELLY

Never Go There

HODDER

First published in Great Britain in 2018 by Hodder & Stoughton
An Hachette UK company

1

Copyright © Rebecca Tinnelly 2018

The right of Rebecca Tinnelly to be identified as the Author
of the Work has been asserted by her in accordance with
the Copyright, Designs and Patents Act 1988.

A CIP catalogue record for this title is available from the British Library

Paperback ISBN 978 1 473 66449 4
eBook ISBN 978 1 473 66448 7

Typeset in Plantin Light by Palimpsest Book Production Limited,
Falkirk, Stirlingshire

Printed and bound in Great Britain by Clays Ltd, Elcograf S.p.A

Hodder & Stoughton policy is to use papers that are natural, renewable
and recyclable products and made from wood grown in sustainable forests.
The logging and manufacturing processes are expected to conform to the
environmental regulations of the country of origin.

Hodder & Stoughton Ltd
Carmelite House
50 Victoria Embankment
London EC4Y 0DZ

www.hodder.co.uk

For Aoife and Ruadhán

Prologue

The metal is cold, her arms aching from the weight as she lifts it.

In the window she sees herself, her hands gripping the object, her fingers in a claw. The moon seeps into the tableau from the black sky outside and obscures her features in the process, her face lost to the bright round orb. If she stepped forwards or back, she would see herself clearly, see the twist of her lips, the arch of her eyebrows, the tremble of her shoulders as she readies her arms.

If the other woman looked up, looked up right now, she would see their reflection in the single-glazed window.

But she doesn't.

The other woman stares, instead, at a Polaroid, held in her thin-fingered hands, her right thumb stroking the face of the man in the white-framed square.

'Thank you,' the other woman mutters, almost under her breath, and it's not clear if she's talking to her or to the man in the picture. 'For giving me this, thank you.' Her voice cracks at the end, on those difficult words.

One hard hit should be enough to knock the woman clean out.

She holds her breath.

She is ready, calm.

The other woman, the woman in front with the picture in her hands, moans. The sound is low, filled with longing, regret, her thumb still stroking that face.

That face.

That man.

Her man.

Her arms reach their summit, hands high above her head, wiry muscles taut, ready.

The thud of her heart in her chest is so strong she's sure the other woman can hear it.

Her fingers tighten around the object in her hands, her pulse beating against the cold metal, beating out the rhythm of those words. The sides of her mouth turn down, her face setting in a foul grimace.

A distant gunshot rings from the bleak hills outside, from lampers out hunting, the sound making the other woman lift her eyes to the window. Her gaze lands on their reflection.

The other woman's mouth freezes in an O.

The first thump is clean, no mess, only noise.

The blood comes with the second sharp blow, the face in the Polaroid now marked with a red spatter.

Her hands lift and pound, lift and pound, opening the other woman's head like a crushed, boiled egg.

If she looks up she would see her reflection. She would see eyes wild, open and blue, her mouth a clenched mass of teeth, dripping with spit.

But instead she looks down, at the head that's no longer a head, her hands covered in the other's blood, the man in the photograph smiling through the dark liquid.

Her original plan, the idea of a clean death, is rendered obsolete. The idea that any of this could be clean is a bad joke.

She can still make out his face, that face that's been ceaselessly haunting her. She draws her arms up then back down, again and again and again until the Polaroid drowns in the other woman's blood.

She is oblivious to the world around her, to the noises outside, to the cheers and barks from the hunters on the hill as another rabbit is shot and killed.

Her hands beat the metal through skin and through hair, through layers of skull, through the soft, squelching mass of pulped brain.

The moon the only witness to what she has done.

To what she has been driven to do.

Nuala

Friday, 17th November, 2017

It wasn't like she had imagined. The pictures online had been blue-skied, not night-dark. The branches above her car, those thin wire fingers from the stunted oaks, hadn't featured at all. But here they were – this was the road, the hill, the place.

A crack and scrape of metal, a rock hitting the car's underside. She wasn't even driving on tarmac any more, just dirt, the creaking sound reminding her of the letter box opening that morning.

She felt for the letter on the passenger seat, the paper already soft from re-reading despite having had it for just a few hours, her finger tracing the words in the dark.

The trees were close, the half-moon hidden by their thin branches, twisting to meet each other inches above the car. She could feel the thud and bump of the aerial bristling against bark. No leaves, of course, not in November with the wind lashing the hill. She knew about that, the wind. But she had always, regardless of his warnings, expected sunshine. Her fault for leaving London so late in the day. Her fault for waiting until November when she should have come in May, but it had taken her months to stockpile the courage.

Three miles to go, the Sat-Nav said. Nearly there.

Too late to call on *her* now, especially as it was unexpected. She would have to wait, do it in the morning, in the blessed sunlight.

At least there was somewhere she could stay. He had told her about the pub, about the woman there: his neighbour, friend, the woman he'd turn to when his mother's attention got too much.

That's two people in the village who would welcome her. She was sure they would, even if she *had* come alone, ignoring his warnings about the kind of place this was. Not like London: the neighbours they used to nod to but never converse with, the endless hem of pavements, the anonymity. This place was different. Close was the word he had used, his mouth in a sneer as he spoke. Neighbours in each other's business, in each other's houses, lives. No privacy. No understanding. No desire to change.

But surely it *would* have changed?

Because places do change, people do change, in seven years. Even he would have admitted that, Nuala was sure of it.

The moon shone through the car window, the wood behind her now, an expanse of night-grey grass in its place, a glint of dark sea in the distance.

Nuala was here. Even if the letter had been addressed to him only, asking him to come, Nuala was here. She could already feel the arms around her, the press of a palm on her back and a 'Come in, come in!' The warm vapour of tea in the air. The insistence that she should stay, for as long as she wanted, needed.

The moon vanished again, hiding behind a cloud this

time, the reflected light dirty grey. And the road was sinking down.

Two miles to go.

The headlights caught a sign, low gear advised, the slope steep. The track lurched into the combe, winding between more stunted trees and barren hedges. A dip, a corner, and the road plummeted downhill.

Nuala gripped the wheel, reduced her car to a crawl. No option for a low gear, not in an automatic, and she had visions of the car skidding down, gathering speed until the bitter end, when metal and glass would meld with the stunted oak trees and their writhing branches would claim her.

But the wheels held true, the car slowed and the tyres gripped the road.

The letter had slipped from the passenger seat and lay in the foot-well, shadowed. The envelope remained on the seat, showing his name above the address of the house they had shared in London, scrawled in a harsh, black hand and bearing the postmark of a town she had passed nearly an hour before.

Nuala had Googled Taunton many times, so too the Quantocks, but the village she was heading for remained a stubborn mystery. The most she had found was a petition from the local newspaper, trying to force BT to install decent broadband for the residents. It had failed.

The road carried on down, lower and lower until the bleak plateau seemed a dream. The trees became bigger, trunks thicker, branches heavy with dying leaves, protected from the wind by the banks of the combe.

Everything looked bleak at night, that was all. In the sunlight it would be beautiful, just like she'd imagined, and the hills would protect Nuala, keep her safe, help her heal.

But the road sank down and her gut went with it.

Half a mile to go.

The trees thinned, hedges remained, the road levelled out. The first house of the village lit up in the glare of the headlights. Cracked plaster, sagging thatch.

She had reached her destination.

She left her car at the side of the road, outside the house she had come all this way to visit. The clock on her dashboard read 7.30 p.m., but the lights in this house were all out. Nuala didn't like to knock in the dark. A woman living on her own may not answer, and she needed that first impression to be a good one, considering the news she was bringing.

She grabbed her bag, slipped the letter into her pocket. Her empty back pocket. Idiot. She'd forgotten her phone, again. Probably no reception here anyway, but the torch from the camera would have been useful. There wasn't a single streetlight.

She picked her way between piles of rotting leaves and horse shit, her boots made for pavements, not dirt. The moon, at least, was visible again but the wind had returned, nipping her through her jeans and sweater. No coat. *Idiot.*

The road bent round and then there was the pub he'd told her about, spoken of fondly enough, for Nuala to know it was safe. That Maggie would be there, that she would surely look after Nuala just as she had looked after him.

It looked more like a house than a bar, a small cottage with a sign above the door and lead hatching on the windows, the glass a warm red that told her a fire was lit somewhere inside. She had the urge to knock but held back, took a breath, and stepped in.

The warmth hit her first, a wall of heat from the fire,

sending her nose and eyes streaming, vision blurring. She could make out the shape of a man at a table, the orange glow from the hearth, a figure behind the bar. The smell of spilt ale, wood smoke and cider.

'All right?' A voice came from behind the beer taps.

Nuala blinked her vision clear and sniffed, hiding her nose with her hand. The room was just as he'd described it. Low ceiling, small, stuffed with three chairs, the card table, a sleeper bolted to the wall in place of a bar and it was too much, too accurate, he should have been there with her.

Why had she come alone? She needed him here, needed him to tell her what to do, what to say.

'All right?' Louder this time, impatient, and the woman at the bar was staring. Her hands, red and raw-looking, were drying glasses with a rag. Blond hair hung either side of her face, a face far younger than the state of her hands would imply, her top lip bitten between her teeth.

Nuala had no idea who this woman was, there were no stories she fit into. She was expecting Maggie, older and greyer and fatter by far, not this young thing with thin arms and narrow shoulders, the small, pointed features of a nymph.

Places change, she'd told herself. People change. What if too much had changed? What if none of it was as she'd been told?

A cough from the man at the card table, a whiff in the air of stale clothes.

'I was looking for a room . . .' Nuala tried to stay steady but the heat, after the cold wind outside, made her body sway, pulse jump.

The air was so damn close.

The woman at the bar put the glass down, threw the rag

on the floor out of sight. Her lips were tight together, brow furrowed and Nuala was sure she was about to say no, no you can't, but then the woman sighed and rubbed the creases from her brow.

'How long for?' she asked Nuala.

The man at the table got up, lumbered to the bar and Nuala noticed his feet, shod in work boots, were impossibly small. Size four, maybe five.

'Just tonight,' Nuala said, hoping it was true, hoping that, by tomorrow, she'd be somewhere else. Have someone else. That she hadn't come all this way for nothing.

'I'll take you up.' The voice came from the man, his back still to Nuala, the curls of his grey hair growing over the collar of his red plaid shirt. His trousers were corduroy, a dirty, pale brown, and he was short, five foot three and an easy four stone overweight. He hid his mouth in the crook of his elbow, coughed into the fabric. 'We've just the one room.'

The voice was all wrong, the cough clearing the airway, making it softer. It wasn't a man after all.

Nuala had expected Maggie to wear florals and aprons, her hair short but femininely styled. She never pictured her wearing men's clothing, never thought her grey hair would be so short at the sides, a curled mullet growing to the nape of her thick neck.

'Give us your details, then I'll take you up,' Maggie said, turning around. And there was the scar he'd described, running from her cheek to her jaw bone and disappearing into the folds of her double chin.

'Do you take credit cards?' Nuala asked, searching in her bag for the wallet she knew was hiding inside, somewhere. Her fingers, still cold from outside, fumbled and missed, the wallet falling to the floor and skidding to a halt by the serving hatch. 'I'm an idiot,' she said, to herself more than Maggie. 'Such an idiot.'

'No, you're not, it's easily done.' Maggie bent down and lifted the wallet, and offered it back with a smile, her scar creasing. 'Cash only, don't take cards.' She nodded to the young woman behind the bar, who in turn looked up like a doe caught in headlights, 'Give Emma your name and a tenner as deposit. Any bags?'

Nuala thought of the baby clothes in bin bags at home, of the suitcases full of jumpers, coats, jeans she'd left behind in her London attic, two hundred miles away.

'Just this one, I can handle it,' she said, even though it was dragging her shoulder down, even though her heart sank at the reminder of the bags and bags of things she'd left behind.

'Name?' asked Emma, a blue-covered exercise book appearing on the wooden sleeper in front of her, pen poised above the empty page.

The letter throbbed like a heart in Nuala's pocket, her own pulse weak in comparison. *Come back,* it read, reminding her of why she was here, who she was here for, *please come back to me.*

'Mrs James,' she said, averting her gaze as Emma wrote it down.

Mouth dry, she turned and followed Maggie up the stairs, telling herself it wasn't an outright lie, just a fib, that everyone gave a fake name when they went away, it was normal. That it was best, for now, that they didn't know who she was.

She'd tell them afterwards, when she'd been to see *her*, explained about *him*.

And the letter throbbed on in her pocket.

Emma

Friday, 17th November, 2017

The woman had a Burberry bag. Emma had clocked it as soon as she walked in. She'd kill for that bag, for those well-cut black jeans, for the boots, for the jumper, the lot.

The woman had arrived two hours ago, hadn't been downstairs since, hadn't asked for any food, no drink. What was she doing up there? And why was she here, out of season, not dressed for walking, nor hunting, clearly not a tourist?

Women travelling solo, complete with designer bags, didn't come to a place like this. *Emma* wouldn't be in a place like this if she didn't have to be.

She looked into the room from behind the bar, pretending the bag, jeans, boots were on her, pretending she, for once, was an outsider seeing the pub for the first time.

An old man in a gravy-stained cardigan, falling asleep at the fire. Windows that let in a draught, their frames either cracked or warped with damp. Damask armchairs that, a decade after the ban, still smelled of stale cigarettes. A floor that looked dirty, no matter how many times Emma got on her knees and scrubbed her hands red raw on the stains.

A pit. She'd see a pathetic pit not even half full on a Friday night, the main custom coming from a table of twats drinking the cheapest beer on offer, one blond prick, in particular, keeping his back well turned to Emma.

She'd see a glimpse of Emma's life. Emma's future.

It was meant to be so much better than this.

What's *her* life like, Emma wondered, looking at the slice of light filtering through the floorboards from the guest bedroom above. The woman hadn't made a sound upstairs, no footsteps on the creaking floorboards, no tap running or water glugging in the chipped sink.

But the light was still on, she must be awake.

What was she doing up there?

Emma looked at the register, the blue-covered exercise book, staring up from its place by the till. *Mrs James,* she'd called herself.

The name, *that* name, was a ripple, a shot of adrenaline, bursting from her innards out. Even the penmanship was shaky where Emma had written the name down.

That name. *James*.

It was a common one.

A coincidence.

But if Emma had been in charge, had been alone when the woman arrived, she would have taken more details. She'd have taken her first name for starters, her address, phone number, written down her debit card details.

Maggie was too desperate for the income, that was her problem. Too eager to keep the charge cash-in-hand, off the books and away from the tax man's sharp eye. Didn't care who stayed there, as long as they left their deposit.

But Emma: she would have got enough to Google the woman, find out who she was, where she lived, how she afforded a bag like that one.

Her finger slid over the screen of her phone, one eye on the bar to make sure no one was watching.

Dwelling on Mrs James would get her nowhere, would only bring up memories she'd rather forget. And if she typed that surname into Google, the auto-fill would suggest the rest of a different name, and she wouldn't do that, search for that. She hadn't searched that name in months.

She put her phone back down on the counter, noticed the splash of beer on her jeans, the bleach mark on her cheap, black t-shirt. Told herself not to care what people thought of her, a mantra Emma had been repeating since the age of fourteen when she left home (*left*; as if the choice had been hers) and moved into Maggie's, her godmother's, spare bedroom.

At least she had a job, even if it was shit, made her hair stink of rotten fruit and dried yeast. At least she was educated, had A Levels, GCSEs and bloody good ones at that. And so what if her father hadn't talked to her, properly, sincerely, in the seven long years since he'd blamed her for . . . for what? Which part of that terrible time had he laid flat down at her feet? She didn't know. He wouldn't talk to her and she had no other living parent to ask. But she had Maggie, she wasn't alone.

What did she care what some blow-in thought of her anyway? But her eye caught the corner of the register again, remembered the name inside.

She looked into the bar, the place she was never meant to stay for so long.

Closed her eyes, clenched her fingers around the edge of the counter, remembered the face, the man, the shitty mess seven years ago that had led her to this point.

'Beer, ta.'

She opened her eyes, clocked the blond prick at the bar. Plastered a smile on her lips, softened her eyes, said, 'Of course, I'll get right on to it.'

She kept the smile there whilst the beer flowed into the glass, her fist tight around the cold, brass lever.

'You're looking pale,' Toby said, leaning over the bar and taking his drink from her hand. 'You all right?'

Emma looked up from the beer tap, smile still fixed on her face, met his eye, held it. 'I'm fine; why wouldn't I be?'

Toby smiled back, had the audacity to look sheepish. 'I was worried I'd upset you,' he said.

What a prick.

He lowered his voice, looked behind him at the table of his friends by the window, back to Emma and said, 'You understand?'

'There's nothing to understand.' Her cheeks were aching with the smile she wouldn't give up, not for him. 'I'm over it already.'

He looked relieved, brushed back his blond hair with one hand. Gave her that look, the half-smile that brought out the laughter-lines on one side, made his bright blue eyes crease at the corners.

'So,' Toby looked over his shoulder again, made sure no one was watching, 'you up for tonight?'

'Up for what, exactly?' Hands beneath the bar, she picked at her fingers, at the old bleach scars adorning her knuckles.

'You know,' Toby said, looked behind him again, moved his arm across the bar and stroked the bare skin on her arm, his touch light and swift, goosebumps spreading from Emma's wrist upwards.

She looked at him standing there, his childlike blond hair and blue eyes, his breath full of hops. Thought how, two days ago, two weeks ago, a month, she had thought him so damn hot that it hurt.

'You want to come upstairs?' she whispered, leaning in. 'Take the room opposite mine, sneak over once Maggie's gone to bed?'

She kept her eyes on his, still aware of the chink of light coming through the floorboards above, of the woman upstairs, of the room she had taken, the room Toby had slept in last week. And the week before that.

Toby craned forward, nodded, said, 'Yeah, let's do it.' Licked his lips and Emma thought of his tongue, of his mouth on hers, on her naked body, and shuddered.

She leant in further, her mouth by his ear, just the wooden bar separating their bodies.

'We're over,' she whispered, her breath brushing his earlobe, making him quiver, 'I deserve better than a fuckwit like you.'

He jumped back, blushed and looked back over his shoulder but none of his friends bothered looking up.

'Come on, Em,' he said, louder this time. 'Don't be like that.'

'Like what? Pissed off that you told me we were together, a cute little item, yet you denied me, completely, in front of your friends?'

'Keep your voice down,' Toby said, looking backwards again, his friends laughing together, oblivious.

'See?' Emma said, laughing to herself, wanted to add, you're a twat, but it would get her in trouble. 'Go sit down,' she told him instead.

She watched him walk back to his table of friends, saw him shrug off her insult, melt back into the conversation.

It was true, she deserved better than this.

Better than a small, crappy pub in the middle of nowhere, nothing to offer her but ignorant locals. Toby was laughing, along with his friends, looking at her and laughing again.

She shouldn't be here. She should be somewhere else, living a life so very different from this. She shouldn't be here.

'Yours, is it? A new one?'

Emma's ears pricked, head tilted towards the table, listening to Toby and his friends discuss an unfamiliar red car parked in the village. She lifted a pint glass, started polishing it with a cloth, hands occupied to cover her eavesdropping.

'Not mine,' said Timmer, a fat ginger lad with a Barbour thrown over his chair. 'Some grockle's, most likely.'

Was it hers then, upstairs? There was no car outside the pub, Emma had checked. If it was hers, the woman must have parked somewhere else and walked over. If she'd parked outside, Emma would have taken the details, registration, gone online to see what she could find.

'Why the fuck are they visiting Shore Road?' asked Robbie Burrows, son of the old man half asleep by the fire.

The glass dropped from her hands, smashed, all the men looked up, stopped talking.

Shore Road.

Mrs James.

Emma dropped below the bar, leant her back to the counter, bottom on the floor, pretended to clean up but she could barely move, barely breathe.

She had only been half serious, suspecting a link. Had thought it a coincidence, nothing more. But the location, the name, the possibility started seeping in, turning her blood cold even though her cheeks burned.

The memories started flooding in, her mind ticking backwards, ignoring the customers, Edward Burrows, the old man sitting by the fire, calling out, 'You all right?'

She heard footsteps on the stairs, Maggie coming up from the cellar. Thank God, Emma needed to get out, needed to walk the memories away, leave the bar to her godmother for the night.

Emma had always known that one day, this would happen.

Maggie

Friday, 17th November, 2017

Maggie gripped the gas canister between her hands, the cylinder thicker than a man's neck. She lifted it up without a groan of complaint or a struggle and hefted it to the wall, clicking it securely in place. Her arms tingled from their load, reminding her of her age, reminding her, too, of her strength despite it.

A crash from upstairs, a glass breaking.

A thump on the floor, directly above Maggie's head, as though someone had slumped to the ground by the till.

Emma.

Maggie looked around her; the last of the barrels not yet hooked up, the letters strewn on the third step down and the landline phone, still warm from where her hand had clutched it, lying face up beside them.

She couldn't leave it like this. Emma might find them, the typed letters received in the post, Maggie's reply handwritten and ready to send. She couldn't work that computer upstairs, not even after Emma tried giving her lessons. Besides, a handwritten note was more sincere, more likely to tug at the heartstrings, draw sympathy. And if she typed it up there was a chance that Emma might see.

And she couldn't let that happen.

A curse from upstairs, slurred around the edges but concerning nonetheless. What was the cause of the smash, the thump? Was it the customers upstairs getting rowdy? She needed to get up there, help her goddaughter.

Maggie picked up the letters, knees groaning as she bent them, begging her, please, to lose weight. She stuffed the sheets of paper in a plastic folder, slid the folder between the barrels at the back.

The phone she left in its place. There was a chance Arthur might call back, given that she'd just hung up on him. She couldn't risk Emma hearing the landline ring, didn't want her picking up the call and hearing her father's voice on the end of the line.

'What choice do you have, Maggie?' His words still rung in her ears, her cheek and scar hot from the pressure of the handset. She had looked at the letters from the bank, her name, Mrs Bradbury, on the top line of each, cursed the fact that she shared the same name with the man on the phone, her husband's dark-hearted cousin.

Maggie headed up two steps at a time, out of breath at the top and pulse thrumming. Sixty-five next June. She was getting too old for all this.

She spread her hands on the wall by the cellar door, leaning into them to catch her breath.

A cold, wet slick on her palm, her hand reeking of mould. Damp.

The last thing she needed. It already had its grip on the rooms upstairs, the hallway carpet boggy and wallpaper black. If it was down here, too, if it reached the barrels, the stock – she closed her eyes, wouldn't think of that, she'd do something, fix it. But the letters downstairs, the empty bank account, overdraft, mortgage, the loan she hadn't the money to repay. How could she fix anything?

'Emma?' She opened her eyes, saw her goddaughter, sitting bottom down on the floor behind the bar, splinters of glass all around her.

'I'm all right,' Emma said, not trying to get up.

'What happened?' Maggie rushed to her through the archway cut out in the kitchen's plasterboard wall. 'Someone's upset you, who was it?' She looked over the bar at the room. Edward Burrows, the old man, was sitting upright in his chair by the fire, his hands raised as if to say, 'Don't ask me.' His son Robbie and his friends were sitting at the table nearest the door, shrugging in unison when Maggie looked over.

Emma shook her head, held on to Maggie's sleeve, pulled herself to standing, her face pale. Her mouth was set firm, eyes hard, but Maggie could tell, from the way her goddaughter's hands were shaking, that something had upset her more than she was willing to show. She lifted the hatch, stepped into the bar, one hand squeezing Emma's shoulder.

'Ignore them,' she whispered, still thinking it was a customer's fault, that someone had said something, some piece of gossip that had inadvertently upset her. Talked about her father, perhaps. Some new business deal raising eyebrows, or perhaps an old grudge. Memories were long in these quiet, cut-off places, Maggie knew. She only hoped, for Emma's sanity, that they hadn't been talking about the girl's own past.

She looked down at Emma's phone, lying screen-up on the counter. The screen said No Connection but the search bar was open. She'd been looking for something again. Looking for some*one*.

'I always ignore them.' Emma offered her a smile, lifted the phone and slipped it into the pocket of her jeans.

'Go put the kettle on,' Maggie told her, squeezing her shoulder again. 'I'll sort this lot.'

She should find out what had happened, who had said what and, if necessary, bar the lousy toad responsible, set an example. But she could see the table full of young, thirsty customers, the empty glasses waiting to be refilled, the wallets of cash resting among them ready to pay, thought of the bank statement she'd hidden in the cellar, the side of her face still hot from where the phone was pressed to it, *'what choice do you have?'* playing again in her ear.

'That true, what Timmer said?' A man's voice drifted over from the fireplace. Maggie turned to see the bald head of Edward, Robbie's father, visible above the top of the damask armchair.

It was out of character for the man to comment on others' conversations, to draw Maggie into talking at all. Normally his vigil by the fire was a silent one, drinking until nine o'clock when he would stumble back home to his wife of forty-five years in the terraced house they rented (on the cheap, Maggie suspected) from Arthur. The change in Edward made Maggie stop, pay him attention.

'Is what true?' she asked, rubbing the mark on her cheek where, years ago, the scar tissue had turned keloid from picking.

'There's a car out there that no one recognises,' he said, hands hugging his dimple-glass tankard. 'I wouldn't care, only it's parked right outside Lois's front door.'

News to Maggie, but she withheld her surprise, kept her face neutral to keep Edward talking. The only newcomer she had seen in the village that day was the woman now resting upstairs. But she had said nothing about a car, and Maggie couldn't be sure it belonged to her at all. She kept quiet, not sure yet what Edward was trying to tell her.

'Has Lois asked someone here, do you think?' he said.

Maggie thought of the stranger in the room upstairs, the way she had gritted her teeth, called herself stupid for something as simple as dropping a purse. If that was her car, if she was here to see Lois, then Lois would eat her alive. 'I hope not,' she said.

'So do I.' Edward looked up, his face dappled with age spots that matched the gravy marks on his white shirt. 'She's no business dragging strangers here.'

'Tea, Mags,' Emma called from the bar, placing a mug on the sleeper before slipping back out to clean up. Maggie hid the mug behind the till on the counter, cooled it down with a capful of gin.

'It's probably nothing,' Maggie said, sitting down by the fire with Edward. She could sit down for five minutes, rest her back and her arms from the strain of the barrels. Rest her head from the ache of bank statements. 'I doubt whoever owns the car means any trouble. It's too quiet around here, that's the problem. People are eager to read drama into the mundane.'

The woman upstairs hardly seemed a trouble maker. Her clothes were too neat, her manner too meek. But then again, there had been something in her eyes, when she'd given her name, handed Emma the tenner deposit. Was she a lawyer, perhaps? Or a reporter? But what story could she be looking for, way out here? And why now? Nothing of significance had happened in years, no scandal, no showdowns, nothing grisly. The last untimely death in the village had been that of Emma's stepmother, Elaine, nearly a decade before – and even though it had broken Emma's heart, losing her step-mother like that, it hadn't made the local papers. No, the woman couldn't be a journalist.

Edward shook his head, his knuckles white against the pint glass, his eyes staring into the fire. 'Arthur won't be happy if Lois has been talking out of turn to some blow-in,' he said, his mouth closing tightly before any more words could escape. He was Arthur's friend as well as his business secretary, predominantly involved in collecting the rent from the three local farms and ten houses that Arthur owned. Edward had run so many errands for that man, over the years, that Maggie was certain he knew all of Arthur's tricks for getting his way, as well as a few of his darker secrets.

Maggie remembered Arthur's voice, not half an hour beforehand, as it whispered into the phone held tight to her ear.

'What other choice do you have?' Arthur had asked her. He was family; her late husband's cousin, Emma's father for God's sake, but he hadn't offered any help, he just saw an oppor-tunity for his own gain.

She'd demanded how he knew, who he'd bribed or back-scratched to get such information, *confidential* information, about her finances.

'Trust me, Maggie,' he'd said and she'd blanched, the very thought of such a thing turning her stomach. How could she trust a man who had turfed out his own daughter when the girl was only just fourteen, when she had needed his under-standing and support the most? When she was left reeling after the death of her stepmother? Not that Maggie wanted

Emma to stay with him, considering what had happened, but she had been horrified by Arthur's response all the same.

'*I want to help you.*' The offer had sounded more like a threat.

'If someone *is* here to dig something up, with Lois that is, something to do with the past, with the –' Edward paused and looked up to the bar, made sure Emma wasn't listening in before he continued – 'with the *fire*, then Arthur won't be happy at all.' Edward's mouth drew into a tight, set line.

Maggie hadn't thought about that, that Lois could have called someone about the fire in her old house years before, the building next door to the pub. That she could be trying to blame Emma for it, again.

'The fire at Lois's house was an accident.' Maggie said sharply, trying to quash the idea before it had a chance to take root, before Emma had a chance to overhear them. 'Everyone knows that. Why would Arthur be worried about it now?'

Edward coughed, rubbed his eyes, looked away, his face suddenly showing his years. 'Forget I said anything.'

'Why would Arthur be worried?' she tried again, anything to get leverage on the man who had too much of his own, using it to get Maggie's situation laid out by the bank manager. Where else would he have found that out, knowing Maggie was down on her knees?

But Edward's jaw tightened and he looked on, clearly regretting his mistake already.

Arthur *wouldn't* be worried about the fire, Maggie reasoned, or about protecting his daughter. He hadn't done a thing when malicious gossip pointed the finger at Emma at the time; she doubted he'd intervene further seven years after the fact.

There was no other reason, as far as Maggie knew.

'You've got to ask yourself, why?' Edward muttered to the glass, the fire throwing shadows on his face. 'If it's Lois they're after, why now? And what the hell are they trying to dig up?'

Maggie wanted to say, 'Nothing, you're drunk, paranoid, that's all.' But a change in the light forced her eye to the bar before the words even left her throat.

Emma was back by the kitchen door, an apple in her hand and her eyes upturned to the ceiling, her face set in a look, a horrible look, that Maggie hadn't seen in a long, long time.

'What is it,' Maggie said, 'that he's scared they'll uncover?'

Nuala
Saturday, 18th November, 2017

Nuala woke in the same position she had slept, her arm stiff, mouth dry, questions pin-balling round in her mind. No bleary first moments of ignorance, not for her. Painfully awake, cruelly aware, from the moment she opened her eyes. The misery she felt was absolute: distracting her, blinding her to the squalid conditions of the guest room she had slept in.

The progression of dawn played out from her window, the light crawling through the trees, creeping over hills, laying bare the dull brown earth.

Years of fantasy, for this?

Her thoughts shifted to the Greater London parks back at home, to the deer, the willows, poplars, the man-made ponds. She took a breath. Another. The lush, wood-flanked fields she'd imagined had been revealed as empty plots of ploughed earth, fending off the winter with threadbare coats of frost. Dirt tracks pocked with gravel, tyre marks gouging wounds in the mud. She thought about the letter: the reason she was here. It lay folded on the bedside table. She needn't look at the words, she knew them by heart. But only two were repeated, over and over, prickling with a horse-fly of a sting:

my darling. Loving words, comforting words. A mother's letter.

She closed her eyes and pretended the letter was for her. Pretended the mother she was here to see was hers.

Maybe she wouldn't have to go back to those parks full of willow trees, the houses, roads, pavements full of strangers. Maybe this place was it. Maybe he'd told her not to come because he knew, if she did, she would never want to leave.

She waited for signs of life to emerge, for birds or scurrying foxes, but the only evidence was audible: the soft, consistent lowing of cows that rose and fell like bells, echoing from the other side of the combe.

More sounds, as if the village existed only to be heard: doors closing, engines turning over, a barking dog.

A knock, at her door.

Emma stood in the hallway, her skin pink from being scrubbed, hair still damp from the shower. She didn't smell of soap or shampoo, but rather bleach.

'Breakfast is ready,' she said.

Downstairs, the bar seemed changed, smaller even. Dark splashes marked the floor, real ale staining the wood. Nuala looked up, to where she'd been sleeping only hours before, and saw the whitewashed floorboards were stained tar-yellow.

'Different in the daylight, isn't it?' Emma spoke from the hatch, a ghost in Nuala's periphery. 'We keep the lights low at night, so it looks less like a living room and more like a bar.'

'It's the only pub here?' Nuala coughed, hoping the tremor in her voice was disguised.

Emma tilted her head, lips smiling but blue eyes cold, searching Nuala's face. 'Know much about the village?'

'No,' she said, cheeks hot. 'I just didn't see any others when I arrived.'

'It's the only pub, yes. We'd do quite well too if the locals would pay their bloody tabs. Robbie's the worst for it. His dad, Edward, too. Know them, do you?'

'I don't know anyone here.'

'If you say so.' Emma's smile returned and she nodded into the room. 'Breakfast's over there.' Turning her back she ducked, out of sight, below the hatch.

Cold toast with coagulated butter, a mug of milky coffee and an apple shared the end table by a faded damask armchair at the hearth. The chair, as she sat, heaved out a cushion-full of fetid air, stale from cigarettes, sour from spillages. She closed her eyes, pining for the perfume she'd long ago stopped wearing, appetite all but gone.

'That seat's the favourite.' Emma's voice had changed, becoming light, even friendly. It drifted from the serving hatch, nothing more than a hole in the wall between the bar and the pantry behind it. 'But be warned; you'll never make it out once you're comfortable.'

Nuala followed the sounds of Emma's movements: the harsh scratch of a scouring pad, a heave of breath. Then there was another, stronger, whiff of bleach. She was cleaning, vigorously, and Nuala realised that she wasn't damp from washing, but from work.

Emma continued, voice like a song. 'The weather's dry; good for walking, if that's why you're here?' She had stopped scrubbing. 'We get tourists, sometimes. It's the remoteness they're after but they're always disappointed when they arrive. No internet, no signal, no decent TV. That why you've come? A little peace and quiet in the middle of god-knows-where?'

Nuala blocked out the words and concentrated on the sound of Emma's voice, the heavy notes, the musical timbre, trying to repress the fear that Emma could see straight through her, that she knew why Nuala was there, who she was there to see.

Emma popped up from the hatch like a rabbit, a wry smile playing at the corners of her mouth. 'Will you be staying again tonight?'

The question, unavoidable, forced Nuala to open her eyes, bringing herself back to the bar and the chair and the one-sided conversation.

And then she saw them: hundreds of faces staring at her from the red brick fireplace.

'What are those?'

Emma jumped over the sleeper into the room, her hand brushing Nuala's shoulder in the small space.

'Polaroids. Maggie's been taking them forever.' She flicked a picture with her bleach-reddened fingers, the skin along her knuckles scaly. 'Some have been there so long they've melted to the wall.'

Nuala began working through them, realising they were of locals, all taken in the pub. She scratched the sides of her jeans with her bitten-down fingertips. When she looked to the side she saw Emma was staring at her.

'I thought you didn't know anyone here?'

'I don't.' Nuala's eyes darted back to the photographs, moving from left to right, left to right, upwards a fraction each time, heart beating like a hummingbird.

'You're looking for someone.' Emma stepped back, her own eyes darting from Nuala to the wall, following the other woman's progress.

Nuala's eyes fixed on their prize, her shoulders softened and dropped.

Halfway up the brickwork on the far right-hand side there he was, staring back with a lopsided grin from a face seven years younger than the one she remembered.

'Who is it you're looking for?' Emma spoke carefully, her tone friendly once more.

He wore the same flat cap she teased him about. A murky-looking pint glass was cradled in one hand whilst the other was raised to his brow in British military salute, soft sandy hair falling into his face, cheekbones high, eyes narrowed in that mocking way of his.

He took her breath away, all over again.

She was aware of Emma's words but had no sense of their meaning. Nuala wanted to dive into the photograph, rest her head on his chest, feel his arms wrap around her. She imagined him sitting next to her, taking her hand and telling her the story behind the photograph Blu Tacked to the wall of this tiny pub in the middle of god-knows-where.

She heard his voice, clear as glass. *Never go there, Nuala.*

She tried to breathe it away but only managed a sharp, raw gasp.

'Are you all right?' Emma was standing in front of Nuala and blocking her view, breaking the daydream.

'I'm fine, really.' She met Emma's eye and forced a smile, willing it to look natural, but couldn't hold it. Her gaze flitted back to the picture on the wall. 'I should be getting on. I'll let you know about the room.'

'Wait!' Emma blocked her way, her face a ruddy pink. 'I need your details; your *real* ones before you go.'

Nuala stood too quickly. She could feel the colour leaving her face, wondered if the barmaid had noticed too, wondered how the hell Emma had known the name Mrs James was a lie.

'I don't care that you made it all up. Everyone does it when they go away, don't they?'

She was so close that Nuala could see the beginnings of fine lines across her forehead.

'I'll need your name,' Emma's lips flickered into a smile, so brief Nuala almost missed it, 'if we're going to keep the room back.'

Nuala's chest heated, the blush spreading along her throat.

'Of course.' Her voice wavered. She pressed her lips together, rubbed her sweating palms along her thighs and told the barmaid her real name. 'It's Nuala. Nuala Greene.'

She waited for a flicker of recognition, the realisation, maybe pleasant surprise. But there was no smile, nothing.

'Greene, was that?'

'That's right.' Her jaw ached from clenching her teeth, waiting for the barmaid to double-take as she wrote the name on the back of her hand. Surely she should recognise the name?

'No Greenes in the village that I know of.'

'No.' Nuala's blush paled, mind blanked. She wished she had the letter to hold on to, the fragment of hope it offered, but she'd left it upstairs with her bag.

'Why'd you not tell me the truth yesterday?' Emma asked, scanning over Nuala's sweater, jeans, black boots.

'I'm sorry, I don't know why, I just—' Nuala trailed off, not knowing where to start, only knowing she couldn't tell Emma the real reason, not yet. Not until she had spoken to *her* first, told *her*.

Emma shrugged, looked up. 'It doesn't matter now. You're here to visit someone?' Waiting for the answer as if she was going to write that down too.

Nuala nodded, mute, whilst inside she screamed, *you should know who I am. Why don't you know who I am?*

'But not family?'

'I have to go. I'll come back, to sort out the room.' Nuala fled outside, leaving Emma alone in the bar.

Before she walked away, Nuala looked back through the lead-panelled window, watched as Emma moved towards the fireplace and stared again at the picture on the wall. Carefully, delicately, the barmaid lifted the photo and slipped it into the pocket of her jeans, leaving a paler square of stone in its wake.

Nuala

Saturday, 18th November, 2017

*Y*ou *mustn't go there, Nuala.*

His hand on her shoulder, tanned, coarse fingers digging in, forcing her to look into his eyes, wide open with urgency.

Or, perhaps, with guilt.

Never visit, never contact them. How many times had he warned her?

Yet here she was, breaking her promise.

And there was no way he could stop her.

The streets were empty, the footsteps from her leather boots amplified by the wind as she walked back towards her car. That same wind bit through her cashmere sweater, prickled her spine.

She had imagined a pretty little place, a quaint Somerset village, but the reality again proved very different. There was no uniformity: each house was made from different stone, those plastered were different colours, thatched roofs beside tiled.

The place was accessible by a single road stretched out over the hills, the road she'd driven along last night. It arrived, turned around and ran away again, fencing the community in or, possibly, keeping the world out.

Never go there, Nuala, he had said.

I'll tell her about you, I'll write, but never go there. Please, never go there.

James's voice, at its most sardonic, rang in her ears; how *pleasant* and *charming* it all was.

It had been unlike him to show such outright loathing. Normally it was hidden between soft touches and kisses: a critique of the dinner she'd cooked or a sharp look as she parked the car, making her realise, too late, she had done it wrong. And it was unlike him not to keep to his word. He had promised to tell them about her. He refused to visit, to phone, email, but he had promised to write.

He had lied.

That girl, Emma, had no idea who Nuala was, no clue as to her significance.

She could picture him here quite clearly, thanks to the photograph. There he was swinging on branches, running through the rain with his eyes obscured by drenched hair. She saw him stumbling drunk from Maggie's pub, throwing his arm around his friends.

She saw him.

He haunted her, hunted her until the cold air on the back of her neck became James's dark breath repeating her name, telling her to go, to run.

Something caught her eye. She stopped dead, front foot suspended mid-air.

Was that a movement in the cottage beside her? Was someone watching her, a shadow behind the net curtains?

She passed another house.

She looked at the terraces across the street, the windows and shadows of the place she had promised to stay away from.

No one was there. No one watched, looked out at her. It was a memory she could feel, of James's careful eyes on her back, waiting for her to slip up.

What was she thinking, acting alone?

She turned back to the road and walked on.

She could do this.

She had to.

She would get to her car, sit inside and calm down. She would gather herself before knocking on that door, seeing *her*, telling her—

She looked ahead, kept her eyes on the road, felt the slippery slick of sweat on her palms.

She lunged forward on unsteady feet, boots skidding on the damp, muddy track. The wind bit her face, her cheeks freezing as the weather chilled them faster than her own blood offered warmth. She had no coat, no hat, no scarf. Idiot. She was such an *idiot*.

Through eyes blurred with tears, she saw her car, bright and red, a radar. She fumbled for the handle but felt something else: a rough slice, papery metal curled up at the sides.

She stepped back, blinking her vision clear.

The door of her car had been mauled: four, five, six scratches hacked into the paint, exposing gunmetal-grey bodywork beneath.

Nuala traced the first of the slashes with her index finger, a whimper strangling in her throat.

She stepped closer but her smooth boots slipped on wet leaves, her hand planing the full length of her car door as she stumbled, forcing her fingertip into the sliced metal and paint.

It cut.

In an instant her finger was in her mouth, tongue searching

for the wound, wanting to seal it with her teeth, and the first retch came.

Air pushed its way out of her lungs, stomach heaving as she gagged. Bent double at the waist, her free hand holding onto the car for support, she retched.

She could smell it more strongly now: the urine, the stale smell of someone else's piss that had stained her car, running across the bodywork in wind-blasted streaks and leaving its smell to linger.

It covered her hands, her cut finger, her teeth, her lips, her tongue, the taste just as strong as the smell.

She searched for the door handle, biting her lips to stop sobbing, pulling herself in and locking the doors, forcing her eyes to close.

She tried to concentrate on regulating her breathing but all she could see was the slash to her car, the red paint flaking to the floor like dried blood. All she could feel was that cut on her finger.

Her hand reached up for the thin gold chain she wore, pulling it, fondling its charm and hiding it beneath her jersey, only to seek it out again immediately.

She raised her hand to her chest, just as she'd been taught, and felt the weight of it on her skin, the rise and fall of her ribcage as her heart beat against her palm, willing its pace to slow.

It doesn't mean anything, she told herself, opening her eyes and staring in the rear-view mirror. The scratch to the car was an accident, a child or a dog with a stick.

Her reflection didn't believe her. Void of makeup she looked corpselike, emaciated beneath her jersey and jeans, her hair limp, cheeks hollow, accentuating her bloodshot eyes.

Maybe this was why James had begged her not to come.

She pushed away those words – '*don't ever go there*'– tried to forget about the scratches and concentrate on the reason she was here.

The hope she would still be made welcome, despite what had happened so far. That she would still feel those arms around her, holding her, telling her it would all be OK.

Rehearsal, she needed rehearsal. Body language, tone of voice, the exact words she would say. She thought about it all, visualising the scene that lay before her until her heartbeat slowed and her breathing was even and deep.

As the last set of phrases took shape she opened her eyes and saw the note.

A page of plain A4, damp from condensation, had been laid down flat between the wiper and the windscreen. By turning her head to the side Nuala could read the words in all their cutting clarity, written in a scrawl so angry it had, in places, torn the page.

> *THINK BEFORE YOU PARK*
> *YOU SELFISH MORON.*
> *IF I WERE A FIRE ENGINE*
> *I COULD NOT GET PAST.*
> *SOMEONE COULD BE DEAD IN A FIRE.*
> *DEAD!*

Nuala's chin trembled, the corners of her mouth turning down, eyes hazy to the narrow street and all its shadows.

Her fingers worked her necklace, the charm moving back and forth along its chain. Her eyes were glued to the note.

She reminded herself that they didn't know who she was.

That the note was a mistake, that if they knew who she was they would never have written it. They would have been kind. Surely, they would have been kind?

But all she could think of was that horrible truth, that they didn't know, that James had never told them, never written, emailed, phoned.

That even his mother had no idea who Nuala was.

She should have parked in front of the pub, last night, and walked to the house, she knew that now. Her car would have been saved. But, her mind forever caught in the London suburbs, she'd taken the space that was located so attractively outside her destination: the house of her mother-in-law, a woman she'd heard of, talked about, imagined, but never met. A woman who clearly delighted in writing venomous *do not park* letters.

She knew, before looking up, that James's mother was watching from her window. There were no curtains for the woman to hide behind.

Outside the car, Nuala picked her way along the gravel path, uneven and weed-ridden. The cottage was tiny, a front door and one bay window beside it, the thatched roof mouldering, the rendering cracked. Her feet landed on the front step and the door sprang opened an inch, the security chain like a rusted moustache across the other woman's face.

'This about your car?'

Nuala was speechless, her rehearsals null and void.

She felt herself blush but could do nothing to stop it. She hadn't prepared herself for such a likeness, had not expected the woman to be so *young*.

'I'm looking for Mrs Lois Lunglow.' A redundant statement: the similarities between mother and son were evident in every sharp feature, every flick of her sandy hair. Even her voice had a flavour of James.

'You can't park in front of *my* house in *my* space. What if I had a car? Where would I have parked if I had a car? What if there'd been a, a—' she looked past Nuala, scanning the street either side, – 'a fire? What then, hmm?' She pulled her cheeks in, accentuating her cheekbones, high and sharp like James's. 'Well?'

'I'm not here about the note.'

'It wasn't me who did the scratches.' Her eyes met Nuala's, blue eyes, as cold as the weather. She seemed devoid of softness, the very opposite of how Nuala expected a mother to look, the opposite of what she had hoped for. 'It was *them.*'

'I don't care about the scratches. I'm just looking for Mrs Lunglow.'

'What do you mean? I'm standing right in front of you.' She closed the door with a slam only to open it again, the security chain unfastened, revealing Lois in all her James-like glory. 'Move your car.'

Lois folded her arms, pulling her cardigan closer with one hand. The sleeves didn't match the body, didn't even match each other, as if the woman had created the cardigan from a mismatch of others. With her other hand, fingers pressed tightly together, she tapped at her chest, a tic. Tap, tap, tap.

'I was hoping I could come in, Mrs Lunglow?'

'I don't know you. Why would I let you in?' She leant her head forward. 'Move your car.'

'I'm Nuala, Mrs Lunglow, Fionnuala Greene.'

Lois looked at Nuala as though she were mad, her face showing no signs of recognition, her fingers still tapping her chest, the tap, tap, tap of a pulse.

He had promised to tell her.

'I'm here about James.'

Lois untangled her arms, the fraying end of one sleeve catching her fingernail. Her face lightened, softened. 'My James?' She smiled at his name, her teeth exposed.

'Yes, your son—'

'How do you know him? You're from London, are you? Has he sent you?' She began scanning the street again, looking through Nuala, the tendons in her neck twitching as her hands smoothed and neatened her hair.

'I'm his wife, Mrs Lunglow. Won't you please let me in?'

'His wife? *His wife?*' Another stab to the gut, each word from Lois twisting the knife. 'No, no, no, he's not married, you're not his wife. I would know if he had a wife; I'm his mother, he would have told me. He *would*. Is he here with you? Is he coming?'

Six months ago

Nuala

Thursday, 11th May, 2017

Nuala was in the bathroom when the doorbell rang. Her mind had been preoccupied that day. She'd achieved a vast amount, full of manic glee. The carpeted rooms had been hoovered and dusted, the wooden floors swept, laundry hidden away. The aroma of garlicky lasagne hung in the air as their supper waited patiently to be devoured and (hopefully) praised. Nothing, at all, that could be complained about.

Lastly, with manicured hands, she had hidden a half bottle of Bollinger at the back of the fridge.

She noticed the time: past six but, outside, the sky was still light. Half an hour until he was home, until they could share their favourite supper, pop the champagne cork, touch glasses.

She pictured James riding home through the park, remembered guiltily how she'd chastised him for picking flowers there the day before, how upset he'd been with her for doing so, calling her ungrateful whilst he stabbed the stems into a vase. Those same flowers, pickerel and Joe-Pye weed, columns of purple loosestrife, were sitting in the crystal cut vase beneath the open window, their vague scent wafting through the room, mingling with the musk from her perfume before being overwhelmed by the smell from the oven.

She went to the bathroom whilst the dinner was cooking, heard the doorbell sound as she pressed the flusher.

Two navy blue shadows darkened the frosted glass, a head in height between them.

Their ears pricked, no doubt, to the flush of the toilet.

She couldn't shake it, imagining the shadowy figures sniggering to each other as they rung the bell, the sound of the flush echoing down the hallway, and she blushed as she opened the door.

Police.

They stood with their hands behind their backs. One looked directly at her; a woman, short black hair, the pits of acne scars across her brow. The other, taller and older, was a man, his eyes to the ground as he rocked on his heels.

'I'm PC Woollard, from Kingston Police Station.' The woman spoke, nerves making her sound impossibly young.

The sight of their uniforms, their serious faces, stole her breath, her voice.

'Are you Fionnuala Greene?'

Why are you here? She failed to ask.

But she knew.

She backed away from the open door, watching as they glanced at each other, the man holding back and letting Woollard lead the way.

'Is there anyone else here at the moment, Mrs Greene?'

James hadn't phoned all day. He would normally call at lunchtime, or during a coffee break.

Nuala had reached the end of the hallway, her back to the door of the kitchen, the smell of dinner leaking through. James's dinner.

Where is James? Did she say that aloud? She couldn't tell.

'Is there somewhere we can sit down, Mrs Greene?'

Why are you here? But the words wouldn't come. She couldn't move.

Woollard turned her head, looked at the silent man blocking the light from the open front door. He nodded, keeping his eyes to the floor, hands behind his back.

The woman took Nuala by the arm, led them through the kitchen and sat her at the table, sitting opposite. She could hear the man rifling through the kitchen, the flick of the kettle and the rumble of its boil, the waft of tea and strong coffee when he eventually found the right cupboard. She couldn't look at him, couldn't take her eyes away from PC Woollard and her small, ringless hands.

'I need to talk to you about your husband, Mrs Greene.'

'He'll be home soon.' Was that her voice? It sounded muffled, quiet, only the vague trembling of her throat telling her she had spoken at all. Her fingers moved to her wedding ring, spinning the plain gold band.

Her eyes darted to the door, expecting it to open, for her husband to walk through and tell her not to worry.

Woollard held on to Nuala's hands, stilling the spinning gold ring.

'Mrs Greene, I'm afraid he's been involved in a very serious accident.' Woollard lowered her head, tried to make eye contact but Nuala couldn't do it, could only look at their hands on the table, her wedding band hidden.

Her eyes filled, the salt stinging and her eyelids suddenly so heavy, so burdened with tears. She opened her mouth to ask if he was OK, if he was coming home, but her voice wouldn't come.

'Mrs Greene,' the woman said, looking away, her jaw

tightening for the briefest of moments. 'I'm afraid he died at the scene.'

Nuala shook her head, horror silencing her, the blood draining from her face.

'It happened at lunchtime. He suffered an aneurysm whilst cycling away from the park.'

She should have known something was wrong.

'He entered the ring-road from the left.'

She should have known when she didn't hear from James during the day. She should have felt something, surely.

'Witnesses saw him slump on his bike and then swerve into oncoming traffic. It would have been very quick, painless.'

Nuala was talking, after all, the same words spilling out of her repeatedly. 'I didn't know.' And her mind shouted, of course you didn't know, how could you have? She realised that this, too, had been said aloud and clasped her hands over her mouth.

She should be screaming.

She should be hugging herself, rocking back and forth, biting her fist to stem the tears.

She shouldn't be sitting here mumbling uncontrollably, tears refusing to fall, blood cold in her veins, her hands, fingers, feet beneath the table, all numb.

'Everyone is different, Mrs Greene. There is no right way to react.' And again, Nuala realised she had been speaking constantly, that Woollard was trying to comfort her and didn't realise Nuala's mortification. She gave into the trembling that started in her hands and spread up her arms to her shoulders and chest and up to her lips and jaw and her teeth began to chatter.

'You're in shock, Fionnuala.'

She wondered when they had started calling her Fionnuala, and if she had given them permission or they just presumed to call her that to create an air of familiarity and, perhaps in familiarity, comfort.

But it didn't give her comfort; it just made her long for her mother.

A hot, sweet smelling tea was placed in front of her and the heat of the vapour and the sugary smell turned her stomach. She was aware of the smell of the lasagne and this too was nauseating. She remembered the bathroom and what she had been doing there before the police officers arrived.

She stood and walked towards it.

She heard Woollard's chair move as she, too, stood to follow.

The test was on top of the cistern. Nuala turned it over to read the positive result, her hand flying to her belly, just as the other woman asked, 'Is there anyone I can call?'

Maggie

Saturday, 18th November, 2017

Arthur would have killed James Lunglow had he ever shown his face again, Maggie was sure of it. That's why Lois had snuck the lad out of the village when she had. Arthur would have killed him without a moment's regret. But that was seven years ago; even the bad luck of a broken mirror would have faded by now.

What was the point in Emma dragging it all up again, when James had been gone for so long? When he'd left, run away, not come back or checked in? Why was Emma wasting her energy thinking of him, just because a woman from London stared at his photo that morning?

Maggie walked on down the main street of the village, the sky thunderous but withholding its rain. She walked away from the pub, from her goddaughter, the centre line of the road ahead marked out not in shining white paint but by a band of inch-thick mud.

Nuala Greene, Emma said her real name was. Not Mrs James, after all.

'They all do it,' Maggie had offered in reply, coat already on, fingers on the door handle ready to make her Saturday morning pilgrimage, when Emma appeared from the kitchen and sprung the news on her. 'They all give a false name. Nothing to worry about.'

'Then why was she staring at *him*?' Emma held a photo aloft between her red fingers, the image shuddering in the draught from the door. The photo she'd taken down from the wall of Polaroids, after Nuala Greene had left. 'Why did she call herself Mrs James, like she was his wife or something? She wasn't wearing a ring, unless maybe she took it off?'

'Stop it, Emma. Just because she was looking at his photo doesn't mean she has anything to do with him. Don't start dragging all that up now. Look,' Maggie had said, softening her tone and holding Emma's shoulders between her two hands, hoping to still the girl's nervous trembling. 'Sort the bar, clean the floor, get the shopping in, take your mind off Mrs James or Mrs Greene or whatever her name is.'

And then she'd left, before the uncomfortable memory of her conversation with Arthur's right-hand-man, Edward Burrows, of his talk of Lois and lawyers and the fire next door showed too clearly on her face.

'Arthur won't like it,' Edward had said from his seat by the fireplace and Maggie still wondered what it was he didn't want Lois talking about, still hoped it was something she could use in her favour.

Maggie walked on towards something more important, a Saturday routine that would never be broken. Walked away, with the pub, Nuala Greene, those photographs all left behind her. All except one, held safe in the breast pocket of her coat, the picture she always carried with her.

She lifted it out and looked at it, allowing her feet to tread the familiar path along the roadside, muscle memory leading the way along the tarmac, edged by dead leaves. Tom, her husband, smiled back, hunched in the damask chair by the fire, one hand holding a cast-iron poker and the other hugging a tumbler of whisky, the drink's colour faded from amber to dull brown with age. In the background, beside the kitchen door, were Lee's white trainers.

Nearly twenty years ago, that photo had been taken. A time when her future was mapped out in an easy path by her relationship to the men in her life. Wife to Tom, the village landlord. Mother to Lee, a young teenager with a good academic record and a solid history of Sunday school attendance. She couldn't call herself either of those things any more. Widow was her label now, failed mother to boot, and she hadn't stepped inside a church in twenty years.

At least she still had Emma to look after, Maggie's role as godmother still stable.

Emma had said that she couldn't even remember Tom's face any more, without looking at his photo. Was it the same with James? Had she forgotten his face yet, other than the photograph, or was he embedded in her memory?

Emma still searched for James online, Maggie knew that much even if she couldn't use the computer herself. She'd seen Emma type his name in. Knew from the sighs and huffs of frustration that she'd never found him, not yet.

Seven years.

She wanted the girl to stop looking, give up. There were other men in the village, in the town down the road, more people who would be better suited to Emma than him. And Maggie wasn't stupid, she'd seen Toby sneak out of Em's room at half five, seen the flush on the girl's cheeks all next day. Wouldn't it be better to focus on Toby, rather than stalk someone online who was living way off in the city? Or at least he was according to Lois.

Maggie walked on, past the terraces that opened right onto the road, through the lopsided wooden gate at the front of the yard, towards the stone building with its crumbling steeple.

The grave was at the front, protected from the wind by blackthorn and a lone silver birch. Flakes of white bark had fallen onto the headstone, a promise of the snow that would no doubt come with the deepening of winter. She tidied them into her side pocket. Felt the brush of the bank manager's letter there, too.

The inscription on the headstone was clear. Nothing extravagant, just his name: *Thomas Luke Bradbury,* and a single date, 12th August 2000.

Below was an empty space, waiting for Maggie, the neighbouring plot already bought, paid for with the last of Tom's life insurance, saved for the day she would join him. She pressed her palm to the void on the stone, her hand-span filling the gap. The seeping cold of it ran through her fingers, jolted her brain with the frozen image of the doctor, sleeves rolled up and bubbles of carbolic soap gathering in the hairs on his forearm, speaking the words she couldn't quite decipher. They had come through a fog, the doctor's mouth filled with cotton wool, Maggie's ears ringing as she tried to make sense of it.

Everything Tom had left her, their son, their land, their pub, had slipped through her fingers like sand when he died.

She knelt, oblivious to the cold soaking through her trouser knees, and brushed away the light covering of moss growing across the rim of the stone, felt the stone rub against the wedding ring she wore on her thumb. Tom's ring.

'I'm sorry, my love. I'm so sorry,' she said, her fingers lingering beside his name, her mind on the letter from the bank in her pocket.

She rested her head on the gravestone, the rim catching in the creases on her brow, tracing Tom's name with her fingers. She relives the car crash that killed him every day. Every time she starts her car, drives over the hill and sees the place where the car went over, where Tom's head smashed through the windscreen, where his body broke against a tree. Every time she looks in the mirror and sees the thick, purple scar on her cheek, the shrapnel from the crash permanently marking her.

So many years and Maggie still hadn't recovered. Could she really blame Emma for still thinking of James after seven? After everything he'd done?

Maggie leant forward, head on the gravestone, knees wet and cold on the ground. Tom would have chased James down and . . . and what? Made him come back? What good would that have done anyone?

'What would you have done, Tom?' she asked him. 'What would you do now?'

But Maggie knew Emma would never forget the past, just as Maggie had never forgotten her own.

'Fix him, please fix him,' Maggie had begged the nurse, the doctor, the woman who cleaned the ward floor. 'Fix him, please fix him.'

'The damage was severe,' said the nurse with strawberry blonde hair, her cap like a striking white halo. 'There wasn't anything we could fix. I'm so sorry.'

The crash had been total, Tom's car slicing through trees, trees slicing through the car. Three days afterwards, when

Maggie awoke, alone in a hospital bed, she thought Tom was waiting somewhere nearby, ready to rush in with flowers the second she woke up.

She had thought it would all be OK.

But it hadn't been.

And now things were getting worse, she was losing it all. She never thought she'd have to do this alone.

She thought of the land, the last scrap of land that Tom had left her in his will, waiting high up on the hill. Just the right size for a bungalow, a view of a thin strip of sea on one side. Space for a garden, vegetable patch, greenhouse, a wooden bench to sit upon with her husband, retired and relaxed, leaving the pub for their son to run.

But their son was long gone. She didn't even know where he was. At the time social services had told her she wasn't allowed anywhere near him. It was for his own protection, they had said. He was a fully-grown man now, but had never tried to find her. Why would he, after all Maggie had done?

'What's the point of building our bungalow,' she said, sitting on the wet, grassed-over earth, leaning her back on the grave, 'if I have to live in it without you?'

What was the point of a garden bench, a vegetable patch, greenhouse, without her husband to tend to it with her?

And she had no money to build it anyway.

So, what was the point in keeping the land? Why was it so hard to sell up?

She pulled out the letter from her overcoat pocket, began tearing the paper to shreds, tiny confetti she plugged into the holes on the vase built into the grave. She'd leave it with Tom. Maybe, somehow, he'd be able to tell her what to do.

She couldn't risk throwing it away at home, wouldn't even risk it on the fire, in case somehow Emma saw it and found out.

And she couldn't let Emma find out, not after the girl had entrusted the last of her paltry savings to Maggie, seven years ago. The money left to Emma in her stepmother's will.

Maggie leant forward, her gut pressing against her thighs and her hands holding onto her knees.

'I was meant to look after it, save it for her. I thought the pub was an investment, a safe bet.'

She tugged on the curls at the back of her neck, watched sparrows hopping through the branches of the blackthorn, dismissing the still-too-hard sloes.

'I can't tell her. I can't.'

She rolled onto her side, grabbed hold of the gravestone and used it to hoist herself up. She could still see the white shreds of the letter through the holes in the brass-topped vase. If she'd had any spare money she'd have come with some flowers, or if it had been summer she'd have picked some from the fields, and hidden the letter's fragments under their stems. As it was, she let the white flecks sit unadorned, under the lid of the vase.

Now wasn't the time to tell Emma the money was gone, Maggie reasoned. Not when someone was here visiting Lois Lunglow, not when she might finally have something to hold over Arthur's head.

Maggie turned back to the yard, looked at the graves, the crumbling church steeple, the silver birch shedding its bark. But her mind was elsewhere, thinking not of money, or Emma, or land. Thinking of Nuala Greene, wondering if it *was* her parked outside Lois's house, wondering if anyone else had seen her, Arthur Bradbury at the top of the list.

Wondering, too, if that waif of a thing, who'd looked ready to drop with exhaustion, knew what she was letting herself in for.

Nuala

Saturday, 18th November, 2017

'It was instant, the police said.'

Lois didn't speak, hadn't said a word since Nuala had told her the news. Her arms gripped each other, one hand tapping her chest; tap, tap, tap, the sound echoing off the walls of her living room, the cold somehow amplifying the sound.

'He wasn't in any pain.'

On the doorstep, Lois had crumpled before Nuala could explain. She'd had to carry her mother-in-law inside, the woman light as a child. She hadn't cried, or screamed, or denied the very possibility of her son's death, she had just fallen to her knees.

'He would barely have registered what was happening, it was so quick.'

Nuala sat opposite, rubbing her arms against the cold and looked around her. Two fraying, upholstered chairs, one brown and one blue, a cracked coffee table and a duvet folded in the corner of the room. No photographs hung on the walls. Even the light bulb, hanging from a wire, swung naked.

'It was an aneurysm, the pathologist reported; it couldn't

have been prevented,' Nuala continued, staring at her hands, at the window, at the bare floor. Anything but the woman's face. 'James was dead before he hit the ground, before his bike even swerved into the road.'

The only discernible change in Lois was her pallor, each word from Nuala reducing it by a shade until it became translucent, skull-white.

'I'll make us tea, shall I?' No answer but, after twenty minutes of silence, Nuala hadn't really expected one.

The same lack of homeliness, the same deep cold, haunted the kitchen. A table accompanied by two chairs. A single cup, bowl and spoon drying by the sink. An unopened packet of out-of-date biscuits beside the teabags, undoubtedly left in the vain hope that visitors might call. Dark chocolate digestives: James's favourite.

No television, no computer, no mobile phone that she could see, though what struck her most was that the cooker was missing. Space had been left for one, the edges of the work surface sawn away so it could be slotted in. On the counter was a two-ring hotplate. Presumably a life of beans on toast for Lois, but then Nuala noticed that there wasn't a toaster or grill.

Her parents' kitchen had been quite different: countertops a mess of gravy-stained medical journals, old birthday cards and letters displayed on the window sill, love notes Blu Tacked to cupboard doors. The walls throughout their house were once saturated with photographs, so much so that when, as a child, she had raced through the hallway her home became a zoetrope of familiar, shifting faces.

This house showed no life. The only object offering any hint of personality was a cast-iron doorstop shaped like a dog, black with dirt, the breed indistinct. Nuala touched the animal with the toe of her boot, wracking her mind for any mention of a dog from James's early years. She came up blank.

She had braced herself for James. She had expected to be surrounded by him, his very childhood should have leaked out of the walls, but there were no photos, no reminders of him, no evidence he had ever existed. Maybe James had been right all along when he told Nuala about his mother.

But still, Nuala reasoned, she deserved to know the truth.

And maybe, once the shock of the news had sunk in, she would let Nuala help her through it. They could get through it together. Nuala was sick, sick and tired and broken from doing it all, all alone.

She left the kitchen, walked back to the living room carrying the tea.

The tapping finally stopped.

'You won't look at me, at my face. Why is that?' Lois clasped her hands in her lap, the tendons on her knuckles showing white through her skin, just as James used to do when tense.

'You look so alike.' So alike it was painful. The same thick, sandy hair, the same heavy-lidded eyes, slim nose, strong jaw. The similarity was exacerbated by Lois's age: early forties at a push, with a son who, this year, would have celebrated his twenty-sixth birthday. Had she really been so young when she had him?

'I'll have to take your word for it. I hadn't seen him in seven years, not even a photograph.' Her face brightened. 'Did you bring any?'

'No, I didn't think.' And she cursed herself for her empty back pocket and the phone, full of photos, lying, forgotten, back home. 'There was one at the pub, though. I'm sure they'd let you have it.'

'And I'm sure they wouldn't.' Lois pulled her cardigan closer, the seams at the shoulder stretching, betraying their handsewn stitches.

'Is there anyone I can call for you?'

Lois waved her hand, swatted the question like a fly.

'There must be someone. A friend, relative?'

'No one.' Lois pressed her fingers to her mouth, her brow furrowed as she bit back the tears. 'No one now James is—'

Nuala looked around the room, the heat of the tea making the cool air feel colder by contrast, and realised it was probably true. Who would let a friend, a relative, live such an existence?

And then she thought of her own empty home, the phone that never rang, the door only deliverymen ever knocked at.

'I knew that I was never going to see him again.' Lois huddled into the chair, her shoulders hunching up against her ears.

Why was she so alone? James's father was dead, had died in a fall down the stairs when the boy was eleven years old. Had Lois been alone since?

'What must you think of me?' Lois's eyes, bloodshot from holding back tears, were upon her, moving from the top of her head to her boot-clad feet and back again.

'I've only just met you, Mrs Lunglow.'

Lois reached for her tea, her hand trembling. 'Most people would ask me, "Why?"'

'I'm sorry?'

'I just told you I had never expected to see my only son again. Most people would ask me, "Why?" You said nothing.'

There was nowhere to look other than straight at Lois, to

either meet her grief head on or stare obviously, awkwardly, at the blank wall.

'And still you say nothing.'

'None of it matters.'

'Of course it matters. Why won't you answer?'

'It's not going to change anything. Please, is there anything else I can do for you?'

'Tell me what you think of me. Tell me what James said. Tell me.' Tap, tap, tap on her chest. 'Tell me.'

'He didn't tell me anything!' The words were hurled into the room, Nuala's throat dry in their wake. Her skin felt bruised where her hands gripped her thighs, pinching the skin. Her teeth clenched to dam the words that screamed inside her head: *He told me you were unbearable, a vindictive, manipulative misanthrope. He told me you hated him, regretted him, pushed him away. He told me you were cruel.*

She held her tongue, flushed, remained silent. What an idiot she had been for not believing him, for thinking he had exaggerated. For thinking, perhaps, Lois had changed from the mother he had left behind. She could picture his face as if he were still alive, the tell-tale twitch of his eyes and the stiffening of his smooth, strong jaw, the disdain that would seep into his expression as he asked her, *'Why didn't you just do as I asked?'*

Lois's hand shook as she raised her cup, the other still tapping her chest. 'How long were you married?'

'Six years.'

'I never wanted him to marry young. What were you? Nineteen?' She pressed the cup to her closed lips, the set of her mouth completely hidden, her red-rimmed eyes turning cold.

'He was nineteen. I had just turned eighteen.'

'You must have met as soon as he arrived in London.'

'A few weeks after.'

'And you married so soon? Whilst he was still studying?'

'He had left university by then.'

'Left?' Lois's face blanched and Nuala had to remind herself that all of this was news to her, that the last seven years of her son's life had been lived through imagination alone.

'University was too much for him, all the people and noise.' Nuala shifted her weight in the chair, trying to see Lois's face behind the cup but Lois mirrored every movement. 'We met in the park, actually. He liked the space, the wildlife. He got a job there, eventually, as a groundsman.'

Lois nodded at her to go on.

'He loved his job, and he was so good at it, really he was.' She held back telling Lois about the four years it took him to find work, or that it was Nuala and her inheritance that kept them comfortable, that the house they lived in belonged to Nuala alone. He had instructed her well to keep those things to herself, because it shouldn't matter whose money it was: they were married. And if he could love her as much as he did in spite of her legion of faults, her stupidity, her laziness, then surely she could forgive him his humble background. Was she really so materialistic, so shallow, to think that these things really mattered? No. No, she wasn't.

Nuala looked to the ceiling, following the hairline cracks in the plaster as she spoke, trying to ignore the memory of the bitter look of resentment on James's face whenever she took out her credit card to pay for the dinner, the shopping, the gas bill.

Instead, she kept faithfully to the script, James's script, the lines he encouraged her to spurt out to his friends on the occasions he allowed her to meet them: the country holidays, the flowers and vegetables he grew, the house they had renovated, the OU course he had started. But any ground Nuala felt she had gained was taken by Lois in one fell swoop.

'You've rehearsed all of that, I can tell.' The other woman put her cup on the table, brushed invisible crumbs from her knees.

More than ever Nuala wished that there was some element of life in the room, something she could look at other than the uncannily familiar face of her mother-in-law.

Lois took a deep breath, as though mustering her composure, her voice sharp when she did speak again.

'So, you lived for six years in a merry-go-round of happiness and fairy tales? Rubbish. I can't imagine James marrying *you* out of love.' The *you* was spat out like poison on her tongue, as though the very notion of loving Nuala was a venomous draught in itself. Her eyes stayed on Nuala, her spit landing on Nuala's knee, her judgement set on the woman her son had married. 'There must have been something else. Money?' The woman looked over Nuala again, her designer jeans, expensive boots. 'That's it, isn't it? Money.'

'Money?' Nuala felt her own cheeks grow hot. 'How dare you? How dare you insinuate that he—'

But Lois held her hand up for silence, the same movement James used to use whenever Nuala had said something stupid and she was dumbfounded, again, by their resemblance.

'You can hardly blame him,' Lois said. 'Look where he grew up, look at this village. It's not as if I could ever offer him all he deserved.' Her forehead creased again, eyes rimmed with red, and she stopped talking, looked down at her lap whilst she took another deep, composing breath.

'Six years and you never forced it out of him?' Lois's voice was still sharp and Nuala's cheeks still burned from the talk of her money. It was the grief, Nuala decided, making Lois talk this way, she had to be patient, had to be kind, remind herself that the woman had only just found out James was dead.

'Where are your guts,' Lois said, 'your backbone? He could never love someone so spineless. No, it was far too soon for him to fall in love again.'

Again.

Nuala's breath caught in her throat.

What did Lois mean, fall in love *again*?

She tried to push the thought away, tears pricking. She focused on what James had told her; that his mother would lie. Don't believe a word she says. There wasn't anyone else, Nuala was the first. The only. James had said so himself: there had never been anyone else. It was what made their connection, their *love*, so special.

But there was no time for Nuala to react, stand her ground, defend her marriage. Lois's next question came like a punch in the gut.

'So, did he leave me any grandchildren?'

Three months ago

Nuala

Tuesday, 23rd August, 2017

I t was a boy.

It seemed right, somehow, that she would have a son. He'd be named Maxwell, after her father. She had been thinking of moving back to Oxfordshire, where she had lived as a young child, taking a house in Woodstock or Yarnton, join mother and baby groups, make some friends of her own. Sell this house, their house, the house where, in the rose garden he had loved so much, James's ashes were buried.

But, best laid plans . . .

At twenty-two weeks, the baby stopped moving.

Three days of running up and down stairs, drinking iced water, eating chocolate and sugared doughnuts, prodding her belly, massaging her belly, singing to her belly and praying to God that her son would move, would punch, would hit, would somersault and kick her in the ribs, would do anything, anything.

On the fourth day, she lay on the hospital bed, the lights turned to their lowest, the ultrasound screen showing the white limbs of her son, his stomach and head, his heart still as the moon.

It was the same sonographer she'd had at the twenty-week

Rebecca Tinnelly

scan; the young man with jet black hair who had shown her all the organs inside Maxwell's body.

'Here are the lungs . . . heart looks healthy . . . left ventricle, right ventricle . . . keep still you cheeky monkey: your son, not you, don't worry.'

The stillness had stolen his joviality. He left the room, a touch of her ankle as he walked past. 'I'm just going to ask for a second opinion.'

She never saw him again.

The consultant, all thick grey hair and tortoiseshell glasses, hadn't been able to meet her eye when he broke the news. 'A silent miscarriage, no rhyme or reason behind it,' looking down at the squares of blue linoleum beneath his feet, their colour, like the colour of his skin, turned to ash in the dimness of the room. 'Sometimes, these things just happen. But I am sorry, so sorry, for your loss.' A tear slid down his cheek, glistening in the light from the monitor.

He turned the machine off, a fuzzy scratch of noise as the screen died, the silence behind it breathtaking.

'Turn it back on, please.'

'Mrs Greene, there really isn't—'

'Turn it back on!'

He breathed a hoarse sigh and the monitor came back to life, the screen split into four squares and an image of her boy in each.

'From the measurements taken, we think he died about a week ago.' He stood behind the bench, his hand lightly on her shoulder and his back to the screen. 'Normally it's longer, three or four weeks sometimes before the mother finds out. A week may sound like a long time, but it really is comparatively quick.'

Her son had changed since the last scan. His legs and arms looked longer, head rounder, nose and lips distinct. She could see the shell-like shadows of his ears, the dark zig-zag of his intestines that she couldn't see before, maybe because of the angle the pictures were taken, maybe because, for these images, he wasn't moving.

She listened to the doctor talk about her options, his voice gentle, tired, explaining to her the differences between hospital delivery and home, medical intervention and natural birth, the drugs they could offer her, the test they could do, the decisions she would have to make.

She didn't listen. How could she? The room around her, the man behind her, all receded into the black hole, her ears deaf to the constant talking, her eyes blind to everything but the four images of her son.

A week ago. He had died a week ago, and what had Nuala been doing? Painting his bedroom pastel green, ordering thick curtains so he could nap in the day, putting together his cot because at last, it was safe to do so; his twenty-week scan was all clear.

'I want to go home. I want to take him home.'

Another sigh behind her, the sound of his hands rubbing his chin. He was talking again, something about the risks of infection, the safety of a hospital, availability of diamorphine.

'I'm going home.'

The doctor stood in front of the screen, blocking her view of the monitor and staring into her eyes for the first time, the sympathy gone from his voice, replaced with frustration, anger.

'It could take weeks for it to happen naturally, don't you understand?'

No, she wanted to say, I don't understand. How can I?

He left shortly afterwards, leaving her with a nurse. They wanted to move her, take her to a quiet room somewhere to talk but she wouldn't go, wouldn't leave the images of her son on the screen, not even when they offered to print them for her.

The nurse was red-haired and freckled, lines around her eyes and mouth and neck.

'I've finished my shift,' she said as she walked in, 'so I can stay as long as you need.' She dragged a stool next to the bed, looking at the monitor with Nuala, reached over and held Nuala's hand, her fingers covered in rings, the metal warm and rugged in Nuala's grip. '"Silent Miscarriage" doesn't do it justice, does it?'

Nuala held a little tighter onto the woman's hand, the first tear of many spilling over.

They sat together, hand in hand, for an hour before the nurse spoke again.

'You might feel scared about the pain.' She passed Nuala a prescription for painkillers the reluctant doctor had left behind. 'But the pain won't be the worst thing about it.'

And for the first time since James died, Nuala felt someone understood.

'Will there be someone with you at home, when it happens? A friend? Your mum, maybe?'

'My mother?' Her voice cracked and the nurse had nodded.

'That's good,' she said, patting her shoulder. 'Your mother will help you through it.'

And Nuala knew that no one would ever understand.

Her mother had died seven years earlier. James only three

months ago. And her son had perished inside her, whilst she painted his room pastel green.

No one would ever understand.

She was alone. Completely alone.

The nurse had been right, though; the miscarriage was far from silent, but the pain, nearly unendurable, wasn't the worst thing about it. When it was over, and she lay shivering on the bedroom floor, she realised that the worst was yet to come.

Because her baby was just that: a little baby. She had expected a small alien-like creature, like the pictures in pregnancy books, but what she held in her hands was a little boy. The reality of his eyes, his nose, his tiny pursed lips delved inside and tore her apart because he was so perfect, complete in everything but his size and his breath, because there was nothing she could do, because it was cruel, needless. Because she didn't understand.

For two days, she held him to her chest, skin to skin beneath her shirt, singing *Seoithín, Seo Hó,* just as her Irish mother had done. His body, curled like a foetus, never got cold. His skin was thin and soft and his head, when she had cleaned away the blood and vernix, showed the first strands of hair. Not blond like her, or the sandy brown of James but dark, nearly black, like her mother's.

His eyes were closed, she would never see the colour behind the lids but she supposed they would be blue. Newborns mostly had blue eyes, or so she'd read.

On the third day, she woke in bed, the sheets damp from her milk, and he was not on her chest as he had been, nor had he fallen into the crook of her arm.

He lay, uncovered, on James's side of the mattress. She reached for him, pulled him towards her and onto her chest but the softness of his skin had gone. She could smell the end of the umbilical cord where it hung from his belly.

He was cold.

And Nuala was all alone.

She wrapped him in his blue cotton blanket, a pattern of elephants in white parading along, and took him to the garden, to the rose bush and the willow casket that waited beneath its roots.

She lifted him from his place, nestled against her breast, and kissed his little cheek before settling him down with his father.

There was a woman out there who didn't know her son, her only son, was dead. James had always said to never contact that woman, no matter what happened. Nuala had burned and buried James without his mother. She had done it alone, just as she was doing this alone. How cruel that was, she now realised. How cruel, that they were both alone, but needn't be.

There was someone, in that place she'd promised never to go, who might understand. Who could be there for her, help her, who could be the mother she needed.

Eyes closed, she replaced the lid, filling the hole with blind, empty hands, singing all the while. 'I'm here by your side praying blessings upon you, hushaby, hush, baby sleep for now.'

Nuala

Saturday, 18th November, 2017

'No.' Nuala looked beyond Lois to the window, to the sky, grey with clouds. 'No children.'

'Didn't you want any?' The tapping sped up. Lois's knees started bouncing, her ankles and feet jerking in rhythm. 'Worried a baby would interfere?'

Nuala kept her eyes on the window, biting the inside of her cheek and reminding herself that this woman had just had a shock, had been plunged into a state of sudden grief, that surely this attack was a reaction to that.

The clouds were darkening, and the room with it. The light wasn't on. Nuala looked up to the bulb swinging above her head, covered with grime and dust. There was no heating, no lighting, no cooker, no life. Nothing. This woman had nothing.

But what did Nuala have herself?

'James always wanted children, always wanted a son. Married for five years and you have nothing to show for it.'

'Six years,' Nuala said, trying hard not to grit her teeth. 'We were married for six years.'

'You are listening then! I thought you were ignoring me. Or maybe I'd just hit a nerve.' Lois leant back in her seat, her eyes brightening as she hit on Nuala's weakness. 'So, you were married to my son for six years. And in all that time, he never told you why he wouldn't come back? Why he refused to contact me?'

Nuala changed tack, studied the floorboards instead of the sky, the tip of her tongue held tight between her front teeth.

'Does your silence mean no? If so, why don't I believe you?' Lois said. 'You expect me to believe he never told you about me, never told you about this village?' Lois cocked her head to the side, her thin smile adding crows-feet to her red-rimmed eyes. 'Did he ever tell you about *her*?'

Nuala's right hand jumped to her left, feeling for a band of gold that wasn't there. She thought back to the letter, tried her best not to wince, but it was instinctive.

The words in the letter had been loving. Kind. They'd shown that the sender was longing for James to return, had given Nuala hope James's mother had changed, was no longer the woman he had described.

Nuala didn't think Lois could write such kind words, feel such longing.

But if she didn't write them, who did?

Because James had promised her that she was his first, just as he had been hers. That in a village of people like *this*, there was no one he wanted, no one he loved. Not until he met Nuala.

He wouldn't have lied about that.

And then Nuala remembered the odd look on Emma's face when she'd given the name Mrs James. The look on Lois's when she told her James was married.

Again she thought of James, not just the oath that he swore over six years ago, claiming he was a virgin like Nuala, but the look on his face as he made it. His eyes wide and earnest, lips parted. It had melted the last of Nuala's doubts and made her lie down in submission. It was an expression she came to know well. He wore it when she failed to show up for her art school interview and had lost her place as a result: they must have dialled a wrong number, talked to the wrong household, because they never spoke to James and left him the details, regardless of what the Head of Admissions had said. And it was the same look he had worn the morning after their wedding, eating a breakfast of croissants and jam, when he had promised Nuala he would tell his mother he had married.

Lois kept on smiling, her grin growing wider until her teeth showed, little yellow razors in her mouth. Nuala was reminded of the note left on her car, the scrawl of angry words.

'Would you like *me* to tell you?'

Yes, Nuala wanted to shout, *tell me, please,* but the words wouldn't form and she shook her head instead.

'A part of you must be curious, on some level at least. After all, if he'd never left here, he would never have met you, isn't that right?'

Nuala stared at her knees, her fingers knotted in her lap.

Lois continued, 'Or maybe you thought it was all fate, is that it? He was fated to leave this place because he was fated to meet you? You were *meant to be*?' She mooned over the words like a school girl, hands clasped to the side of her face.

'I love him!' she shouted and Lois stopped, hands still caressing her cheek. 'I loved him.' She winced at the tense. 'And he loved me. And you wouldn't understand, you could never understand because I know you never had that in your own damn marriage!'

James had told Nuala that he knew his mother never loved his father, how could she? Jim Lunglow had been a brute of a man, James had said. His idea of affection was a cuff round the ear for his son, or a punch on the arm so hard it could never be thought of as fond. His final birthday present for James, when the boy turned eleven, had been a second-hand porno, its pages curled at the edges. James told Nuala he had opened it and cried, disturbed by the looks on the women's faces. Jim had slapped him so hard he had felt his jaw pop, then he had gone off drinking, come home so blind drunk he'd fallen down the stairs and broken his neck. James said it was the best birthday present he could have asked for and Nuala had known, by his sober voice, that he meant it.

Jim had been a violent, bad-tempered imbecile nearly thirty years older than the girl he got pregnant, the young woman who became his reluctant wife. What James had failed to tell her was just how young a woman Lois must have been when her son was conceived, fifteen or sixteen by Nuala's guess.

Silenced, momentarily, by the slight on her marriage, Lois's hands dropped down to her lap. Her eyes followed suit until they fell to the floor, resting on Nuala's leather boots.

'And you really think he loved you *first*?'

'He did!' Nuala said. 'He found me alone and he made me whole, we put each other back together. And yes, we were young and naïve and hopeful but we were never, either of us, carefree. But we cared for each other and split our worries between us from that very first moment, from the second I saw him and he saw me. It's worth fighting for, that connection, the rarity of being each other's first love in every sense of the word.'

She stopped, out of breath, her head awash with James, all of his expressions, his moods, those sudden little changes in manner that made her stomach flip, never sure if it was his praise or criticism she'd be receiving. Remembering his hands on her body, gentle as if he were holding a newborn, his hands in her hair, combing it through with his fingers as she lay with her head on his chest. It had been their connection, he'd always said, their special connection, his body craving her body because it had been the only one he'd ever known. It made up for the times he was silent, or sullen, or told Nuala she was an idiot for something or other. For believing she could ever get into St Martin's, for example, after she missed the admissions interview. Or that any of her friends would want to come to Nuala's birthday, because why would they? Really, why would anyone, apart from James?

They had a very special connection, and it would always see them through.

'You lied to me,' Lois said.

'No.' Nuala blinked, her mirage of James melting away and revealing, in its place, his bitter mother. 'I didn't.'

'You said you knew nothing, yet he clearly told you about his damned father.'

Nuala got ready to defend herself again, to tell this woman she was wrong. But then Lois said, 'He lied to you, too. He said you were his first, but you weren't.'

Nuala shook her head because she was sure of what she knew, what James had told her from the very first time.

Lois lifted her eyes from the ground, drinking in Nuala's jeans, her sweater, neck, face and hair. 'He lied to me, too. Made promises, before he left, that he never kept.'

'I'm not like you.'

'I didn't say you were. I said he lied to you, just like he lied to me. He lied to everyone he cared about, it would seem.'

That 'everyone', that hint that there were others, turned

Nuala's stomach. She felt the rising surge of bile burn her throat, thought of every time James had called her stupid, foolish, an idiot, such an idiot, but it was OK because they loved each other, because their love was special, would outlast every other relationship in existence, no matter what stupid thing she did, or hurtful thing he said, or the way the money in her account made him green.

'You weren't his first,' Lois said.

Nuala closed her eyes, tried to gather her thoughts, but was already aware nothing would work. There were no coping mechanisms that could help her navigate this woman's venom. She should never have come.

'I want to go home.' It was meant to be internal, whispered inside her head, but one look at the disgust spreading across Lois's face told her she had whimpered it aloud.

She wanted to go into her garden, lie down on the rosebed above Maxwell.

Lois stood and moved to the window, her back turned, and Nuala knew the mother she needed wasn't to be found in this room. The mother she needed was already gone, had died with Nuala's father when Nuala was only just eighteen.

She was suddenly eager to get out of that house, that tiny cold house, and feel the hard, creased leather of her steering wheel in her hands. Even the guilt she felt over imparting such bad news couldn't make her stay any longer.

'Look, time is a great healer.' Nuala didn't even wince as the cliché slipped off her tongue, she was so eager to escape. 'James would want you to find some kind of happiness, to move on.' She spouted out the phrases, one on top of another, desperate for their meeting to end, repeating the tired platitudes she had hated so much, that had made her turn away from the few who had attempted condolence after James's death. 'It's important to remember the good times you shared, the happy memories.' She massaged her temples, trying to concentrate on the words and not the feeling in her gut telling her to run.

'Whatever happened between you, whatever you said to each other, I'm sure he would have forgiven you in time.' She looked up.

Lois turned back from the window, her lips tight. 'Is that what you think? We had some measly argument? That I was waiting for his *forgiveness*?' She gripped the windowsill with one hand, the other pointing at Nuala, spittle spraying at every word.

'Don't *you* force your presumptions onto *me*, Nuala. I wasn't waiting for his forgiveness.' Lois looked back to the window, to the road, to the drip of pedestrians, to the sad grey sky. 'I was waiting for him to come home. They all think I did a terrible thing, that I told lies and kept secrets to keep him away from *her*, but they never tried to understand. They never knew what it cost me, sending my only son away.'

Her fire was gone. She returned to her chair and sat, slumped and still.

'Tell me this, though,' she said, 'was he happy?'

'Yes!' Nuala said, and tried to believe it. 'We were happy.' She tried to ignore the words Lois had said earlier, the horrible possibility that James had lied to her, for so long.

Lois closed her eyes. 'James cried when he left, did he tell you that? He cried like an infant because he was scared. I had to be cruel, I had to stop him crying. I had to send him away from me, away from *her*.'

Nuala winced at Lois's final word. 'I let him cry,' she said. 'If he needed to cry, I let him.'

Lois just sneered. 'And that's probably why he never amounted to anything. A gardener, what a waste.'

'A groundsman, actually.'

'I always thought he'd make a good businessman,' Lois said, 'like his father.'

'I thought his father was a mechanic.'

'And *I* thought he never told you anything.' Lois's lip curled sadistically. 'He would have come back eventually of course.'

'I'm sure he would have.' Nuala placed both feet squarely on the floor, readying herself to stand, to leave.

'You don't understand. He would have come back, but not for me.'

Nuala thought of the letters, always the letters, the brief notes of longing she had hoped were sent by his mother.

'Please, don't,' she said though she knew her objections were useless. She didn't want to know who they were from, who had been writing to James for years, who had been begging him to return.

'Oh no, I'll go on. It's my turn now, Nuala.' Smiling, Lois leant forward, elbows on her knees. 'He would always have come back for *her* eventually, married or not.'

Nuala stood, brushed herself down, held her head high, chin up.

She needed air, fresh air free from the sourness of embittered grief, from the spite that was filling the room. But her way was barred. Lois shot past and stood at the door, one arm blocking the way and the other gripping Nuala's shoulder, her nails clawing through the fabric.

'You think you can be the only one to devastate? That you

have all the bad news? You held on to this for *months* and didn't tell me! You think you can burn him without me, mourn him without me, and not pay for that?'

Nuala tried to wrestle Lois off, but her grip was too strong.

'You were nothing to him, understand? You didn't know him, not like I did. You couldn't have loved him, not without truly knowing him. *I* loved him!' Lois's eyes were terrifying, her stare boring straight into Nuala, her face so close that Nuala's cheeks were dewy from her breath. 'But there was someone else, someone he kept secret from you, but I've known about her for *years*! *I* was there when he left, I know *why* he left, I knew who he was leaving behind him!'

Nuala turned her head from Lois's open mouth, the rank bitterness making her want to retch. She had to escape. She nodded.

'So you do know something, then?' Lois persisted.

'There were letters.' Her shoulders sagged beneath Lois's grip.

Lois was still so close, her face only inches away. She could feel the air around her ebb and flow with the tide of the woman's lungs.

'*There were letters.*' She stepped back and her arms returned to their familiar pose, one resting on the elbow of the other, her hand tapping at her chest. 'I can tell you who sent them.' She looked Nuala up and down again. 'I can tell you her name.' Tap, tap, tap.

'I don't want to know,' Nuala managed to speak, though her lungs ached for a breath she couldn't pull. She sidestepped Lois and ran into the hallway. The front door was within reach, but she could feel Lois at her heels.

'Oh, but you do.'

Lois's voice turned soft, caressing.

Nuala tried to ignore her, began fumbling with the latch, but when it finally sprang open she was still trapped, the chain across the door barring her way.

Lois reached out and slammed the door closed, resting her weight against Nuala, her chest against Nuala's back, her mouth by her ear.

Nuala shrugged herself free, wrestled the chain loose, the metal cold and slippery beneath her fingers. Lois stayed behind her, still close but not touching, her hand tapping her chest.

'You've met her already, Nuala.'

Tap, tap, tap.

'Her name is Emma.'

Tap, tap, tap.

'Emma Bradbury.'

The name, like a bullet, shot through Nuala. She heard Emma's voice inside her head before picturing her face. She could feel the blood drain from her cheeks, her legs sway. Seven years ago, Emma couldn't have been more than fourteen, James nineteen. Surely he wouldn't have touched a child?

Nuala had come here for closure, for comfort, for the warm arms of James's mother wrapped around her. To find that those letters weren't maternal but romantic, to find out her husband, the father of her poor baby, had lied to her, kept them hidden, was too much.

The door opened and Nuala stumbled through, gasping for breath, smelling the dung from the surrounding fields.

A gunshot rang out from a crow scarer, the sky darkening with black birds as they fled from the closest field, the sound of the shot, the flap of the wings, pounding through Nuala's skull.

And still, Lois wasn't finished. She waited until Nuala had reached the gate, had fumbled with the lock on her car, waited until she was just about to enter the safety of her own space. 'James got her pregnant, Nuala. Did he tell you that?'

Emma

Saturday, 18th November, 2017

Maggie had ordered her upstairs to rest, but she went to the bathroom first, washed the bleach away, rubbed moisturiser into the cracks on her wrists, avoided the inflamed skin on her knuckles.

'Jesus, look at your hands!' Maggie had cried when she got back from the graveyard, holding her hands up to the light. 'You have to dilute it, Em!'

Maggie had overreacted, Emma thought, and the way the old woman kept looking around her, furrowing her brow and stroking the scar on her cheek, made Emma think she had something else on her mind.

'I've been cleaning, that's all.' And she had been, all morning, her mind so preoccupied with James, by the memory of her fourteen-year-old self, of the very last things James had told her, that she hadn't felt her skin start to wrinkle, fingers throb, as the bleach worked its way up her hands. For the first time in seven years she had called herself *an idiot*, immediately hating herself for it.

'With neat bleach? Did you even use a cloth? It looks like you've been scooping it up bare handed!'

And then Maggie noticed the gap in the photographs was

still there, that James's picture was still in Emma's pocket. And though she tried to change Maggie's mind, none of her arguments, her reassurances, removed the pity from her godmother's eyes.

'Upstairs,' Maggie said, rubbing the base of Emma's back, kissing her forehead, 'get some rest.' As if the memories were a hangover she could sleep off.

Emma still thought of James, not every day but often enough. Of the last time she saw his face, and the last words he had said to her.

Even her bedroom reminded her of him, of who she had been with him. Maybe it would have been different if Toby had stayed over last night, left his scent on her bedsheets and clothes, but he hadn't. And she didn't want him to, she reminded herself.

It was an adolescent's bedroom designed for a different girl: single divan bed (bedspread faded yellow, base of the bed marked with black and grey spores) small desk and plastic school chair (for what? She'd always wondered. University papers she'd never have the chance, or the funding, to write?), mould-spotted pink curtains. It had been the spare room before it was opened up for the not-quite-grown-up Emma, though why she wasn't given Lee's old room she never knew.

It's not as if he was ever coming back.

Three apple cores sat on the radiator, the bedroom full of the rotting sweetness as they dried, the smell reminding her of Toby's drunk breath as he whispered in her ear. At least it covered up the smell of damp. The wallpaper, at the base, was black with mould, the only dry patch of wall around the radiator where the apple cores lay.

The two from this morning were still fresh and wet, but

the one from yesterday evening, the husk wrinkled and matt, was just dry enough.

She sat at her desk, the apple core in front of her, the drawer, with the half-filled jars and the blunt-edged knife, open at her side.

Emma moved her tongue in her mouth, felt the soft, wrinkled flesh of the scabs on her lip, the light metallic taste of them, the sharp jolt through her jaw and into her nose and she scraped the scabs with her teeth. The shiver of that name beneath it all.

James Lunglow.

She held the knife by the handle and pulled the flesh of her lip into her mouth until blood leaked in an iron tang on her tongue, nose smarting. So, too, the scars on her belly.

And now it wasn't blood in her mouth but something else, a memory of a different tang, different taste, and James above her hidden by wheat shafts, her mouth full of him as his whole body shuddered.

Her eyes continued to sting, but not from the pain of her lip. She had been such a fool, back then. Such a silly, naïve school-aged fool. To think he would stay. To think he had wanted her for anything other than her body, her mouth, her hands.

Angry that she still thought about him, after all this time. Still hoped that she had been wrong and he would, after all, come back home. Where had her backbone dissolved to?

She could smell him in the sweetness of the apple core, in the vague scent of the chip pan that had followed her everywhere since the fire at his old house, next door, could sense him in the blunt edged knife in her hand.

'Mama!' came a call from outside.

Knife dropped, the apple seeds splayed, a click as their hulls hit the desk.

Who had said that?

And her empty hand itched to hold that child's hand, for a small, sticky palm in her own, remembering the daydreams she used to hold on to.

'Mama?' The voice muffled by the glass and the distance between houses, a boy in a garden down the road.

She could see him outside, not the child but his shadow, calling, 'Mummy! Mama?' down the street.

How easy it would be to run outside, to lift him up and pretend he was hers, that James had left her with something she could keep, something he would come back for. To pretend that the last seven years of pain, abandonment, destruction never happened. To wash away the ghost of that chip pan fire, the speculation, the suspicion, the unofficial blame which had dogged her, with the smell of talcum powder and milk.

An open front door and a woman's voice calling, 'John, I'm right here, come on in.'

And the taste of blood returned to her mouth. Emma had been to school with that woman, had seen her waddle through her pregnancy at nineteen years old, still a teenager, heard her complain of tiredness, lack of help. Emma should never have seen all this, should have been far away (with him, yes, with him) with bumps and babes of her own, or university papers to write, a future to plan.

The apple seeds glistened mahogany, a white stripe of soft flesh showing through. They had cracked in the fall, rendered useless.

'*Now*, John!' called the woman outside and Emma wanted to call back, 'Don't shout at him, please!' but instead just listened to the slap-patter-pat of his little plimsolls along the garden path, imagined his creased thighs and dimpled wrists as he ran into the hug from his mother and Emma's head fell, chin down on her chest, and she stared at the broken seed husks.

Useless, useless.

Couldn't even get that right, couldn't even get a few poxy seeds from a dried-out core without messing it all up.

Except it wasn't her who fucked it up this time, made her hands shake and crack the damn seeds. ('Don't swear,' Elaine would have said. 'It does you no favours.' And the memory of her step mother made it worse.)

It was Nuala Greene for bringing it all back, making her think of him, making the scar on her belly throb.

Making her hope that maybe she wouldn't need the apple seeds and lye, or the powder she'd made from the two. That maybe some kind of life was salvageable, because he was coming back for her, regardless of what he had said in the past, and she could tell him all the things she had been burning to say.

John was laughing outside, the laugh bursting her hope, all hope.

'We've everything we need right here, you've a future, a career, right here,' Maggie had said, the one time Emma mentioned going back to school, studying. 'No better people, no better place.' And despite Emma's joke of an existence Maggie believed it. And, despite herself, Emma was glad that she did. At least one of them was happy.

Maggie could be right. It could be the best place on earth and how would Emma know? She'd never been anywhere else. And if she couldn't make it here, she wouldn't make it anywhere so what was the point in obsessing? If even Toby had stopped coming by, if the old men just stared at her chest and the women looked down their noses and ushered their children away, what made her think it would be any different anywhere else? She couldn't even pluck out a few seeds without damaging them: what made her think she could do anything else? Raise a child, build a home, a relationship?

What made her think Toby would be any different from James?

And the apple seeds winked in the light and the jar of powder at the back looked like smoke.

She'd had enough now, had done for weeks, so why wait?

'Nuala Greene has nothing to do with James,' Maggie had said, after the kiss to her forehead downstairs, 'I promise you, whatever reason she's got for coming here, it's nothing to do with him. He's not coming back.' And she was right. Why would he come back for someone like Emma?

What did she have to offer anyone?

Why wait?

Her hand on the jar, not of seeds but of powder, the lethal promise of nothingness held in its grains. She could dissolve it in whisky and drink it with her father, show Arthur Bradbury what she thought of him abandoning her when she was so young, leaving her to deal with Elaine's death, with James's flight, all alone. Leaving her with Maggie, who needed looking after herself and had been in no fit state, back then, to care for a teenage girl.

She could visit Lois and shove some down her throat. Force the woman's jaws open, those deceitful jaws, and pour some down her gullet. Show her what it's like to be on the receiving end of someone else's venom.

Another noise below, the door creaking open. Someone else was in the bar.

Emma's hand stalled. Who had come in?

She left the jar alone, cocked her head to one side.

A smash downstairs, a plate or mug breaking.

Something else for her to clean up.

Her eyes moved to the floor, saw the knife she'd dropped earlier lying there, drifted to the divan and thought of what was inside: the brown holdall which had been left for her on the doorstep of the pub on that day, years ago; on the day of the funeral she was banned from attending. It contained the last letter she had ever received from Elaine. Her eyes glossed over as she tried to focus on what she could hear from downstairs. Maggie was talking to someone, but she couldn't make out a clear word. Couldn't make out a single name.

James? Were they talking about him?

Was he here, was Maggie wrong?

And what would James find? A woman at twenty-one with no future, a jar of oblivion in her hand, contemplating who should receive the first dose when she knew, full well, she should bloody well take it herself.

('You're still so young!' Maggie had said, at her birthday that year, the big two-one no one else had remembered. 'Not here, I'm not,' she'd spat back and Maggie had looked so hurt Emma had made out she'd been joking, laughed and ate the dry cake her godmother had bought, kissed her cheek, cleaned up the crumbs and gin splashes later.)

Wiping her eyes with the heels of her hand, she took a breath to steady herself, calm down, still aware of the muffled voices downstairs. All wasn't over, not yet.

Maybe James *had* come back.

Maybe everything would work out, one way or another.

She picked up the butter knife, the jar of apple seeds, the one of powder, and returned them all to the drawer, her bleach-burnt knuckles catching the writing paper at the very back: folded letters in her handwriting hidden from view, the written words desperate and begging for help. How many of those letters had she written, now? How many pages were filled with her black, crabbed writing, filled with her longing?

She slammed the drawer shut on the whole damn lot, inched herself closer to her bedroom door. Opening it, just a crack, she tried to catch the words floating up from the bar.

She heard Maggie, her thick West-Country tones warm, familiar.

She heard Nuala, the regionless, well-to-do accent marking her out.

And she heard his name, heard them *both* speak it.

James.

Maggie

Saturday, 18th November, 2017

S he'd felt sorry for Nuala Greene, until now.

When the woman had first walked into the bar, Maggie had seen someone who needed a good night's rest, a few decent meals and someone to make her smile, lift her spirits. She thought this woman might be the turning point for the pub; a sign that B&B and tourism could offer a way forward, the first small step out of debt and into the black.

But then she'd seen Emma's hands, worked to blisters like they hadn't been for years, not since the aftermath of the fire next door. All because this ridiculous woman had come here from the city, stared at a photo on the wall, and stirred up painful memories.

Now she just wanted Nuala Greene to go away, leave her in peace to sort out her bankruptcy and fragile goddaughter. She had too much to worry about already without adding this stray to the list.

What the hell had Emma been thinking? Why was she so convinced that the woman was here because of James? And what did it matter, after seven years, if she was?

But then the door handle turned and Maggie's body locked

with tension in the damask chair, the gin-nipped tea in her hand held still.

'I've come to sort out the room,' the voice said, from the door.

Maggie stayed motionless, facing the swept-out hearth that Emma had forgotten to lay, the greasy crumbs from a bacon sandwich collecting in the creases of her blue striped shirt.

A thick snot-clogged sniff. 'I won't stay another night after all.'

Maggie felt her hand tighten around her mug, her insides clench against the sandwich in her stomach. The stress from the bank's letter, the phone call from Arthur, the pink shock of skin across Emma's knuckles, wound in Maggie's gut.

'I shouldn't have come,' Nuala said, her voice breaking slightly on the last word, taking a deep breath before she continued.

'Then why did you?' Maggie wanted to shout, but her jaw wouldn't unclench and she couldn't get Emma's hands out of her head, the burns on her knuckles, the bleach-scoured floor.

She thought of the letter, in shreds, at the bottom of the graveyard vase. Thought of the bungalow she would never now build.

She lifted the cup to her lips and sipped, tried her best to keep calm. No point getting cross with a stranger, with a woman who, so far, had done nothing wrong. She had more important things to concentrate on.

'I'm sorry,' Nuala said.

And Maggie couldn't take the last word. Her bacon-greased fingers slipped against the mug, lost their grip. It fell from her hand, the sound of the smash bouncing off the stone walls, spilling the tea and the gin on the wood. Maggie thought of Emma, imagined her bending to clean up the mess, saw her pale face, red fingers, the way they shook as they held out the photo of James.

'You're here because of *him*.' It wasn't a question any more. Maggie felt she had known it all along, ever since the woman walked in reeking of nervousness, desperation. Because it *would* happen now, when Maggie was on her knees and trying not to show it. Of course it would happen now.

'I didn't want anyone to know,' Nuala said, her voice slightly fainter and wavering as she inched her way back to the door. 'Not till I had a chance to see his mother.'

Maggie turned her head slightly, saw Nuala pressed to the door, her wide-open eyes staring at the remnants of the mug on the floor, her blond hair hanging lank to her shoulders.

'Who are you to James Lunglow?'

Nuala straightened her back, tried to keep her head high even though her chin trembled. 'James Greene, actually.'

Maggie saw the woman had been crying, her face blotchy, eyes swollen, cheeks damp. Yesterday Maggie would have gone to her, held her in her arms and helped her to calm down. But not now, now she knew who the woman was here for.

'He changed his name?'

'He took mine when we married. He didn't want me to become a Lunglow, hated the idea that I would be called Mrs Lunglow, like his mother.'

'You *married* him?' Maggie got up from the chair with a heave of breath and turned, face on, towards Nuala. 'That worthless piece of – you married *him*?' But beneath the question was another, one that Maggie couldn't bring herself to ask out loud. Why did James marry Nuala? She must have reminded him, every day, of the girl he had left behind. All she needed was the scaly red knuckles, the scar by her eye and the habit of biting her lip.

Nuala spat the words, 'He's dead,' like an insult. They wiped the disgust from Maggie's face.

Maggie looked again, reassessing Nuala under the weight of the news. The lines on her young face, the shadows beneath her eyes that told of more than just sleepless nights, the unnaturally waifish body. Her frailty.

She rubbed her face, felt the scarred ribbon of flesh on her cheek, whispered 'he's dead' into the palm of her hand. She looked towards the ceiling, then to the bottle of gin by the bar.

On top of everything else she had to contend with, James was dead.

'Emma knew you were here about James. She told me your name, that you'd been looking at his photo, that you were here because of *him*. "No, Emma," I said, "she's just a grockle," I said. "We'll have forgotten all about her by the weekend." And do you know what she said to me?' Maggie shook her head clear, ran her fingers through the grey hair, flecks of dandruff falling on her blue striped cotton shirt. 'She said you weren't wearing a ring, that at least you're not his wife! What the hell am I supposed to say to her?'

Maggie sniffed back the mucus from her nose, her eyes raw from unshed tears, gritty from troubled sleep. She paced the room, Nuala still pressed against the door, and made it to the bar and back in eight strides.

'He was meant to come back for her. We all thought he would, we were all waiting to give him the beating of his bloody life. But Emma? She was just waiting. She just wanted him back.' The room darkened, the sun outside dipping behind a cloud, shadows creeping from the window across the floor and shrouding Nuala's expression. But Maggie could sense it, even if she couldn't see it, the narrowing of the other woman's eyes, the tension in her jaw as she thought of Emma waiting for James.

Maggie stopped, out of breath, and leant on the wooden sleeper. She spoke into her chest, the shirt covering her mouth, softening her tone. 'I've been trying to put Emma back together for seven years. And all this time, all this time that I've been helping her, getting her to move on, picking up the pieces that he bloody well broke, he was swanning around London with a posh little wife.'

'How could you marry a man who had done what he did?'

Nuala looked away to the lead cross-hatched window.

'He never told you?'

Maggie watched as Nuala picked at splinter of wood on the card table beside her, flicking it upright to a spike.

'And you never asked him why he left? Never forced it out of him?'

'He would have told me, one day.' Nuala grazed her finger across the splinter, smoothing it down, lifting it up. 'He didn't like me to pressure him. He didn't like it at all.'

Maggie sighed, 'You didn't want to know.' She tried a small laugh but the sound was hollow and flat. 'Thought he did something so terrible it might change your feelings for him, that it?'

'I love him.' Nuala winced at the words, pushed her fingertip down and the splinter buckled beneath. '*Loved* him. Nothing can change that.'

The building creaked and Maggie jumped, looked up at

the ceiling, cocking her head to one side to listen. She glanced
back at the kitchen door.

'So James Lunglow's dead.' She rubbed her face, wiped
her nose with the sleeve of her shirt and headed for the
kitchen. 'I need another tea.'

Maggie returned minutes later with a large mug in her
hands, fresh biscuit crumbs lining the creases of the shirt at
her bust and the bulge of her stomach.

'What happened?' she asked, sitting at the card table. Her
face was paler, the news beginning to sink in, draining the blood
from her face as it did so. 'I'll need to know so I can tell Emma.
She'll have questions, I want to be able to answer them.'

'I want to tell her myself.'

'Absolutely not. She's already in a state after this morning,
I'll not let you do any more damage.' Maggie's mind spun
back to Emma, hopefully resting upstairs oblivious to all this,
the bleach marks on her hands starting, tentatively, to heal.

'She's been writing to him,' Nuala said, frowning as she
leaned back against the wall. 'For the past five years, at least.
I want to tell her myself.' She tried to keep her jaw relaxed,
face calm and Maggie noticed the effort it took her.

Maggie paled further, imagining Emma at the computer,
on her phone, disappearing to the library in town where the
connection was better. She had found him after all. Found
him, but never told Maggie. Why hadn't she told her?

'No,' Maggie said, disbelieving. She took a mouthful of tea
before coughing into the crook of her elbow. She could smell
an undertone of gin on the echo of her breath, hoped Nuala
wasn't close enough to catch it. 'Tell me what happened. I'll
let Emma know after you've gone.' She looked up at the
ceiling again, cocked her head again. 'Better still, just leave

now. You don't even have to pay: I just want you out. I'll tell her myself.'

And what would she tell her? What the hell was she going to say? How would Emma react to the news? But if Maggie got rid of Nuala now, made her leave, then maybe—

'No, you won't,' Nuala said, her voice stronger, determined, the tremble in her chin no more.

'What?' Maggie flushed, her nose turning scarlet as Nuala read her thoughts aloud.

'You won't tell her. You just want me to leave so you can make it all up, let her carry on thinking he's going to come back.' Nuala rubbed her temples, her thin fingers bulging at the joints, her neck tensed, the sinew and tendons visible.

'It'll destroy her if she finds out.' And again Maggie thought of Emma's red raw knuckles. 'She just needs more time.'

'It's false hope.'

'It's better than nothing.'

Nuala moved one hand from her face to her belly, clutching the jersey where it hung from her body. 'What about the baby?' she snarled, mouth grimacing as she bit down, hard, on the littlest finger of her spare hand. 'Or should I say, child? It must be seven years old by now.' She kept the finger in her mouth, biting at the nail, the flesh around it, ripping a slice off with her teeth.

The baby.

Maggie's face flushed with a wash of red, swallowing her face with its violence. She looked up from her place at the table, caught Nuala in the cold of her stare. 'Who *the fuck* told you that?' She spoke quietly, the venom all the more forceful.

'Lois.' The inflection in her voice making it sound like a nervous question.

Maggie punched the table with both fists, startling Nuala and spilling more tea. A jolt of pain moved from her hands to her shoulder, reminding her of her age, that she should be getting ready to retire, relax, hand the business over to Emma, instead of her son, like she'd planned. Not to sit here and clean up the mess that another man had started, a mess his mother had made worse seven years ago and was still making worse now.

Nuala's hands flew to her mouth, worrying away at the bitten flesh on her finger.

'If Lois thinks she can dig that up again, she's got another think coming. I will not stand for it!' Maggie straightened her back, her cheeks damp. 'I will not stand for it.'

Nuala inched forward, a deep v forming between her eyebrows. 'Tell me what happened?'

Maggie shook her head.

Nuala stepped forward again, lifted her hand, tentatively touched Maggie's shoulder. 'Please.'

'You really don't know why he left?' Maggie stared at Nuala, confounded by her ignorance. She wanted to push her away and send her out, but she thought of Lois, of the story *she* would tell Nuala given the chance. Of the damage it would do to Emma if she heard.

'I'll tell you.' A creak from upstairs. The soft thud-thud of footfall. 'But not here.'

Nuala creaked open the door, slid outside into the cold and Maggie followed, wondering what else this strange woman might reveal.

Two months ago

Nuala

Wednesday, 13th September, 2017

'Hello.'

The woman in the park stopped, looked around her, behind her, raised one hand to her eyes and scanned the distance.

'I'm over here.'

The woman looked again, dark bobbed hair swishing as her head turned, sending a breeze of Chanel over the low hedge and into the garden. She saw Nuala staring back, skin as white as the clouds, neck and shoulders as thin as the branches she was peering over.

'I have a pram.' Nuala's lips were dry, small cracks radiating from the centre line. This was the second person she had spoken to that day, her lips sore from the effort.

'I'm sorry?' The woman in the park let her mouth hang open, her pretty young face confused. The hand that had shielded her eyes now gripped the strap of her handbag, the other jumped to her cashmere swaddled bump and Nuala felt her own small bump, flaccid and empty but still there, itching sympathetically beneath her clothes. 'Do you want it?'

'The pram?' The woman in the park avoided Nuala's gaze and instead looked behind her to the garden, frown lines deepening as she took in the overgrown grass, unruly hedges, the wilting rose, the weedy hemlock strangling the herb garden.

'Yes.' Nuala followed her gaze to the rose bed. Lingered on the dry, brown plants, the hemlock's poisonous flower heads.

'No, thank you.'

'Oh.' Nuala hung her head and began to shudder, the movements sending her own perfume over the bush; greasy hair, unwashed clothes, her dehydrated, stinking breath.

The woman in the park rubbed her bump, the yellow wool rippling under her hand. She gave a weak smile. 'We're not ready for one yet.' She stepped back, about to walk away, but stopped when she saw Nuala's chin tremble.

'I didn't mean to offend. I'm superstitious, that's all. I won't even put the cot together until the baby's here, let alone buy a pram.' She gave a little shrug, another smile and waddled away, her hips swaying with the weight of the bump.

Nuala felt her stretch-marks burn. The other woman looked over her shoulder, saw Nuala watching and sped up, her mobile phone now pressed to her ear. And Nuala wondered what that would be like, to hold the cold, hard plastic to your ear and talk to your husband, or mother, or friend.

Nuala turned her back on the park, walked past the dying rose and through the kitchen door. Tiny flies buzzed around her, others formed a black mass in the fruit bowl, feasting off the putrefying bananas. More crawled across the fridge, lapping up the milky yellow juice that was seeping beneath the seal.

The smell was too much, the air dusty with mould spores and sweet from rotting food, but to leave the kitchen would mean walking into the hallway. It would mean walking towards the cardboard box that had been delivered that morning, the picture on the side of a smiling mother gripping the handle-bars of a pram, the feet and hands of a squirming baby poking from beneath the hood.

She had bought it after her twenty-week scan when Maxwell still wriggled inside her. They would deliver it closer to her due date, they told her. That way she wouldn't have to store it herself, they told her. She wouldn't be tempting fate.

She'd have to send it back, tell them it was no longer needed.

She closed her eyes and walked through the hall, one hand feeling the wall until she reached the bannister, lifting her feet to walk up the stairs.

Something brushed her calf.

She jumped back, the corners of her mouth splitting open as she screamed, her hands grappling for something, anything.

She fell to the floor with a smack.

It was the pram that had brushed her leg, the corner of the box tickling her calf. The woman in the picture looked out with a grin, triumphant and condescending, laughing at Nuala's fall, laughing at her sagging belly.

The baby in the pram kicked and kicked. 'You can't have me,' it seemed to say between giggles and dribbles of spit, 'you can't have me.' And it kicked on and on and on, the woman pushing the pram laughing, laughing, laughing.

Nuala half lifted herself up, crawled on hands and knees up the stairs.

She stopped at the top. The nursery was straight ahead. The door was closed but inside the walls were pale green, the carpet the same light grey wool that covered the landing, the cot a fresh white, the nursing chair, the little chest of drawers, the changing table, the toy chest – all white.

She took the door beside the nursery, the door leading to her bedroom.

The bed where they had made love, the cupboards that still held his clothes, the table where his flat cap lay, Maxwell's pictures tucked inside.

The sheets were yellow but once they, too, had been white. Her side of the bed was spotted with dried, stale milk spots, though her milk had dried up weeks ago. His side of the bed was spotted with Maxwell, the dark red blot from his umbilical cord, a black smudge of meconium.

Nuala crawled across the floor to the wash of dried blood that she had never cleaned up.

She stood up at last, on the rusty brown stain, the carpet dry and matted beneath her feet, eyes out of focus, memory sharp to that day.

She was alone.

She was all alone.

Her friends from school had been out of touch since she had married James, feeling snubbed perhaps that they weren't invited to her wedding (why invite them when it's none of their business? Wouldn't it be more romantic, just the two of them? And how could she invite all her friends, her distant cousins, when James had left all his far behind him? Did Nuala really want to rub it in his face, how alone he was? Did she really want to make him feel so lonely on what should be the best day of his life? Was she really so cruel? And of course she wasn't, of course not, so she had left her old friends behind her.)

All of James's new friends, the ones from his work at the park, were awkward, didn't know what to do or to say, even more so since Maxwell, none of them really knowing her that well at all.

And there were no more of her own, no friends from a job or a course or a hobby. No one suitable, in James's eyes (and, by proxy, Nuala's). And what would she want with girlfriends who would drag her from pub to club, morals as low as their necklines, drinking and flirting and doing what most women do? What *other* women do? Nuala was different, special, because she had saved herself for James. She was his and his only, untouched by the dirty masses like so many other women out there. She didn't need those women as friends. She didn't need anyone else, and if she had to talk to someone then why not talk to James, tell him everything, because wasn't he everything to her? Wasn't he? Well? Because she was everything to him, and it would have killed him, *killed him*, if he hadn't been everything to her.

And there was nobody she could think of to turn to. Nobody that James, dead or alive, would want her near. Her parents were both dead, her maternal family made up of strangers in Ireland, father's parents passed before she was born. And his family was one woman only; a mother so terrible he couldn't bear to be near her, so terrible he had changed his name, cut her off.

When she finally lifted her head, the room had gone dark, the streetlights glowing through the blinds.

Nuala walked past the bed to the other side of the room, through the door that led to the en-suite. The room stank, the smell far worse than the kitchen. The toilet hadn't been flushed in days. Why bother to flush a toilet? What was the point?

She opened the mirrored cabinet above the sink and stared at all the bottles and packets within. Paracetamol, ibuprofen, aspirin, sleeping pills, temazepam, antihistamines, hypnotics,

Prozac, Sudafed, flu tablets, codeine and a small, purple bottle with a white lid, a smiling baby on its label.

She took them all into her bedroom and emptied them, packet by packet, onto the duvet. She filled her mouth in handfuls, washing the pills down with the Calpol and let herself fall, face down, on the blood stain.

Emma

Saturday, 18th November, 2017

The side of her face still pressed to the gap in the door, she paused. Her blood ran cold, her body frozen. Except her ears, burning with the name she had heard.

James.

Nuala Greene had spoken it, the name like a whisper carrying up from the bar.

The woman *was* here because of James. She'd been right.

'It'll destroy her if she finds out.' That was Maggie.

What would destroy her, and why? What the hell were they talking about?

Emma opened her bedroom door further, craned her neck into the dank little hallway, trying to hear more, the floorboards creaking as she stepped out.

Silence following her footfall.

'I'll tell you, but not here.'

Maggie was going to tell her.

Tell her everything.

After all Maggie had said to Emma that morning, urging her to forget about the stranger, telling her how harmless she was, how she had nothing whatsoever to do with James.

And now Maggie was going to tell this woman everything.

Some trumped up blow-in from London was going to find out all about her past. Because Emma's story was woven with James's, Maggie wouldn't be able to tell Nuala why James left the village without explaining what happened to Emma.

If only Emma had heard more of the conversation, instead of snippets when voices were raised.

She heard the front door close. In the street, there was the rumble of an engine and she moved to the window, watched Maggie climb into Nuala's small red car, the same car that had caused all the whispers in the bar last night. She watched it drive away, following the road out of the village, the thick-necked shadow of Maggie visible in the passenger seat.

She could hear the car long after it had disappeared from view. She listened until its noise vanished, the sound lost to that of the wind, of the cows in the dairy behind them, of the crow scarer blasting off gunshots in the fields either side of Shore Road.

She needed to clean the bar up, sort out whatever Maggie had spilt downstairs. She needed to lay the fire, clean the glasses, make sure the bar was ready for service that night, needed to go to the shop and buy food. She should get to work. Take her mind off Nuala Greene, take her mind off whatever Maggie was telling her.

Her hands began to throb, the burn from the bleach stinging again.

She should get to work, carry on as normal.

But outside her bedroom, in the hallway that ran the length of the house, she couldn't take her eyes off the guest room.

She reached for the door, pulse galloping as it opened inward.

A single bed. A sink fastened at the corner, no mirror. The wallpaper spotted with mildew, black with damp at the bottom edge. One bedside table, the drawer at the top missing and the surface covered in old cigarette burns from when Maggie used to let people smoke inside.

But she hadn't let that happen since the fire next door, even though it was caused by a chip pan, not a fag. Even though *that* fire had been set on purpose.

On the floor by the foot of the bed was that Burberry bag, and Emma's jaw clenched at the label.

Knees on the ground, the thin woollen rug protecting against the splintery wood beneath, she opened the bag and looked through it.

A small, quilted toiletry bag held tiny bottles, Clarins, Arden, Molton Brown on the labels, a gold tube of Touche Éclat.

The cashmere jumper Nuala had worn the day before. Reiss, the label read. The jeans were there too, Diesel no less, and even her underwear was by Morgan Lane.

Emma hadn't worn anything like this since moving to the pub, since Maggie started footing the bill. Her own lovely clothes, bought by her stepmother, Elaine, from the department stores in town, were gradually replaced by supermarket own brands, the underwear in plastic packs from Primark. She still had the last cardigan Elaine had bought for her, a soft, pale-green wool. She held it to her nose sometimes. She used to be able to smell her dead stepmother's perfume, a mixture of gardenia and clean cotton. The real scent was long gone, she just imagined it, remembered it, now, never having the money to buy it herself.

There was no perfume in Nuala's bag, but Emma suspected that, had there been any, it would have been Chanel. Even Nuala's socks were Bridgedale, for Christ's sake. No holes. No worn heels.

And this woman was about to find out all about Emma's sad little life, all about the girl James left behind.

She held Nuala's jumper up to the daylight, the cashmere too thick to let the sun through. Emma pressed it to her body, thought what-the-hell and tried it on, pushing her head through the hole in the top and feeling the soft wool stroke her cheek.

She had forgotten how nice good wool felt.

As she hugged the fabric to her she noticed something else.

A small piece of paper on the side table.

Keeping the jumper on, her hands still stroking the front, she stepped away and picked up the paper.

An envelope.

Addressed to James.

Why would Nuala have this? And where was the letter that came with it?

What right did she have to open this when it wasn't hers?

It was for James.

How did she get it?

An idea, like a seedling, took root in her head. The letter was addressed to James Lunglow, the name Emma had been searching for online for seven years.

Hands shaking, burns stinging, she prised her phone from her back pocket and held the handset up to the window, the top right-hand corner where sometimes she would get a bar or two of reception.

In the search bar, she began to type his name, James Lunglow automatically coming up as a suggestion. Her guts writhing, stomach weak with the horrible possibility that Nuala was his wife after all, she deleted the Lunglow, changed it to Nuala's surname, Greene.

She waited for the results to come in, hoping she was wrong, that James hadn't forfeited Emma for this woman, with her money and nice things.

But what came up in her search was far worse.

The blue and white homepage for Facebook.

James staring back from the photo in the top corner.

And comment after comment, stretching back for six months.

We'll miss you.

Won't forget you.

R.I.P.

Emma dropped her phone, stumbled to the sink by the wall, and retched her breakfast up into the porcelain.

Nuala

Saturday, 18th November, 2017

Not in the pub, Maggie had said, in case Emma overhears, gets upset.

And nowhere inside the village was private enough, suitable for this kind of talk. Someone else may overhear, Maggie had said, and tell Emma. *Poor Emma.*

As if *Emma* was the widow, as if *she* mattered, as if *she* had ever been anything to James.

Nuala gripped the wheel of her car, stared at the road, tried to keep calm, relaxed.

She had agreed to drive Maggie out of the village, up to the hill to find somewhere private. Anything to get to the end of this story, to hear the truth at last.

'Why did you never ask him?' Maggie shook her head for the fifth time since they had driven away from the pub, watching the shallow rise of the hill from her passenger window. The houses were gone, replaced by the odd stunted sessile oak, the occasional glossy holly.

'I'd have forced it out of him. If it were my husband, I'd have gotten him drunk, got him to carry on drinking until he'd told all.'

Dark, leafless hedges rose up at the sides of the road, the

twigs and branches obscuring the light. From the corner of her eye Nuala could see Maggie's reflection staring back from the passenger window, the pale grey of her hair stark against the dark foliage outside. Her own features, her brow and eyes visible in the rear-view mirror, were tense as she studied the road.

'How can you live with someone for seven years and not know why they left home?'

The road lifted and dropped, the blind summit swooping down to the plateau. The wind came from all directions, swirling the fallen leaves into tornadoes, stumps of heather and gorse beaten into submission.

They were at the top of the hills, James's village in the valley below them, sheep-dotted scrubland to the left, a drop into oblivion on the right. Nuala steered into the wind, forcing the wheels to obey, slowed the car to a crawl.

'You can't have known him at all, if you didn't know about his past. Take the next side-road.'

'That's what Lois said; I can't have loved him, not without knowing him,' Nuala repeated the words and felt her chest constrict, focused instead on the sounds of the tyres gripping the dirt road.

'Well, I do love him, I do know him. Did know him.'

The side-road was no more than a dirt track flanked by hazel, blackthorn and the odd stump of gorse.

'Seems odd, that's all,' Maggie said. 'Stop over there, that gap in the hedge.'

Nuala stopped the car and Maggie jumped out to open a wide, wooden gate, then waved her through. Nuala looked down to see the skin across her knuckles stretched to translucency where she gripped the wheel.

Maggie lumbered back in, the car's suspension swaying. 'More peace here, no one to overhear us, no one to go back and tell Emma what I'm about to tell you. If you'd come better dressed I'd have taken you walking, found some privacy up on the hill paths.' She gestured around them. 'It was my father-in-law's, this land. I sold most of it to keep the pub afloat after Tom, my husband, passed, but I kept this bit back so I've something to leave to Emma. Land will always be worth more than money, Tom used to say.'

'Why do we have to be so far out of the village to have this discussion?' Nuala asked. 'Why would Emma care?'

'I don't want her thinking I'm talking behind her back. She's sensitive about this business, about anything to do with James.' Maggie rubbed the scar tissue on her cheek. Nuala could smell the earth on Maggie's boots from when she opened the gate, manure and rotting leaves from the field outside. 'As you would know, if you'd ever pushed James to tell you himself. If you'd found out who he really was.'

'You know, James used to smell of the earth,' Nuala said. 'He was a groundsman, his hands smelled like soil, even if he had washed them. In October they would cut back the bracken, burn it in piles once it had dried and use the ash as fertiliser. He used to smell of bonfires in November and that heavy, mossy smell of ferns.' Her hands were at her face, her index finger in her mouth, teeth gnawing away at the edges. When she drew it back she saw the bright pink slice of a raw wound, blood rising up to the surface. 'I *did* know him. He was my husband, I knew my own husband.'

Maggie's face creased with condescending pity. 'I'm sure you believe you did.'

Nuala rubbed her neck, needling the skin behind her ear

with her fingers. 'I know that the hat James was wearing in the photo at the pub came from you.' She thought of it at home on her bedside table, the ultrasound photo tucked inside.

'I didn't give it to him—'

'I know. He stole it. You caught him drinking when he was fifteen. He said he'd never give it back if you told Lois and you said he could keep it, even though it was your late husband's.'

Tall patches of hay-like grass loomed over the car, the strands brushing against the window in the swirl of the wind, their shadows lashing her thighs.

'Well, James never had a hat on his head, even in winter.' Maggie stared into her lap. 'He could have done with one.'

'I know he got textbooks every Christmas, never toys. I know Lois gave him Bird's custard for pudding every Sunday, made with water. I know the holes in his shoes were fixed with cardboard insoles, that when his father died Lois altered the old man's clothes and gave them to James for his twelfth birthday.'

Nuala could hear the grass thrashing the car, whipping the ground, and beyond it the sound of the wood pigeons' pitiful repetition. The sound brought back more memories of James, of the hum that escaped with his breath when he found the album of her childhood birthday parties, the pony she was gifted at eight, his face sad and sullen as he told her he'd never had a birthday party as a child, not one and certainly nothing like this, his hand flicking the picture of Nuala's new pony, a *happy birthday* hat perched on its head. James's voice had been sharp and if it hadn't been for the sad look in his eyes, Nuala would have thought he was jealous. But he didn't need ponies and parties and gifts to prove his worth. And he certainly wasn't jealous of *her*, why would he be? Why would anyone be jealous of *her*? The thought made him laugh and he did. He did.

No, the photos of her parties reminded him of his mother, led to a rare mention of her, how shit she had been, how she'd done nothing for him, nothing. The first woman in his life to disappoint him.

'I know that, in the holidays, Lois made him redo the schoolwork he had failed. I know he hardly had any friends because nobody was allowed to play with him.' She looked to the sky and saw the swirl of pale grey clouds, whiter where the sun tried to break through them, darker where they tempted rain. Thought of James telling her, again, that they would never need anyone else, just each other, no need for outside interference.

'I know he used to dread the winter because his house didn't have central heating, because his mother would make him share her bed to keep warm.'

She could hear James again, ordering her *never to go there*, to just do as he said *for once*. She wished he was alive, safe at home, warm beneath a blanket or in front of a fire but he wasn't, he was here with her, waiting in the mud, the wind and grass whipping his frame whilst he stared at her, his face telling her what a fool, what an idiot, she had been not to listen. That she was disappointing him, again.

'And I know he loved you, Maggie.' Her chin wavered and she swallowed, tried to remember all the good things James had told her. 'You taught him to ride a bike the summer his dad died, you let him into the pub when it was cold, gave him cider to warm him up even when he was too young for it, gave him the cream from the top of the milk and the fat from the bacon, fried to a crisp and wrapped in buttered bread.' She breathed in, the damp rot of leaves and mud invading her senses. Even with her eyes closed she could see her husband, hear his voice in her head as he told her stories about Maggie, his tone far softer than it normally was.

'Someone had to watch out for him. He took his father's death terribly hard, happening, as it did, on the boy's birthday.' Maggie stared at her knees, clearly moved by what Nuala had said. 'I'm surprised he remembered all that.'

'He told me more about you than anyone else, it's the reason I came straight to your pub, how I knew I would be safe there with you. He told me,' Nuala reached out, touched Maggie's shoulder, waited for the woman to look up before she went on, 'you were the mother he needed when his own mother failed him. He said you were the mother he wished he had had.'

'Lois was too young, could barely cope, and her parents would have nothing to do with them. I helped when I could. But then my husband died and I really was in no fit state, I couldn't even look after my own—' Maggie stopped, looked out of her window and sighed.

Nuala's hand was still on Maggie's right shoulder. 'I know you can't hate him, Maggie. You looked after him and he loved you for it. I know that, whatever he did, you loved him too, because seven years later, you still have his photograph on the pub wall, even if you won't let anyone speak his name.'

'Did he really say that?' Maggie asked, her mournful voice tinged with regret. 'About me being the mother he wished he'd had?'

Nuala nodded, her eyes on James's phantom in the grass. The wind was momentarily still, outside quiet. Maggie shifted in her seat. 'Maybe it's best you don't know. I don't want to tarnish your memories, I know how precious they can be.'

'No!' Nuala spoke too loudly, her cries frightening James away, his body fading to nothing in the mud. The skin on her finger was burning now, the blood leaking out from the gnawed-raw wound. 'You have to tell me. I can't go until I know what happened.'

'You're sure?' Maggie said, still looking away, clearly trying to find the right words. 'Because once you know, you can't go back.'

Nuala was firm. 'I want to know.'

Maggie drew in a breath and began.

Seven years ago

Emma

Tuesday, 10th August, 2010

Emma lingered, watching her stepmother walking ahead of her along the road, an empty carrier bag in her hand, before catching her up.

'It would be so much easier if Daddy just taught you to drive; you wouldn't have to carry them back so far.'

At the sound of her voice, Elaine turned with a smile. Emma did her usual quick scan, checking her stepmother over for new bruises or marks to her skin, but found nothing.

'There's no need, everything I want's within walking distance. Besides, your father needs the car for the farm, you know that.'

Elaine linked arms with her stepdaughter and Emma could smell the gardenia from her perfume, a vague undercurrent of Persil. Emma stiffened, aware suddenly of her own smell, the smell of *him*, emanating from her body. Could Elaine smell it too?

His scent clung to Emma's skin, as it always did, the smell making her dizzy as the breeze lifted and wafted it around her. She could still taste him on her lips and the skin of her arm, bare in the summer heat, ran with goose bumps from where his skin had touched hers.

'Don't tell anyone,' he'd whispered just as she left, the same

words he said every time. *'Not a soul.'* His grip on her wrist had been a little too tight but the tone of his voice was so soft, so loving, she quickly forgave him. *'You'd get me in trouble if you did, and you don't want that, do you? Well? Do you?'*

'Have you had a good day?' Elaine was smiling and Emma breathed out, her heart resuming its normal, calm pattern.

She nodded, dispelling the image of James above her, the ears of ripening wheat blowing around them, showering them with grain, tickling her bare calves and wrists.

'Just been out in the sunshine,' she said and her voice sounded, to her own ear, somehow older, as though James had infected every part of her. 'Took a book up into the hills and sat reading.' She dug the book out of the bag on her shoulder, holding out the proof of her lie. Could Elaine detect the change in her voice? Had she been following the progressive changes in Emma over the past two months, noticed how every time she'd been with that man in *that* way, she'd felt even more like a woman herself? The self-awareness, the confidence, the way, sometimes, she would blush in the mirror, seeing herself the way James saw her.

'You're no little girl,' he'd said to her that day, *'You're all woman with me. You're my woman.'* And the thrill of being his, of belonging to James Lunglow, a man so good-looking he was surely half God, made her giddy.

'You needn't look so worried.' Elaine squeezed her elbow, making Emma jump, making her wonder if her stepmother *did* know, if she'd known all along since that very first time, eight weeks ago now, in the barn at the back of the farm. James had put his hands on her then; first her waist, his fingers moving up through her blouse buttons with ease. They'd used that same blouse to wipe up afterwards. She'd had to clean the blouse herself, in her en-suite washbasin, his stain tougher to remove than she'd imagined.

But she'd had to do it herself. She couldn't let Elaine see, or worse, her father. And she certainly couldn't wear the blouse, stained like that, to school.

Elaine leant in even further to Emma. 'I shan't tell your father.'

Emma paled, felt her arm tremble beneath Elaine's hand.

Had Elaine seen James lead Emma away that very first time, had she seen him unbutton his jeans and show Emma, so nervous she was shaking from head to foot, what she should do, how she should kneel, where she should look, exactly how far she should take him in her mouth?

She didn't need to be told any more, of course, she knew his rhythms by heart, that initial fear, uncertainty long melted away. But what use was that knowledge, that instinct, when they were about to be unmasked?

The road curved around and they were greeted by a breeze, melting the heat from Emma's skin, leaving her cold and pin-pricked with worry.

What had she been expecting, anyway? For things to continue indefinitely? The wheat that had hidden them through summer would soon be harvested, the sky would cloud over into autumn, the birds singing to them from the trees would fly away.

'Not that your father would mind that you went off to read for a few hours, of course,' Elaine said with a smile. Emma stalled, confusion slowing her step until relief sank in and she realised Elaine didn't know anything.

'He doesn't expect you to work on the farm for the whole summer; you are only fourteen, after all.'

Emma tried to smile, but the crease in her brow remained. She tried to see herself as Elaine saw her; as a young, fresh girl on her summer holidays, gearing up for a new year of school, escaping to the hills so her father wouldn't make her work all summer long. Not the half-naked nymph lying beneath a fully-grown man only hours before, hiding from her parents in a field of three-foot high wheat.

Just the thought of them finding out turned the blood in her veins to ice. She bit her lip, remembering James above her again, the patches of fine hair on his chest, the stubble on his jaw, trying to feel ashamed of herself, as her parents would be if they knew, but the shame didn't come and the underside of her collar stuck to the back of her neck.

'You're *my* woman,' he had said and she was, she was.

'You have to have some fun, even your daddy understands that.' Elaine squeezed her arm again.

'Yes, your father *would* want you to have fun.' Lois Lunglow, feet feline silent in their leatherette pumps, had sprung on them from behind. She was wearing a cardigan, despite the heat, two of the buttons gone. 'As long as it's the right sort, of course.'

Emma could hear the blood rushing in her ears. She forced herself to stay calm, to remember that nobody knew what she'd been doing with James Lunglow only hours beforehand, least of all his mother.

'Emma's just been out walking, enjoying the sun, Lois.'

Why, in God's name, did Elaine have to talk to that woman? Why couldn't she just follow the trend and ignore her?

'*You* clearly haven't been out walking, Elaine. I'd be surprised if you've lifted a finger all day, dressed like that?' Lois fell into step beside them, her eyes drinking in Elaine's dress. 'It's very nice. New, is it? Arthur buy it for you, did he?'

It was the cold smile Emma hated the most; the way Lois's lips would thin and disappear, her mouth no more than a slit across her face. Thank God James didn't have her smile. His lips were fuller, firmer, their touch opening her to him, making her yield.

Emma felt herself blush again, the skin on her forehead clammy.

'He likes to treat me.' Elaine's eyes flicked to the right, to the row of neat cottages set back from the road, the cottages owned by Arthur and let out. The income from those alone was nearly double what the average labourer earned, probably triple the sum Lois claimed from the state.

'Must be nice, to be treated. I wouldn't know.' Lois had noticed the look and followed it to the little houses, their double-glazed windows, their leak-free roofs.

Emma sped up, forming the point of the three-person arrow as she led them away from Arthur's cottages, Elaine's cottages, and on towards the shop. Head down, eyes to the floor, she noticed Lois's shoes again, the sole coming away from the toe on both feet.

When they reached the shop Emma waited for Lois to leave, but she stayed, her smile fixed.

'Of course, I'll know what it's like to be treated soon, once James graduates and gets himself a good city job.'

Emma's ears pricked up but she stayed silent, not wanting to seem keen, not wanting people to think that she cared about Lois or her son. She looked into the shop, saw Jennifer Hill and her son Toby meandering through the aisles, Jennifer glancing up at Lois and Elaine. No doubt she was trying to listen in.

'Graduates? Have you plans for him to go to college?' Elaine asked.

Lois scoffed and Emma hated her for it. 'I don't have any plans *for* James, he's old enough to make his own and none of his plans involve him staying *here*.'

Lois was wrong. James was going to stay here. He was going to stay close to Emma whilst she finished school, he'd get a job, start a career, earn enough money to take care of Emma because by then it wouldn't be so bad if people found out, if she was older and he could support her. That's what he'd told her. That's what she believed. They'd be together forever. Forever and ever.

As soon as she was old enough to leave home.

Elaine nodded, her arm around Emma's shoulders, and still Lois's eyes were upon Emma. 'We have our own high hopes for this one,' she said. 'Arthur has it all mapped out for you, doesn't he, Emma? No settling down early for *you*, no getting married too young. Not like—' Elaine stopped abruptly, suddenly aware of what she was saying.

'Which of us are you referring to there, *Mrs Bradbury*?' Lois moistened her lips with her tongue and her fingers flexed in and out, each time making a fist so tight her tendons bulged.

'Oh, no,' muttered Elaine, 'I meant—' but her words slipped into silence, her eyes fixed on the ground.

Lois looked at Emma, with her thin mouth and sharp cheekbones, her eyes boring straight into Emma's.

Emma felt sick, lightheaded.

What would happen to James if they knew? Emma had read enough, seen enough on TV to know James could be charged with statutory rape. Her parents would never forgive him, never forgive her, they'd punish them both. They wouldn't care that it was true love, that James would never do those things to her if he didn't love her, didn't intend on staying with her forever.

'Thankfully,' Lois said, her eyes darting back to Elaine, 'James is to start at university in September, even has a job lined up part time whilst he studies.' She paused for effect, looking behind her to make sure Jennifer Hill in the shop was listening, would be able to spread the news to the rest of the village whilst they stocked up on milk and fresh bread. 'If he's any sense he won't return.'

'You're pale, Emma.'

Her father spoke from the other end of the table, his glasses perched on his forehead.

'I'm fine, just tired after my walk.' She hadn't been able to eat a thing, the chicken lying congealed in its sauce on her plate. Even the glass of water was difficult to swallow.

James was leaving.

He hadn't told her.

'Your mother worked hard, cooking that.' Her father sat back in his chair, frowning, his own plate empty. Emma often called Elaine Mum, always referred to her as her mother, but when Arthur said it, it sounded hollow, a reminder of why Elaine was here instead of Emma's birth mother, a reminder of the first mistake Emma had ever made because, as her father often told her, if it hadn't been for Emma her mother would still be alive, would never have developed grade four tears during labour, suffered catastrophic blood loss, died on the operating table.

'I'm sorry.' She fumbled her words, fiddling with her napkin, feeling the familiar nervous heat prick her neck. 'I'll eat more.' She pulled the plate towards her but her hands felt weak, shaky. She put them in her lap to hide them from her father. He wouldn't like to see her so nervous, wouldn't like it at all, would interrogate Elaine about it after Emma had gone to bed and Emma couldn't bear the thought of it, Elaine taking the heat for Emma. *Because* of Emma.

If only she could get a hold of herself, stop her heart from racing like this, stop her stomach from churning.

Lovesick, that was her problem. Lovesick for a man five years older, who'd probably got bored of his fourteen-year-old pet.

'Go on then,' her father said. 'Eat up.'

Emma pushed James out of her head, steadied herself with a deep breath and lifted a forkful of chicken. Every mouthful, she told herself as she ate, would be one less mark on Elaine's white skin.

She chewed, and chewed, the food like dust on her tongue. She looked at Elaine, who was pulling her cardigan further down her arm, a vague purple bruise on her wrist. She caught the slight shake of Elaine's head. Arthur was watching Emma, his hands in fists on the table, and she forced the food down her throat.

Her whole body felt sweaty, prickled with heat, the food churning in her angry stomach.

Why hadn't James told her he was leaving? Why, when she was lying naked in his arms, grains of wheat catching in the hairs on his chest, did he not tell her?

What would she do, when he was gone?

How could she cope with all *this*, without him?

She hadn't seen anyone else the whole summer, had let friendships slide, had neglected invitations to spend more time with James, to devote herself, her mind and body, to him. All they needed was each other; he'd said so many times. No one else. She was *his*, wasn't he hers? Did she really need to spend time with immature little girls when she could spend time with him instead?

'That'll do,' Arthur said and Emma realised that she had forced down half her meal in a trance, her eyes glazed over. Elaine offered her a sad, thankful smile.

'You're lucky, to get a good, hot meal every night.' Her father's voice was cold, his hands still in fists and Emma thought how very black her luck was. But still she said, yes, I know, thank you and Arthur didn't say any more, his eyes set on Elaine.

It was a few moments later, as Emma left the table and bent down to kiss Arthur's offered cheek, that the first pulse of nausea hit her. She smiled through it, so her father wouldn't notice.

Another hit as her foot touched the bottom step of the stairs. She doubled over, the food rising up her throat with a stomachful of bile.

Upstairs it came in waves, pulsing through her as she lay on her bed. Instinctively she curled into a ball, her duvet hugged against her body. Her forehead was damp, hands clammy, tongue thick and dry in her mouth.

It couldn't be food poisoning; she had barely eaten all day.

It didn't feel like the flu.

She tried to remember the last time she'd had her period, but she'd only had three so far and they had all been maddeningly irregular.

She had to speak to James. She wouldn't call him, never did for fear of being overheard. Couldn't text him either, because her father was in the habit of checking her phone. She would see him instead, face to face.

She could still picture James, his whisper in her ear telling her not to worry, that he'd be careful, wouldn't finish inside her and besides, she was only just fourteen, she should trust him, trust him, trust him, she was far too young to get pregnant.

But a dull ache throbbed down in her belly.

Maybe James would have to stay after all.

Because he couldn't leave her, not now.

Seven years ago

Emma

Tuesday, 10th August, 2010

The following morning the cramping pain was still there, so too the sickness. A deep wash of nausea enveloped her from the moment she opened her eyes.

She couldn't tell anyone she was pregnant, let alone that the father was James.

'Pregnancy is dangerous, Emma.' Her father's warnings echoed in her ears, repeating with each thud of her heartbeat. 'Your mother was proof enough of that.'

How many times had he told her what had happened to her mother? He reminded Emma on each of her birthdays as they walked to her mother's grave to lay flowers – no birthday present for the girl who killed her mother. It was Elaine who cured those birthday heartaches. Elaine who, in secret, would get her a gift. A new cardigan, a bar of chocolate, sweet-smelling shampoo, wrapped up in ribbon.

She passed the pub, dark and quiet at this time of the morning, and thought of Maggie, the few memories she had of her before Tom died ten years before. A time when her godmother used to bake with her, kiss her cheek, tell her stories, treat her the way Emma would treat this baby, with love. Not that Maggie didn't still love Emma, Emma knew that she did, but now

Maggie's attention was stained with grief for the son she had lost to the system, for the husband who had died in the crash. James had told her that, when Maggie talked to him, she sometimes slipped up and called him Lee.

She pushed open the gate to James's house, next door to Maggie's pub, the sound of metal scraping concrete grating her nerves.

Her whole body hurt, the pain radiating like a white hot ripple from the centre of her body. She had to tell James.

He would help her.

She didn't know what to do.

She knocked and the pain winded her, a flash of red eclipsing her vision.

A head looked out.

Two hands grabbed her, pulled her inside.

The door slammed, the sound making Emma jump and her vision clear.

'You're roasting, what's wrong with you?' It was Lois, not James, her tone lacking any concern. She put her hand to Emma's head, guided her to the stairs and lowered her onto the bottom step, her actions only marginally more gentle than her voice.

Emma gripped the woman's arm. Her hand brushed something soft: one of James's jumpers on the step, waiting to be carried up, his scent emanating from the cloth. Lois followed Emma's gaze, her eyes lingering, too, on her son's sweater.

'Why are you so pale?' Her voice was accusing as well as questioning.

Emma moved her mouth to reply, but no words came. She tried to focus on Lois, but she was mesmerised by James.

All she could see was James.

The walls along the hallway were studded with frames,

alternating between his photograph and his certificates from school, twenty frames opposite her at least.

'He's not here.' Lois said, watching the young girl stare at the photographs. 'He left early; *university* business. Won't be back for a while. My God, what's wrong with you? You're white as a sheet.' Lois's eyes stayed on the pictures of James long after Emma's gaze had fallen away from them. The skin around Lois's eyes and mouth was tense. Fearful. 'What is it you want with my son?'

Emma's head began to spin.

She felt for Lois's arm, tried to cling to the fabric but her fingers felt numb.

She shouldn't have come. She should have gone straight to her stepmother, or to Maggie. Shouldn't have risked Lois finding out about her and James. Emma would lose him, she knew she would, if his mother got in the way. She could sense it in the other woman's tensed arms, in her voice laced with that odd mixture of protectiveness for her son and aggression towards anyone else.

Lois would see Emma as an obstacle to her son. A rival.

Emma asked for Elaine, asked to be taken home, but the pain made words difficult to form.

'You need to talk slower, Emma, I can't understand you.' The woman prised Emma's fingers from her arm and Emma cried out, Lois's touch like icicles on her flesh. But the woman carried on, one hand feeling the glands on Emma's neck, the other reaching for her mobile phone, her eyes flickering from Emma to the pictures of James, suspicion rather than sympathy in her actions

'Dammit!' Lois flung the mobile onto the floor. No reception. Emma tried to stand, but her arms and legs wouldn't hold her. The world turned sideways. She was on her back on the hallway floor, the light bulb above burning her eyes.

Lois gasped and kneeled by her side. 'I need your phone.' Panic made her voice shake. 'I need to call an ambulance. I need to contact your parents.'

'No!'

The force of Emma's cry made her wince, her stomach and torso contracting, but she couldn't let Lois call her parents, not yet. She couldn't tell them what she had done, or with whom.

'You need to tell me what the matter is, Emma,' Lois cajoled, her voice edged with fear. 'Tell me, so I can help.'

Tears prickled and she tried to speak again, wanting Elaine, wanting James to take her away, keep her safe, stop the pain that was ripping her in two.

She parted her lips, her eyes closing against the swirling, shifting images above. She knew Lois wouldn't want to help her. But who else could she turn to?

'I need James,' she said, and Lois's face came closer, her eyes only inches from Emma's. 'He's the father.'

Lois sprang back. Stared at the girl on the floor, at Emma's belly, shook her head and her face paled to white. 'No, you can't be, he wouldn't!'

'Don't tell my dad, please.'

'Your dad?' Lois raised her hands to her face, hid her mouth. 'No, you're right, he can't know.'

'Please help me,' Emma said, voice broken. She couldn't hold it in any more and her hands slid down to cradle her belly. 'Please.'

Lois didn't move. Emma could see the disgust in her face, the disapproval. She wished she had gone to Elaine more than ever, knew that her stepmother would have held her close and stroked her hair, promised her that everything would be all right.

Lois managed to shake the horror from her face, moved forward urgently. 'You mustn't tell Arthur that James is the father. Understand?' She grabbed Emma's shoulder, tried to make her agree but Emma couldn't talk any more.

Head foggy, she was aware of footsteps, Lois running to the building next door: Maggie's pub.

Painstaking moments of silence followed, the pain kicking her, grinding her.

'She's through here,' she heard Lois say at last, and Emma cried out in relief when it was Maggie who appeared, dear Maggie, holding Emma up in her strong arms, carrying Emma through the door.

'Ambulance will take too long, forty minutes they said, at least,' Lois said to Maggie, guiding them out of the house. 'They told me you should drive her on in.'

'What about Arthur and Elaine?' Maggie asked, her eyes never leaving her goddaughter's face.

'I tried but there was no answer.' Emma knew that Lois's mobile phone lay on the floor, discarded. Lois met her eye for an instant, then looked away. She was lying: for whatever reason, she wanted to keep this from Arthur as much as Emma did. 'You can ring them again from the hospital.'

'Shouldn't we try again? We could drive past their house—'

'For God's sake, look at her! There's no time!'

'What's wrong with her?' The panic in Maggie's voice made Emma ache, but she had no strength left to tell her herself.

'She's pregnant, Maggie,' Lois spat. 'The stupid girl's gotten herself pregnant.'

Seven years ago

Maggie

Tuesday, 10th August, 2010

Maggie's arms ached with the weight of the girl, the strain making her stomach tighten. She was still wearing her pin-stripe pyjamas, hadn't even gotten around to brushing her teeth before Lois had banged on her door.

'She's only fourteen, how the hell can she have got pregnant?' At the sound of Maggie's voice Emma opened her eyes, closed them again, lying limp and heavy in her godmother's arms.

It was the horror of the situation that was making Maggie feel queasy, the reality, that her goddaughter had been violated in this way, nauseating. Nothing to do with the gin she'd been drinking last night, or the restless, drunken sleep that followed.

'Same way you did, Maggie,' Lois said, her eyes on the teenage girl. 'Same way I did.' She opened the back door of the car, swept away the crisp packets and stale-smelling cardigan that littered the rear seat.

Maggie bent forwards and lay Emma down, the heat from the sun-baked car hitting her as soon as she ducked her head inside it. She wound down the rear window, then opened the front passenger door to let Lois inside.

But the other woman had turned away, was making her way back to her house.

'Lois!' Maggie called, then looked around, side to side down the street, to make sure there was no one around. She didn't want to cause a scene, didn't want anyone to know about Emma's situation. 'Get in, we need to go!' The last few words hissed through her gritted teeth.

Lois didn't turn back.

'Lois!' Maggie called again, louder, Emma mewing on the back seat, her eyelids flickering but not opening.

'Go then,' Lois said, turning back with a cold, hard stare. 'I'm not stopping you.'

'You're not coming?' Maggie looked at the girl lying prostrate on the seat, a slick of sweat glistening on her forehead, her skin worryingly pale.

'That's why I came for you,' Lois said. 'You're her godmother, you deal with it.'

'She's a child, for God's sake, and she's pregnant!' Maggie cried. 'Pregnant, Lois! You of all people should want to make sure she's OK.'

'Me of all people?' Lois repeated the words with venom, teeth bared, face hard. Her gaze flickered to the car. 'She's got nothing to do with me,' she hissed.

A flash of understanding hit Maggie, almost winded her into shocked silence. Why Emma had run to Lois's house, why Lois was so frighteningly hostile. So *frightened*. 'It's James!'

'You don't know anything.' Lois spat the words, the tendons in her neck pulled taut. '*Nothing*.'

But the reaction, the fear in her eyes, told Maggie she was right. 'He's the father.'

The whimpering from the car reminded Maggie there wasn't time to argue or ask more.

'Is he here?' Maggie asked. Lois shook her head, folded her arms.

'He's gone to London.'

'You need to contact him, get him to come home.' Maggie pleaded with Lois this time. 'If James is the father he'll need to know.'

'He's not!' Lois cried. 'He *wouldn't*! She's—' And a sob escaped, stifled only when Lois pressed her hands to her mouth.

'She's only fourteen.' Maggie finished the sentence for her, pointing to the girl who needed their help. 'Just a year younger than you were—'

'Don't you *dare* compare me to *her*!' There was an edge to Lois's tone, a remnant of the angry, sarcastic teenager she once was, or turned into once she was married to Jim Lunglow at just sixteen, pregnant with his baby. Maggie remembered the shouting she would often hear from next door, the arguments between Jim and Lois in the first few years of their marriage, the years that were meant to be blissfully happy, not spent engrossed in rows whilst their baby son cried upstairs.

It had raised a few eyebrows, Jim Lunglow, then forty at least, marrying a girl still in her teens. Those eyebrows turned to frowns when it was revealed that Lois was already pregnant, the wedding deemed *shotgun*, the young woman labelled as cheap, easy, a slut who was getting what she deserved for sleeping with a much older man.

Some said she got pregnant on purpose, to trap Jim into marriage, to give herself an easy life.

Some said she'd slept with other men, though nobody ever said who.

No one, Maggie recalled, blamed Jim.

This was the man who had raised James, this had been James's role model.

And now James had skulked into his father's depraved footsteps.

'If she's lucky, she'll lose the baby,' Lois spat. 'At least that way, she *won't* end up like me.' There was some dark thing in her expression as she caught Maggie's eye, then she turned on her heel and went angrily through her front door, slamming it fast behind her.

Maggie wanted to follow, to make Lois look at Emma, wanted Lois to come with her to hospital and explain to the doctors exactly what had happened. But the need to get Emma to safety, get her seen, overrode everything else. She dropped heavily to the driver's seat and turned the key, Emma groaning as the car came to life.

As she drove out of the village she tried to push Lois from her thoughts, the hostility in her voice, the anger. She tried to think about Emma, about getting her to hospital as quickly, and safely, as she could.

The car bounded along the track, the fields either side bright green, purple heather growing along the banks, the white dot of sheep far off to the left.

Maggie looked over her shoulder at Emma's young face, her eyes closed and lips parted.

Was Lois thinking of her own past? Was that why she was hostile when faced with a child in the same state Lois had been in herself? Although Lois had been one year older when James was conceived.

James.

He was nineteen, five years older than Emma, a grown man.

He wouldn't have gone near her, would he? He wouldn't be so low as to do that?

But another image played inside her head. That of James, nineteen, a fully-grown man, taking little Emma's hand and leading her into the darkness.

Maggie stroked Emma's hand, feeling the tube that pierced the skin, the coarse white tape that held the tube in place. The girl had been out of surgery for just half an hour, was yet to wake up.

The room was light, the day still early and the sun outside bright and hot. The drip beside Emma's bed clicked and beeped, the monitor attached to her chest beeping in sync with her heart, a constant, rhythmic bleep-bleep that should have been re-assuring, but wasn't.

The sound reminded Maggie of waking up in a room just like this one, ten years before. The monitor was the first thing she had heard upon waking, registering the noise even before her eyes had opened, focusing on its sound as the doctors told her that she had survived the crash but her husband was brain dead, that she would have decisions to make, papers to sign. It was the sound she had listened to, the bleep becoming a constant drawl, as she held Tom's hand whilst they switched off the machines that breathed for him, as his heart stopped beating and he left her for good.

On Emma's bedside table were several empty plastic cups, the water going someway to relieve Maggie's aching head, but a slight pain remained at the back of her skull, a throbbing sense of dread. It wasn't the gin from the night before (she hadn't drunk *that* much, just a little over half a bottle, hadn't even been sick for goodness sake.) Nor was it caused by these memories, the sounds of the hospital, the smell of boiled food and harsh bleach, forcing Tom's death to the forefront of her mind like a barbed hook she couldn't pull out.

No. It was the phone call she'd made an hour or so ago, the phone call to Emma's parents.

'Why didn't you call me straight away?' Arthur's voice had been a growl, the receiver obviously close to his mouth, making his words sound muffled and wet. She could hear his footsteps as he paced the hardwood floor of his hallway, his heels sounding out a slap on the wood.

'I couldn't get through before,' Maggie had lied, not telling him she hadn't even tried, had viewed making the phone call in the way one might approach holding an unpinned grenade. She had hoped Elaine would answer, that Arthur would be out at the farm. She had put off making the call until she really couldn't put it off any longer, the staff asking her, once again, when Emma's parents would arrive. 'She's in surgery,' Maggie had told him, avoiding explanations. 'If you drive down now you'll probably be here in time for her to wake up.'

She had hoped the revelation would spark his sympathy, dissolve his anger. It hadn't.

'Tell me what's wrong with her,' he barked down the phone. 'Why the hell's Emma in surgery? What *happened*?'

She swallowed once, twice, the impossible words, 'Your daughter's pregnant,' drying out her mouth. She couldn't tell him.

'The doctors will explain everything when you're here,' she had said instead, her mobile phone slipping against her clammy cheek.

'Maggie,' he spoke her name quietly, a threat in his voice, 'tell me what's wrong with my daughter.'

She couldn't, wouldn't, be that messenger.

'I have to go,' she had said instead, ending the call and turning off her phone.

Now she looked at Emma lying motionless on the bed, the drip embedded in her thin arm, the heart monitor beep-beeping beside her. Had Maggie done the right thing, calling the girl's parents? Was there something else she could have done instead?

But on the bed, Emma looked so very childlike that Maggie knew there hadn't been another option. Of course there hadn't. And, despite Maggie's opinion of Arthur, he had a right to know that Emma was in hospital. Besides, her low opinion of his character was based only on the way he had treated Maggie herself. The rest of the community loved him, applauded him, had him to thank for countless jobs in his farms, dairy, warehouse, and cheap rent in the houses he owned. Perhaps she was wrong, had misjudged him. Perhaps he would be kind, understanding, calm.

But Maggie knew she was fooling herself. She had experienced his cruelty first hand, ten years ago.

'*Sign the fucking papers.*'

Maggie had been half cut on the gin Arthur himself had bought her, head lolling on the table of her empty pub as he pushed the papers towards her. Tom had been dead less than a month. Arthur's sympathy for her loss had disappeared as soon as she said no to his offer. '*What the hell do you want with that land, Maggie? Wouldn't it be easier to sell it?*'

'*It's my land. My boy's land. I'll keep it for Lee,*' Maggie slurred. She had drunk too much.

But she had said no. Even when drunk, she stood her ground.

And then Edward Burrows, Arthur's right-hand man, came to see her, stopping by for a pint a week later, a week that Maggie had spent in the pub all alone, not a single customer gracing the bar, the till empty save for the float. *'It'll get worse,'* Edward had warned her. *'I doubt anyone will come drinking in here, not with Arthur angry with you the way he is.'* And it had got worse. Not a soul entered the pub for a month, the business nearly down on its knees. By the time Maggie gave in and sold the land to Arthur, save for one small field, she was broke. All the money from the sale had gone into saving the pub. But, at the time, she felt she had little choice.

'Maggie?' The name came out as a croak, the sound drawing Maggie back from her reverie.

She jumped, pressed the call button on the bed, held Emma's hand properly at last.

'You're awake.'

The girl had her eyes half open, blinking lazily. 'What happened?' she asked, her lips dry, their edges cracked.

Maggie reached for a cup from the table. She held it to her goddaughter's lips and helped the girl drink.

'I'm pregnant,' Emma said when the cup was removed, her lips trembling. 'Aren't I, Maggie?' Her right hand, free from needles or drips, rested lightly on her belly, pulling away again as soon as she felt the bulk of gauze and bandages beneath her gown.

Maggie lifted the hand, held it in her own. 'The pregnancy was ectopic, Emma,' she said gently. 'The foetus was growing in one of your fallopian tubes; they had to remove it.'

'But the baby?' Emma asked, her voice high pitched and childishly hopeful. 'It's going to be OK?'

'Sweetheart, they couldn't save it.'

Emma's face crumpled, tears filling her wide, blue eyes. 'Oh,' she said, opened her mouth and closed it again.

'I'm so sorry.' Maggie squeezed Emma's hand, but the girl withdrew her fingers to wipe the tears from her eyes.

Maggie took a deep breath. 'Emma,' she began, wondering how long she had before Arthur arrived, 'was James the father?'

Emma's eyes widened, the last of the weak colour draining from her face. 'Don't tell Daddy,' she whispered, grabbing Maggie's hand and squeezing this time. 'Please.'

'I'm sure he'll understand—' Maggie tried, but she knew it was useless, could tell from the desperate look on Emma's face that the girl was petrified of her father's reaction. 'He's your father, love, and you're only fourteen. Of course he has to be told.'

'But he doesn't have to know about James, does he?'

'He'll find out eventually, these things have a way of coming out.' Maggie shifted her weight, static building between the plastic chair and the back of her thin, cheap pyjamas. The collar stuck to the back of her neck, sweat prickling under her short, grey curls. Why was Emma so protective of James?

Maggie had looked after him often enough as a child to know how charming he could be. He had an inquisitive nature, a sharp wit, a way of focusing his attention unwaveringly upon you, making you feel like you were the only person in the world who mattered. But Maggie knew, too, some of his other traits. His constant need for attention, his jealousy. Had Emma seen this side of him?

'I'm not going to tell anyone about James. I won't.' Emma kept Maggie's eye as she spoke and Maggie realised that the girl thought she was in love.

'I won't tell your dad if you don't want me to,' she said carefully, 'but I can't promise you he'll not discover the truth.'

Emma nodded and sniffed, her chin quivering as she tried

her best not to cry. 'Does James know?' she asked, looking down at her belly. 'Is he coming back from London?'

Maggie thought of Lois at home, of her determination to protect her son and keep well out of it all. Would she have told James by now? And, if she had, would James bother coming at all or discard Emma like he had so many toys in his boyhood, desperately wanted when they were new, fresh, untouched, and discarded as soon as they were blemished? The football, no good once mud soaked its threading. The books discarded because of broken spines. He had been poor, practically penniless, yet the sudden ease with which he rejected, found fault, had never ceased to amaze Maggie.

'I don't know,' Maggie said cautiously, not wanting to upset Emma further.

'He can't come to the hospital. If he does and Daddy finds out, he'll kill James, Maggie, I know he will.' Emma's hands clutched the sheet so tightly that the veins bulged, the needle on the back of her left leaking blood and staining the white surgical tape red.

Maggie shook her head, wanted to say don't be silly, of course he wouldn't, but she stopped herself. Emma looked frightened, even more so than Lois had done earlier that day.

'Emma,' Maggie said urgently, and leaned forward so her whisper could be heard, so she could reach out and hold Emma if needed. 'Has Arthur ever—'

Hurt you? Or Elaine?

But her words went unsaid, a sound from outside robbing her of her chance.

Heavy footsteps, a nurse saying, 'Your daughter's through here.'

Emma tensed up, held her breath.

The door behind Maggie swung open.

'Emma!' Arthur's voice was soft, full of relief. 'My girl,' he said, then again, 'my girl.'

Maggie looked at him: his brow was creased with concern, eyes moist with tears, his mouth set in a warm, reassuring smile that, to her, looked forced and unnatural. On the bed, Emma shrank into herself.

Arthur turned to the nurse.

'I can't thank you enough,' he said, sincerity dripping from each word. 'For all you've done, for saving her. My God . . .' He stopped, ran his fingers through his hair, thick and flecked with grey.

'It was a close call, but she pulled through. The important thing now is to see that she rests.' The young nurse smiled. She was plump and blond-haired, dimples gracing her cheeks and a blush spreading up from her neck.

Arthur touched her shoulder. 'Thank you,' he said again, and the nurse's blush deepened. 'And please thank your colleagues on my behalf, for saving my little girl.'

Maggie watched him in awe, his face a picture of paternal concern. She had forgotten how charming he could be.

It was as the nurse turned to leave that Maggie noticed Elaine, standing in the doorway behind Arthur, silent and unmoving.

The nurse walked out and Arthur watched her go. Then he closed the door and turned round, motioning Elaine towards the bed.

Elaine obeyed and sat down beside Emma, her gait careful and controlled. But when her eyes met Maggie's, she could see the fear in them.

Emma remained tense, her gaze fixed on her father.

Maggie braced herself, looked across the bed at Elaine, who

was gripping Emma's other hand. She noticed, on Elaine's exposed wrist, a deep purple bruise in the shape of a thumbprint.

Arthur opened his mouth to speak, wiped his hand across his lips when he noticed Maggie.

'You can go,' he said to her, coolly. 'Thank you for bringing her in.' The charm he had used for the nurse, the sincerity, had long gone. He had nothing for Maggie but ice.

Emma found Maggie's hand and held it.

Maggie didn't move from her seat.

'You're welcome.' Maggie looked at Arthur and kept her voice steady. 'But I'll stay, if it's all the same to you. She's my goddaughter, after all. I want to make sure she's OK.'

Arthur glowered and turned away, looked instead at Emma.

'The father,' he said. 'Who was it?'

No one answered.

Arthur rubbed his hand over his face. Said again, more fiercely, 'Who was it?'

'I'm sorry, Daddy,' Emma said, her voice so childlike, the words a desperate plea.

'Who fucked my *fourteen*-year-old daughter?' His fists clenched and unclenched as he spoke. 'Tell me his name.'

'Arthur, *don't*.' Elaine squared her shoulders but her hand, holding on tightly to Emma's, was shaking. 'Please don't speak to our daughter like that.'

The sweat on the back of Maggie's neck turned cold, her pyjamas sticking to her skin. She tried to swallow but her mouth was too dry, the ache in her head returning with a vengeance. She could only imagine how Emma must be feeling.

Arthur exhaled, a long, menacing breath, so loud and deliberate that Maggie could hear every clot of mucus rattle in his airway. 'Don't you *dare*—'

'We can talk about the details when Emma's better.' Elaine kept her gaze downcast, as though not wanting to push things too far. Maggie saw from the way her chest had stopped moving that Emma was holding her breath.

There were footsteps outside as someone walked past the room, reminding them they were not alone.

Arthur relaxed his hands from their fists.

Maggie inwardly sighed in relief, though the feeling was very shortlived.

'What was she doing at the pub, anyway?' Arthur turned his attention to Maggie, scanning her from head to toe, judging her unbrushed hair, unwashed skin, her pyjamas.

Maggie tried to swallow again. 'She wasn't,' she stumbled. 'She was at Lois's, next door. Lois called me over and I drove her here.' Too late she remembered the fearful look on Lois's face, her desire to keep her name out of it, and Maggie wished fervently she hadn't said anything.

'At Lois Lunglow's?' He looked back at his daughter, pale on the bed, scanned over her with the same look of disgust he'd used on Maggie. 'What the hell were you doing with *her,* Emma?'

Emma stared at her hands.

'Why were you with *that* woman?' Arthur's seething anger was palpable, replacing the room's summer warmth with a dread-filled chill. Then he paused, and Maggie could practically see the paternity puzzle falling to place in his mind as he realised that James also lived in that house. But he said nothing.

Elaine looked from Emma to Arthur, and Maggie saw the indecision in her eyes, the desire to placate him oozing from her. But she kept silent, perhaps too frightened of saying the wrong thing, making it worse than it already was. Maggie looked again at the bruise on her wrist.

When Emma still didn't answer, Arthur turned away from them all. 'I'm going to talk to the doctor,' he snarled, and walked out.

The warmth returned to the room as soon as Emma's father left it.

'Oh, Emma.' Elaine wrapped her arms around her step-daughter, bent her head to Emma's head and kissed her crown, breathed her in.

Emma unfroze, the fear melting into tears. Her face crumpled, eyes squeezed shut, sobs wracking her shoulders as Elaine kissed her.

'I'm sorry,' the girl said, sorrow, loss, shame leaching out of her with those words.

Elaine hushed her. 'Just rest,' she said, stroking Emma's hair away from her face. 'Concentrate on getting better.'

Maggie looked away.

Thought of Lee, curled in a ball on his own hospital bed, Maggie trying to fight her way in but the orderlies stopping her. She remembered wanting to stroke Lee's sweet, bruised face the way that Elaine was stroking Emma's, had wanted to put her arms round her boy's broken body and sob her regrets into his ear. She had been led away, taken to a room and strapped up to a drip until the alcohol had been flushed from her system, had been told she wouldn't see her son until she was sober.

But she never saw him again.

Maggie felt the sting of tears behind her eyelids and sniffed back hard.

As Elaine murmured inaudibly, soothingly to Emma the girl clung to her stepmother like an infant, her fingers clutching the fabric of Elaine's cardigan, her face buried in her chest.

Maggie stood up, sensing the two needed to be alone. 'I'll

be back in a minute,' she said, but neither Emma or Elaine looked up.

She opened the door and walked through, her slippered feet sliding beneath her, reminding her of how inappropriate she looked in her pinstripe pyjamas; more like a patient than a visitor.

'Is that her mum in with her now?' asked a dark-haired nurse, the same woman who had wheeled Emma into the recovery room just an hour before. 'Typical teenager; they hold it together until they see their mum and then they all fall apart, bless 'em.'

Maggie smiled politely, moved on up the corridor.

'Are you all right?' said the nurse, her warm hand resting on Maggie's arm, her large brown eyes searching Maggie's face. 'You look pale, come and sit down.'

Maggie nodded, said 'I'm fine, really.' But realised that something felt wrong.

What was it? An uncertainty, dread, in the pit of her stomach.

She looked either way along the long corridor, searching for Arthur.

'Excuse me?' She called the nurse back, suddenly understanding why she felt so uneasy. 'Emma's father, do you know where he is?'

The nurse smiled, and Maggie realised Arthur had most likely charmed her too.

'He's gone, said he had to go home, but that he'd be back in later. He's a lovely chap, isn't he? Emma's clearly doted on; he wouldn't leave till he had us all swear we'd watch over his little girl.'

Maggie's heartbeat was galloping. She knew that Arthur hadn't gone back to the farm.

She thought of the bruises on Elaine's arm, of the fear on Emma's face in the presence of her father.

Arthur had gone to find the person responsible for Emma's condition. And Maggie had inadvertently led him to guess who it was. He'd gone to find James.

But James wasn't there. It was Lois whom he'd find, home alone.

Nuala

Saturday, 18th November, 2017

'You're lying to me.' Nuala turned the key in the ignition, not wanting to hear any more, her skin crawling from the tales Maggie was telling her, knowing that it couldn't be true, that James would never have touched a girl so young. 'And besides, you only have her word for it that it was his baby at all. Maybe he left because she pointed the finger, wrongly accused him to protect someone else. That's why he never told me, because he was scared, because he couldn't bear to relive the accusations and wanted to protect me from them, too.'

The evening had drawn in whilst Maggie was talking, the air cold and close round the car, heavy with the smell of damp leaves. The rain had stopped but the wind remained, ripping through the long grass, beating at the car.

'You haven't let me finish, I haven't told you the last of it yet. Maybe if you let me tell you, you'll understand.'

'They're lies.' Nuala's fingers were slippery from chewing, the ends gnawed to a deep, shiny pink. The saliva, the blood, made it difficult to grip the key and she had to try three times before it turned and the car came to life. 'He told me everything, nearly everything. He told me about his friends, schoolwork, his A Levels. He told me about summer holidays walking the hills, swimming in rivers, climbing rocks.' And she remembered him sneering as she told him about hers, about the Caribbean cruises, the month-long sojourns to Greek islands, how it's all right for some having a rich ma and pa, despite the fact that hers were both dead.

'He never told me about Emma. He would have told me about her.' How many times had he reassured her, promised her, that she was his only? That that was what made him love her so much, that she was his first, that he was hers, that they shared that special bond.

'He never told you about Emma at all?'

Nuala shook her head, her foot ready above the accelerator, eager to go, to leave this abandoned field, to leave Maggie's lies, because they must be, *must be*, lies.

Outside the moon found a gap in the clouds. In the moonlight, Maggie's short curls shone like silver, Nuala's skin brightened, lost the yellow tinge of malnutrition, the grass outside casting long, thin shadows on the car, lashing the bodywork like whips.

'I'm sorry. It's hard to hear, but it was all true. He did have a relationship with Emma,' Maggie said. 'And the baby *was* his.'

Nuala's cheeks burned, the hot embarrassment of her ignorance. She thought of James in the park, the first time she'd ever seen him. Sandy hair falling into his eyes, tears clinging to his lashes.

'And I haven't told you everything, there's more . . .' Maggie said, but her voice barely cut through, her words lost to the daydream.

James, thin, dirty, tired. The most beautiful thing Nuala'd ever seen.

'It wasn't just Emma he left.' Maggie's voice grew urgent, Nuala's refusal to hear her more obstinate.

James, the look in his eyes so intense it had stopped Nuala in her tracks. The ends of his jeans were frayed, trainers worn through and thick with mud. No sleeping bag, no begging bowl, yet she knew he had nowhere to go.

'He left his mother, too. He left Lois, even though he knew what happened to her, what Arthur did to her. And for all her spite, all her lies and all her vindictiveness both before and after the event, she didn't deserve what happened. No one deserves to be treated like that . . .' Maggie was trying to make Nuala look at her, was trying to tell her the rest of the story, but the words didn't connect. Nuala refused to listen.

She ignored Maggie, blocking out the lies, thinking of her husband, the man who looked after her even when she was such a disappointment, loved her even when she was an idiot, such an idiot, and did things wrong all the time.

When they'd first met the look on James' face had been like a mirror, his pain calling to her fresh, orphan's grief.

Nuala had answered his loneliness with her own desperate need to cling to someone, anyone, to not be alone.

Maggie's hands grabbed her shoulders, shook her. 'Don't you understand?' She was shouting at her now, her breath tinged with gin, spit landing on Nuala's sweater.

Nuala pushed Maggie back, swatting her like a fly. 'You don't know the pain he was in! *You don't understand!*'

'You're still protecting him after everything he did?' And Maggie didn't look angry any more, her face pale, save for the dark circles under her eyes. 'Not just to Emma, but to Lois?'

Nuala looked at Maggie, but away again when she saw the

sad pity on her face. She wanted to see out of the window, wanted to see James hiding in the grass but the glass had steamed up and she couldn't see out. She could only hear the wind, the grass lashing the car, the mournful *towoo* of an owl.

'I've heard enough.' She bit the side of her thumb, scraping the cuticle with her teeth. 'I don't want to hear any more.'

It was lies, it must be lies.

A distant bang, sharp and unfamiliar, rang out and Nuala jumped.

'The noise,' Maggie said. 'It's lampers, shooting rabbits. Wind like this is perfect for it, takes the hunters' scent away.' Another shot echoed. Nuala turned the heater to full, the sound masking the wind. The bottom of the windscreen was clear already. She could see a shape in the grass, could imagine his shins, knees, thighs curled up against the cold.

Maggie turned the heater back down. 'James turned everyone against each other. He twisted everything, and then ran away when he should have stayed and helped, abandoned the people he was supposed to love to save his own bloody skin!' Her exhaustion showed in her voice, cracking and wavering as though relieved to have finally told the truth, relieved that Nuala now knew. She reached into her pocket, pulled out a paper bag, translucent with grease. She unwrapped the parcels, revealing pastry and an overwhelming smell of sausage meat. 'Nuala,' she said before taking her first bite, 'why did you really come?'

The mist clung to the windscreen, James only semi-formed outside. Nuala could see his hands, could make out the glint of his wedding ring. The letter burned hot in her back pocket, the envelope left in the room at the pub.

'I came to tell Lois that he was dead,' she said, and reached for the chain around her neck, feeling for the matching rings that hung from it, clutching them in her fist.

'Why won't you go back there?' she had asked James in those heady early days when she still had the courage to say such things. *'What are you afraid of?'* The violent look on his face had warned her not to ask.

But Maggie's lying, Nuala told herself, relaxing her vision so the world became an easy, safe blur. It's all irrelevant, because she's lying.

'You could have told Lois over the phone,' Maggie said, 'could have written an email, found her online. Why come all this way, six months after the fact?'

Nuala thought of the blood stain on the carpet at home, the buggy still unpacked in the hallway, the door that no one ever knocked at, the phone that never rang, the mobile that stayed silent, the Facebook page with a dwindling count of friends.

'My parents died when I was eighteen,' she said, unsure as to why she felt able to tell Maggie this, remembering James telling her he used to talk to Maggie too when he was young. 'I have no one else.'

'What about friends? Siblings?'

'No,' she said, and thought of how sad that must sound, how pathetic. 'I didn't need friends, I had James.'

'He was always a wary child,' Maggie said, eyeing Nuala sidelong, 'always liked to be the focus of attention. Not in a crowd, or a group, but when it was just you and him. He always liked to make sure your attention was fully on him. It's what he was used to at home, of course, when his father wasn't there causing trouble. He was used to it being just him and Lois, to being the centre of that young woman's world.'

'You don't know anything.' Nuala looked out at the grass, the mist on the window nearly cleared, James nearly in full view. Any second now his face would appear, his beautiful, sharp features, and Nuala would know it was all lies. That he discouraged her friendships because he loved her company. That he dissuaded her, time and again, from getting a job because he genuinely didn't want her to have the stress, that he understood she was set for life if she was careful with her inheritance, that she could spend her time on hobbies and reading books. Not because he wanted to keep her his, in his control, bending her to his will alone. ('Yes, just like that!' he had said, when she had got his dinner just right, whilst he watched her from the kitchen stool. A baked potato; simple but cooked to perfection. Crisp skin, butter melted throughout and so tender that, when pressed at the edges, the fluffy insides plumed from the cut in the top. He had spun her around, held on to her waist and looked into her blue eyes with his. 'I knew it,' he said, kissed her softly on the lips, one of the kisses that made her stomach turn over with lust and relief. 'I knew you'd get it right, eventually.' And his hands skimmed upwards, brushed her breasts. He made love to her on the kitchen counter, wrapping her legs around his waist. Afterwards he threw it away, the potato. It was cold. Nuala had stared at it, eyes brimming, and he had laughed at her sentimentality. 'You know how to do it now,' he said, rubbing the base of her back with his knuckles. 'No excuses.' But she had never made it again, that simplest of meals.)

'So you came here looking for a family? I thought you said James told you what Lois was like; why did you think you could rely on her?'

'I thought she might have changed. I thought we could comfort each other.'

'Lois will never change, you're better off without her.' Maggie swallowed a bite of her roll, held out a matching paper bag. 'I've another, look, if you want it?'

Nuala looked away.

Maggie filled her mouth, turning the second sausage-roll sideways and shoving it in in one go. She looked at Nuala, then away, sucking and chewing on the mouthful.

Nuala didn't say anything, couldn't, somehow. Her mind only lingered on home, on the rose bush at home, on the precious boy buried beneath it.

She flicked the heater back on, turned it up full blast and watched the glass clear. Slowly, slowly, there was her husband. She just needed to see his face, and she knew all the doubt and worry would disappear. She would know she had been right to trust him. That his love for her was real. That he moved in with her because he wanted to, really wanted to, not just because he had nowhere to go. Her hands tore at each other, picking at her nails, reopening the wound on her finger until the blood oozed, wanting to *feel it*.

Maggie turned the heater off, used her greasy fist of paper to clear the windscreen, wiping it across the glass, replacing the mist with streaks of distorting fat and pastry crumbs.

'No!' Nuala batted her away but it was too late. James looked up at her, highlighted by the headlamps from the car, his face and body writhing, ugly through the film of grease and a smear of blood from her finger.

Swaying in the wind, his face grotesque, the grass whipping around him. Nuala flicked off the headlights, but the darkness did nothing and still James stared back, his mouth a gaping black hole, sucking into it the last of her hope.

'What about Emma?' she asked, knowing now what she had to do, that she had to find that girl, talk to her, make her tell the truth. Make her tell Nuala why, seven years on, she was still writing to the man who supposedly abandoned her, begging him to come home, take her with him.

The wind picked up. A light pattering sound hit the windscreen.

'Emma?' Nuala asked again.

Maggie stared outside, her eyes following the pattern of the leaves. 'She saved my life, do you know that?' She turned towards Nuala, the gear stick disappearing into the rolls of her belly. 'I fell apart after my husband died, shortly after Emma's fourth birthday. For years afterwards I was a mess. I drank, I didn't look after myself or my . . . I did a lot of things I'm not proud of. Emma moved in with me when she was fourteen, after all this business with the pregnancy had blown up, and even though she had so much to contend with she still managed to look after me. I was her godmother, her responsible adult, her carer but it was *she* who cared for *me*. She forced me to look outside of myself. She stopped me from falling apart completely because I had something in my life again. I had *her*. And she's never complained about it once; not about me, not the treatment from her father or Lois, not about what happened to poor Elaine. And she's the only one, save for Lois, not to say a bad word against James. Despite everything she still loves him, still believed that what they had was real love. I don't know what she'll do when she finds out he's gone.'

Nuala straightened her posture, lifted her chin. 'Do you promise to tell her?'

Another shotgun sounded and this time Maggie jumped, her knees smacking into the glove compartment.

'You better go home before the weather turns,' Maggie said. 'They say rain's coming. Look, you can let me out here and I'll walk back, take the short cut over the stile and back through the fields, I'll be home within an hour. You can go straight on, save yourself the petrol.'

Nuala closed her eyes, her right hand moving to her temple. 'Promise me that you'll tell her.'

'I promise,' Maggie said and felt inside her coat. 'I'll tell her as soon as you've gone.'

Nuala could see, in the moonlight, the shape of a hip flask in Maggie's breast pocket.

'There's a small bag of my things, just a change of clothes, a few toiletries—'

'If you leave me your address I'll send them to you, in the post. If you go now.'

Nuala nodded. 'Emma has it already,' she said, testing Maggie's resolve with the lie. Emma would have told Maggie if she'd had her address, she was sure of it, but Maggie didn't challenge it, didn't even ask for it again just in case. Instead, Maggie's face lightened with relief. She opened the car door, let herself out, waved to Nuala as she climbed over the stile, watching keenly, waiting far too eagerly for her to drive off.

And Nuala knew, as Maggie turned her back and took a swig from the flask in the shadows, that she was lying.

Maggie wasn't going to tell Emma about James.

Nuala could drive home. Forget this place, burn any letters that arrived. Move on.

But she thought of the rose bush, her baby, her empty home, the memories, the loss and despair she felt there.

She thought of what she had tried to do to herself a few weeks ago, the oblivion she had craved.

She couldn't go back, not yet. She couldn't face those empty rooms, give in to despair all alone, all by herself.

It was time for Nuala to take control, one last stab of control. James wasn't there to show her the way any more, to tell her what to do. She had to do this, alone. It was time to find out the truth.

Nuala had an hour, by Maggie's own estimate, to find Emma.

Two months ago

Nuala

Friday, 15th September, 2017

The smell woke her before her eyes opened, before she could scrape away the sleep and crust that glued her lashes to her cheek.

Her nose told her she was still alive, still very much alive. The smell of vomit, the acidic notes of bile, the sweetness of Calpol, told her she'd spewed it all out, all hope of escape, of an end.

She hadn't even managed to do that properly. She couldn't even end it all without messing it up like an idiot.

She knew what her mother would have said. Too much too soon, a weak stomach saving her life. Remembered her lamenting the loss of a patient to an overdose, the despair in her mother's face when she had recounted that the dead woman had taken just the right amount, not so much that she would sick it all up, not so little that she came round and died slowly of the after effects of liver and kidney damage. Just the right amount.

Nuala had been told this, she knew this and still, she had messed it all up. What a pathetic idiot.

The first thing she saw, when her eyes opened, was the blood stain on the bedroom carpet. Up close the smell of the blood was erased by that of the vomit.

Darkness outside, the room grey around her. Sick on the carpet, hanging in lumps and sticky drips from the duvet, sprayed out against the door and the wall. Sick down her front, in her hair, on her back, in her hands.

She had no idea what day it was or what time. Didn't know if the sun was setting or rising again. Had no clue as to how long she had lain there, face squashed into the blood on the carpet, body languishing on urine-soaked pile.

Her whole body ached, arms weak as she pushed herself up from the floor. Legs shaky as she moved to the window, gripping the sill to keep from falling.

The sun was coming up, she could see that. It was rising over the park, highlighting the trees and bracken fronds, illuminating Nuala's long stretch of garden, picking out the rusted trowel in the sage pot, its wooden handle turned black with rot, the hemlock taking over the borders.

Looking down on it all, from the window upstairs, she could see the sad little grave. The ground still uneven from digging, the rose above it dry and failing to flower.

The rose was dying.

It was meant to flourish, thrive, wrap its roots around Maxwell and keep him. It wasn't meant to die. It couldn't die.

Maybe she had watered it too much. Perhaps the roots had never recovered from all the digging. Or maybe it had got tired of her, lying with her face to the dirt, ants crawling into her hair, her earlobes and nostrils.

Her knees finally gave way. She took a step towards the bed, keeled over. Landed, belly down, on the old, dark splash of meconium.

Her eyes closed, room dark, impassive to the smell of stale vomit.

Outside jackdaws crowed, cars passed, rain fell and Nuala lay asleep, oblivious to it all.

The sun rose, set, rose again before Nuala awoke.

The curtains were still open and from her place on the bed, she could make out the garden outside, the herbs and the grass and the hemlock.

She could see the rose, its failing buds, dried-out thorns.

A test, perhaps. A sign.

Maybe it was James, telling her not to give up yet, to look after the rose and when she'd looked after the rose she should look after herself.

Her clothes were stinking, crisp as cardboard from dried fluid, the remnants of vomit gritty against her skin. She pulled them off, one by one, piled them into the basket in the bathroom (the toilet still unflushed, the smell rank) and layered new, clean clothes over her dirty body.

Up the stairs, to the top floor.

It was meant to be a studio, one day. A place for Nuala to paint, draw, write, sculpt or whatever the hell she wanted to do with all her time because wasn't she lucky, so lucky, that she didn't have to work, that her parents left her everything, *everything*, she could ever need whilst James had grown up poor, cold, hungry. ('But I'd rather have them,' she'd told him. 'I'd rather have no money, a small house, cheap clothes but have them.' And he scoffed at her and walked out of the room, and she'd never said it again. Not worth the risk of losing him too, because then what would she do? Who would look after her then? 'You're such an *idiot*, you can't even look after yourself,' he'd told her, when she'd burned her thumb on the edge of the hob. 'Aren't you lucky, aren't you so lucky, that I'm here?' He'd held her thumb under the cold tap, his hand tight on her wrist, smiling.)

The room stretched across the top floor of the house, windows at either end letting in light all day long. A desk at one side, the computer she used to sit at whilst James was at work, use Google, Facebook, Twitter, the lot to try and find out something about the place he grew up in, find anything more about why he left, wouldn't go back.

Until, one day, he'd found her search history. He was angry, of course, so disappointed in her, but he didn't hit her, didn't lash out. He wasn't *abusive*. In the end, when her tears had dried up, when his anger had subsided, he'd laughed at her. Wasn't it funny that someone as stupid as her thought she could find something out?

As if Nuala could do that.

As if she could do anything.

And then he'd forgiven her, kissed her, and made nice, told her all that she needed to know, all the things he'd already told her about his mother being terrible, someone he wouldn't want her to know, about Maggie who was story-book kind, about the hot summers, the cold winters, the lack of friends for poor James to play with. Told her again that, whilst she was sunning herself in Greece with her wealthy parents or riding the pony they'd bought her, he was huddled under a shared duvet with his mother, no money for central heating, his shoes lined with cardboard insoles cut from a cornflakes packet. And he would never go back to that life, he'd told her. He wouldn't take her to see his humble origins, the people who would latch on to her wealth like leeches, who would suck the goodness, the purity, from her simple soul.

'This is the last time,' he'd said to her. 'Understand? We're never going there, we're never meeting any of them, we're going to leave the past where it belongs, far behind us. And Nuala . . .' His thumb and index finger held her chin, she couldn't look away. 'I'm not going to tell you again.'

They'd watched a film afterwards, *Point Break*, his arm round her on the sofa, him filling her wine glass, fetching her popcorn, saying, 'Isn't it nice when we just get along?'

Beside the desk was the old sea chest, dark brown wood with black iron hinges. It was her father's, once. Nuala had kept it after she'd sold all the other furniture that still smelt of her father and sometimes smelt of her mother's perfume too. James had liked it, claimed it, used it to store his paper-work, his certificates, his gardening manuals that could possibly, possibly, tell Nuala how she could save the rose that was dying in the garden, its roots wrapped around her lost child.

She had to save the rose.

The house was cooler up here, draughty despite the Velux windows and extra roof insulation. It didn't have the hot, sour atmosphere of the rest of the house, or the stink of the master bedroom.

The chest's black iron clasps unlocked with a click. A flurry of dust as the lid was lifted.

And inside she could see all his things, all James's papers, papers she'd read many times before. (He didn't know that, that she'd been through his things in those early, early days when the look of fear in his eyes had made her curious, when she thought that, if she knew the truth, she could help him release that fear and be free. But that was before she'd learnt to appreciate her own limitations, her stupidity, her inability to do anything right. It was before she'd been caught out.)

She lifted out the papers, put them to one side and picked up the jumpers that were beneath them, placing them on the floor. She took a blanket that lay inside too, wrapped it round her shoulders, stroked it against her cheek, held it beneath her nose and smelt him.

In the grimy half-light James's fingertips walked along her skin, stroking the soft down of her belly, tracing the arc of her ribs. His hair brushed past her collarbone, resting near her ear as he kissed her.

She could feel him, the smell from his clothes in the trunk forcing him back to life, reawakening his tongue inside her mouth.

She curled her toes against the blanket wrapped around them, the same woollen blanket they used to lie on before the fire, or in the woods where no one would find them. Its scent invaded her nostrils, removed the insults and criticisms from her mind, made her remember only her bare skin against his.

She stroked her finger over the wooden chest, remembered her finger stroking him, let it glide against the hard flat surface as though it were his stomach, his tight muscles, his skin.

She forced her eyes closed, tried to hold on to that feeling, that good feeling of him, how he loved her. Kept the tears, the gut-wrenching reality, out of her mind, tried to pretend, to feel him with her, inside her.

She arched her neck, thought of his hands on her throat, on her breasts, held her chin up to the ceiling as though he were kissing her.

Her hair fell across her face with the movement, the strands catching her nostrils, her nose smelling the vomit from downstairs.

Her eyes opened.

Pretending was useless.

Her gaze landed back on the chest.

There were the gardening manuals, thick and well thumbed. But, beside them, something else.

A cardboard box, dark brown with a swirl of white writing across it. The shoe box for the Louboutin pumps she braved when she had to see her lawyer or accountant in person, the smart shoes for dealing with her dead parents' generosity.

She lifted it out, felt the weight inside shift and slide as she lifted.

The lid was soft and frayed at the edges, one corner broken at the seam from frequent lifting.

Beneath the lid were sheets of paper, folded in half and stacked in date order. Dozens of letters. Forty-nine in total addressed to James's university, the place he'd stayed at less than a term.

He must have paid for them to be redirected.

He must have wanted the letters to come.

And then he had hidden them, kept them secret, not wanting his wife to find them.

She opened the first. 'I need you, come back, come back to me.' Nothing else, no signature, no name, address, no hint of who the author was.

The second. 'I miss you, I'm sorry, please come back.'

The third. 'I'm lost without you, I don't know what to do.'

And so on, and so on, desperate and pitiful, repetitive, needy, full of regret.

James's mother had pushed him away, he told Nuala that final time, done things he could never forget, never forgive, had lied to him again and again.

He'd told Nuala his mother was poisonous, a viper, the

opposite of Nuala in every way, that she would lie to Nuala, turn her against James, tell her things about him that simply weren't true.

But these letters were postmarked from that village, the place he said he would never go back to. Had he written to his mother, like he'd promised in the days after their wedding, told her he was married, happy, fulfilled?

Had she responded in kind, writing and letting him know she still loved him, wanted him to forgive her, forget the past and move on? He hadn't given her their new address, obviously wanted to keep his mother away. But he had kept the letters, so did he still feel something for her?

The woman who wrote these wasn't a viper, wasn't malicious but lonely, missed James as much as Nuala did now.

People change. Places change. Seven years is a long time, after all.

These letters told her someone wanted him back.

It must be his mother, she told herself again. He never mentioned anyone, no other woman, of significance.

It must be his mother.

It must be.

Emma

Saturday, 18th November, 2017

Emma sat at the kitchen table, staring at the dust motes
that hung in the air, each one representing a fragment
of the messed-up, messy story Maggie must be telling Nuala
right now. *Emma's* story. She should be angry. But all she felt
was the heaviness in her limbs, an emptiness in her chest.

What did that matter any more, that Maggie was talking
to a stranger about Emma? What did any of it matter, now
James was never coming back?

Maggie had stuck a note on one of the yellowing cupboard
doors before she'd left with Nuala.

Keep the pub closed tonight. Back later, with news.

Emma knew, though.

James was dead.

He'd run off, left her, married that woman.

Nuala didn't seem his type somehow. Too thin, hair too
dull and greasy, no backbone, no spirit.

*'You're a firecracker, Em. A firecracker wrapped up in this
little girl costume, all innocent.'*

'Which would you rather? The firecracker or the innocent?'

'What do you think?' And a kiss, soft at first then harder, his tongue working its way through her closed lips and teeth.

Even now, seven years on, she could practically feel the points of his hips pressing her flesh, the wheat grazing her ankles, tickling her wrists, the sound of his sigh in her ear. She would dream of him tonight and oh, dear God, the things she would do to him in that dream. Her back arched, the top of her spine pressing into the wood of the chair, lost in imagination. She'd show him what a real firecracker she was, she would show him what she could really do, now she was older and so, so much wiser.

Her eyes sprang open. She remembered.

He was never coming back.

She would never see him again, never do those things she imagined.

She brushed herself off and stood, taking a cup of tepid tea to the sink, leaving it there with the detritus of her unfinished dinner. Slovenly was the word that came to her mind, the word Elaine would have once used, the thought of her stepmother a stab to the chest. Normally she wouldn't leave a mess, normally she would scrub and clean and polish and sweep and dust and tidy and scrub some more until her nose bled from bleach fumes.

But how could she do that now, when James was dead?

She picked up her phone, opened the contacts, stared at Toby's name.

She could invite him round, tell him the bar was closed and did he fancy a lock-in? A sleepover?

She could wipe away the memory of James with the body of another man. Pretend, for one night, that James never existed. That she was here, in this shitty pub with this shitty job, crappy life because she wanted to be, not because James and his mother ruined everything.

Toby wouldn't be interested anyway, regardless of what he'd said the other night. Why would he be interested in her? He hadn't even wanted to tell his friends they'd been together, had wanted to keep Emma a secret. Just like James.

Memories of Elaine swarmed in her head. The last day she saw her stepmother had been the last day, too, that she had seen James. When she thought of Elaine she could still remember her touch, the feel of her thin arms holding her close, telling her everything was going to be all right after all those terrible nights at home, when Emma's father had drunk too much or had decided the way Elaine looked at him hadn't been quite right.

'You deserve better,' Elaine would say to her now if she could see Emma's thumb hovering over Toby's name. 'Don't sell yourself short.'

But what else was she meant to do?

Forget it all, move on, suck it up and keep moving forward?

That's what Elaine would have said.

Keep moving forward.

She pushed her phone away.

She would leave.

No one could stop her, not now. She had nothing, no one, to wait for.

She had some money, a few thousand pounds from the savings account set up by Elaine years ago, the account Maggie had been watching for her these recent years. She would tell Maggie to give her the details, withdraw the money, go to university or move away, get a job somewhere else.

Maggie would understand.

Emma got up, head light.

She would clean downstairs, sort the fire, stock the bar. She would butter Maggie up, relax her, then tell her it was time to move on.

Maggie couldn't begrudge her that chance, could she?

If Emma showed Maggie how determined she was, that she needed to do this, needed to feel her life wasn't over, that she wasn't worthless and pathetic, then how could Maggie refuse?

She couldn't.

She wouldn't.

Emma wiped down the table, brushed the floor, swept the hearth and prepared a fresh fire. She checked the fridge; there was enough food for a nice dinner. Bacon and cabbage fried in butter, mash with the skins on, onion gravy with a dash of Guinness, just how Maggie liked it.

Emma held on to the door of the fridge, the cold air hitting her thighs, and pressed the heel of her hand to her mouth. She was smiling. She could feel her cheeks stretching, her head light with this feeling she hadn't felt in so long.

James was dead, he was dead, but she didn't need him anyway.

It was going to be OK.

She would move on.

Leave him behind her, take her life into her own hands at last.

She closed the fridge, went to the cellar to check the barrels.

She had missed this year's enrollment but maybe she could start university in September next year, take her time choosing the right course, the right place.

She took the stairs in twos, giddy by the time she reached the bottom, jumping off the last step.

She checked the gas levels on the canisters by the wall. All fine; Maggie had changed them only last night.

She could try a university in the North, far away, maybe even Edinburgh if she fancied it, why not? Maggie had persuaded her against it at eighteen, told her to wait, stay on at the pub, help build the business. She should never have listened, but in her naivety, after all Maggie had done for her, she had felt duty-bound to obey.

She checked the bitter, ale, dry cider. All were fine. Only the sweeter cider was looking quite low.

She would get the barrel ready, it'd make changing it easier for Maggie when the time came.

She could study one of the sciences like she'd always planned to when she was younger. She already had good A Levels in chemistry and biology. Maybe an access course first, see which discipline she liked the most. Something to stretch her, get her mind working.

She rolled the sweet cider barrel towards her, shifting its weight with a heave and a groan and wondering how Maggie still did this at her age, nearly sixty-five.

The slap of something falling, the rustle of paper on the ground. Emma looked behind the barrel, lifted a plastic sleeve of letters from the floor, letters from the bank.

The room grew darker by a degree, the damp, whitewashed bricks closing in.

One hand on the wall, the other holding the letters, she let herself fall onto the bottom step, the step she had jumped from, jubilant, hopeful, only moments before.

Letters telling Maggie the accounts were all empty.

The door at the top of the cellar stairs was still open, a draught working its way down, stroking Emma's neck with the cold, bringing the smells from the kitchen down with it.

Overdrawn.

The smells worked their way round Emma. She could taste the old fat from the frying pan, the dry, stale teabags by the sink.

Late payments.

Spoiled milk and yeasty, rotten cider.

Bankruptcy.

She gagged but had nothing left to bring up, the food from earlier splashed on the edges of Nuala's sink, another round heaved up in the toilet. Her stomach was empty, her gags were painful, dry.

The money was gone. All of Emma's money was gone.

She looked up from the letters, hands shaking.. She was cold, her head light and empty.

She had nothing.

No one.

Standing, hand on the wall for support, she felt inside her jeans pocket for her phone. She would look online, see what her options were. But her phone was upstairs, on the table in the kitchen. All she found in her pocket were apple seeds. Who was she kidding? She didn't have any options at all.

Nuala

Saturday, 18th November, 2017

The car filled with Nuala's cries, her head thrown back and mouth wide open, the sound like a banshee's wail. The car rocked as she pummelled the steering wheel. Her fingers dug into her palms, wanting to cut, wanting to see the black flow of blood but her nails were gone, gnawed to the quick.

She raised her hands to her mouth and bit down, ripping open the top layer of skin until blood began to flow, dripping into her mouth and clotting beneath her tongue. All the while the images from Maggie's story echoed, the memory of Maggie's voice brimming over with blame, disapproval, disgust for the man Nuala loved.

She continued to bite, but the physical pain did nothing to quash that other pain, that darker pain, impossible to reach with fingernails or teeth.

She couldn't go on.

Below her, she could see the lights from the village houses, the winding streets of the combe. She had come here, to this place she had promised never to go, to find solace, comfort, the embrace of a mother in as much pain as Nuala. She had read the letters, up there in her attic at home, and saw hope, saw a lifeline, someone she could go to at last.

What a fool she had been.

She thought of her baby, her little boy, buried in the garden at home. Thought of James' arms around her, kissing her, telling her he was sorry for calling her names, so sorry, didn't she know he loved her, only her?

Only her.

She thought of all the times she had forgiven him. She thought of all the times she had bitten her tongue until she had lost the ability to speak altogether.

Was it the letters that had caused his foul tempers? Was it the reminder of what he had left behind, run away from, that made him lash out?

If Emma had never sent them, would James have been different, would he have remained the kind, caring man she'd first met?

Those first few months. Waking up early and bringing back coffee and fresh pastries from the Starbucks down the road. Cooking her dinner. Laughing *with* her when she burnt the cake she'd baked for his twentieth birthday. Looking at it now, she was sure that the number of times they laughed together, shared a smile or a joke in those first few months, outnumbered all of their moments of post-nuptial camaraderie.

Maybe that was when the first letter arrived, Nuala thought, remembering how James would twist the wedding ring around her finger, calling her 'Mine', in a soft, low voice. 'You'll always be mine.' And she had said, 'Yes, yes of course I'll always be yours.' And he had laughed, said 'I know,' and she realised he hadn't been looking for reassurance. He was stating a fact.

James was her husband.

Hers.

She hadn't spent years perfecting her role as his wife, working

and working and _working_ at being the woman he had wanted
her to be, for someone else to lay claim to his memory, to plant
themselves in his biography when he had built his life around
Nuala alone. She wasn't going to let Emma mourn him as _the
one that got away_, or Maggie taint him with her disapproval.

'Besides,' Nuala said, 'you shouldn't speak ill of the dead.'
And laughed when she realised she'd spoken aloud.

She wound her car through the village's dark streets, the
moon hidden.

She passed the school and its sad little park. She passed
side-roads that led to farms and barns.

Which one did Emma claim to have fucked James in?

She stopped the car in the middle of the road, not bothering
to pull over.

What an idiot she had been.

Why did she assume Lois had written those letters, when
James had warned her about his mother, told her what she
was like?

Why had she come here, driven all this way, for something
she would never find?

Comfort.

Understanding.

Love.

It had all gone, died with James, with their son.

And not one of them knew about it. James never told them
about her, they didn't know who she was, what she'd put up
with to build up the family she had wanted for so long.

They didn't understand what she had been driven to, how
desperate she had become.

She had to make them see.

She had to make Emma understand.

Maybe then Nuala would find some peace.

She looked at the clock on her dashboard; she still had fifty minutes. More, if Maggie was a slow walker which, due to her size and girth, she suspected she was.

She drove on.

Past the shop, past more houses, the pub up ahead and in sight.

As she reached the pub she noticed the building beside it, another house set back from the road.

A fragment of Maggie's story came back to her. Maggie had said that Lois and James lived next door to the pub, that Lois was Maggie's neighbour.

Then why did Lois live on the opposite side of the village now? What had made her move?

Nuala parked the car and got out, walked over to the building next door to the pub.

The house itself was set back, a forgotten garden at the front, a tumbled down wall surrounding it, scorch marks licking the edge like tongues. The burnt out remains of Lois's former home.

The roof was missing, the door too. The windows, staring out from the blackened stonework, were glassless, frameless holes.

From the state of the building, the destruction, Nuala knew that nothing would have survived the fire. Furniture, gone. Books, curtains, photographs.

Nuala knew how it would look inside; like the monochrome setting of a silent film. Wallpaper, grey and delicate, curling away from the walls. Melted, distorted furniture, the white ash of unidentifiable objects scattered around, after the fire moved through like a hurricane.

She had seen it all in her parents' house in Oxfordshire. Her father, asleep on the sofa, holding one of the lit cigarettes her GP mother always nagged him about, had burned their house to ruin. Her mother upstairs, asleep in bed with the door open, had choked to death on the fumes. Nuala slept in the far end of the house, the big yellow bedroom with the strong, closed door that the firemen said had saved her life.

She could smell the heady scent of wood smoke and melted plastic, even the smell of burned hair where the fire had caught brushes, dog beds. The dogs.

At the time, they'd told her that it was her imagination, there was no way you could isolate the different smells from a pile of cinders. But she could. She could smell the hair, the plastic, the burned flesh.

The clouds shifted with the wind and the moon broke through, brightening the ivy in the house's doorway and windows.

She thought she would die, too, in those first few months afterwards. Thought she would die from loneliness, pain, guilt, from the sympathy of overbearing neighbours, from the stifling hugs of her friends' mothers who would hold her and tell her it is all right to cry, dear girl, cry away.

She didn't die, not then.

Someone had saved her. James.

She thought of him walking barefoot on the grass in front of this house, with the sun behind him. She thought of him as a child playing in the street, imagined the sound of Lois calling him in for a dinner of mackerel and toast.

When she turned to the burned-out house there he was, smiling in the doorway, waving and beckoning her inside.

But he wasn't waving at Nuala.

Another phantom swept by, a phantom with soft, dimpled arms, blonde hair flowing over her shoulders, laughing as she ran to him and let him hold her waist and kiss her neck, his lips caressing the space above her collar bone.

She watched as Emma's hands disappeared beneath his T-shirt, tugged at the fly on his jeans. It was Emma, all Emma, biting his neck and guiding his fingers inside her knickers, filling his mouth with her tongue.

Here, James did not belong to her, he would never be remembered as her husband. It was a love story they didn't have time for.

He would only be remembered, here, as Emma's lover.

The phantoms receded, hidden by the shadows so only their naked limbs could be seen, James's feet moving with the rhythm of his body, Emma's legs open either side of his, her knees raised, toes curling against his calves.

Nuala looked away.

Looked to the pub, its lights on, shadows moving inside.

Emma.

She stepped along the pavement, feet quiet, close to the pub and peered in through the window.

She could see her, behind the bar, staring into the mid-distance, her face blank, eyes glazed over.

Nuala carried on watching as Emma picked up a glass from the washer, dried it on a rag, put it on a shelf. Emma didn't once change her stance, look up or to the side, as though she were working on pure automatic.

Oblivious.

Carrying on as normal, unaware of the pain she had caused.

Not knowing that the letters she sent, those goddamn letters, were delivered to another woman's husband. That those letters had caused him anguish and upset, caused him to close himself away from his wife, become distant, unpredictable, mean.

It was time to make her understand.

Emma

Saturday, 18th November, 2017

She was standing at the bar, glass in one hand, rag in the other, eyes fixed on the empty mid-distance of the room.

She had nothing.

No money.

No one she could trust. Not even Maggie.

Her chin quivered but she stopped herself crying. She had never once cried in this room, punters or no punters to witness it. She wasn't going to start now.

She sniffed hard until the air hurt her nose, smelled the dirt and the damp from the rag in her hand, realising too late the cloth she was using to dry the clean glasses was filthy.

What did it matter?

This was it now. This was her lot.

Was Nuala Greene the reason that James never came back? The reason he never returned and told Emma he was sorry, so sorry, that he would make up for everything that had happened to her?

Was Nuala the reason Emma never had the chance to make him pay for what he did to her, what he took?

She had loved him.

Given herself to him, her young body, her soul, her future.

Nuala had rocked up with her Burberry bag, her nice clothes, her miniatures of Molton Brown, not knowing who Emma was, or what James had done.

Emma abandoned the glasses, left the dirty rag in the bar. She walked to the kitchen, flicked on the old black kettle out of habit, the wire fixed in three places with tape.

She had nothing.

Eyes on the window to the side of the room, she saw Lois's old burned-out house glaring back at her from outside and remembered how glad she had been, how happy, to know that that woman's possessions were all gone. That she had nothing. And after all she had done to Emma, she knew that nothing was all Lois deserved.

Did Maggie tell Nuala that too, about Lois and what she did? How she sent James away from her, split them apart, the lies she made James believe? How, if she had just helped Emma instead of hindered her, that Elaine might still be alive? That Emma would still, possibly, have her stepmother to cling to?

The steam rose from the kettle, clouded the air and stuck to the window pane in a mist.

The house next door was replaced with a silver fog of condensation, the colour of the glass reminding her of the jars in her bedroom drawer, of the powder she'd made from the apples and lye.

She could hear them calling to her, their promise of release and blessed nothingness, an end to this painful existence made worse now that there was no way out.

But her thoughts were interrupted.

Someone was knocking on the locked pub door.

Nuala

Saturday, 18th November, 2017

'I know,' Emma said to her, not stepping aside to let Nuala in. 'I know who you are, now.'

Emma's face was pale, but her cheeks were tinged scarlet; she looked almost feverish, the colour adding to her otherwise insipid complexion.

'And what is it,' Nuala said, 'that you think you know about me?'

'You're James's wife. You're the one who—'

'Who kept him away?'

'I suppose so, yes. The one who kept him away.' Emma moved away from the door, and Nuala could feel her eyes on her as she stepped inside. Could feel the jealousy, in all its forms, seething beneath the surface.

She closed the door behind her and stood in the warmth from the fire, the cold wind, the threat of rain, left outside.

Emma turned the light on in the kitchen, the one, too, above the bar till. The room still looked dark, cramped with furniture that cast shadows on the floor and walls, the absence of customers making it feel smaller still.

'You're wearing my jumper,' Nuala said, looking at Emma's

red hands, imagining them rifling through her things, surprised that she didn't really care. What did it matter, if Emma touched her clothes, her bag, wore her jumper? Another time in her life she would have felt violated, spied on. But really, these were such trivial things.

She had far bigger complexities to work out.

'I know,' Emma said, and she crossed her arms over her chest. 'I know he's dead.' Her voice cracked as she spoke, her eyes filled with tears.

Nuala felt no sympathy. Emma was thinking only of her own loss. No care for Nuala, how she was feeling, how she had coped. Just selfish, inward grief, claiming James's death as her own source of pain, no one else's.

How *dare* she.

The clock above the bar reminded her that she didn't have long; only forty minutes or so until Maggie came back. But still, that should be more than enough.

'Don't apologise, about the jumper,' Nuala said, switching the topic back, making sure she took the lead in the conversation. She watched as Emma peeled the cashmere from her body, stood before her in a black T-shirt, goosebumps on her bare arms, showing the nervousness of someone caught out. Wondered if this was how James had felt, when Nuala had stood, unsure, before him when he was in one of his moods.

'Why are you here?' Emma asked at last, holding out the jumper in her scaly, red hands, looking straight into Nuala's eyes without blinking, only her flushed cheeks and slight tremble giving away her nerves.

'You're shaking, look,' Nuala said, tucking the jumper under her arm and taking the other woman's hands, feeling their trembling give her power. 'It must be the shock.' Nuala's own hands were steady. Her wedding ring felt warm on her chest where it hung from the chain around her neck. The jumper in her hands had been a present, last year, from James. He had been hers, the truth of that fact giving her strength. 'You weren't expecting me to be his wife, were you? Weren't expecting him to be married at all. Did you think he was waiting for you?'

Emma had no idea what was coming. She looked as if she wanted to take the upper hand, as if she was steeling herself for a fight. But she had no idea what she was really dealing with, what Nuala was preparing to do.

'He never even mentioned you, never uttered your name in our house,' Nuala said, stepping forward and closing the already small gap between her and Emma. 'He told me all about Maggie, his mother, some about his father. But never *you*. And never your baby.' Nuala paused, watching Emma's reaction, horrified disbelief on the other girl's face.

'I'll take this upstairs, sort out my things,' Nuala said. 'Then we can talk before I go.'

'You're leaving?' Emma said, clearly still shocked by Nuala's last comments, blindsided by her sudden change in direction, uncertain of what she should do. Nuala watched the woman's gaze flitter from the bar to the kitchen door, then settle on the cashmere jumper under Nuala's arm.

The beat of Nuala's heart sped up as she enjoyed Emma's uncertainty, the feeling of power from putting her on the back foot.

'Why would I stay *here*?' she said, emphasising the last word, watching Emma's jaw tighten as she did so. 'Why would anyone?'

Emma seemed to know what she meant. She sank down in the damask chair by the fire, and held her head in her hands, chewed her lip.

'As I said, it's the shock. It all must have been such a shock.' Nuala smiled sweetly at Emma, so sweetly, a plan forming in her head. 'I'll make you some tea, fix you something to eat. Yes, I know it's not my place but don't argue, I don't mind.' She patted the air in front of her as Emma tried to stand up, object, made it clear in both her tone and her stance that she meant every word she said, enjoying so much this feeling of dominance, how easily addictive it could become. 'Then we can talk before I go.'

Upstairs, alone, the bravado wore thin.

She felt along the hallway towards the guest room, the image of Emma's heartbroken face filling her vision in place of the worn-down carpet, the stained ceiling, damp walls. In the room she packed the jumper away, checked her bag to see if anything else was missing.

In a minute, she would go back downstairs, to the kitchen. She had said she would make them both tea, just as she had done with Lois earlier that day. Before she had found out what Lois was really like, and learned what lies Emma had been spewing all these years.

As if her husband would fuck a fourteen-year-old, get her pregnant.

Then her eyes alighted on the envelope by the bed, and she reached into her back pocket for the letter.

Come back to me, my darling.

If Emma had only left James alone. How different their lives could have been.

But she would make Emma see, make them all see, that it

was *she* who'd loved James all along, who really knew him.

Nuala walked out of the room, down the stairs and into the kitchen.

The room was dingy, the grey walls were splattered with grease and tea stains. Through the hatch into the bar, Nuala could see Emma, her head still in her hands as she sat in front of the fireplace, thinking, no doubt, about James.

Her husband.

And suddenly she was calm.

'My husband,' she whispered to herself. '*Mine.*' She closed her eyes and let the word fill her mouth.

Emma looked up, her gaze questioning, but Nuala didn't falter. Instead, she met the other woman's eye, held it, smiled.

As the water boiled, Nuala looked up, to the window above the kettle, the glass misty with steam. The reflection she saw in the window, the older woman staring back at her, made her stomach drop.

Thick, straight black hair pulled into a low ponytail. A clear oval face, high pink cheeks and round green eyes. Nuala could see that her right incisor was damaged, the enamel a whitish grey where the root had died.

Nuala froze, too scared to turn in case this vision of her mother vanished. She was desperate to put her arms around her, smell her perfume, feel her heartbeat. To have that sweet voice telling her she didn't have to do this after all, because her mother was back and Nuala wasn't alone any more.

Wasn't that why she had come here? So that she wouldn't be alone?

But not one person had offered her their condolences, as though oblivious to the fact her husband was dead.

Because here, she remembered again, James belonged to Emma.

The girl spreading lies, writing to Nuala's husband, trying to tempt him away.

That's what Nuala had found, coming here. Not comfort, not understanding.

All she had found was that girl and her lies.

And a final sense of purpose.

She kept her eyes closed, thinking of her mother, what her mother would say.

'Go home,' she'd advise, her voice warm as ginger biscuits. 'Now you know why he left, why he didn't want you coming back. Just go home, leave all this behind you.'

Only Nuala didn't have anything to go back home for. A dead rose bush, dead husband, dead son.

She opened her eyes.

Her mother was gone. And she knew what she had to do.

Her own reflection stared back at her, her eyes wired with that new sense of determination, not tired-looking any more.

She finished making the tea and placed each cup on a saucer, added biscuits to Emma's from the pack she found by the kettle, and walked back into the bar.

'Here you go,' she said, a saccharine smile directed at Emma. 'I've added sugar, they say it helps with the shock. I've biscuits here, too.'

She passed a saucer to Emma, and, holding her own, settled into the opposite armchair by the fire.

'You've been waiting for James to come back,' she said. 'But he was *my* husband!' Her words were too loud for the small room, but she didn't care. 'You had no right trying to lure back my husband.'

'I wasn't trying to lure him,' Emma said, her young face defiant, her cheeks still flushed.

'But you wanted him back. You wanted him to come back here, to find you.'

'I didn't know he was married.'

'Would that have made a difference?'

And Emma looked down, didn't answer, and Nuala smiled.

'No,' Nuala said, 'It wouldn't have made a difference, not to you. You would have carried on regardless.'

Emma pulled her top lip into her mouth, chewed it to keep herself from speaking, talking back, and Nuala smiled wider, felt the stretch of her cheeks as her teeth were exposed. How well she knew that feeling, the feeling of holding back. How good it felt, now, to let it all go.

'Spreading your lies. Your dirty lies about what my husband did to you, lies you made everyone believe.'

'They're *not* lies,' Emma said, her lip springing free from her teeth, her free hand curled into a fist.

'James never touched you. He wouldn't have slept with a fourteen-year-old girl, a *child*.'

'He *did*.' Emma's chin had dropped, but her eyes looked up at Nuala, dark and forbidding beneath her brow.

'Stop lying to me!' Nuala's shout was high pitched, spittle spraying with her words, tea splashing over the edge of her cup and landing on the arm of the chair.

Emma gritted her teeth. 'I'm not lying,'

'How pathetic you are,' Nuala said, 'to cling on to the lie even now when you know that he's gone, that my husband is *dead*.' But the last word choked her and she looked away, to the wall of photographs.

'He's gone.' She said it again, meaning the photos this time, her finger pointing out the gap where the Polaroid had been. 'Where is he?'

'I took it down,' Emma said.

'Give it to me.'

'No.'

'He's *my* husband! Give it to me!'

Emma stood up, her half-drunk tea placed on the table beside her, the biscuits untouched, and took the crumpled photograph from her back pocket.

She walked towards the fire and Nuala could see her intention, the photograph inches from the flames.

'Don't you dare,' she said, rising.

'I'm not lying,' Emma said, 'He did do all those things. He *loved* me, he left me, no matter what you say.'

'Give me his photograph,' Nuala said, arms outstretched, taking a step towards Emma and the fire. 'He's mine! Give him to me!'

Emma's hand moved closer, the flames highlighting the bleached skin on her knuckles.

'What do you care? It's just a photograph. And what does it matter to you if I'm lying or not? *Why do you care?*'

'He's all I've got!' Nuala screamed, lunging for Emma, grabbing her arm. 'He was all I ever had, you can't take him away!'

'I can't take him away if he's already dead!'

'You're claiming him, saying he's yours, that he loved you when the only woman he loved was me! He told me so! It's what kept me hanging on through all the bad times, all the— if he was lying, then what am I left with? What does that make me?'

She yanked Emma towards her, grabbed the photo and held it, safe, to her chest, pressed it against the wedding rings hanging from the chain around her neck.

'I'm *not* a pathetic fool who followed a man blindly. I'm not a sad, desperate orphan who clung to the first person to show her love. I stayed with him because we loved each other, and you're trying to turn me into something else!'

'No, I'm not. I never said anything like that!'

'You think—'

'I don't think anything about you, I don't *know* anything about you!'

'Let me finish! You think I'm beaten, downtrodden, that I let a man walk all over me, take my money, my home, my body because I was desperate not to be alone, is that it? Is that what you think?'

'I know nothing about you.' Emma backed away, her arms held out in front of her, eyes wary and Nuala realised her outburst had frightened her.

'Do you think I'm going to hurt you?' Nuala asked, the words sounding insane, delicious. 'Do you think I'm going to hurt you for the lies you've been spreading about James?'

'James told me he loved me,' Emma said, teeth gritted. 'He promised he'd look after me. We were waiting until I was old enough so we could run away. He had nothing to keep him here, in this village, except his mother and you know what she's like. And besides,' she said, 'it's in the past, you can't change it.'

And she laughed, her cheeks flushed. 'At some point, Nuala, you have to let it go.'

'Don't take that tone with me.' Nuala stepped forward, closer to Emma, closer to the fire. 'Don't talk as if you're above me, wiser, more experienced, as if you have the upper hand. I know what you did. He had to leave here because of you, because he knew if he were to return he'd have to deal with all your stupid little lies, because you're such an idiot, such a stupid fool, such a pathetic, useless creature, that you blamed him for your stupid mistakes. You're just an idiot, you're an *idiot*!'

'My God,' Emma said, stepping away from the fire. 'You sound just like him. Idiot. He used to call me an idiot all the time, but sweetly, like it was a pet name even though I knew he really meant it. And he'd say it for the stupidest things, if I missed a button when doing up my school blouse, or caught my tights on the ladder up to the barn loft—'

'Stop it!' Nuala screamed, her throat vibrating, fists clenched. She hated that Emma could echo him so perfectly, that she had known him in this way. Hated that James had spoken to another girl in the way that he had spoken to Nuala, his *wife*. She took another step towards Emma. 'Stop trying to turn it around now, it's too late! I know that you were writing to him.' Another step forward, her face only inches from Emma's. 'I know you wanted him back, *my husband*.' She raised her hand, pushed Emma backwards with a jab to her chest.

Emma stumbled, faltered, eyes wide from the shock of the attack. 'I don't know what you're talking about,' she said, hands held up, palms outwards, 'I don't know what you think I've done, but—'

'Stop lying!' Nuala lunged, pushed Emma again, forced her against the wall by the fireplace, the heat from the flames growing stronger.

'Why would you think I would still want him after he left me like that? Left me to face everyone alone?' Emma shouted.

'I can see it in your face,' Nuala said, pushing Emma into

the brickwork, holding here there with both hands. 'The effect he had on you, the longing you still have for him. Why else would you write him those letters?'

Nuala's voice broke, a split second of weakness and Emma turned, shoved her hard, watched Nuala fall, stumbling back, holding on to the side of the armchair to stop herself falling.

'As if I don't have enough to worry about!' Emma cried. 'Why would I write to him, beg for his attention, when I have *so much more to worry about*?'

Emma moved towards the fireplace, the hearth cluttered with tools for the fire, a penknife, coal shovel, tongs. She turned with a cast-iron poker held firmly in her fist.

'When I have Maggie to look after, this pub to sort out? When everything around me is falling apart?'

The tip of the poker gleamed dangerously as she held it aloft.

'Go ahead!' Nuala shouted, not cowering. 'Hit me, hit me as hard as you like! It won't make the least bit of difference!' She started to laugh, the laugh growing manic, her shoulders shuddering and face contorted. 'I came here to find family, solace,' she said. 'But that was all wrong. You see, my family is gone, they can't be replaced. I'll show you how much they meant to me, how far I'm willing to go to prove my love for James. To prove that our love was *real*.' She darted forward, grabbed Emma's wrist and yanked the poker cleanly away.

Emma lunged, hands reaching up to grab at the weapon but missed, fell at the floor between Nuala's feet and the hearth.

The poker was hard and hot in her hand. Nuala raised it above her head.

Emma scrabbled behind her, desperately trying to find something to counterattack with.

But Nuala was faster.

Emma screamed as the poker came down.

Seven years ago

Maggie

Tuesday, 10th August, 2010

Maggie had to reach Lois. She had to make sure she was OK.

Her car dipped over the hill, making the final descent into the village, the sun burning through the rear windscreen and turning the car into a furnace, even with the windows down.

There had been no argument from Emma and Elaine when Maggie had burst into the room, told them where she suspected Arthur of having gone. 'You have to go,' Emma had said to Maggie. 'You have to stop him.' As if it were the simplest thing in the world.

She drove on through the village centre, her pub up ahead, beside it Lois's house.

Lois's garden gate was hanging loose, one of the hinges broken away from the wall.

The front door was ajar, something dark smeared on the white surround. Surely it wasn't blood?

She slowed the car, tried to look inside the house but she couldn't see a thing.

Frantic, she parked by the roadside, in between the pub and

Lois's house, stepped out of her car onto the pavement and nearly collided head on with Arthur.

Wild eyes, filled with a savage expression.

They were the first thing she noticed.

'Where's Lois?' Maggie asked nervously, looking past him, seeing the door to Lois's house was open.

'Where the fuck were *you*?' Arthur said, his teeth bared in a dog-like snarl. 'Where were you when *he* was doing those things to my daughter?' His spittle landed on Maggie's cheek; he raised a hand and jabbed her in the shoulder. 'You're her godmother! Where the fuck *were* you?'

Maggie couldn't answer, rendered mute by the expression in his eyes. She had never seen him like this, his whole being consumed with pure rage.

He wiped his mouth on the back of his hand, stormed away. His hair was dishevelled, his clothes too.

Above his collar, on the back of his neck, was a fresh scratch seeping blood onto his shirt.

Maggie looked towards the open door, and ran straight for Lois, calling her name as she entered the house.

The hallway itself was the same as it had been that morning, though the air hung thick and ripe with tension. She could feel it ooze across her skin, lift the hair on her forearms.

She heard a muffled cry, like a sob wept into a pillow.

It had come from the living room.

Maggie lunged forwards, barging open the door with her shoulder. She paused at the threshold, out of breath, her body frozen in shock.

She hadn't expected Arthur to go so far.

She hadn't predicted *this*.

Lois sat slumped on the floorboards by the sagging beige sofa.

Blood leaked from her right nostril in a thin line.

One eye was swollen shut, the eyebrow above it cut, blood smeared across her forehead and crusted black at the hairline. Her throat was ringed with red, a purple thumb mark on the side of her neck. Maggie thought of Elaine's bruised wrist and shivered.

A smear of blood marked the sofa cushion behind her.

'Oh my God, Lois! I'm calling the police.' Maggie said, one foot already pointing out of the door.

Lois gave a muffled sob, opening her good eye. 'No police!' Her words were thick and slurred and Maggie could see blood on the edge of her tongue. 'Arthur said he'd report James if I called the police!'

Maggie was still turned to go, desperate to report Arthur, draw the police in, but Lois managed to stand and grab her arm before her weak legs failed her. Maggie noticed that her knees were scuffed red with carpet burns.

'No police,' Lois said again, frantically. Her bottom lip was swelling before Maggie's eyes. 'I won't let this ruin my son's life.' There were marks beside her left ear, small half-moons the shape of a man's fingernails. At some point, Arthur must have grabbed Lois's ear, dug his claws into that sensitive flesh.

In the hallway, through the living room door, Maggie could see the school portraits of a young, smiling James. She knew that Lois would take countless more punches to protect her only child. It's what Maggie had always suspected she had done with Jim: taken the hit from her husband to save her boy. Until the night that Jim fell down the stairs, broke his neck, and finally Lois was left alone.

'OK.' Maggie held Lois's elbow, helped her steady herself, 'But you're coming next door with me. I'm not leaving you like this.'

Lois winced, but stayed still, didn't cry out in pain.

'Nearly done.' Maggie lifted the cotton, dabbed in vodka from the bar because she'd long ago run out of antiseptic.

'I need to get back,' Lois said again, the third time since Maggie had dragged her to the pub to clean her up. Lois had nothing at home, no plasters or gauze, nothing to clean a wound with other than tap water.

'You can stay here, tonight, if you want to.'

'I don't want to.' Lois wouldn't look at Maggie but kept her eyes on the door. 'I knew he'd blame me,' she said. 'I just wanted to keep out of it, but you wouldn't let me, you had to tell him that Emma had been here.'

'I didn't think he'd do this!' Maggie said. 'I had no idea!'

'Neither did I,' Lois said, looking down at her hands, her fingers worrying in her lap.

The light in the bar didn't help Maggie much, the dimness perfect for drinking but not much else. She touched Lois's chin, tried to get her to look up, to make sure the wound above her eye was all clean.

Lois flinched, squeezed the bloody tissue in her hand.

There was something unsettling about that tissue, held in her hand, something about the way Lois wouldn't quite meet Maggie's eye. Maybe it was the light, highlighting the youth in Lois's face, maybe it was the purpling cheekbone, reminding Maggie of her son, Lee, how his face had bloomed with bruises beneath her fist during that one, terrible time when she had lost her senses completely, drunk on gin and wallowing in grief.

'I really wish you'd let me take you to the hospital. I can

patch you up, but the cut on your eyebrow will probably scar. A nurse would do a much better job.'

'I'm not going to the hospital.'

'And your tongue needs looking at, too.' The underside of Lois's tongue had been ripped, the frenulum torn. 'What the hell did he do?'

'He pulled it out between finger and thumb. Wouldn't let go till I promised not to tell anyone about *this*.' Lois' gestured towards her bruised face and neck, tried to say more but her chin began to quiver.

Maggie dropped the cottonwool ball, 'Jesus, Lois! We have to tell the police, he has to be held accountable for this!'

Lois shook her head. 'I just want to go home.'

'Why? There's no one there. Someone needs to look after you.'

'What do you care?'

'I'm trying to help,' Maggie said, and lifted the cotton ball back up, inhaling the vodka evaporating from the wool.

'You're too late to help!' Lois held her chin high. 'You're always too late.'

Lois was looking at her at last, eyes flaming, lips trembling. Beneath her defiance was something else, a fragment of her teenage self. The blood on Lois's face, the sight of the tissue in her hands, reawakened a memory of Maggie's.

Lois at fifteen, standing in the village's main street on a humid summer's day, her father's oil-marked hand between her shoulder blades.

Maggie had seen her, had watched from the aisles of the shop.

'Go on then!' he'd shouted through fag-stained teeth and Lois flinched, her eyes on the ground, as he pushed her towards three of the village's most recognisable figures. Arthur Bradbury, who was swiftly making a name for himself as a businessman. Dark blond hair slicked back from his forehead, a brown tweed blazer on over his broad, farmer's shoulders and a year-old wedding ring glinting on his left hand. A third of the locals were in Arthur's employment already, working either on his farm, in his dairy or in his production yard. Next to him was Edward Burrows, Arthur's secretary (though *lackey* was the term Maggie's husband Tom favoured, having never taken a shine to his cousin's right-hand man). And then there was Jim Lunglow, the only unmarried man between them, steel-capped boots on his feet and mechanic's overalls on his back, completing the trio. All three of them were in their forties; a powerful group of imposing men, and were rarely seen without each other.

'Ask 'em then, girl, ask 'em.' Lois's father spat on the pavement, his spit yellow and thick. 'You want a lift into town, and I'm not going to bloody well take you!'

Arthur flicked his cigarette to the floor, looked towards the shop and caught Maggie's eye. She looked down, back at the tins of soup on the shelf. Lois's father raised his foot and stamped the cigarette out.

The young girl mumbled something.

'I'll drive you to town,' Edward offered. He dug the corner of his elbow into Jim's side, winked at him when Lois's father wasn't looking. Jim, his open mouth adding to his air of idiocy, rubbed his hands on the flank of his overalls.

'Well, wha' d'you say?' Lois's father again, pushing her forward so she stumbled and Edward caught her by her upper arms, his fingers denting her flesh.

'Thank you,' Lois mumbled. So unlike her, Maggie thought. Where was the rudeness she was used to, the obstinate lack of respect? In all the years she had known her, and she had known the girl all her life, she had never once said thank you for anything.

'Where's it you wanna go to, lovely?' And Edward's fingers moved from her arm to her waist, waving the girl's father away with his spare hand.

Lois's father walked off, visibly relieved he didn't have to drive his daughter himself, a plume of cheap tobacco smoke left in his wake.

Lois watched him go silently.

Maggie moved closer to the open shop door so she could catch what was said. She couldn't take her eyes off the young girl outside, off the older man holding her waist.

Maggie looked around. No one here was paying the scene any attention at all.

Not entirely sure what she was going to achieve, other than the very fact she was doing *something*, Maggie stepped out of the shop.

'Hello there, Lois. Want me to walk you home?' she said. 'I'm heading that way now—'

Edward's stare turned dark at her approach. 'You're not needed here, Maggie.'

Lois was silent, her face blank, and Maggie said, 'You all right, Lois?'

'Why wouldn't she be?' Jim squared his shoulders and stared Maggie down. 'What are you implying?' He was taller than Maggie by a head, the muscles on his thick arms flexing as he took a step towards her.

'Nothing.' Maggie backed away, wished Tom was there with her. 'Just wanted to make sure Lois was all right.'

Arthur folded his arms, looked at Jim grimly with his eyebrows slightly raised. The mechanic followed the silent orders and stepped down.

'You're fine, aren't you, sweetheart?' Edward's tone was light, almost jovial, his eyes on Lois as he waited for her answer.

The girl nodded, eyes on the floor.

'Say hello to Tom for me,' Arthur said by way of goodbye, putting an end to Maggie's involvement.

'Right you are,' she said awkwardly, not wanting to leave but feeling she had little choice.

When Maggie looked back, from inside the shop, Arthur was talking seriously to Jim but Edward was still holding Lois by the waist. Maggie tried to reassure herself that he was doing the young girl a favour, giving her a lift. That there wasn't something intrinsically off.

Lois was just a kid, after all.

Wore too much makeup, used language unfit for a lady, but she was just a kid.

Edward was a decent married man, for God's sake. And Arthur was Tom's cousin. He was trustworthy; a businessman with a reputation to protect. Lois would be perfectly fine with him.

Later that day, when Maggie was walking back from the church after sorting the flowers and dusting the pews, she saw them again.

Edward had beckoned her over to his green Ford Cortina with a beep of the horn.

'All right, Mags?'

She was nearly home. She was tired. She wanted to see Tom, was confused as to why Edward would call her over.

Maggie glanced in through the passenger window. The car was hot and the inside smelled sour, of sweat and hot skin. 'I'm just back from town, took Lois to the library,' Edward said, jauntily. There was no sign of Arthur, or of Jim.

She noticed Lois then, so still on the backseat that Maggie hadn't realised she was in the car. Her face pale, eyes red rimmed, a hanky in her hand.

'Everything OK, Lois?' Maggie asked.

But Lois didn't say a word. She pressed her lips together and gave the slightest shake of her head. Her hands were in her lap, worrying the hanky between them, knees tight together beneath her skirt.

'She's fine,' Edward said and Maggie looked back at him, his easy confidence, relaxed smile, off-white teeth. 'Just taking her home to her folks, safe and sound.'

Beside Lois was a dark, damp patch on the tan corduroy seat, and another tissue lay scrunched up by the seatbelt.

Maggie caught her eye and the girl looked away, her bottom lip quivering again.

'She's had her little trip to the library and now I'm bringing her back. Looked after you the whole time, didn't I, little girl?'

Maggie wondered what the point had been in calling her over. The heat from the sun on her shoulders was getting stronger, and her bent back was beginning to ache. 'What are you after, Edward?'

'Just wanted to say hello, that's all. Anything you want to say, Lois?' He turned so that his expression was hidden from Maggie. 'You're the one who wanted to talk to Maggie, isn't that right? Isn't that what you said to me earlier? Well, here she is, what was it you wanted to tell her?'

Maggie rubbed the sweat from her brow. 'What is it, Lois?'

Lois said nothing; dropped her eyes to her knees. Edward turned back with a smile. 'She must have forgotten,' he said. 'You know what teenagers are like.'

'I'll be off then,' said Maggie, still confused by the exchange, not knowing if Lois had really wanted to talk to her or not.

As she went to leave, she saw Lois raise the hanky to her eyes again.

A label was sticking out of the hanky, a BHS label – the kind found in the backs of girls' knickers.

Maggie stepped back, opened her mouth in shock, but the car drove away and she lost her chance to speak.

She hadn't seen anything concrete, she told herself as she walked home. She didn't know anything for sure.

Back at home she had helped Tom set the bar up for the evening, cooked dinner for the family. She poured pints of cider, ale, bitter, the occasional gin. Helped Tom tidy up after last orders.

But she couldn't get the image out of her head, couldn't stop thinking about the girl in the car, the hanky that might, or might not, have been a pair of knickers scrunched up in her hand, tissues in a ball by the seatbelt.

She began to take notice of how often she saw the young girl in the company of that tight group of three, Edward, Jim and Arthur. Sometimes it was Edward who drove Lois out of the village, sometimes it was Jim, Arthur seemingly never directly involved.

Eventually she heard the village gossip, mostly from customers at the bar, once from Lois's mother herself who came in to drown her shame in cheap wine. Arthur had for once driven Lois home, practically thrown her on the doorstep of her father's terrace house, and told the man that his daughter was a disgrace, a bloody disgrace, that Lois had come to him and begged him for money to help her and how dare she do that, how dare she, when it had nothing to do with him? That she'd been sleeping with Jim, like a cheap little whore, tried throwing herself at Edward too, but he was married, of course, so refused her.

There were no tears by that point, no knickers dabbing damp cheeks. After that, Maggie only saw Lois with dead eyes, snarling lips, hands balled into fists by her side and a baby growing inside her.

The rest had all happened so quickly, or so Lois's mother told Maggie: her sixteenth birthday present was a cheap white dress, not the abortion Lois begged her throat dry for. The wedding to Jim was held the next day, the man salivating and eyeing up his young bride throughout the short church service. Lois's mother pretended to be overjoyed with the pairing but the fake smile was too difficult to maintain. She didn't even wait until the birth of the child before upping and leaving with her husband to live in a town near her sister, the *shame of it* driving her away. Maggie hadn't seen her since. She doubted Lois had either, even though they lived less than fifty miles away.

Coming back to the present, Maggie breathed in, filled her lungs, smelled the vodka. She looked at Lois and remembered the young girl, her knickers in her hands.

'I'm sorry, for what happened with Jim.' Maggie said. 'I should have—'

'Don't!' Lois snarled. 'Don't you dare pity me.'

'I'm not—'

But Lois pushed back from the table, stood up to go home, grabbed the butterfly stitches and told Maggie she'd do it herself.

'You can't do it yourself,' Maggie had called after her, getting up a second too late, 'you'll need help!'

But Lois had gone, the door swinging shut. Maggie let her go, tried to take her mind off it, off Emma, James, Lois, the past.

She wiped the bar clean, threw away the blood-stained cotton-wool, the tissues, the shallow dish of blood-pinked vodka. She heated a pie, chips and gravy to have for her dinner, made a cup of tea and added a splash of the liquor to help cool it down.

And when, an hour later, the door sounded again, Maggie thought Lois had changed her mind. Thought the woman needed her help after all.

But it wasn't Lois she found on the threshold.

Seven years ago

Maggie

Tuesday, 10th August, 2010

Elaine stood at the door, a suitcase at her feet. On the right side of her face was a shining bruise.

'Jesus!' Maggie pulled the woman inside, pushed the case over the threshold with her foot. She closed the door, bolted it shut and guided Elaine, feather-light and easy to move, into the chair by the card table, then lifted the fringe from her face.

The skin beneath was red, swollen and raw, the bruising spanning her eye, nose and cheek. The second beaten face at the hands of that man, as though his anger could not be sated by attacking one woman alone.

'I can't do this any more, Maggie.'

'My God, Elaine. He's a monster! '

She left Elaine for a moment, filled two tumblers with brandy, for the shock. The hair on her head was standing on end, the curls at the nape of her neck frizzy from the heat and the sweat she'd built up through that day.

How long had this been going on? How often had Maggie sat in their kitchen with Tom, when he was still alive, and chatted about the farm, the land, oblivious to this streak in Arthur's nature? She thought of him throwing the fifteen-year-old Lois on her father's doorstep, Maggie and Tom keeping away because it was none of their business, now, was it? She remembered Arthur after Tom had died, plying her with gin and pressuring her to sign over her dead husband's land. *'Sign the fucking papers.'*

Publicly, Arthur's mask had never slipped, always pretending to be the fine village businessman, the salt of the earth, relying on Edward Burrows to lash out most of his threats or Jim Lunglow to take the fall for his mistakes. Elaine had never said anything. How had she managed to keep her own mask in place, living up to her role of wife, mother, hostess, all the while hiding the bruises her husband had given her?

Did Emma know? Did Arthur hurt his daughter, too? Is that why she was so fearful of her father's reaction to her pregnancy?

Maggie put a brandy glass in front of Elaine and took a sip from her own.

Remembering the marks she'd seen earlier, Maggie lifted Elaine's arm, with no resistance or question from Elaine, and peeled back her sleeve. There were four bruises along her wrist, a fifth larger bruise on the underside. The shape of butterbeans – or of fingers.

'That was an accident,' Elaine said and, in the dim half-light of the bar, Maggie could see her eyes were glossy, glassed over. 'I don't think he meant it that time.' Elaine lifted the glass of brandy to her lips, took a sip, her trembling hand making the glass rattle against her front teeth. 'Sometimes he means it, but sometimes he says he doesn't know what he's doing, that it's not his fault, that I make him do these things.' She couldn't keep her hands still; Maggie had never seen her actions this frantic, her body language so at odds with the empty, dead look in her eyes.

Maggie put her glass down, the action as strong and

commanding as her voice. 'You can stay here as long as you need to. You and Emma.'

'I can't stay here. He'll find me.' The pitch of Elaine's voice heightened with each word, desperate. 'He'll make me go home.'

And Maggie knew that it was true, he would. And unless someone was brave enough to call the police, he'd succeed. And who would call the police in a small place like this, over ten miles away from the nearest station? Where everyone had something to protect, where everyone was employed by Arthur or rented one of his cottages or had a child, sibling, friend who did.

'Do you need my help, to get away? Do you want me to drive you into town?' Maggie took Elaine's hand in her own. 'You could stay in a hotel, maybe one near the hospital, plan your next move?'

'I know what my next move will be,' Elaine said, and she squeezed Maggie's hand with her trembling one, 'but I do need your help with something else.'

'Of course, anything, anything at all.'

Shame filled Elaine's eyes as she tried to speak, fear evident in the tight lines of her mouth. The mask had truly fallen, the façade of the happy wife long gone. Left behind was Elaine's pain, her uncertainty, her terror. A woman who couldn't take any more.

'I need you to look after Emma,' Elaine said, the effort of those words showing plainly on her bruised face.

Emma. The girl couldn't go home to her father, couldn't live in a house with such a man.

'Don't you want to take her with you, once she's been discharged?' Maggie asked, taking another sip of her brandy, letting it mix with the earlier vodka inside her stomach. Looking at

Elaine she knew the woman was in no position to look after the girl, or at least not whilst she was in such a state. A couple of weeks, Maggie could look after her goddaughter for a couple of weeks whilst Elaine recovered, found somewhere safe for them both to stay. Maggie could do that.

'I want to stay with her, of course I do. But I have to stop being so selfish. I have to put her first for once.'

'You always put her first.' Maggie knelt down in front of Elaine, tried to make eye contact, but Elaine's eyes darted, wouldn't settle on any one thing, least of all Maggie's earnest face. 'You're a great mother,' Maggie tried again and Elaine crumbled, her shoulders caving in. There were no tears, her eyes still gaping and dry, but the sound that came from her throat was a sob.

'I've let her down. I have. It's my fault, that's what he said, that it's my fault. I should have been there for her, should have known what she was doing, should have put a stop to it and kept her safe, but I failed.' Elaine gripped Maggie's forearms, her fingers digging into Maggie's sleeve. 'I failed her.'

'No.' Maggie shook her head. 'You have not failed her. This is not your doing.'

'Don't you see? If I hadn't been so worried about myself, if I hadn't been so scared of making a mistake, upsetting Arthur, then maybe I would have known what Emma was doing. I could have put a stop to it and we wouldn't be in this position now.'

'Please, stop blaming yourself,' Maggie said, softly. 'They hid it from everyone, there's no way you could have known. Emma knew that James would get in trouble, being so much older than her, she kept it a secret from everyone to protect him, and herself.'

Elaine forced a smile and held Maggie's hand again, patted it as though she were a child, her fingers so, so cold. 'You're very kind, Maggie. You've always been so kind.'

Maggie lifted herself from the floor, holding onto the back of a chair for support.

She took Elaine's glass and refilled it along with her own at the bar.

When she turned, Elaine was standing, her movements silent. An envelope was on the card table next to her, bearing Emma's name.

'There's a house, on one of the little terraces.' Elaine's voice was trembling but her face was expressionless, the mannequin returning. 'I always had my eye on it for Emma. I liked the thought of being in the garden and looking up to see Emma in her own kitchen, pottering away.'

'Emma can still do those things. She got carried away, made a mistake or two. She's not *dead* for Christ's sake.' Maggie's eyes rested on the suitcase Elaine had brought with her.

'The bag is Emma's,' Elaine said. 'I was hoping you'd agree to collect her from hospital. That's what I need you to do, that's how you can help me.'

Maggie eyed the bag, unsure of what exactly Elaine was really asking, but nodded consent all the same.

'Arthur won't have her in the house. I can't change his mind. I've never been able to do that.' Elaine swayed slightly. 'It's not safe for her there, not whilst he's so angry. I've packed some things for her. I've packed everything, actually. I didn't realise how little she has. It's rather sad, isn't it?'

Maggie didn't know if it was Emma's lack of possessions or the fact that they had been packed away that was meant to be sad. Elaine touched the envelope, her face crumpling as she brushed her fingers over Emma's name. Maggie tried to usher her back into the chair but she wouldn't move.

'Are you asking me if Emma can stay here, Elaine?'

Elaine nodded, then let out an abrupt sob and put her hands over her face. 'For God's sake!' she said, her voice breaking. 'I worked so hard to make sure she didn't make these mistakes.'

'She'll be OK, I'll look after her.' Maggie moved forward, pulled Elaine towards her and wrapped her arms around her body. Thought of all the times she didn't stop by, call in, check to make sure she was all right, just presumed that she was because Elaine had her husband to support her, she was *lucky*, when Maggie had been left all alone.

How could she have been so thoughtless, so blind?

But at least she could help now.

'I'll look after Emma,' she said again. 'I'm her godmother, after all.'

Elaine kissed Maggie on her left cheek, whispered a thank you into her ear.

'I just need to know Emma will be looked after,' she said.

Maggie rubbed Elaine's shoulders, wanted to say yes, of course, she'll be well looked after, but her mind wandered to her son Lee.

How could she look after a fourteen-year-old girl, even if it was only for a couple of weeks? Just a year younger than Lee was the last time Maggie had seen him. Maggie had been deemed an unfit, unstable mother. Was she really capable of caring for Emma? What would she do if Arthur came after her?

'Emma's always loved you, Maggie,' Elaine said, reading the landlady's mind.

'I'll do my best,' Maggie said, choking out the words, hoping it would be sooner rather than later that Elaine came back and took Emma away with her, somewhere else, somewhere safe. At the same time, she thought of the infant Emma, the balled-up fists, red face, puckered rosebud mouth, her heart swelling at the memory of the baby.

Elaine stepped back, smiled and her frown lines disappeared, leaving her face looking eerily calm. 'That's how I know Emma will be safe with you, Maggie. Because you're kind. You've always been so kind.'

'You're leaving now?' Maggie said, 'Right now? Are you sure you'll be all right? Won't you let me take you to wherever you're going?'

Elaine shook her head. 'There's no need,' she said, and swayed slightly on her feet.

'God, Elaine, I'm so sorry,' Maggie said, slumping into the chair by the table, thinking of how she should have guessed what Arthur had been doing to Elaine. She hung her head in shame. 'I'm so sorry.'

'It's not your fault, Maggie. None of this is.' Elaine's voice sounded high and strained, a manic look replacing the calm on her face. 'I need to go now.'

'It's not your fault either, Elaine.' Maggie's voice was heavy with sympathy, and with guilt. 'Please don't blame yourself.'

'Don't you worry about me,' Elaine said, tears in her eyes. 'I'll be fine. I know what I have to do to make things right.'

Elaine unbolted the door, walked out into an August night only just beginning to darken.

'I'll tell Emma you'll see her soon. I won't let Arthur come near her,' Maggie said before the door closed on her friend. 'I'll tell her that you'll come back and take her with you. I'll keep her safe until then.'

Elaine gave Maggie a nod, only the good side of her face on display. Then she turned and walked away.

And if Maggie had known what was going to happen she would have followed, chased Elaine and held her back, kept her safe in the pub forever.

But she didn't know.

She let the woman walk away.

And Maggie returned to the bar, to the bottle of brandy. She didn't think of Elaine, of where she would go, what plans might be running through her head, what might happen to her. No. She drank the brandy in greedy, self-pitying gulps and thought of Emma, dreading having to tell the girl what her father had done, how Elaine had gone away. How Emma would be looked after by Maggie from now on, when both knew she was in no fit state to parent.

Maggie

T he rest of the story played on in Maggie's head as she walked across the dark fields back towards the pub, the words she didn't get a chance to say to Nuala. Nuala had wanted to know what happened seven years ago to make James flee the village and never come back, Hopefully Maggie had told Nuala enough to make sure *she* never came back either, enough so that she had closure and would leave the past, and Emma, well alone.

What was the woman doing now? She'd be nearly on the M5 with any luck, nearly out of the West Country, out of their lives for good.

Maggie shone her torch straight ahead, but the bulb was weak, battery running low, and the beam of light was barely stronger than that from the moon.

Maggie could hear the blast of the shotgun further up the hill, echoed by that bloody crow scarer in the fields below.

Why had she insisted on walking back home at night in the cold, clouds threatening rain, men with loaded guns stalking rabbits nearby? She thought of Emma, of James, Nuala, what happened to Lois, what happened to Elaine and knew she had made the right call, that it was best to keep

Nuala away from Emma. There had been something about Nuala that hadn't sat well with Maggie, something off balance.

Maggie pulled her coat around her, felt the bulge of the flask in her pocket and pulled it out, took a sip to stave off the cold, just a sip.

At least she had her boots on, their thick-soled grip keeping her upright, but her knees were killing her. And she could barely see a thing with that pathetic torch. She heard another gunshot, envious of the lampers and their search lights.

Twice her face was scratched by a bramble, their thorns tough and dry now the berries were gone. They stuck out like thin arms from the hedges, grappling to get hold of anything in their way, including the pockmarked, scarred face of a woman in her mid-sixties.

She was out of breath by the time she reached the second field, the pull of her lungs the loudest noise in the field by far, save for the gunshot on the hills. She almost took a detour then, through the land that used to be hers. Before she sold it to Arthur. Before she invested the money into the fast-sinking pub. She knew the lay of the land even better than the scar on her face, the instinctive knowledge from having grown up here.

But the detour would take her through the land beside Arthur's house. She would have to walk past the barn, and she didn't want to do that, not with the memory of what had happened inside it seven years ago.

She slipped out the flask again and took a nip. Just to warm her up.

The colours were muted by the moonlight, different shades

of shadow. The ground began to rise and she knew, on the other side of the hillock, was the stile that led to the final field.

Not long to go now, thank God.

How far left had Nuala Greene to go, until she reached London, the house by the park she'd told Maggie about? Would she stay away, for good?

Another gun blasted, followed by cheers and the bark of a dog. Maggie hoped the poor rabbit had been shot cleanly, died quickly, rather than waiting for the dog to shake it dead.

She walked on, used to the cold now, used to the dark, her mind on Nuala.

Maybe she would walk a bit further. Take another detour. There was no rush to go home if the pub was closed for the night. No rush to see Emma.

To explain.

What was she going to say?

She thought of the bar, of the money, the land, the phone call from Emma's father yesterday lunchtime. *'What choice do you have?'* ringing fresh in her ears.

Did she have to tell Emma anything? Why worry her? Why talk of money, failure, loss?

Why tell her, at all, about James?

And what would Emma do, if she did find out that the man she was waiting for was dead? Maggie wasn't stupid, she knew Emma had been searching for him, trying to find him, get in touch. She knew that one of the reasons Emma hadn't tried to leave was the fact that James might come back. Part of Emma had been forever trapped in her fourteen-year-old self, the girl with ideals, hopes, dreams of the man she thought loved her.

If Emma knew he was dead, would she leave? Ask Maggie for her money, the money Maggie didn't have?

She took another sip from the flask, emptying the dregs down her throat, the thought of Emma leaving her stinging more sharply than the gin. She had a second flask in her back pocket but didn't reach for it, not yet.

The ground was boggy in this field, the fallen leaves beginning to mulch. She couldn't see more than a few meters in front of her, kept her head bent to study the path.

What would she do if Emma left? She had no one else, her son had never tried to get back in contact, despite being an adult and free to see her if he so wished. Emma was all the family she had; she couldn't imagine living without her.

She would tell her about James, she would, but not yet. She'd wait until the pub was doing better, until she had clawed back some of the money she had lost. If the business was doing well maybe Emma wouldn't want to leave. Especially if Maggie signed her onto the deeds, offered to go into business with Emma, give her half the pub now and the other half when Maggie retired.

Light starting seeping through the trees, and Maggie knew she was nearing Shore Road. One more stile, then an alley cut between houses, then onto the tarmacked road home.

The road to Emma.

She eased herself over the stile, her knees and hips screaming at her to stop. She sat on the plank, felt the moisture on the wood seep through her trousers.

She could tell Emma the truth. Do the right thing.

But if Maggie kept her in the dark, wouldn't it be for her own good?

She could stop the story now, tie up the one loose end that

would leak the news of James's death to the village . . . and to Emma. There had been a shift in Emma's mood of late, a bleak obsession with the past that didn't sit well with Maggie. News of James's death might push her too far towards turmoil, when Maggie wanted her to brighten up, look ahead to the future, help her get the business back on track.

Maggie got up, headed down the alley. The street ahead was empty, dark save for the lights from the houses, one house in particular catching Maggie's eye.

She could turn left, go home to Emma, tell her everything. *Do the right thing.*

Instead, she turned right, crunched her way along the gravel path and knocked on Lois's door.

The windows were dark, but Maggie knew they always were whether Lois was at home or not.

She pressed her ear to the door, swayed slightly, off balance.

She knocked again, heard a deep sniff from inside.

Maggie lowered herself down, knees on the doorstep, opened the letterbox with a finger and peered through.

She could see Lois, sitting on the stairs, hands hugging her knees.

'I can see you,' Maggie whispered. 'Let me in.'

Lois didn't answer.

'It's me, it's Maggie,' she said. 'I know about James.'

The words were like magic, always had been with Lois, and the woman eased herself up, came to the door and opened it.

'Nuala stayed at the pub last night, she told me today what happened to James. I need to know if you've told anyone, Lois. I need to manage the situation if I still can.' Maggie was out of breath from the walk, queasy from the gin. 'Have you told anyone?'

Even in the darkness, Maggie could make out Lois's red-rimmed eyes, swollen lids, bloodshot whites from an afternoon spent crying. Lois was shaking, one hand tapping at her chest with the nervous tap-tap she'd developed since the fire took her old house, robbed her of every possession she owned, every picture of her son, stealing every last bit of empathy and generosity from her already weak spirit until she became the bitter, suspicious woman she was now.

'My son is dead.'

'I know, Lois. I'm so—'

'Don't you dare!' Lois' breath was dry and smelled foul, her lips cracked with white scum at the edges. Her shoulders heaved with a sob but her eyes remained tearless. 'Don't you dare pretend that you care.'

Lois stepped backwards, hand on the door ready to close it but Maggie pushed back, gently easing the door open and stepping inside, feeling callous, heartless, shamefully cruel.

'I'm sorry, Lois.' And she was, she really was, but she still had to think of Emma. 'I just wanted to know if you've told anyone.'

'Leave me alone!' Lois shouted again, but it came out as barely more than a rasp, and her face crumbled in on itself.

Maggie moved towards her, put her hands on her shoulders, tried to draw her in, but Lois pushed back like a feral cat.

'I'll tell who I want! Whoever I want! He's my son! He's my—' The words failed in her throat, her mouth moving silently, repeating *my son*.

'Let me get you some water,' Maggie said, stepping to the side, but Lois stopped her.

'Get out of my house,' Lois said, her hand tap-tap-tapping again. 'I don't want you here. Get out and leave me alone!'

Maggie tried again to hold her, to comfort her, said, 'Lois, please, let me help you.'

Lois pushed her away. 'You don't care,' she said, standing up straight, putting all her strength into remaining composed. 'You didn't come to offer your sympathy, or to bring one of those fucking casseroles that everyone else gets when they're bereaved. You don't care how I might be feeling, how hard this is. You just want to make sure I didn't tell anyone so Emma fucking Bradbury doesn't find out, doesn't get hurt, run away, leave *you* all alone like I am now. Well, I don't care if she does! I don't care if anyone does! My son is dead, he's *dead,* Maggie!'

Lois covered her face with her hands. Maggie stepped forward, hands hovering in front, not sure whether to touch Lois or not.

'It's hard for you, I know. It's going to be so, so hard, and I am so sorry.' She touched Lois's elbow. 'It's going to be hard for Emma, too, if she finds out.'

'If it wasn't for Emma he would never have left!'

The blame on her goddaughter was too much, and Maggie drew her hand back. 'You cannot put this on Emma's shoulders!' Maggie said, remembering the final piece of the story. 'And besides, you're the one who sent James away!'

'I wanted him to be safe, away from this damned village, away from *her*!'

'She was fourteen, just a child, it wasn't her fault. James should have known better, he was five years older, a fully-grown man. He ran away and left her to deal with her father, *alone,* he saw what Arthur did to you and *still* he left, he knew what happened to Elaine for Christ's sake, he should have stuck around to help Emma get through it! He behaved like a callous, selfish coward, took of advantage of a young girl and ran when it all got too real.'

'Her parents should have done more. She should have stayed away—'

'She was a child—'

'She was his sister!' The words burst out of Lois with crude force, plunging them both into a horrified, pregnant silence.

Maggie faltered. 'What do you mean?' she finally asked, nauseated, but she already knew. Lois's eyes darkened to black.

She remembered Jim staring at Lois when the girl was fifteen, Edward's fingers on the curve of her waist. And Arthur, always a step behind, always watching, always there, silent, arrogant, above suspicion.

'It was only ever Arthur,' Lois began. 'Edward and Jim would bring me to him, drive me to wherever he wanted to have me, and wait, listen, take it in turns to *watch* whilst he, he—' Lois's chin quivered and she sniffed, rubbed her dry eyes on the sleeve of her cardigan. 'Arthur would let the other two touch me, have me sit on their laps whilst they felt me up, their goddamn dicks getting hard on my thigh. But when it came to fucking me, it was always, *only* Arthur,' she said, her voice cracking. 'Until I fell pregnant and asked him to help me, to pay for an abortion. But they had an agreement, those three men, from the very beginning. Edward got money from Arthur for keeping his mouth shut. Jim, the man I would be forced to marry, live with as husband and wife, refused the money. Instead, when it all went wrong, he got to pretend he was the father, he got to keep the *damaged goods* that was me, a teenage girl all to himself to fuck whenever he wanted to, raise Arthur's son as if he were his own. He used to remind me all the time as he held me down, my face pressed into the pillow. He'd tell me that I was Arthur's little whore, that he knew all my dirty little secrets, that he was my keeper now and I better do as he said or he'd tell James everything, tell him what a dirty, disgusting, filthy little girl his mother was.'

Sickened, Maggie remembered watching him, Jim's eyes on Lois, mouth wet as he drank the girl in.

'Did James know?' Maggie asked. 'Did you tell him?'

Lois's face fell and she nodded. She stilled her tapping hand and tried to take a deep composing breath, but when she finally spoke her voice was thin and cracked with pain.

'The morning we found out Emma was pregnant, James had been in the house all along. I told Emma he'd gone to London; I *had* to keep them apart. When you left to take Emma to hospital I woke him, I told him what had happened, that he needed to stay in the house and hide because Arthur was going to be furious. I told him I would look after him, protect him like I always had done. And he listened to me. But I couldn't tell him the rest, I never wanted him to know, it was too much to even bear thinking about, especially when I discovered he'd been sleeping with Emma, for God's sake! But he was still in the house that day, he was there when Arthur—' Lois's voice broke again and Maggie filled in the rest of the words.

'When Arthur attacked you?'

Lois's eyes bored straight into Maggie.

'He saw it all.' The pain in Lois voice, in her face, too, mixed with anger, bitterness, and an undercurrent of fear, even now, seven years after the event. 'He heard me telling Arthur that he didn't know Emma was his sister, I was begging him to leave James alone. Then I looked up and realised that he was watching from the top of the stairs.'

Maggie remembered that day: Lois slumped in her living room, face swelling before Maggie's eyes. The smear of blood that ran up her face from her nose to the tip of her hairline. The bruising around her neck. The torn frenulum and the blood that seeped from her tongue.

'And James saw Arthur do that to you . . . and did *nothing*?' Maggie tried to fathom it, tried to understand how anyone could possibly stand by and let someone do that to their mother, to *anyone*.

'He didn't know what to do! He was confused, scared!'

'He was an adult!' Maggie said. 'He was nineteen, fit and strong. He could have pulled Arthur off, he could have stopped him. He should have protected you!'

Lois shook her head, 'I should have been the one to protect him.'

'It's not your fault, Lois!' Maggie cried. 'What happened then? When I arrived, why did I find you alone?'

Lois dropped her gaze, no longer able to look Maggie in the eyes. 'Why would James want to come anywhere near me?' Her voice had lost its ferocity, her tone as meek and vulnerable as she now looked. 'Why would anyone? After Arthur left, my son looked at me as though I were vermin, a disgusting rat half dead on the floor.' Her words were punctuated with sobs and gasps for breath and Maggie stared open mouthed, horrified, as Lois went on.

'He didn't have to say anything, I could read it all in his face, how pathetic I am, how worthless.' She met Maggie's eyes, the broken look on her face bringing a lump to Maggie's throat. 'Why would he want to help me? Why would anyone?' The wall Lois had spent years building, hiding behind, crumbled before Maggie's eyes. The hostility, the anger, the bitterness dissolved and Lois looked fifteen again, young and naïve without anyone to guide her, manipulated by three adult men.

'He wouldn't speak to me after that,' Lois went on. 'Before he left for good, the next night, I tried to talk to him, make it right. He pushed me away, my son pushed me away and told me that I'm a slut, a liar. That I'd ruined his life. And he was right.' Lois stopped then, turning her face away from Maggie as though she could no longer bear to be seen.

'None of this was your fault,' Maggie said, Lois's vulnerability, her thin frame shaking with cold and misery, too much to bear. She softened her voice, masking her disgust at James with her sympathy for Lois. 'You were only trying to protect James. If everyone had known the truth, what really happened to you –'

'*You* knew,' Lois said and Maggie's head shot up.

'I didn't! I didn't know a thing!'

'You knew something was wrong. That's why you asked me if I was all right when you saw me with *them* by the shop, tried to walk me home. I knew that you knew, from that first day in Edward's car when I tried to tell you, tried to show you, what had happened to me. But you ignored me. Like everyone else.'

'But I didn't see anything, I didn't have any proof!'

'You didn't need any! You just needed to talk to me, or tell someone, but you didn't. You kept silent. You kept their secret.'

Maggie shook her head, stepped back, away from the stairs, away from Lois and those eyes, those dark, accusing eyes.

'I didn't do anything wrong,' she said, feeling the shame of the lie burn in her cheeks. 'I did nothing wrong.'

'You did *nothing*, Maggie,' Lois said, her hands still by her sides. 'You did nothing. So don't ask me to help you now. *My son is dead.* I'll tell whoever I need to.'

Maggie took a step backwards, away from Lois, and caught the step, falling and landing with her hip on the ground.

She looked up at Lois, standing on the threshold.

Her eyes filled with pain, Lois slammed the door shut on Maggie, turned the lock.

Head swimming, Maggie stumbled to her feet, felt saliva flood her mouth as she tried to digest what she'd heard.

From behind the closed door she could hear Lois sobbing, a dry, rasping sound, crying for the dead son who had slept with his own sister.

Maggie walked away, knowing that Lois wouldn't answer again if she were to knock, knowing, too, that she couldn't bear to hear any more.

She thought of the rare glimpses she'd had of Emma and James together; a *hello*, a brief hug here and there, James's libidinous stare as he watched Emma walk away.

Maggie lurched along the street on unsteady legs.

The garden walls began closing in; the pavement felt too narrow. She concentrated on walking: right foot then left foot.

Had she really done nothing? Told no one? It had happened in the world she shared with Tom and their son, a world where she was content, happy with their lot and less concerned, perhaps, with the lots of others.

Maggie's head ached, the road swimming before her eyes.

It was fate, or so it seemed, that she would end up where she did, the graveyard calling to her.

How many other people had suspected? Why hadn't anyone helped Lois?

Why, for Christ's sake, hadn't Maggie done something?

Her mouth felt dry, eyes heavy. She didn't want to go home, didn't want to see Emma or tell her about the money, the pub, about James. Didn't want to tell her about who he really was, didn't want to look her in the eye and admit how she'd failed Lois.

Would she have to tell her everything? Even the fact that James was her half-brother? It would destroy her, disgust her, but still Maggie knew that the truth would finally have to be told. It would be better coming from Maggie than from Lois, and Maggie didn't trust the other woman not to speak out. Now James was dead she had no one left to protect.

Maggie looked up at the church, the cross standing proud on top of the steeple. It was Arthur who deserved the anger; it was his fault, and Jim's and Edward's. Maggie had done nothing wrong.

She had done nothing at all.

She stumbled on, tripping over grass and pebble until she finally came to Tom's grave, her place of solace, reassurance, comfort, but for once found no comfort there. She rested her head on the gravestone, traced his name.

'Oh Tom, my love, Tom.' She squeezed her eyes shut, the tears stinging behind her lids. 'I need you here to tell me what to do. I don't know any more. I don't know how I'm going to tell Emma, I don't know how I'm going to fix this mess with Arthur, Lois, the lot.'

The rough stone grazed her forehead but she didn't move, just kept tracing Tom's name over and again, trying to focus on that, and not the horrible story Lois had just told.

She pictured James with Emma and clung to her stomach as she retched, spilling thin vomit across the grass to her right. It was James's fault; he was the one who did wrong, as though his father's immorality was inherent, woven into his own DNA.

She spat on the ground, her bile tasting of gin, of regret and of guilt. If she'd said something to someone about Lois's abuse, none of this mess would have happened. Lois would be a different person entirely. James would never have existed, Emma would be free from the pain of his memory, her step-mother might still be alive.

The thought of Elaine was too much and Maggie couldn't hold back any longer, bursting into tears as she clung to Tom's grave.

The sound of Maggie's cry rang out through the church-yard, echoing from the tombstones and the graveyard walls.

With her final wail, she raised her head, letting the cold air quiet her tears, the wind dry her eyes and cheeks and longing for Emma to come, to take her home and put her to bed and promise her that it would be better tomorrow, that it would all be better in the morning.

Emma, it all centred around Emma. It was she who had put Maggie back together again after Tom had died and Lee had been taken away. Emma had given Maggie hope, made her look forwards instead of wallowing, drunk, in the past.

Emma had tried to make Maggie forgive herself. She had helped Maggie contact social services, counselled her when they wouldn't pass on a single detail about Lee, said one day he would understand, Lee would forgive her for what she had done in the years after Tom's death.

Emma had turned Maggie round completely, stopped her drinking, kept her sane.

And Maggie had failed her. Good God, she had failed herself. She had always seen Emma as her daughter, ever since she'd looked after her as a babe. But she had never truly lived up to her role as godmother.

She stood up, knees wet and joints sore but at least her hands had stopped shaking.

There was still time to fix things. She would claw back the money, Emma's money. Give the girl a future to be proud of. She would tell her the truth, the whole truth, and be there to help Emma through it.

She looked behind her to the church, the steeple and cross, hoisted herself up from the ground and stood tall.

No more excuses.

No more gin.

No more lies.

She hadn't failed Emma, not yet.

Maggie wiped her mouth and her eyes with the back of her hand, turned to the gate to head back home.

She would tell Emma tomorrow, tell her everything, and set about changing her ways.

The ground was damp underfoot from wet leaves and wet mud, but her boots held firm as she walked. She reached into her back pocket for the second hip flask of gin, the last she vowed she would ever drink.

From low down on the hill came the shot from a gun, the sound closer than the last round of lamping.

Maggie sipped from her flask again, walked on towards home, her mind straying to the small, frightened animal.

Poor rabbit.

Maggie

Sunday, 19th November, 2017

Maggie woke up, neck stiff and head sore, her eyes squinting against the weak morning sun.

She was downstairs in the bar. She must've fallen asleep by the fire.

Where was Emma?

Maggie looked around her, saw the empty glass on the floor by her foot.

Why was her head so sore? Just a nip was all she normally allowed herself, a mere capful here and there. Even the two empty hipflasks, lying on the sleeper, held no more than a few measures each. But beside the flasks was an empty tumbler, a half-empty gin bottle behind it. What the hell had made her slip up and drink so much she fell asleep in her chair?

Why hadn't Emma woken Maggie up, taken her upstairs, unpeeled her dirty clothes and put her to bed?

Maggie ran her hand over her hair, over her face, down the front of her shirt and felt the crispy remnants of bile.

The fire was out, her legs felt cold and stiff. The fire poker was lying on the floor, on its side. Had Maggie dropped it there, left it?

She looked up to the bar, saw the clock. Just gone ten in the morning. Emma was always up by now, would normally have cleaned the bar, laid a fresh fire, sorted breakfast and thrown a wash in. Where was she?

She gingerly walked to the sleeper, peered over it into the kitchen.

'Emma?' she called but could see her goddaughter wasn't there. It had been cleaned up, though.

The kettle was pushed back and wiped down, a stack of clean mugs and saucers by the sink. The rubbish had been taken out, too, an empty bin liner in the bin by the door. Maybe Emma did all that last night before bed. Maybe she was asleep before Maggie came home. Maybe she was still in bed.

Alone?

Maggie thought of Toby, the way he had crept out of Emma's room a few weekends before. Maybe he had called round last night. Maybe he was up there now.

Maggie left the kitchen behind her, walked up the stairs, knees and hips complaining more than usual. Why were they hurting so much? Why couldn't she remember?

The hallway was dark but Emma's door was ajar. Maggie pushed it open.

Empty.

The bed had been made and the room smelled of stale air, faint notes of apples and bleach.

She turned around on her heel, spotted the guest room across the hall. Remembered Nuala.

Remembered that James was dead.

Remembered, with a twist to her gut, that he was Emma's half-brother.

Had Emma somehow found out?

She thundered downstairs, ignoring the pain everywhere.

'Emma!' The silence was too much, bearing down from every angle.

The kitchen was empty, the bar was empty, the bathroom beneath the stairs empty too.

Maggie's car keys, normally hanging above the kettle, were missing. So too was the familiar brown smudge through the frosted glass. The old Rover wasn't there. Which meant Emma was—

'Emma!' Maggie ran through the door, ignoring the pain in her knees and shins, ignoring the burning in her bile-stripped throat.

She'd gone.

'Emma!' Her shout more of a sob.

Maggie stumbled out into the street but it was empty, not a person or car in sight.

Lois.

What if she had called, told Emma everything? What if Emma had gone to Shore Road to hear it from Lois in person? The idea caught and Maggie knew it was true, knew that that's where Emma had gone.

She began to run, feet slipping on the pavement.

She tried to breathe through her mouth but it filled with saliva, her throat burning when she swallowed, her body too fat and weak to keep the pace.

When she turned the last corner she saw her car, that familiar brown smudge. She lurched toward it, knowing Emma was close, knowing she had to find her and hold her and explain, before Lois could.

Maggie rang the bell, but there was no answer. She tried

the handle and it opened, the house quiet and still. Perhaps Lois and Emma were upstairs.

It was colder inside this house then it was on the street. Damp spotted the paintwork in hazy black dots, the paint flaked and powdery. But worse than the cold was the silence. No movement, no breathing.

A light caught her eye, from beneath the kitchen door.

Odd, she thought, that a light would be on at this time of day.

Her hand paused above the handle.

All was quiet.

She took a deep breath and pushed, opening the door.

The first thing she noticed was the blood, the ocean of blood, with the viscosity of black gloss paint. A cast-iron door-stop shaped like a dog sat primly in the centre of the kitchen table, covered in the congealed liquid, pieces of hair, bone and flaccid flesh sticking to its etched-on fur.

Then there was Lois, sitting on a chair, bent over with her face pressed into the tabletop and the back of her head a beaten mess.

And finally there was Emma, always Emma. Sitting beside Lois at the table, her clothes, shoes, hands, covered in blood. Her blond hair was lank, the ends rusty with dried blood, some of it hanging at her shoulders, some of it sticking in matted clumps to the wall behind. The shotgun was in her lap, its barrel pointing to where her face should have been.

Maggie

Monday, 20th November, 2017

'My name is Detective Sergeant Pale.' He had a city voice; was trying hard to cover his accent. Bristol, perhaps, Bath at a push. 'This is my colleague, DC Ali.'

If this was the 'interview suite' then Maggie never wanted to see an interrogation room. The walls were dirty beige, and there were no windows.

'Good afternoon, Mrs Bradbury.' Ali held out her small, thin hand for Maggie to shake. She reached for it over the table, until Pale coughed, shook his head and Ali's hand retreated to her lap. She smiled instead, opened her mouth to apologise but closed it again when she saw Pale's face.

'We're here to talk to you about the events that unfolded on Saturday night,' Pale said, turning back to Maggie.

Maggie rubbed her dry eyes. She hadn't slept since the sedatives the paramedic administered had worn off. Because every time she closed her eyes she saw them.

The blood.

Lois's head.

Emma.

Always Emma.

Maggie blinked and saw it all again, the blood and the lumps of hair, the cast-iron dog.

'You need to look for Nuala Greene.' A drip of sweat slid down Maggie's neck. She wasn't sure if she'd said it aloud or not.

The room was too small, too dark, for this conversation, the ceiling too low, not enough air.

She shifted her feet beneath her. They had taken her shoes away, the sturdy boots that were covered in mud from the walk on Saturday night, the soles covered in blood from the scene she'd discovered on Sunday morning. Instead, she was wearing thin ballet pumps. She'd never worn a pair of ballet pumps in her life, and her feet were sweating.

Her arms were sweating too, and her back and the folds of her belly. A cold sweat, constant, making her shiver when a draught caught her skin. She hadn't eaten anything. She hadn't drunk anything other than coffee, the rehydration she'd received from the drip they'd inserted the day before long worn off. But she didn't feel hungry or thirsty.

All she felt was horror, abject horror.

When she had eventually come round, earlier that morning, she was tucked up in a bed she didn't know, a room she'd never been in. A two-litre bottle of water at her bedside, the room so clean you could smell the laundry detergent on the duck-egg blue bedclothes, no hint of damp, smell of mould, in the air. She had heard footsteps, hushed murmurs, the flush of a toilet somewhere downstairs. She had climbed out of the bed, made it all the way to the door, padding along the soft carpet, before she had remembered. Before she had closed her eyes and seen the blood, the blood everywhere, the blood.

Staggering back she had landed bottom down on the bed, let out a cry.

Jennifer Hill had burst into the room, the cry drawing her up from downstairs, and Maggie realised where she was, at Toby's parents, Jon and Jennifer's house, the dairy farm that backed onto the pub.

'It's all right, it's OK,' Jennifer said, her hands on Maggie's shoulders, easing her back down onto the bed. 'It's all right, it's all right.' And she tucked Maggie in, Maggie's eyes already rolling, head lolling on the soft cotton pillow.

But she couldn't sleep, couldn't close her eyes. She had never been good with blood, not since Tom's accident.

'You're OK,' Jennifer had said, and in hushed tones, her voice low, told Maggie what had happened. How the paramedic had sedated her, to help with the shock of discovering the scene, how Jennifer had taken her home.

But the sedatives had worn off now, long gone. Maggie didn't think she'd ever be able to close her eyes again.

Once she'd felt able to stand and had drunk some water, she had demanded to go straight to the police. And a good job too, as they had been waiting for her, needing her statement as the first on the scene of the crime. The drugs pumped into her system had been an awful delay in the procedures that needed to take place.

'What we need to do at this stage,' DC Ali said, resting her hands, palms together, on the table and looking sympathetically into Maggie's eyes, 'is to identify—'

'Emma?'

'Yes, it's about Emma. We hope that—'

Maggie felt the squeeze on her stomach again, the same

one that had caused her to contaminate the crime scene with her vomit the day before.

'She has blond hair, the colour of pine. Blue eyes. Tall for a woman, about 5-8, 5-9. Never wore heels, just trainers or wellies. She was wearing trainers on Saturday, with a black T-shirt and jeans.' Emma never wore skirts, they made her feel vulnerable. But she wasn't vulnerable, she was strong, capable, brave. Oh, Emma.

She closed her eyes, an involuntary, instinctive blink and there it was, all that blood, there it was again.

It must have shown on Maggie's face as DS Pale's voice softened when he said, 'Mrs Bradbury, you really don't . . .'

But Maggie held up her hands for quiet. She could do this, she could be strong. She could remember her goddaughter with her face intact, her hands clean. It was the first step, she reasoned. Identify Emma, then identify her killer.

'She has three small scars on her tummy, from surgery. And she wore a necklace: a silver chain with a gold band hanging from it.' It had been Elaine's, left in the envelope for Emma, along with a letter Maggie had never had the courage (or the invitation) to read.

'Mrs Bradbury, you don't have to identify—' The detective touched her arm with a tanned, manicured hand. Maggie looked at him, but all she could see was the ceiling pressing down, the sickly yellow light from the bulb above her, Emma's missing face, missing chin.

'She had another scar beside her right eye, about an inch long. Got it when she was seven.' Whenever she smiled, the white scar crinkled, nearly disappeared. 'She wore an old gold watch and a gold ring on her little finger. Right hand, both of them.' They were her mother's, her real mother's. She used to complain she'd inherited her father's working hands and the ring wouldn't fit on any other finger but the littlest.

'Mrs Bradbury, you misunderstand. You don't have to identify her, that's already been done.'

'What?' Somewhere in the building, a phone began to ring. 'Who by?'

'Her father.' Pale rested his arms on the table, leaning on his elbows, his voice weary. 'We took him to the morgue this morning. He confirmed the other details: hair colour, eye colour, height, her penchant for cleaning with neat bleach, hence the damaged skin on her hands and fingertips. Gave us her dentist's details for the X-rays, not that they were much use considering the damage to her jaw.'

'It should have been me,' Maggie said, even though she knew it was petty and pointless. 'I knew her far better than him.'

'He's the next of kin; it's standard procedure,' Pale said, then softened his tone when he saw the look on Maggie's face, how her shoulders dropped. 'It was a technicality really.'

Maggie's tongue, stuck to the floor of her mouth, felt immovable as a vast lead weight. She wanted to say, 'She meant nothing to him, I'm the one who loved her, looked after her.'

But Ali spoke up before Maggie could find the right words.

'What we really want to ascertain,' Ali said, spreading out a few sheets of paper that Maggie couldn't bring herself to look at, 'is Emma's state of mind over the last few days, the triggers as it were.'

'Triggers?' Maggie said at last and looked up at the detectives in front of her. Pale was, despite his name, very dark.

Clean shaven, olive skinned, those dark, dark eyes and dark eyebrows. He wore a navy blazer like a schoolboy, his dimples only adding to the effect. It was the lines on his forehead, around his eyes and the sides of the mouth, that gave his age away as being closer to forty.

'Yes,' Ali said, meeting her eye and keeping the business-like quality to her gold and brown gaze, 'the triggers. We've been through the pub, of course—'

'You've what?'

'Been through the pub. Nothing forensic, not considering the evidence we've already gathered. But it will help to give us an insight into her frame of mind, the things she had been doing, what she had been searching for online, and so on.'

'You've been through my pub, without my permission?'

Pale narrowed his eyes, cocked his head, his expression assessing. 'There was no need for permission,' he said, 'on the basis that a serious crime had taken place, and your pub was home to one of the deceased.' He reshuffled the papers in front of him, sat down and poured water into three glasses, pushing one towards Maggie with a nod.

He waited until Maggie had taken a mouthful of water, then said, 'I understand you're under some financial strain?'

She spluttered, her mind on the letters hidden behind the cider barrel in the pub's cellar. 'It'll work itself out,' she said. 'I don't see what that has to do with—'

'Did you tell Emma about the money problems?' Ali asked, and Maggie turned towards her.

'There was no need, I was sorting it out. Why are you looking at me like that? What?'

'We found letters from your bank, statements and demands,

strewn across the cellar floor. We believe Emma found these letters—'

Maggie groaned, covered her face, needled the scar with the pad of her finger. 'No, no, she couldn't have done.'

'Can I surmise from your reaction that you hadn't told her? There were letters relating to Emma's savings fund, the account you were named as trustee of until Emma reached twenty-five, though it was empty, had been for some time. Was she aware of this?'

Maggie held her face in her hands, shaking her head from side to side. Emma died knowing Maggie had failed her. Worse, that Maggie had lied.

'What we want to know, at this stage,' Ali continued, 'is if there was anything else that might have caused Emma to lash out in the way that she did?'

Maggie's hands flew away from her face. 'What do you mean?' she said. 'Lash out?'

Pale pressed his lips together, looked at his sheets of paper before speaking again. 'We are still investigating this case and nothing has been finalised, not at all. But you should know that, considering the quantity of evidence that supports the theory, we are working on the basis that the crime was a murder-suicide. We believe Emma intentionally killed Lois Lunglow before turning the gun on herself.'

'No,' Maggie said, standing up from her chair, so forcefully it crashed away from the table. 'You're wrong, you're all wrong. She wouldn't do such a thing, she couldn't.'

If Maggie had been expecting comfort or platitudes, she was mistaken. Pale sat back. 'You mean to tell me that Emma had no cause for grievance against Lois? That her life hadn't recently taken a downturn: the breakup with a boyfriend, Toby

Hill, the discovery her savings were gone, the continued estrangement from her father?'

The detective surveyed Maggie, his dark eyebrows raised. 'You don't think these would have had an effect?'

'How can you be so blind?' Maggie shouted.

'You want me to believe it wasn't Emma?'

'It was Nuala Greene!'

Pale sighed and the sigh grew into a yawn, hidden behind his hand. 'Who is Nuala Greene?' His voice sounded tired, his face looked weary and stressed. He drew out a notebook from his blazer pocket, a small pencil with it.

Maggie told them about Nuala's stay, from her arrival on Friday evening to the crimes she must have, *must have*, committed on Saturday night whilst Maggie walked home. There was enough time, Maggie surmised, for Nuala to have knocked Emma out and driven her to Lois's house, where she killed both the women and set up the scene so no one would suspect her, all while Maggie was asleep in the chair at the pub. The lampers had been out all evening, the crow scarer had been going off, too. Who would have noticed one more gunshot?

Then a terrible thought struck her, weaving through her senses like a poisonous spider's web. Of the three people in the village that Maggie knew for certain Nuala had spoken to, only she, Maggie, was left alive.

'I can't believe you're not looking for her already! She's two days ahead of you, for Christ's sake!'

There was a knock at the door. The two detectives exchanged a glance then Ali stood up and walked out, with a small smile for Maggie as she closed the door behind her.

DS Pale, left behind, looked at Maggie. 'There was no

evidence of another woman at the crime scene, no mention of her by the other witnesses.' He put the notebook down. 'Did you take her details when she came to the pub? Her full name? Address? Registration?'

'She gave us a different name: Mrs James. I didn't take her address or her registration.'

'Did she pay by credit or debit card? Something we can follow up?'

Maggie curled her fingers in her lap. 'She didn't pay at all.'

Maggie could hear Pale's foot tapping on the lino, and thought of Lois's tap-tap-tap.

'Emma would never harm anyone, she's good as gold.' Maggie could feel the cloth from her shirt digging into the wet, salty skin of her armpits. 'She would never kill herself, never. And Lois's front door was unlocked. Unlocked!'

'So what are you saying?'

'She never left it unlocked! She was paranoid about it; always locked it with the security chain in place.'

'And what's your theory?' Pale was holding his pencil but Maggie knew he wouldn't make any more notes, she knew the detective was placating her.

'I think she knocked Emma out, dragged her to Lois's house and set the whole thing up. I think Nuala Greene battered Lois to death and I think Nuala Greene shot Emma.'

DS Pale nodded and for a moment Maggie's headache lifted.

'Any idea where we might find this Nuala Greene?'

Maggie sat straight, shoulders square. 'London.'

'London.' Pale looked up to the ceiling, his fingers running through his thick, black hair. 'Mrs Bradbury, do you know much about London? Ever been?'

Maggie looked down, shook her head.

'Have you any idea how big it is? How many people live there?'

The door opened and Ali walked back in, passed a sheet of paper to Pale with a sideways glance at Maggie.

'But I know about *her*. I know her parents are dead, that she's half Irish, that she lived with James near a park. I know James used to work in one of those London parks, and it had deer in it. I know she had a red car that was new; a foreign make.'

'That information could have been found anywhere, Mrs Bradbury,' Ali said, giving her partner time to read the new notes. 'And we know from Emma's phone that she had been looking up James online that day. We know, from her search history, that she looked for him fairly regularly, though usually by his former name of Lunglow.'

'What are you implying?'

'We just have to look at the evidence from all angles, Mrs Bradbury.' DC Ali looked to Pale as he finished reading the sheet of paper.

Maggie said, 'What, what is it?'

'They found a note. It was tucked into the pocket of Emma's jeans.'

'What did it say?'

'It's a suicide note.'

The room fell silent, the phone outside, the hallway footsteps, all hushed. Even Maggie's head, still wracked with pain, stopped ringing.

'It must have been Nuala who wrote it.'

Pale leant back in the chair, chin down. 'Had Emma ever tried to harm herself before, Mrs Bradbury?'

Maggie shook her head, unable to speak, unable to look Pale in the eye. No, she wouldn't do that. She wouldn't.

She tried to take a sip of water but her hands shook, the water spilling.

'We found a further three suicide notes in her bedroom. The oldest was from seven years ago, the most recent eighteen months, each stating that she wished to end her life. All were written in the same handwriting, Emma's handwriting. It seems clear to us that she had suicidal tendencies.'

'No.' Maggie wiped at the spilt water on the table with the cuff of her shirt.

'Can you think of anything from, say, seven years ago, that may have instigated Emma to first try and—'

The facts ran through Maggie's mind, snowballing horrifically together. Emma losing her baby, James fleeing. Her father refusing to have her in the house, the death of her stepmother. . .

And then there was the fire, Maggie thought. The fire that ruined Lois's house next door to the pub, a thunderous force of heat and flame that burned every one of her possessions, starting only hours after James had fled. A chip pan fire, a simple mistake, Lois forgetting to turn off the hob after dinner, her mind no doubt preoccupied with James leaving. But local gossip painted a different picture, pointing the finger at Emma, an act of revenge on Lois for keeping James away, and on James for leaving her. Back at school, no one would talk to her. In the street her old friends turned their backs.

But Emma was strong, a fighter, had been since the day she was born and Maggie couldn't believe she would kill herself, that she would feel so low without reaching out to Maggie for help. She *wouldn't* believe it.

'No!' Maggie shouted, faithful to her goddaughter to the end.

'Are you sure about that, Mrs Bradbury?' Pale's eyes narrowed, his lips in a moue. "Nothing that would have ignited anger towards Lois?'

Maggie caught on one word, *ignited,* and all its insinuations. Did Pale really think Emma had not only started that fire seven years ago, but had intended to kill Lois then too? The rest of Pale's words sunk in and Maggie realised someone must have told him about Emma, about James, about why Emma hated Lois so. It could have been anyone, anyone.

Half the village bore witness in the end.

Seven years ago

Emma

Wednesday, 11th August, 2010

' I was waiting all night for someone to call me, to tell me what happened after Daddy left.' Emma was looking out of the car window, watching the hospital slide from view as Maggie drove her home, the glass reflecting the purple half-moons beneath her eyes.

'You've no need to worry,' Maggie said firmly, but Emma knew she was lying. Maggie wouldn't look at Emma, that was the tell; had barely met her eye since she arrived to collect her. 'It's all in hand,' Maggie said, 'I'll tell you everything once we're home.' Her voice was strong but, on the final word, trembled. Emma found herself worrying more.

'I thought Elaine might phone, let me know what had happened,' Emma pushed, waiting for her godmother to say more.

Maggie coughed, stared at the road ahead.

'Did Daddy talk to Lois?' Emma said, trying to convince herself that Arthur wouldn't have lashed out at Lois, that he only ever behaved like that at home. 'Have you seen him since, Maggie?' She tried to hold on to a bright cheery tone.

Maggie opened her mouth, as if to speak, but closed it again, looking sidelong at Emma's belly. 'Let's just get you back home,' Maggie said at last, reaching over and patting Emma's knee. Emma could smell alcohol on her breath, sour and stale, hoped it was from last night and not this morning. She was painfully aware that Maggie had avoided her question.

Her godmother looked tired, almost as tired as Emma felt, a night of constant worry robbing her of sleep.

'Is Mum OK?' Emma asked in a small voice, pleading for Maggie's attention. 'Why didn't she come with you to get me?' Maggie didn't answer, the silence only adding to the dread in Emma's gut, the feeling so tangible it pulled at the stiches on her belly.

'Just give me a minute, Emma. Let me concentrate on the road.' Maggie rubbed her face with her left hand.

Emma shrank in her seat.

Did Maggie know how Arthur treated Elaine? Would now be the time to tell someone, tell Maggie in the safety of the car, where she knew her father would never overhear or find out? Could this be the chance to tell all? To explain why, when another man came to her, offered her comfort, affection and more, she had taken it so greedily? Drinking up the praise and the attention in whatever form it manifested itself?

James understood what it was like, living in a home like hers. He had watched his father hit his mother more times than he could count. Had watched Lois take beatings to save him from his father's anger, though James suspected she hated him for it, suspected she hated having had him in the first place. He said that he knew what it was like to blame yourself for the actions of your parents. And wasn't it lucky that Emma had found someone, found James, who knew just what that feeling was like? Wasn't that wonderful, that she had found someone like James to love her? Because no one else would, after growing up in a home like hers. No one else *could*.

Would he be waiting for her when she got home?

'Has James come back?' she asked Maggie. 'Did you see him?'

'He's still away; Lois says he won't be back until next week at least.'

Emma fell silent, hands resting on her tender belly. Had no one told James what had happened? Wasn't he coming straight home to see her, make sure she was all right? Didn't he want to find out what happened to their baby?

Emma slumped in her seat, chin on palm, top lip pulled into her mouth, head filled with thoughts of James. She watched as they passed the old youth club, now a rehab clinic, and drove on through the streets of three-storey council flats. The car was warm, another hot day, the dull rumble of the tyres soporific, gradually lulling her. She tried her best to stifle it, but she let out a long yawn, so wide her mouth cracked at the sides. Just as she was about to fall asleep, her godmother finally spoke.

'Emma,' Maggie said, 'I need to talk to you, before we get back.'

Emma's eyes shot open. The serious tone of Maggie's voice told her she must stay awake, hear what had to be said.

'What is it?' she asked.

Maggie paused, her eyes on the road ahead.

'I looked after you, as a newborn. You know that?'

'Of course I do. That's why you're my godmother, you looked after me when Daddy couldn't, after my mother had—'

'That's right,' Maggie said. 'Tom and I looked after you for those first few months of your life. Arthur was still weak with grief, but you were strong, a little fighter. You slept in the basket by my bed, slept right through from when you were six weeks old, as though you knew by instinct that we all needed to keep up our strength because we all had to keep fighting.'

'And then Daddy met Elaine and they got married,' Emma went on, knowing the story by heart. 'Elaine looked after me then, and they asked you and Tom to be godparents.'

'And I've never stopped loving you, you know that?'

This was new; the story normally ended at Emma's last sentence.

She looked up at her godmother, still staring at the road.

'I know,' Emma said.

The road narrowed, the surface rougher and dotted with potholes. The path ahead growing darker as they reached the woods.

'Emma, I need to talk to you about what happened yesterday—'

She hesitated, her face dappled in shadow as they drove through the trees.

'What is it, Maggie?' The knot in Emma's stomach was growing Something about Maggie's voice, the way her knuckles whitened as she gripped the steering wheel, played on Emma's nerves, made her anxious.

Maggie took a deep breath. 'You're going to be staying with me for a while, my dear girl. You see, Emma, your father got very . . . cross last night. After everything at the hospital. Elaine's had to go away for a while, to find somewhere safe for you both to go—'

Cross. An understatement. Emma knew immediately that it meant her father had done something to Elaine. Had punished her for Emma's mistakes, as was his twisted habit. As if he knew that, whenever he hit Elaine instead of Emma, he was punishing his daughter's psyche, wreaking far more damage than a punch to the girl's stomach could inflict.

Emma felt the familiar guilt work its way through her body, like ice, until she felt that dread chill from her head to her toes. She had gotten pregnant. And her father would lay the blame on Elaine.

'What happened?' she whispered, the words hurting her throat, mouth and tongue because she could guess what had happened. She pictured what her father would do to Elaine, the word *cross* still ringing in her ears. 'Is Mum . . .?'

'She'll be fine,' Maggie said, too quickly to be believed. She gripped the wheel more tightly.

'What did he do? I have to see her!' Emma cried, the tears starting to fall.

Maggie pulled over to the side of the road, held Emma firmly in her arms as she cried.

'Emma,' she said, 'Emma, you have me, I'll look after you.' Emma smelled the gin on Maggie's breath and cried harder, her shoulders juddering, her tears soaking Maggie's shirt, her tender belly made sore by the twisting angle of the embrace.

Maggie held her tightly, didn't let go, held her and hushed her until her tears had subsided. 'I'll look after you, sweetheart,' she said again, but Emma didn't want her to. She wanted Elaine. She wanted James. She wanted her father to be the one to go, run away.

Eventually she quietened, wiped her eyes on her sleeve, pictured Elaine in a hotel away from Arthur, from his anger, and the image fuelled the last vestiges of her strength, helped her to sit up straight and look ahead.

'I'll take you home,' Maggie said. 'You'll stay with me until

Elaine sends word, until you can go and stay with her, some-where safe. Because you're not safe with your father, you know that?'

Emma bit her lip to stop from crying again, and she nodded.

As Maggie went to restart the car the rear-view mirror caught a flash of red light, then blue.

They heard a siren, getting louder.

Another siren echoing close behind.

Maggie found the bite point on the clutch, waited for the ambulance and police car to pass them, then put her foot to the floor and sped off, following them.

They were heading for the village.

Neither Maggie nor Emma said a word, both filled with the same certainty that the ambulance had something to do with yesterday's fallout, that the drama and horror hadn't subsided just yet.

As Maggie followed the vehicles over the rough road, Emma gripped the door handle, toes curled inside her trainers, teeth clenched painfully hard in her jaw.

The ambulance dipped down, disappeared down the hill, the police car hot on its heels.

Maggie followed, the noise of the sirens deafening now.

Emma watched the village pass, then Shore Road and the houses her father owned, rented out, then the shop, Lois's house, Maggie's pub.

They flew through the streets, the pavements getting busier, people stepping out of their houses, drawn by the noise, watching as Maggie's car hurtled past.

Emma knew where they were going. She knew where this road led and her heart lurched with that sea-sick feeling of dread.

There was her house, the home she'd grown up in, her father's Land Rover pulled up outside.

They followed the vehicles along the lane which ran beside Emma's house, and came to a stop at the end of the track, the barn in full view.

The wood-plank building was heaving with people, half the village standing outside it. The red-painted doors were flung open, crows perched on the slate-tiled roof.

The paramedics jumped out, abandoned the ambulance to rush into the barn, the officers from the police car following.

Emma was out of the car in a moment, pushing through the small crowd, could hear Maggie's laboured breathing behind her as she did the same.

A paramedic, green shirt and black hair, boots still shiny from that morning's polish, stepped out of the barn. Behind him, discarded on the floor of the barn, strewn with hay and pale sawdust, was a peach cardigan in fine wool, one pearl button catching the sunlight. Emma recognised it as Elaine's, the same one she had worn to the hospital yesterday.

The WPC turned, looked questioningly at the paramedic.

The man shook his head in reply.

The shake of the head said plainly *no hope*.

Emma wasn't the only one to have seen it.

Maggie reached for Emma's hand.

'Oh Emma,' she said, but her words were stamped out, drowned by another, terrible, noise: a guttural scream, repeating the word 'You!' It came from Arthur, who lunged outside through the open barn doors.

Emma had never seen her father like this.

Eyes wide, mouth dripping, his face purple. His hair, normally so neat and combed back, fell across his forehead in damp, sticky strands.

His feet were shoeless, clothed in black and red socks stuck with dirt and old hay from the barn.

'You!' he screamed again, eyes on his daughter, lunging towards her, restrained by the WPC. 'She did this because of you!'

Emma's heart dropped; she could feel its beat echo through the stitches in her belly.

Arthur's hands were covered in Elaine's dried, black blood.

'*You* drove her to this!'

The WPC called for support and two labourers stepped forward, held Arthur's arms by his sides, stopped him from pointing at Emma but everyone had seen, everyone had turned to look at the girl.

'Why couldn't you have been a good girl?'

Blood had soaked into his shirt, his trouser legs, glistening wet and black.

'She'd never have done this if it weren't for you!'

Emma faltered, stumbled forward, the WPC calling to her, 'Please stay back!'

'If you hadn't got yourself pregnant,' Arthur shouted. 'If you hadn't acted like a whore!'

Emma opened her mouth but nothing came out. She turned to face her godmother, needing her support.

'What's happened?' Emma said, but her voice was too weak to carry. 'I don't understand, what's happened to Elaine? What's happened to my mum?' Emma shouted, turning towards the WPC standing by the barn's open doors.

Another policeman stepped out from the barn, white-gloved

hands holding a shotgun wrapped in an evidence bag, the shotgun Arthur kept in the boot room at home, the gun he'd taught Emma, taught Elaine, how to load, aim, shoot.

Emma took one more step forward, the WPC too busy holding Arthur to stop her.

She could feel Maggie behind her. Maggie's gasp turned into a sob, a wail of grief and of horror as she, too, looked into the barn.

Maggie's strong hands pulled Emma backwards, away from the door, held her tight to her chest. She wept openly, her tears falling into Emma's hair.

Emma stayed silent. Her insides frozen, her face paralysed and pressed to Maggie's soft chest. She couldn't close her eyes, couldn't blink away what she had seen in the barn, the sight of her stepmother's dead body forever etched into her four-teen-year-old mind.

So much blood.

Dark and oozing, dried to flaky black pools in some places, wet and thick and red in others.

So much blood.

And Maggie held her and sobbed, her whole body shaking, repeating the words, 'I'm so sorry,' into her ear.

Arthur was crying, his back turned to his daughter, unable to look at her at all.

People whispered behind her, the crowd's muttering a hum of collective shock.

And Emma stood with her eyes wide open, stared at the barn and remembered what was inside it, knew she would never forget what she had seen.

Her stepmother's body, slumped on the hay-strewn floor, the shotgun having done its deadly damage.

Her Elaine.

Elaine, the only mother she had ever known, had ever wanted, had shot herself.

And Emma knew she had done it because of her.

It was all her fault.

Seven years ago

Emma

Wednesday, 11th August, 2010

A numbness washed over her. No tears, no screams, no cries. She sat in the bar, alone. Maggie had gone out to fetch tea, sugar, staples from the shop to help with the shock. Even Maggie, it seemed, couldn't bear to be next to Emma, knowing what Emma had done. What she had pushed Elaine to do.

Was it really her fault? Had she really driven her stepmother to *this*?

She wanted James to come back, to hold her and tell her . . . what would he tell her? That yes, it was her fault, like everything else, but he still loved her nonetheless. Is that what she needed to hear?

Maybe she just needed his arms around her.

She pulled her knees up to her chest, but her stitches were sore and her stomach tender, her body screaming in pain at the movement.

The chair she was sitting on was swirled with patterns, cream feathery shapes decorating the green fabric. Each looked like a curled up foetus, each like the baby they had ripped from inside her, had killed to save her own life.

And still nothing.

She was empty.

Shock, a voice in her head spoke up. It's the shock.

But Emma couldn't believe it. Couldn't believe there was any excuse for this feeling of nothingness. Her baby was dead, her stepmother was dead, her father hated her, had always hated her and even Maggie had fled her side at the earliest excuse.

She heard a car pull up outside. Looked up out of the window and saw the roof-mounted sign of a taxi.

James.

And suddenly she felt something, she felt hope, relief.

He had come back.

He was home, had come to see her, make sure she was all right.

She jumped from her chair, ignored the pain in her belly, ran to the door and flung it open, ran outside without even pausing to put her trainers on.

There was the taxi, outside James's house.

The driver had stepped outside it, was knocking on James's front door.

There must be a mistake. Surely the car was bringing James home; why was the cab empty? Why was the driver knocking on the door of the house?

Emma slowed, her eyes locked on the door.

It must be Lois, she thought, Lois ordered a taxi to take her to the station or something, she was going to greet James as he arrived on the train.

The door opened.

James stepped out.

He wasn't expecting to see her, she could see it in his face: shock, disbelief, a hint of, what was it, anger? But she pushed that last thought away. He couldn't be angry with her, too.

'James!' She could hear the anguish in her own voice, spilling out with each syllable.

He picked up his pace as he walked towards her, signalling to the taxi driver that he'd just be a minute. He grabbed her by the upper arm, pulled her off the street and into the alley that separated his house from the pub.

He hissed a harsh, 'Ssssh,' looking both ways down the street to make sure no one was watching, listening. 'What are you doing?' he said. 'Haven't you got me into enough trouble already, telling your dad about me, without talking to me openly in the street? What the fuck are you thinking?'

She opened her lips to begin, but where would she start? That she had wanted to see him, she needed him, she'd never have told her dad about them. That their baby was dead, her stepmother was dead, that Emma had fucked everything up and she didn't know what to do?

James ran one hand through his hair, the other still gripping Emma's arm and she knew that she had to choose what to say carefully because he got annoyed when she mumbled or mixed up her words.

But where should she start?

The hardness in his eyes made her throat ache with smothered grief. She wanted to ask him what they were going to do, how he was going to help her, ask him where he had been all this time but she found herself crying instead. The only words she could find, when her sobs receded, were simply, 'It's all my fault.'

His eyes scanned Emma up and down, his top lip lifted at the corner, the way it always did just before he was about to kiss her, run his fingers across her still-developing body.

But he didn't kiss her, not yet.

His grip on her arm didn't let up, his fingers needling her flesh. He pulled her towards him and whispered in her ear, his lips hot and moist against her lobe. 'Your father visited my mother yesterday, after you told him about us. Do you know that?' He spoke quietly, vehemently.

'I'm sorry,' Emma said helplessly and James sneered.

'I have to leave,' he said, 'because if I don't, he'll come after me.'

'I didn't tell him,' Emma shook her head as she spoke. She looked up into his eyes, those beautiful blues that could be so kind when he wanted them to be, so caring.

'You couldn't even keep us a secret, couldn't even do that simplest thing properly,' he said, his face cold. 'I should have known you couldn't handle this, that you're too young and useless.'

He dropped her arm and her skin felt tender and bruised where he'd held her.

She looked down at the ground, struggling not to cry. Just two days ago James had held her in his arms, said, 'Yes, just like that, just like that,' and she had felt so happy, so pleased she was pleasing him, this man who was handsome and strong and brave, lying with her in a sunny wheat field, her hair in his fists as he held her head in position.

And now he was leaving her.

James went on, his voice soft and callous. 'You're just a little idiot, that's all, a stupid little girl.'

Emma snapped her head up. 'Why would you say that? How can you be so cruel?'

James licked his lips. 'You didn't know what you were doing when you came on to me; that's what I've been telling myself. It's much better than what my mother thinks: that you fucked an older man, fucked me, got pregnant, because you wanted to trap me.'

Emma took a step backwards in shock. 'She said that?' Emma followed James's gaze to his childhood home, imagined Lois spitting out those words, surrounded by photos of her son. '*You* don't think that though, James?'

James stroked Emma's cheek, pinching her flesh between finger and thumb. 'You've let me down, that much I know.'

She tried to right herself, to stand tall with her head held high, but she was light headed and dizzy, her belly tender and aching at the sides.

She closed her eyes, tried to steady her mind so she could steady herself, but the image of Elaine's body floated behind her closed lids. The deep-seated feeling of wrongness worming its way inside her, making a nest in her guts.

When she opened her eyes James was smiling at her sadly.

'My mother says I'm better off without you.' He searched her eyes with his own. 'She thinks that you're trouble and will only get me into trouble too.'

'I need you,' Emma said. 'I'm not trouble.'

'Really?' He raised his eyebrows, cocked his head. 'My mum said Elaine's dead. That she shot herself. Is that true?'

Emma nodded, tried to swallow back the tears but the lump in her throat was too big, she felt the threat of a sob rise up her throat. She waited for his arms to engulf her, to pull her back into him and let her cry.

But he didn't.

'Why did Elaine do it, do you think?' he asked, his mouth to her ear, his breath warm.

She tried to say, 'I don't know,' but choked on the words.

'Mum says it's because of you.' His whisper sounded so sweet in her ear, so at odds with his words. 'Because of all the terrible things you've done.'

She tried to say it wasn't true, that Lois was lying, but the words, the blame, felt so at home in her ear she couldn't refute them.

James tilted her chin, wiped her tears with his thumb and kissed her full on the mouth. She felt his tongue squirm inside her, push open her teeth, felt his hands grip her waist and pull her in. She was still crying, trying to digest the things he had said, tasted the salt of her own tears along with his tongue. She stifled a sob and he groaned, lowered his hands to her bottom and felt her.

Her stitches were burning, her throat sore from crying, her hands limp and useless at her sides.

But she needed him.

She loved him.

And, almost as suddenly as it began, it stopped. James pulled back. The cab beeped its horn. He turned away, ready to leave.

'Wait!' she called, her head dizzy with confusion and fear. 'You can't leave me!'

'It's because of you I have to go.' He was still walking away. She followed.

'Are you coming back?' Her voice was small, but something was on fire inside her, her eyes still fixed on his house.

'My mum's right,' he said. 'You're just a filthy slut, a whore, and you'll forget about me as soon as I'm gone.'

'Please,' she choked out, but he had stepped away. The taxi door closed; she heard the engine roar to life. Her mind was numb, her chest hot and hands shaking. She looked away, couldn't bear to see him leave her.

After the taxi drove off, her eyes stayed fixed on that house.

And then she thought of the woman who had poured poison in James's ear.

Who had persuaded him to leave.

Who was leaving her with no one.

Lois.

Maggie

Monday, 20th November, 2017

'But Maggie,' Jennifer said, steering her car through the police car park exit. 'Who else would it have been? I know you thought the world of Emma, but who else would have reason to hurt Lois like that?'

And Maggie looked, open-mouthed, at the woman driving her home, her neighbour for over twenty years.

'I told you,' Maggie said, raising her voice, 'just like I told them. It was Nuala Greene, James's widow. She did it.'

Jennifer coughed, checked the blind spot to her right, her thick, wire-wool hair concealing her expression.

'It *was*.' Maggie shifted in her seat. Outside, rain still pattered the window.

'But what evidence is there?' Jennifer said, her voice strained. Her eyes were red as if she, too, had been crying. Maggie hoped she had. Hoped everyone had been crying for the loss of her goddaughter.

'I know it's hard for you, Maggie, terribly hard, but you can't just go blaming random people.'

'I'm not blaming random people! It was her! She stayed on Friday night, took the room in the pub. There must still be her DNA on the bedsheets, for heaven's sake!'

'Nobody else saw her, let alone spoke to her. Why didn't you tell anyone you had a paying guest? Why didn't Emma tell anyone she was staying? You had a full pub on Friday night, according to Toby, and none of them knew about this Nuala Greene.'

'They knew about her car, though.' Maggie lifted a biro that was rattling in the car door pocket, wrote *red hatchback* on the back of her hand.

'What, the one on Shore Road? That was gone by Saturday morning, no one saw it again.'

Jennifer looked over at Maggie, patted the woman's knee with her left hand. 'It's just your word for it, Maggie. The police won't waste resources based on one person's word, not when they already have so much evidence pointing at Emma.'

'What are you trying to say? That I made it up, that I'm mad?'

'No, of course not! But you've had such a shock and you were in such a state yesterday, understandably. I think that maybe the shock has played havoc in some way with your, you know—'

'With my mind?'

'I just think it's strange that you didn't mention this woman to anyone until after the fact. You said yourself the police found evidence that Emma had been searching for James online, had found details of his death on the internet on Saturday. Could it be possible that you got confused, that Emma told you James was dead, had been married to a woman called Nuala Greene, and that the shock of everything jumbled this up in your head?'

'She was here, I saw her, spoke to her, carried her bloody bag upstairs and you think I imagined it?'

'No! Oh, Maggie, I don't know what I think, but it all just seems so out of place, so odd. And such a coincidence that Emma finds James online the same day you say this Nuala Greene woman comes to the village.'

'Nuala only told Lois about James's death this weekend, that was why she came all the way down here. And Emma probably only searched for James online off the back of Nuala Greene's visit.'

'If Nuala came to tell Lois that her son had died, why would she end up killing her? It doesn't make sense, does it?'

'None of it makes sense!' Maggie closed her eyes, rubbed her temples, and there it all was again, the blood, the iron doorstop, the brain matter on the kitchen wall. And despite it all, the suicide letters, internet searches, the bank statements Emma had strewn across the cellar floor, it didn't make sense.

'I'll have to make them believe me,' Maggie said, her mind winding up, into life. 'I'll give them evidence if that's what they need. I'll make them realise she was here all along. Her tyre tracks would still be in the fields.'

'It's been raining since Saturday, Maggie, the fields are washed clean of tracks.'

'I'll give them a full description, her looks, mannerisms.'

'You could have got all that from the internet, Twitter and the like.'

'I have to make them believe me!' Maggie said.

She knew Emma far better than any of them. She knew the tenacity inside that girl. She couldn't see it; Emma taking the gun, sitting beside the woman she had supposedly beaten to death and pointing it at her face, the barrel an inch below her jaw. She couldn't see Emma pulling the trigger. Couldn't

imagine the desolation she would had to have felt, the loneliness, the despair. Surely she would have noticed it if Emma
had been so low, so close to suicide?

And then she thought of the letters, the suicide letters the
police found in Emma's drawer.

Then she saw Emma's face, her sweet face, ruined by the
shotgun between her knees. The same gun Elaine had used
to shoot herself, the gun Arthur had given to Emma on the
day it was released from police evidence, a sick gift reminding
her, always, of where Arthur placed the blame of Elaine's
death, the gun Emma had kept ever since in a holdall stored
inside her divan.

For the police it fitted so neatly, Emma killing the woman
she blamed for her fall from grace, before killing herself with
that gun, in the home of the man she had never stopped loving.

They drove the rest of the way in silence, Jennifer still
wearing her sympathetic, closed-lipped smile. No other cars
passed them, no cyclists or ramblers braved the rain.

They drove past the track that led to Maggie's field and
she thought of Nuala, her bitten fingers, thin wrists. The look
in her eye when Maggie told her that James had, at nineteen
years of age, slept with a girl barely fourteen.

They drove on through the village, along Shore Road where
Lois's house was still draped with police tape, already sagging
from the near-constant rain. That house had been Nuala's
destination all along; it made sense it would end there for her
too, made sense to Maggie at least.

They passed the pub, also cordoned off, and followed the
road round the back to the dairy farm and the Hill's stone-
built farmhouse, a low wide building with a dark slate roof
and sash windows framed in black wood.

'Another day or so and you'll be back in the pub,' Jennifer said inside, standing in the doorway of the spare room. 'But you know we're always here if you need us, Jon and I. You don't have to deal with any of this alone.'

Maggie nodded, took a breath, her mind sharper now the sedatives had fully cleared from her system.

'Have you spoken to Arthur?' she asked.

'He's not spoken to a soul since he came back from the morgue. Locked himself in his house, won't answer his phone or the front door.'

Maggie nodded again, unsure of what else to say, knowing how inappropriate it would have been to voice her opinion of Arthur under such circumstances. Wishing, too, she was in her own house instead of a guest in someone else's.

'I was wondering if you wanted me to call anyone?' Jennifer said when they reached the spare room, standing very straight and rubbing her hands together as if she were cold. She shifted her weight from one hip to the other.

Maggie kept her eyes on the wall behind Jennifer.

'No,' she said. There was no one left for her to call.

Maggie looked around the bedroom, eyes lingering on the computer at the desk by the window. Imagined Jennifer, her grey hair and thick ankles, the age spots on her cheeks and the backs of her hands, typing at a keyboard, clicking like and share and send. Was it really just Maggie, then, who hadn't succumbed? Who had resisted all efforts to connect?

Emma had tried to get Maggie computer literate, taught her about Facebook and Twitter. She had even tried getting Maggie to create a page of her own, telling her it would be a good way to try and find Lee, to reconnect. Maggie had refused, solidly refused. She couldn't make up for the past by liking a status on a computer screen. The joke of it.

She regretted it now. It would be a lot easier to find Nuala if she knew how to use that machine.

'Is there anything I can get you?' Jennifer asked, one foot in the hallway, the closed-lipped smile back on her pitying face. 'Anything at all?'

Mind on clearing Emma's name, Maggie said, 'Yes, actually there is. Do you have any maps in the house? Maps of the country, London in particular?'

Jennifer stepped back into the room. 'You're not going to London? You're not going to try and track this woman down?' She frowned, placing her hands firmly on her hips to complete the disapproving schoolmarm façade.

And Maggie wanted to say, why not, why couldn't I, but caught her reflection in the wardrobe mirror, the spare tyres floating beneath her blue shirt, the thick arms, thick neck, wrinkled face and grey hair, so instead she said, 'No, of course not. But if I can just get the police to take me seriously, to see that I'm not just making this up as some naïve, desperate attempt for attention, then maybe they'll go see Nuala themselves, bring her in.'

Jennifer flicked the switch on the old computer. She brought up street maps on Google Earth. 'How exactly are you going to do that?' Her voice was chirpy again, cajoling. Maggie knew she was being placated, but she didn't care. She'd make Jennifer see too, knew that one day very soon the police, her neighbours, the village, would see she was right and congratulate her ingenuity, her persistence in making the police follow the right lead.

Because she had to make them find Nuala Greene. She

may not be on social media or au fait with search engines, but why should that stop her? Whatever happened to good, old-fashioned legwork? She would write down everything Nuala had told her, look in every phone book and directory for sign of an N or J Greene, no matter how long it took. She would phone every one of those parks if need be, see if she could find the one where James worked, the park Nuala Greene's house backed onto.

She looked at the image of London on the screen over Jennifer's shoulder, the dark blocks of buildings and houses. She had no intention of going herself, how ridiculous, how impossible it would be for her to even attempt it, but if she could lead the police in the right direction, if they could go themselves then surely they would see?

She looked on at the dark blocks, winding roads, the green swathes of parklands and wondered where in it Nuala was hiding.

Nuala

Tuesday, 21st November, 2017

Steam fills the shower, swathes of foam cover her breasts, hiding her knees and elbows. The soap is expensive, oil filled, rich with the scent of the ocean, yet it's the cheap bar soap she longs for, soap that would strip the grease from her body, rendering her tight and raw.

She marks the steam on the glass door with her finger, leaving loops and whorls in the mist, then washes the patterns away, cleans the shower door to a shine until all that's left is her reflection. But there's a mistake, because this woman can't be her. This woman's hands are scrubbed clean, whereas hers are black with blood.

She moves the same, this reflection. She too reaches behind her for the thermostat, turning it to its highest, her skin flaring red.

But when the mirage with clean hands disappears behind the steam, she looks down. Her palms and nails are still tattooed with blood, her arms aching from the weight of iron in her fist, the gun in her hand.

No matter how hot the water gets, her limbs never lose their tension, the soap never cleans the blood away. Her mouth, closed and silent, never surrenders its scream.

The dead won't let her be.

All the washing was no use, no use at all.

Afterwards, the brush caught a lump in the underside of her hair. Small and pink as lamb meat, it oozed juices through the bristles. It wound round her senses; the taste of ham left to rot in the heat.

She threw the brush to the floor, watching it bounce and crack until it skidded to a halt by the wall. The lump fell too, landing with a moist thud, a putrid ruby of another woman's flesh, glistening on the bathroom tiles.

The extractor fan, like an old man, rasped down her neck.

She pushed the window open, letting it swing wide and blast her with cold from outside.

Layers of toilet paper covering her hand.

She stepped towards that lump, hovered, retreated. Then plunged, picking it up from the floor and flinging it out of the window, not waiting to see where it landed.

But the jackdaws saw and swooped from the trees. 'There!' they cried. 'There!' And the window was open, her body still naked. Were they calling at her or the meat?

Her fingers were sticky, smelling of death, rot, iron door-stops, and gunshot residue.

The tissue had not been enough. She wiped her fingers clean but the smell lingered.

She scrubbed them at the sink, with soap and a scouring pad, but the smell leaked through the almondy hand wash.

She clutched the green bottle from beside the cistern and lurched back into the shower. She emptied it into her hands, the liquid burning rivulets along her belly, singeing the skin at her groin.

She rubbed her hands until they smelt of pine, until the top layer melted and her palms stung. The reflection in the glass watched her wash.

She rubbed harder, swapping the piney bleach for coconut shampoo, forcing her fingers into every crevice, scrubbing every fold of skin until she shone pink.

She turned her back on the glass, faced the tiles, and her mind filled with the image of someone else, someone hunting, chasing, finding her naked with the smell of the dead in her hair.

She closed her eyes, squeezed them shut, but the image remained. A fat old woman with a deep-scarred cheek and clothes that stank of a bar-room.

Maggie

Wednesday, 22nd November, 2017

K eys in hand, Maggie opened the door to the bar.

The sky was dark, clouds low. A few pinpricks of rain spotted the detective's shirtsleeve.

'I'll come in,' said Pale, but he was looking at something past Maggie. She followed his gaze to the burnt-out house beside them – Lois's old house.

Pale's words from the interview on Monday repeated in Maggie's head, his conviction that Emma was to blame, that she had some kind of history of wanting to hurt both herself and Lois. She shook them away, her grip tightening on the holdall by her side.

The wind seemed to tilt the house forward as if, with the next gust, the last of the scorched bricks would loosen and bury them both.

Maggie squeezed the handles of the bag, the plastic nestling into the creases of her palm. It was all she had brought with her from Jennifer's house, a bag-for-life half-full with note-books and maps.

'I expect you want to talk to me about the case,' Maggie said hopefully, standing to one side to let Pale through. He had barely spoken since collecting her from Jennifer's house, his silence making her nervous. 'Want me to show you the room she slept in, where she parked, that sort of thing? I expect the door-to-door inquiries will start soon, won't they?'

Pale ignored her, striding into the bar and looking around.

Maggie stayed in the open doorway. Her feet felt too heavy to step inside, the first time she'd been in the bar since finding Emma and Lois.

The detective's top lip twitched disdainfully as he took in his surroundings. There were the chairs Emma sat in every Monday when it was quiet, reading a book. Maggie suddenly realised that she would never now buy Emma the Kindle she had promised her but could never afford.

Pale raised one eyebrow as he spotted the tar-yellow ceiling. Kept it raised when he caught sight of the hallway doorframe, smeared with greasy finger-marks.

The doorframe Emma used to lean against, eating apples and sucking their cores, watching the drinkers.

'Are you coming in?' Pale asked.

Maggie realised she was trembling. Her lips parted as if to speak, but the words never materialised. She wished Ali was there instead of Pale.

'Well?' asked Pale. Maggie nodded, but she couldn't move from her post in the doorway.

She could see Emma there, eating apples.

She could see her in the armchair, reading Oscar Wilde.

She could see her.

'The SOCOs have left everything in order if that's what you're worried about,' Pale said.

'SOCOs?'

'Scene of crime officers.' And Maggie must still have looked confused because Pale said, 'The chaps who searched for evidence.'

The breeze from the open door spiralled through the room, mixing the sourness of the bar with the smell of rain.

Pale took Maggie by the elbow and led her inside, sitting her down on a chair by the card table. He was firm, forceful and once again Maggie wished for Ali and her gentler hands.

'What's the point in searching the pub?' Maggie realised she was sitting in Emma's seat, not her own, the place she would sit with a coffee and flick through her phone.

'As I said; to gather evidence.'

And Maggie wanted to ask why, why here when the woman you want is in London? But Pale's features were rigid, his mouth a straight line and his eyes were fixed on the carrier bag by Maggie's feet, the bag of meticulous notes she had made, the maps she had studied, the evidence she had collated, all ready to hand over to the DS.

That's why she'd called Pale, why she'd asked for the detective to be the one to release the pub back to her when the crime scene tape had been removed and she was allowed to go back inside.

Because of Emma.

Because of the bag.

Because of Nuala fucking Greene.

The detective nodded to the bag. 'What's inside there?'

And this was the moment. She could feel Emma smiling from the kitchen door.

She pulled apart the handles with a flourish. 'Evidence.'

'Evidence?'

The bag was over half full: a few notebooks, the odd sheet

of loose paper. One corner of a faded map was just visible, a park circled in blue highlighter.

'I've written it all down, everything I can remember: what she looks like, the things she told me.'

'You mean Nuala Greene?'

'Of course I mean Nuala Greene! It'll help when you start the search.' Maggie looked back at the detective. 'No notebook for you this time? Do you want to borrow one?'

'I don't need one at the moment, Mrs Bradbury—'

'Maggie, please.'

'My memory's fine for now.'

Maggie tapped the side of her head, wanting to keep him on side. 'The best always have good memories, Detective. I expect your mind is as sharp as a razor. That's probably why they sent you, isn't it, because you're the best? I suppose you'll be releasing a statement to the press soon, isn't that right? Then it'll be on the news, in the papers.'

Pale's gaze flitted from Maggie to the bag and he raised his eyebrow again.

'It'll help! Give you something to go on when you find her. Evidence to charge her, isn't that what you need?' Maggie eagerly nodded her head and felt her jowls sway with the movement.

'What would be more useful,' Pale said, scanning the hand-written notes poking out from inside the bag, 'is electronic data. CCTV images, for example?'

'We don't have any cameras, not here. Never had the money to install them and besides, we've never had any serious trouble before, nothing that would warrant the need.'

'Until now,' Pale said, his eyes darting back up to Maggie, pausing on the scar on her cheek. 'And are you quite sure you didn't take any details, not even a swipe of her card to hold the room? Seems odd.'

'We don't have a card machine, cash only here. We're too small for it, you see. The cost of the machine would wipe out the profits, unless I put on a minimum spend and, to be honest, that wouldn't go down too well. I'm trying to keep hold of customers, not drive them away.'

Pale looked again at the bag-for-life and Maggie was sure then, knew he would take it, read the notes, find Nuala.

But Pale didn't reach for the bag.

'You told us in your first statement,' he said, smoothing his blazer down, 'that the women had fallen out over the way Lois dealt with Emma when she fell pregnant as a teenager. She apparently bad-mouthed Emma to her son, the baby's father, insinuated to him that Emma got pregnant on purpose.'

'Yes, but Emma had—'

'Had forgiven her?'

'That's right. If I could just show you some of my—'

'What about the fire? The fire that started the night that James Lunglow moved away?'

Maggie froze.

The wind outside picked up. The loose sheets of paper shivered.

'You never mentioned it.' Pale walked to the pub's open door, polished heels gliding across the wood. 'Were you hoping I wouldn't find out? You must have known it would come up, eventually?'

'There was no need, it's irrelevant.' Maggie pulled her sleeves further down her wrists, the hair on the back of her neck erect. 'It was a long time ago. Lois's house caught fire, a kitchen fire. It was an accident.'

'The fire started on the day Emma's stepmother killed herself. The day Emma returned from hospital after losing her baby. The day her boyfriend ran away.' Pale swung the door shut, the latch catching with a bang.

'I think Emma set that fire.' Pale looked at her, a cold smile on his lips. 'Didn't she, Maggie?'

'No!' Maggie shouted, her voice shaking.

'Quite a few people have told me all about it. But you didn't, Maggie; why was that?'

'No one blamed Emma.'

'I found more than a few people who did. Seems it was common knowledge.'

'Then why was she never charged, tell me that?' Maggie folded her arms, trying to ignore the apprehension growing in the pit of her stomach.

'I know how it works in these places. The village takes care of itself without drawing the police in.' Pale looked up at Maggie, his cold manner so at odds with his thick, black lashes and the schoolboy dimples in his cheeks. 'I've read the official report on the fire. Firemen mistook it as an accident, weren't aware of what had happened that day.'

Maggie gripped her arms tightly. Pale watched her, as though waiting for the moment she would break.

She wanted to leap across the table and grab the detective by the neck, wring out the names of the people who'd talked, who'd lied.

But she didn't.

She couldn't.

She needed the detective on side, needed to make him believe, and so she kept her mouth closed.

'It could have ruined Lois, couldn't it? House gone, all her possessions.' Pale turned his back, paced to the other end of the room. 'No family to cling to, no friends, yet miraculously she never went destitute. Why was that, Maggie?'

'The village looked after her, the community rallied round.'

'The *whole* village?'

'That's right.' Maggie tried to keep her voice steady, tried to keep her eyes on the holdall.

'That's not what I've heard.'

'No?'

'No.' Pale leant back against the sleeper. 'I've heard it was one person alone who helped Lois, one person who particularly wanted to make sure she never reported Emma.'

'I did as much as anyone,' Maggie said defensively. 'I sent her the odd bit of food, some old clothes—'

Pale smiled, walked to the fireplace and stood before the Polaroids. 'It wasn't you who helped her, Maggie.' He turned, looked Maggie square in the eye. 'It was Arthur Bradbury.'

Maggie felt the thrum of her heartbeat speed up.

'Who do you think owns her house? Who gave her the furniture, set her up with a miserly tab at the local shop? Why would he do all that if he wasn't trying to protect his daughter?'

And Maggie thought of Arthur's monstrous treatment of Lois on that terrible day seven years ago, remembered the bruises on Elaine's wrist and mouth the night she turned up at the pub, the dirty little secret surrounding James's birth, wondered how far Arthur would go to keep Lois's lips sealed.

But she couldn't tell Pale that.

She couldn't tell *anyone* that, it would be one more thing for them to add to the evidence against her goddaughter.

'Emma tried to kill Lois once before and, this time, she succeeded.'

A distant bang echoed, the damn crow scarer again, the sound bringing back images of Emma's shot-through face.

'It was a house fire,' Maggie said with more conviction this time, eager to bring the talk of the fire to a close and revert the conversation back to Nuala. 'Lois left the hob on and went for a walk. She was distracted, James having just left, and forgot to turn the hob off before she went out. She had a chip pan, an old tin thing, half full of oil; it set alight.'

'Yes, that's what the report says. It was an accident, a run of the mill kitchen fire, the fire chief never suspected arson and, as he filed it as an accident, a police investigation was never conducted. And the house wasn't insured, so there was no motive there. It all looks, on paper, very straightforward. But I think Emma set that fire. I think she poured the oil in the pan, lit the gas burners and waited. It would only have taken twenty minutes.'

'No!' Maggie's knees were jumping beneath the table. 'She went to put the fire *out* but it had spread. It was drawn through the house by the draught from a bedroom window.'

'*Emma* opened the windows upstairs so the fire would travel faster.'

'No! She tried to help!'

'Then why didn't she?'

'You weren't there! I'd come back from the shops and saw the smoke from Lois's house. I ran inside calling for her but it was Emma I found, watching the flames jump from the kitchen to the hallway, the ceiling black with smoke. I had to drag her out, she wouldn't move. She was just standing there shaking from head to foot.'

Pale cocked his head, waiting for her to go on.

Maggie closed her eyes, pushing the heel of her palms into

the sockets. 'Half the village were on their way, the fire engine too, and in amongst them all I saw Lois.'

'I can only imagine how upset Lois must have been.'

'The first thing I did was go back to Emma. She was sobbing, convinced Lois was dead. I told her that it was OK, that Lois was fine. She was *relieved*. Why would she be relieved if she'd started the fire?'

'You tell me.'

'She didn't do it! The only guilt she felt was over her inability to help. She'd frozen, too caught up in what had happened that day to think clearly. Her stepmother had just died, for heaven's sake! She was in shock and grieving, not just for Elaine but for her baby, and for her relationship with James. It was my wake-up call: I realised I had to help her, so she could help herself. So I took her out of the village school and signed her up to the one in town, drove her there and back myself every day so she could focus on her school-work without local kids gossiping and bullying her, which they did, believe me. I encouraged her to do her GCSEs, her A Levels, I taught her how to run the pub as soon as she finished school. I changed my will, so she could take over when I died, so she'd have something to focus on, something to prove she hadn't lost everything. It worked; she came round, was happier than ever.'

Maggie looked imploringly at the detective but he just smiled, shook his head. 'Do you realise you're the only person who's told me this version? I've been told that Emma and James were seen arguing in the street just before he left the village that night. Emma was seen standing, staring, at Lois's house before the fire started. And it must have started so very soon after James had left; maybe half an hour tops.'

Maggie's fists clenched beneath the table. 'Emma had no intention of killing Lois then and had no reason to kill her now. She had her future to think of.'

'She seemed suicidal, or so her notes imply. Perhaps she didn't care about the future.' Pale reached into his blazer pocket and lifted out a letter, smoothing it out onto the table between them. 'It's a photocopy of the most recent note, the one we found in Emma's back pocket. The original's in evidence.'

Maggie lifted the piece of paper but her hands were shaking, blurring the words, and she put it back.

The detective read aloud. '*I'm taking her with me. I can't leave knowing she is still breathing. I should say that I am sorry, but I am not sorry.*'

His eyes lifted to Maggie's. 'Just three lines. Our psych consult tells us she snapped. Her previous efforts were planned; this time she moved on instinct.'

Maggie's arms fell to her sides, her eyes fixed on the note on the table.

'Emma would have written more.'

'She didn't.'

'She would have mentioned me.'

'There's something else.'

'What's that?'

'Cyanide.'

'Wh—?' Maggie's furrowed brow completed the question, tears dried up in surprise.

'We found it in her bedroom, more than enough to kill herself. We're analysing it to see where it came from.'

Maggie's eyes fell back onto Pale. 'Why would a normal girl like Emma have cyanide?'

'I think it's safe to say,' said Pale, 'that she was far from normal.'

That cold smile again.

'You didn't know her!' Maggie's face felt hot, her voice wavering as she tried to maintain control. 'She wouldn't do this, she wouldn't leave me!'

But Pale was getting up, making to leave.

'Please!' The anger had left Maggie's voice. 'Read these and you'll see.' She held out the carrier bag of notebooks, maps and scrawled on paper. 'It was *her. Please!*'

'No one else has mentioned Nuala Greene, Mrs Bradbury,' Pale said. '*No one.*'

'Someone will have seen her.'

Pale was nearly at the door.

'Have you asked Louisa, at the shop?'

He ignored her.

'Have you asked *anyone*?' Maggie cried but still Pale didn't answer.

'I'll find someone.' Maggie grasped at the detective's sleeve, her fat fingers gripping the navy blue blazer. 'I'll make them tell you! I can still help!'

Pale spun round.

Maggie's wrist twisted.

'Are you telling me how to do my job?' Pale's face was an angry red.

'I want to help! I have to do something!' Maggie thought of the tyre tracks in the field, washed away by the rain. Of fingerprints wiped clean. 'You haven't asked anyone?'

'You want questions?' And now his fingers were on Maggie, prising loose her grip on the blazer. 'I can ask questions. Have a premise licence, Mrs Bradbury?'

'What's that got to do—' Did she? Oh Christ, did she have one of those?

'How about a personal licence?'

Maggie stepped back, away from him.

'Does the HMRC know all about the little cash-in-hand room you let out upstairs?'

Maggie curled her hands into fists, her hands trembling.

Pale saw the tremble.

'You don't want me asking questions, Mrs Bradbury.'

'I'll find someone. I'll make them talk, make you see.'

Pale's eyes were on Maggie's dirty boots, her too-long trousers rolled at the hem. 'You will, will you?' They scanned over her belly, bulging out from beneath her shirt, her armpits ringed in sweat marks, the grey-white of her bra peeking from between the buttonholes.

Pale's lips curved upwards, his smile full of pity.

Maggie tried to shout, 'Yes, yes I will!' but her throat was too dry and the words merely croaked.

Pale opened the door, walked through it without looking back.

'I will!' She found the words, but the detective was gone and Maggie was alone in the bar.

Her hands still shook at her sides. Sweat had gathered in the creases of her shirt and between her breasts. She could feel it building at the back of her neck. Her throat was no longer dry. 'I'll find her!'

Seven years ago

Emma

Wednesday, 11th August, 2010

She stood by the sink, the lino already melting at the doorway between kitchen and hallway, the flames leaving tongue-shaped scorch marks on the walls until eventually these, too, set alight.

She could feel the suck of the air, pulling the flames out of the kitchen and on through the hallway, up the stairs and into the bedrooms.

She felt nothing, not pride, not righteousness, no vindication.

A crack of glass.

A thud on the floor, followed by another crack and thud, then another.

The photographs of James, ranging from baby to man, smashed one by one to the ground.

His clothes would be burning, now, upstairs. So too would his bed, his books.

He was leaving.

And it was all *her* fault.

Lois deserved all of this, Emma thought to herself as she watched the flames devour the house.

She had a sudden vision of what could have been. A nice,

white maternity ward, Elaine holding Emma's hand on one side, James holding her hand on the other, all urging Emma on with encouragement and pride, waiting for the moment her baby would be born.

But that wasn't to be. That chance had gone, along with all the people who should have been there to support her. James should be there with her right now, holding her whilst she mourned.

The room was getting hotter, Emma's face red with the heat. Though the windows upstairs were all open, pulling the fire through the house and upstairs, some of the flames were working backwards, inching across the lino towards Emma's feet at the sink.

She closed her eyes, tried to block out the vision, but when her eyes were closed all she saw was her stepmother, her sweet Elaine. All she could feel was the warmth from those hands, a stroke to her cheek, a longing Emma couldn't live with.

The flames were nearer, the smoke growing thick, the air so hot Emma could barely breathe. She didn't move from her place by the sink. She stood, motionless, wondering how many deep breaths it would take to end her life.

A crash from behind, the kitchen door opening.

A gasp.

A scream.

Arms grabbing Emma, pulling her backwards.

Now there was blue sky above her, she was in Maggie's arms, Maggie desperately asking, 'Are you all right?'

She was being carried away from the flames, from the black smoke that had promised to take her away to her stepmother.

She was alone again.

She wrapped her arms round Maggie's neck, the frying oil from her fingers marking Maggie's shirt, and watched as Lois's house burned.

Maggie

Friday, 24th November, 2017

'What happened, Maggie?' Jennifer Hill knelt down beside Maggie's kitchen chair, put a hand on her friend's slumped shoulder. 'It's been years since I've seen you like this, *years*. What happened to get you in such a state?'

Maggie shrugged her hand away, raised her head from the vomit-splattered table-top, gestured at the dead laptop in front of her. 'I tried to find her myself,' she slurred.

What *had* happened last night?

She had reopened the pub. That had been her first mistake. A last-ditch attempt to find someone who remembered Nuala, who would tell the police Maggie was right. None of the lads would talk to her last night, no one would say they had seen Nuala. She had rung the bell, called time, closed the door on them all and bolted it shut.

None of them believed her.

The bar, in their wake, was too big for once. The chairs were all empty, each sat in, at one time or another, by Emma. The photographs on the fireplace wall were frozen images. She thought of Tom, standing in front of the fire, a glass of whisky in his hand.

He was dead too, he was gone, and the bar was far, far too

empty. Maggie walked to the kettle in the kitchen and flicked it on, made a cup of tea, lots of milk and a capful of gin, but this time she didn't put the bottle away.

On the kitchen worktop, beside the entrance to the bar, was the laptop. Emma's phone was still in police custody, her laptop held there too. But this one, ten years old and fixed at the hinge with scotch tape, was technically Maggie's and the police had left it behind. Enough evidence, it would seem, had already been found on Emma's phone and bedroom computer.

Evidence.

No one in the village would help her. They didn't believe her, thought she was imagining things, half mad.

What was it Jennifer had said to her, about the things that could be found online, social media, Google, the like?

Maggie lifted the machine and sat it at the table, lifted the lid and turned the thing on.

No password, thank God, just the desktop screen. Maggie wracked her brain, tried to remember which icon was which, which one Emma had told her to click for the internet. She had never listened, that was the problem. She didn't have the confidence to try it, didn't see the need when Emma was there to do it for her.

Only she wasn't here now; she was locked in a steel drawer at the morgue. The thought made Maggie wince, made her reach for the gin bottle, fill another cap and add it to her tea.

Finger over the mousepad she moved the cursor with painstaking care, watching as the arrow made its way to the internet icon.

She wasn't an idiot. She'd done this before, used a laptop, a computer before. It was just a long time ago. There had seemed such little point in loading the thing up once Lee had gone; no homework to help with and so on. There had seemed such little point in anything.

Until Emma had moved in, needed looking after, made Maggie crawl out of herself and face life.

But now she was gone. Like Lee, like Tom. She was gone.

Maggie poured another capful of gin into her tea, then another, wiping her cheeks dry of the moisture from the mug's steam. Discovered the moisture on her skin was from tears.

She blinked them away, rubbed her eyes. In the darkness, there was Emma, the shotgun, the blood.

There was Lois, bent over the table, her head resting in a black puddle.

Maggie jolted upright, knocking the laptop, its screen flickering. Maggie clicked on the internet icon. Waited for it to spring to life, remembering Emma huffing through the long wait for the page to load.

But it loaded far quicker than she had ever expected, luck perhaps on her side for once.

She moved the cursor again, floating the arrow to the bar at the top, using her index finger to type www. The address for Facebook appeared, as if by magic.

She could log in as Emma, search for Nuala online, search for James.

Emma's username came up in the log-in page and that was where Maggie's luck had run out.

She sipped her tea, added another gin cap, typed in the first password she could think of. *Elaine.*

Password not recognised.

She tried *Maggie*, tried *James, Lunglow, Bradbury*. Nothing got through, nothing worked.

She lifted her mug, realised all the tea had gone. She refilled it instead with gin and plain water. Her fingers were starting to warm up, feet fuzzy and warm beneath the table.

Different tactic.

She moved the cursor to the top again, typed in Google.

Filled the search bar with the words *Nuala Greene*.

Eighty-five thousand results.

She tried again, remembering Emma telling her to be specific, accurate, so this time added to the search: *Nuala Greene, London*.

Even more results came up, mocking Maggie and her ignorance, mocking her with page after page of the wrong woman.

If only she had her address, she would go there right now. If only she had one of those letters Nuala said Emma had written, if only Emma had written that address down.

She took a mouthful, clicked open a page, dismissed it and began again. Drink, click, dismiss.

The light was starting to burn her eyes, the computer screen out of focus. She got up, stumbled to the bar and fetched a fresh bottle of gin.

She tried again, adding *James* to the search, adding *Irish, park, dead parents*, adding *red hatchback* as if that would help.

She didn't know what to do, how to narrow it down, how to make the right page appear.

Then something must have gone wrong, because she stopped clicking and the pages kept on opening by themselves. Page after page came up, closed down, another one swiftly in its place. Images filled her screen that she didn't ask for, didn't want, text boxes, words flashing, photos.

A virus.

And she remembered why she never used the damn thing, how Emma had told her, time and again, to install security software. Why didn't she listen?

She pushed the machine away, far away, watched as the screen finally blacked out.

She tried the on-switch, nothing happened. Tried control-alt-delete but that didn't work either.

She took another sip from her drink.

Then another.

At some point she was sick.

At another point, she fell asleep.

At some point much later, she was woken by Jennifer's cries.

'Oh, Maggie,' Jennifer said now, lifting the empty gin bottles and adding them to the black recycling box. 'You know DC Ali came, earlier?'

'I think I ought to go to bed.' Maggie tried to push herself up but her stomach muscles went into spasm. She swallowed a mouthful of bile.

'She said that they found something in Emma's room, a type of poison.'

And Maggie saw Pale's face as he told her about the cyanide, and she didn't want to hear any more.

'She made it herself, from apple seeds and lye.' Maggie didn't look at Jennifer's face, but she could imagine her expression well enough. 'You know she was always eating apples? She must have collected the seeds. Hundreds and hundreds of apple seeds.'

And Maggie could see Emma, apple in her mouth, sucking on the core, the sound as it cracked in her mouth.

'They found the same poison at Lois's house.'

'Then it must have been planted!' Ignoring her pounding head, contracting throat, Maggie managed to look up. 'Surely that proves—'

'No, Maggie. It was in a packet of chocolate digestives that Emma had sent her, years ago, but Lois had never opened them. The receipt was still in Emma's drawer, underneath the poison and the notes. You know which notes I mean?' And she tried to take Maggie's hand, but Maggie shook her off. 'She's tried it more than once, Ali said.'

The sound that followed was the cry and screech of her heart tearing in two; it couldn't be anything else.

She wanted to scream but her mouth wouldn't open, her jaw wouldn't release.

Her stomach fought against her, fighting the gin from last night, the lies Jennifer was trying to make her swallow.

Just then, a tap at the front door announced DC Ali's arrival.

Maggie pulled her arms around herself, hugged her middle. She didn't turn to look.

'Tea, detective?' Jennifer jumped from her seat.

Ali declined. She didn't take a seat either, so Jennifer remained standing too, hovering nervously at the edge of the table.

Ali didn't say anything, and the silence was thick in Maggie's ears.

'I'm sorry,' Ali said at last, and the apology was unbearable, horrible and sincere. 'The investigation is complete, Mrs Bradbury.' There was no hint of Pale's triumph in Ali's voice. 'We're handing it to the coroner now, so an inquest can be carried out.'

Last night's gin reared up, wringing Maggie's throat, her stomach. 'But . . . Nuala Greene,' she managed to whisper.

'All lines of inquiry have been followed up,' Ali said gently. Maggie could smell her own body, stale and sour.

Ali was still talking, saying something about Nuala writing to Lois months ago and telling her James was dead, but that couldn't be right, Maggie must have heard wrong because she saw Nuala, spoke to her, so did Emma. Did the police really think she'd made it all up?

'Mrs Greene's very fragile . . . agoraphobic . . . hasn't left her house in months . . . '

Maggie could hear little else above the ringing in her ears, the churning in her gut, the see-saw pain in her head. The police had talked to Nuala, but she must have fooled them, spun them lies.

'The GPS on her phone hasn't moved . . . no one saw her leave or return. Maggie, she was never *here* . . .'

But she was, Maggie tried to say but couldn't.

'. . . You could be suffering from symptoms of post-traumatic stress . . .'

Hair of the dog was what she needed. A sip of something strong and she'd be able to concentrate, tell Ali she was wrong.

'Memory transfer is a common side effect,' Ali continued. 'Something that happened a year ago may seem to have happened recently, or vice-versa. Shock can be devastating to the mind.' She put a leaflet down on the table, the letters PTSD staring up. 'There's a number you can call to talk to someone or arrange counselling.'

They thought Maggie was losing her senses, getting confused, mixing up reality with stories she'd been told.

Maggie squeezed her eyes shut, but that hurt too and bright dots floated across her vision. The dots were replaced by Maggie's boy, by Lee, his face screwed up, scared, sorry, missing his father and bracing himself for his mother's fist.

'You all right, Maggie?' Jennifer's hand was on Maggie's. Her skin hurt, her back, her stomach, oh God, her stomach.

She stumbled to her feet, reached for the counter, vomited into the sink.

'Tell her,' she could hear Ali saying to Jennifer, her voice already receding from the room, 'that Pale saw Mrs Greene himself. She's been cleared of all involvement.'

After the detective left Jennifer sat down, sighing with unmistakable relief. For her, it was over: the interviews, the police, the responsibility.

But Maggie, bent at the sink, could see the bag-for-life by Jennifer's feet. The map of London was poking out, the parks encircled in blue. She knew it wasn't over, not yet.

It wouldn't be over until she found her.

Nuala

Friday, 24th November, 2017

She held the letters above the bin. Her fingers were shaking, making the tears uneven. Some of the letters tore in half with precision, but others more clumsily, all with a crisp ripping sound, the fragments cascading down, some falling into the bin, some to the floor.

But her breathing wasn't so laboured.

And she had only showered once today, hadn't even rewashed her hair.

Was that what would happen, now? Every day she'd see a slight improvement, worry a little less, until she could pass herself off as normal?

But she dropped the matches four, five times before eventually one struck and lit. No, it wouldn't be so easy.

She'd had visitors yesterday, unexpected and unwelcome.

Afterwards she knew she would never be normal again.

'Mrs Greene? I'm PC Charlton,' the woman in uniform had said, standing on the doorstep the day before, a dark-haired man by her side. 'I've come from Kingston Police Station. This is Detective Sergeant Pale, from the Somerset constabulary . . .'

Pale looked beyond her to the hall, eyes scanning the dark carpet, ivory walls, the photographs that hung either side.

And then they lit upon her.

'There!' screamed a jackdaw, perched in a pine, beak pointing down to the house. 'There she is, there!' But neither officer looked at the tree.

The thump of her heart felt heavy, her knees and ankles weak. She could see the jackdaw, hear its call, could see Maggie's face in its feathers.

But all eyes were on her and the time had come, *her* time had come. As if she could get away with it, as if it would've worked. What had she been thinking—

'May we come in?' the WPC asked, her lips folded in an apologetic smile.

Then they were in the kitchen, sitting across the table, fruit flies and mould spores in the air. Perhaps she should have taken them to a different room, one less neglected. But which? All the rooms downstairs were the same. And she couldn't let them upstairs.

The letters were upstairs.

Her head was swimming with Pale's citrus aftershave, the sound of the flies.

'Can you tell me when you last saw your mother-in-law, Mrs Greene?'

And the room faded to grey, the calls from the birds let up. 'My mother-in-law?'

Where were the handcuffs? When would they read her her rights?

'Your mother-in-law, Mrs Lois Lunglow. Can you tell me when you last saw her?'

'I've never—' Could she do it? She looked from the woman to the man. Pale's head was slightly to one side, his dark eyes narrowed.

Charlton was smiling, waiting for the lie to complete.

What else was there to do?

'I've never met her,' she said, and the jackdaws woke up, calling her liar and worse.

'James never—' and she started to shake, the tremble spreading down her arms.

Pale stood still and watched her.

He wasn't smiling, just listening. Waiting to catch her out.

They knew what she had done.

She closed her eyes and held out her wrist.

Charlton reached forward, took her outstretched hand. 'Your mother-in-law was attacked at her home,' she said in a low, soft voice. 'I'm afraid she died at the scene.'

They told her how Lois was killed.

How a local girl committed suicide after the attack.

There was no one else involved, they said.

The inquiry had been handed to the coroner, they said.

The tremble in her body grew stronger, her face in agony as she tried to control it. She covered her mouth to stop the screaming, but the tears wouldn't let up.

Charlton kept hold of her hand.

Pale placed a mug of tea before her on the table.

'Have you ever been to that place, Mrs Greene?' he asked.

The tea hadn't been stirred and the milk was dancing, suspended in the dark water.

'Were you there the weekend of the 15th November, Mrs Greene?'

Of course, here it comes; they knew it was her all along.

They would have known the minute the door opened inwards, the second they saw her face. The things she had done were etched into her skin, the blood stained in the creases of her knuckles.

But still, she kept to the lie. 'I was at home last weekend, alone,' she said.

Pale's eyes never left her, narrowed and searching.

Charlton squeezed her hand again, nodded at Pale.

'Just procedure, Mrs Greene. I'm sorry for your loss,' she said.

Where were the handcuffs, where were her rights? Why couldn't they see who she was? A criminal, a murderer.

They had let her get away with murder.

Was it really as easy as that?

Except . . .

Except they could return at any minute.

They could decide to look upstairs.

They could take a closer look around the house, inspect the soiled clothes, the photographs on the walls, the shoe box of letters in the bedroom.

She had barely slept all night, convinced they would return, wondering what she should do, coming to a decision in the early hours of the morning. Now, the metal bin was in the bath, the letters, ripped to pieces, lying in its base, the shower hose ready if the flames got too much.

The match that finally lit did little to the wastepaper bonfire. It burned for a second, a flare of red and the smell of sparks and smoke. The edges burned briefly with a witch's cackle, but the flame was quick to go. The embers kept moving, though, sucking at the paper and turning it to ash, the black-grey spreading like a smouldering rash. The letters crumbled into a heap of fine grit.

The voice in her head said she'd done it, they believed her, she was free.

But, oh, what a small voice that was.

She turned on the shower hose, rinsing the last of the letters away. She would clean the house next, burn the stained clothes, delete the car's Sat-Nav history.

But in her haste to escape she had forgotten something vital, left something behind in that village so far, far away.

The last letter, the envelope with this address on it.

'It will all be OK,' she told herself. 'They won't find it.'

But the paranoia was impossible to shake. The ghost of the doorbell rang in her ears, the noise from the traffic outside all police.

She was convinced that every woman in the street had grey hair, every woman in the park was fat and scarred.

She had to prepare herself, had to be strong, willing to fight without a shotgun or doorstop.

Someone else was coming for her.

Maggie

Monday, 11th December, 2017

'Aren't you ready?' Jennifer stood at the back door, a black coat on over a dark trouser suit.

'It's today?' Maggie gasped, mortified at having forgotten. She stepped back, let Jennifer into the kitchen.

'I did remind you, yesterday.'

Maggie sighed, rubbed both hands across her face, felt the puckered scar beneath her fingertips.

'Have you anything to wear?' Jennifer asked, scanning the kitchen with her lips pressed together, eyes lingering on the pile of unopened letters by the bin, the recycling box half full of glass bottles, the pile of laundry shoved on the floor by the washing machine.

'I'll get dressed in a minute.' Maggie poured hot water into two mugs, reached for the gin bottle and splashed a measure into her own.

'What's this?' Jennifer asked, the Yellow Pages open in front of her. 'Private investigators?' She looked up, eyebrows raised, forehead puckered. 'Really?'

Maggie shrugged. No point arguing, no point defending herself, no point telling Jennifer it was no use anyway because

PIs cost money and Maggie didn't have enough, not nearly enough.

She set the mugs of tea down and slumped in a chair, head in her hands.

How could she have forgotten it was today?

'Let's get you ready,' Jennifer's voice softened as she reached over to touch Maggie's elbow.

Maggie lifted her mug and took a long sip, the tea burning the roof of her mouth. She didn't care. She swallowed, felt it burn her throat too. She stared at the pile of letters she couldn't bring herself to open.

Some were from the bank, wanting money.

Some were from the DVLA confirming the sale of her brown Rover, confirming the refund on her car tax. It had only been a few hundred pounds, but better than nothing. Better, by far, than staring at it every day, thinking of Emma driving it, thinking of Nuala driving it with Emma's body inside. (Was that what had happened, how Nuala had done it? Was that something worth writing down?)

And in there, somewhere, was the letter from the coroner confirming she wasn't to be called as a witness at the inquest in January; enough evidence could be garnered from the police, the paramedics, the pathologist, psychiatric consult. They didn't need an old, fat landlady who had fallen apart the minute she'd seen her goddaughter's blood. They'd already told her that she wasn't needed, was of no use, help, worth at all and would she please stop calling.

She had hoped the sale of her car would go some way towards paying for a private investigator, but she'd been naïve in estimating the cost, the paltry sum from her car not nearly enough.

The more time passed, the harder it got. Fewer people were willing to listen to her. But she had to make them see, understand, had to make them believe that Emma wasn't a murderer, not at all, she was kind and brave and Maggie loved her, still loved her and didn't want to let her down.

She'd thought she could put the money from the car towards today, the service, but Arthur Bradbury insisted that he pay for it. Then he offered, again, to buy the last of Maggie's farmland (*'What choice do you have?'*). He wouldn't talk to her about Emma, hung up the phone when Maggie tried to probe him about how he felt, what it had been like to identify her remains. She had wanted him to open up, prove that he had some humanity left in him, that she wasn't alone in missing Emma. But he'd given her nothing.

She finished the tea, planting the mug on the table, lining it up with an old water ring.

Where had Jennifer gone? She had said something about getting Maggie ready to go.

Oh, God.

Maggie's head cleared and she jumped up, pounded up the stairs.

She was out of breath by the top of them, her lungs burning.

'Don't!' she called out, but it was too late; Jennifer had already opened the bedroom door, seen the boxes.

She turned to Maggie. 'I thought we agreed that you'd stop this? I thought you agreed it wasn't healthy?'

'*You* said it wasn't healthy, not me,' Maggie said, trying her best to keep her voice calm, when all she wanted to do was tell Jennifer to mind her own business.

But she didn't have many friends left. And Jennifer was just worried, she knew that. It was the reason Maggie had promised to stop trying to find Nuala Greene, stop writing notes, making phone calls.

'Leave all this to the police, Maggie,' Jennifer said. 'Give yourself time to grieve properly.'

Maggie sighed, nodded. 'I will. Just leave it for today at least, please.' She motioned Jennifer downstairs. 'I'll get dressed, I'm quite capable.'

The wardrobe door was blocked by the two boxes, each brimming over with scribbled-on notes. To be sent to the coroner, the press (they could still be interested, she'd convinced herself,) the police for when they would inevitably reopen the case. She moved them away, to the foot of the bed, balancing them on another box of ring-binders and maps.

She knew the suit to wear; Tom's old suit, the one she had tailored to fitted her five years after he'd died. It was black, it still fitted her, and today she needed a part of him with her, a part of him holding her close.

She undressed and put her clothes in the laundry basket, which was half hidden behind the largest of three corkboards. This one showed a timeline of events from *that* weekend made out in Post-it notes of varying colours.

Once changed, she took the second corkboard, the one with the road map showing the motorways between London and the West, possible routes Nuala could have taken and service stations that may have caught her on CCTV, away from the mirror to make sure she looked fit to pass.

On the third board was a large map of London, the parks circled in blue, the ones who had agreed to talk to her and confirmed that a James Lunglow/Greene had never worked there crossed out in red. But most wouldn't talk to her, no matter how often she rang them. Confidential, apparently, they could neither confirm or deny the names of their employees, past or present, even if said employees were dead. There were still an awful lot of parks marked in blue. How was she going to find Nuala Greene if she couldn't afford an investigator, if the police weren't interested, if the coroner didn't want to talk to her?

Looking in the mirror, Maggie saw that the curls at the back of her head hung over the collar of her suit jacket, longer now Emma wasn't there to trim them. The sides were longer too, the odd grey hair fading to white.

The scar on her cheek, that purple ribbon of keloid flesh, had wrinkled at the edges. She'd lost weight. Normally the scar's tip was hidden beneath the folds of her chin but she could see it now, the neat point, half an inch below her jawline.

Her skin was pale, the whites of her eyes tinged yellow and spun with blood vessels. She looked just like she did seventeen years ago, when she had lost her husband, had stood at the grave with her crying son and couldn't bring herself to put her arms around him, comfort him, tell him it would all be OK because how could it be? How could it be OK?

She looked away from the mirror, sick of the sight of herself, of the memories her image induced. She found her black boots, put them on, slunk down the stairs to her friend.

'Jon and Toby are meeting us there,' Jennifer said, pulling a pair of gloves on. 'Shall we go?'

Maggie nodded. Paused at the door, took a deep breath. The exhalation shuddered out of her, making her shoulders tremble.

She felt Jennifer's gloved hand slide into her own, felt the squeeze of her friend's fingers. 'It'll be OK,' Jennifer said, and pulled Maggie out through the door.

They walked down the street, Jennifer's hand in the crook of Maggie's arm, huddled together against the cold. All the leaves had fallen from the trees, lay mouldering and wet at the sides of the road.

The sky was clear; no clouds, just a sun low and bright.

Not another soul walked the street. The cows were quiet, so too the cars on the road, the sheep on the hill. Even the crowscarer couldn't be heard.

Ahead rose the church's steeple. As they reached the church's door Maggie moved to open it, but Jennifer stopped her.

'Where are you going, Mags? It's this way.' She pulled Maggie's arm, tried to lead her away.

Maggie dug her heels in. 'What do you mean, this way? Why aren't we going inside?' Her knees felt weak; had she failed Emma again? 'Are we too late?' she asked, voice panicked. 'Did we miss it, the service?'

'Maggie.' Jennifer's eyes dropped. 'There's no service.'

'There's always a service,' Maggie said, feeling in her pocket for the speech she'd prepared a week ago, writing down everything about Emma, every good little thing until her heart broke again and she could write not a single word more. 'It's her funeral,' she said. 'There's always a service first.'

'It's not a funeral, just a burial.' Jennifer stepped closer, resting her hand against Maggie's back.

'But Arthur was paying for the funeral! I wanted to arrange it myself, you remember. I wanted to do it and he said no, pulled the kinship card, took control. He said he was paying!' Her voice was high, anxious.

She knew there was to be no procession, no hearse driving slowly through the streets. She knew Arthur hadn't arranged a wake, a remembrance . . . but no service? No prayers for his daughter, no hymns?

'Arthur didn't pay for a service; just to have Emma buried in the yard.' Jennifer guided Maggie forward, away from the church to the graves at the side.

Maggie's clutched the piece of paper in her coat pocket.

At the back of the church there was Toby, blond hair bright in the sunlight. Beside him was his father, Jon. The vicar stood in dark robes, bible to chest, surreptitiously peeking at his watch.

There was nobody else. No drinkers from the pub, no friends, no old teachers. Even Emma's own father hadn't bothered to attend. How could he do this?

And there was the grave prepared for Emma. Maggie closed her eyes, felt for her friend's arm and held tight to it.

A hole in the earth, six feet long and so dark, so deep, a mound of soil beside it.

The vicar looked up, 'Shall we begin?' he asked in soft tones, his face solemn.

Maggie stared at the hole, at the gravestone next to it. She would have organised a *funeral*. She would have chosen hymns, prayers, readings. She would have made them all come, everyone who had known her, would have stood in front of them all and told them who Emma was, really was, the difference she had made to Maggie. She would have given her goddaughter flowers, music, would have made everyone come back to the pub afterwards to raise a glass to her name.

Beside the hole in the ground was the coffin, waiting in the cold.

It wasn't enough, none of this was enough.

'Like as a father pitieth his own children: even so is the

Lord merciful unto them that fear him. For he knoweth whereof we are made . . .'

Maggie's ears felt like they were full of water. She couldn't see the vicar, or Jennifer, or the pile of soil at her feet.

Instead, she remembered Arthur, neat black suit and black shirt beneath, drunk after burying his first wife.

'*She was born bad,*' Arthur had said, his drunk gaze fixed on the infant daughter he still couldn't bear to hold. '*First thing she did was kill her mother.*'

Maggie had tried to talk him down, but she was drunk herself and made a hash of it.

Emma wasn't born bad, quite the opposite. She grew up to be so very good.

Emma had saved Maggie's life when she moved into the pub, stopped her drinking herself to death on neat gin, limiting her to a capful per cup of tea. All that, on the shoulders of a girl so young, just fourteen, who had already lost so much. '*I can't lose you too, Mags,*' she had said, '*I can't lose you too.*'

'. . . But the merciful goodness of the Lord endureth,' the vicar continued, his thin, tired voice battling the cold breeze, 'for ever and ever upon them that fear him . . .'

Jennifer sniffed, a tissue held to her face.

'*Not a good bone in this girl's body,*' Arthur had slurred to Maggie at the wake of Emma's real mother, twenty-one years ago, knocking the bassinet she was sleeping in with his foot. As Emma grew older and found out what had happened, how her poor mother had died, Arthur never hugged her or reassured her it wasn't her fault, that of course it wasn't her fault. She'd been a baby, an innocent baby and he loved her. Instead, he took her to the grave on her birthday every year, showed her the place her mother was buried and reminded her of her part in it all.

The vicar touched Maggie's shoulder, signalling to the mound of soil by his side. Maggie took a handful, her arms like lead, hands numb to the touch of the earth.

'We commend unto thy hands of mercy, most merciful Father, the soul of this our sister departed, and we commit her body to the ground, earth to earth, ashes to ashes . . .'

But Maggie still wasn't listening. She barely felt the cold, granulated soil move through her fingers, or the wind pick up and ruffle her hair.

The only sound she heard was the earth hitting the coffin, a dry, hollow patter as it landed on the chipboard lid.

The coffin was gradually covered, Jon, Jennifer, Toby each throwing in a handful. Emma's final resting place was a coffin made from unvarnished chipboard, the nails splitting veins in the lid.

It was too much for Maggie, too much because it wasn't nearly enough.

Beside Emma's grave was Tom's. Maggie brushed her thumb over the inscription, knew he would look after Emma, laid to rest in the plot by his side, the plot Maggie had bought and insisted on Emma being buried in.

It was the sole concession Arthur had granted to Maggie.

The thought of Arthur was like a vile taste in her mouth.

So much of this mess was that man's fault and no one had ever held him accountable. Not yet, anyway.

She turned on her heel, staggered back through the graves, against the cold wind that bit at her skin.

She didn't stop to say *thank you, God bless,* to the vicar in his stark robes, ignored Jennifer's call to her.

Her tongue burned with the words she needed to say, her pulse quickening the closer she got to him.

Arthur.

The man at the root of it all.

Maggie

Monday, 11th December, 2017

When she got to the house the curtains were drawn even though it was the middle of the day. His Land Rover was parked outside.

Maggie knocked on the door with her fist, stepped back. She could feel her heart thudding, chest aching from the rush of adrenaline. She heard the shuffle of slippers on carpet, the progress painfully slow.

'I thought you'd come,' Arthur slurred when he finally opened the door, the sun catching the day-old stubble on his chin like fresh frost.

He didn't meet Maggie's eye. Head bent, he turned and shuffled back into the house, the door left open for Maggie to follow.

He'd lost weight, just as Maggie had, but now he looked like a skeleton, wrapped in clothes a few sizes too big. He hadn't got dressed, was still in pyjamas. He looked less like the bully Maggie knew him to be and more like a broken, white-haired old man.

Maybe he didn't come to the church, arrange a proper funeral, because he couldn't bear to bury his daughter, couldn't face choosing flowers for her, hymns, prayers. So he hid at home, wearing last night's pyjamas.

Maybe this was why he had refused to discuss Emma's death with Maggie, at all, until now.

The house hadn't changed in seven years, since the last time she'd been invited inside. The rug was the same, a little worn down the centre line. The chairs were all covered in dust sheets.

Arthur shuffled his way into the study at the end of the hall, Maggie following. His hair was quite white now, his neck wrinkled. The man was in his seventies but looked older, much older.

'I presume you're here,' Arthur said, turning around with a piece of paper in his hand, 'for this?'

He held it out to her.

'It's the right thing to do,' he said as she read it. 'After all, what choice do you have?'

'What choice do you have?' That phrase again, making her think of the phone call from Arthur the very night that Nuala arrived, Maggie hiding downstairs in the cellar at home, the phone pressed to her ear whilst she listened to Arthur's latest demand to buy her land, Emma in the bar above her, still alive, gloriously alive.

'What is this?' Maggie said, staring down at the cheque in her hand, the sum of money insulting, nauseating. Only worth half of his last offer. 'You think I'm here because of this? Because I want your money?'

'You need my money.'

Her cheeks burned, her scar too, and she glared at him. 'Is that what you said to Edward when he kept your little secret safe? What you said to Jim? To *Lois*?' She expected him to baulk, look up in shock, in horror at having been unmasked. She expected him to be as frail and broken as he looked.

He wasn't.

'Well?' Maggie said, but Arthur shrugged carelessly, arrogantly. 'Is that what you said when James was born?' Maggie went on, shifting her weight from hip to hip, her left side hot from the fire. 'Did you offer her money to keep the fact that you were his real father quiet?'

'Are you trying to increase my offer, Maggie? Trying to wring my pockets dry? Because you can't prove anything, you know. Not a thing. But I'll tell you what,' he said, leaning forward, the sides of his mouth crusted with stale spit. 'I'll give you another hundred if it'd make you feel better.'

'I don't want your money.'

He laughed a coughing hack of a laugh. 'You need my money,' he said again. 'You need to sell that land or you'll lose everything else that you own. How else are you going to keep your pub running, keep your home, keep food on the table?' He looked up at her, eyes glinting, the left corner of his mouth twitching back a smile. 'How else are you going to keep gin in your tea?'

Maggie's skin tingled. She crumpled the cheque in her fist.

'How dare you,' she hissed. 'You think I want your money? You think I want anything from you? A rapist? A paedophile? Look at yourself! You're disgusting, pathetic!'

'Call me all the names under the sun, it won't change a damn thing. I'm not the one with a failing business, with no money, no investment. Who's the pathetic one, Maggie?'

His voice was calm, level and low, making Maggie sound high pitched and strained.

'Where were you today?' Maggie asked him. 'Why didn't you come to the church?'

He looked away, his face blank of emotion. She remembered again him kicking the bassinet, telling Emma what a bad little baby she was. Why didn't Maggie do something then? Why didn't she take Emma away with her, then?

Because that was when Arthur met Elaine, at the wake of his dead first wife, and Maggie had let herself believe it would all be OK, that Emma would be in safe hands.

A photo caught her eye, sitting on the edge of the desk, a photo of Emma at twelve or thirteen. Pretty and young, blond hair pulled back from her face, her blue eyes looking up at the camera as she sat on the garden wall.

'How could you not come?' She thought of the pub, her home, how little it all meant without Emma. 'How could you do that to her?'

Arthur didn't reply, his head turned towards the log fire.

'She deserved more!' Maggie shouted, planting herself in front of Arthur, making him look up at her, take notice. 'You're her father, for God's sake! You should have been there! You should have seen her off properly, given her flowers, given her a decent fucking coffin to lay down in!'

'I've done more than enough for that girl,' he growled, his dark eyes shooting a warning to Maggie.

'You've done nothing but hurt her,' Maggie cried in despair, 'physically, emotionally—'

'Who do you think paid off the fire chief?' Arthur leaned forward in his chair, the light from the fire making his face look red. 'Convinced him that Lois's house fire was an accident? I may not have wanted that girl in my house but I didn't want her in prison, either.'

'You did that to keep Lois quiet!'

'Quiet about what?' Arthur asked coldly, his face infuriatingly calm.

'About you *raping her* as a teenager!' Maggie shouted, 'About you beating her up on the day Emma lost the baby! About the fact that you were James's real father!'

'Don't get me started on that boy.' Arthur sat back in the chair, folded his arms and stared back at Maggie, defiant. 'I saved Emma from him, too, not that she knew it.'

Maggie opened her mouth to contest him, but how could she? There was no defence for James, nothing that righted his wrongdoing.

'And how did Emma repay me?' Arthur said in the same sour voice. 'By growing up to be a waste of space.'

'How can you say that?' Maggie pleaded, 'She was a wonderful girl, a brilliant young woman—'

'She was a girl who threw her body around, first with James, her own *brother*, and then with anyone who'd look at her.'

'What are you talking about? She didn't know who he was and she's only had three boyfriends since then, for Christ's sake!'

'She was sleeping with the Hill boy, last I heard. A farmhand, a nobody.'

'She was twenty-one, a grown woman, she could see whoever she liked, do what she liked!'

'No!' He spat the words out, spittle landing on his knees. 'She was a murderer, an embarrassment and a *whore*.'

'She was my daughter!' Maggie cried, and then stopped herself, realising the mistake she had made.

Arthur laughed at her. 'No, she wasn't. She was *my*

daughter, not yours. You were her godmother, a figurehead, nothing more, nothing at all.'

'That's not what I meant,' Maggie said, though she knew that it was, that she'd always felt that way about Emma, always. 'I meant I loved her as if she were my own. I loved her and you pushed her away!'

'The only way that girl could have turned out any worse,' Arthur said, squaring his thin shoulders, 'is if you had been her real mother.'

'How dare you,' Maggie said, but her eyes stung at the words.

'How is your son doing, Maggie? Did Lee ever forgive you for the mess of a mother you were?'

'Don't you—' But it was true and Maggie knew it.

'You call yourself a mother, but your own son won't go near you. You call Emma your daughter but you didn't see this coming! You missed it, all those signs, missed the despair she must have felt, the depression! How did you fail to realise she'd dropped so low, Maggie?'

'I didn't,' she said, stepping back. 'I couldn't.'

'Why not?' Arthur said, leaning forward again. 'Blind, were you? *Drunk*?'

She hadn't been blind, she hadn't been drunk, she hadn't, not once whilst Emma had lived under her roof. Emma had saved her from all that.

There was one reason alone Maggie had missed all those signs, one truth she believed in more than anything.

'I didn't see it,' Maggie said, 'because Emma didn't do it. She didn't kill Lois, she didn't kill herself!'

Arthur laughed at her again, loudly. 'You've lost your mind, Maggie. You've lost all sense of reason.'

'She didn't!' Maggie balled up the cheque, threw it straight at his face. 'She didn't do it!' She turned to go.

'You'll be back,' Arthur said, smoothing out the cheque on his knee and flattening his palm upon it. 'You need this, Maggie!'

But she had gone, left the room, the door slamming closed in her wake, each step onward fuelled by her fury. She would see to it that Arthur was punished for his past, his treatment of Lois, Elaine and his daughter. But more importantly than that, than anything else, Maggie would clear her goddaughter's name.

Emma didn't do it.

Maggie would prove it, somehow. Maggie would show them all.

She would show them how far she was willing to go.

Maggie

Tuesday, 12th December, 2017

What had she been thinking?

Why had she come?

'For Emma, I came for Emma,' she said to herself. Her throat prickled.

She sat on the bench at the far end of the platform. She was shaking.

She didn't want it to show, draw attention.

But it could be too late for that. A fat old woman with a scar down her face, wearing her dead husband's mac and clutching a pink rucksack to her chest, faded pony stickers peeling from the sides, Emma's name written in childish scrawl along the strap.

Why had she thought she could do this, alone?

In Bristol, the platform had smelled of engine oil and stale coffee. But here, in Paddington, she couldn't define it. Petrol, bird shit, sweat, cloves, feet, cigarettes and stale beer.

Two girls in matching velour tracksuits laughed. One pointed a purple-painted fingernail at Maggie.

Pointed at her mullet of short curls, her scarred face, the androgynous clothes she wore.

She staggered on, but the passengers behind were eager to

pass, pushing her this way and that, the occasional 'sorry,' thrown back behind them.

Then there was the guard in uniform, staring at her.

The sweat built up at the nape of Maggie's neck. She could feel them all staring at her.

Once she found the right platform she sat with her head hanging low, hands wringing the pink rucksack.

A memento of Emma. A reminder of why she was sitting in Paddington station, less than an hour from Nuala Greene's front door.

Because she knew now, she knew where she lived. She had *found* her.

What was that noise?

Footsteps.

Maggie looked up, down the platform, watched the clicking step of a woman wrapped up in a quilted jacket, impossible heels on her feet. The other woman didn't look at Maggie, not once, nor at the bag held tight to Maggie's heaving chest.

Breathe, she told herself, breathe.

People kept coming, the benches filling, people standing, people leaning against the wall, people everywhere.

She looked at her phone in her pocket, checked the time. The old phone she never updated, had resisted all attempts by Emma to modernise, download apps, social media, email. This one did everything she needed, phone calls and the odd text, and worked as a pocket watch too.

They would be missing her by now, at home.

She thought of Jennifer banging on the pub door, finding the letter Maggie had left for her, explaining, begging her not to tell anyone, not to follow.

She imagined Jennifer calling the police all the same, telling them where Maggie was heading.

And she thought of DS Pale going through the pub, Ali close behind, finding the letter she'd left addressed to them both. The letter detailing Arthur's actions, what he'd done to Lois all those years ago, how Edward Burrows was the last living witness. She didn't want Arthur to go unpunished. She left it on the kitchen table, just in case she got caught up in London, never came back. Nuala Greene had already killed two people, after all.

She turned the phone off, slipped it beneath her on the bench. She would leave it behind. She'd watched enough television, read enough books, to know the phone signal could lead the police straight to her.

Maybe that's why Nuala had left her phone in London when she had come, weeks ago, to the village. That's what Ali had said, that the GPS hadn't moved on her phone for weeks. It had formed part of her alibi.

Nuala Greene.

The name was like lemon juice at the back of her throat, making her jaw clench, tongue prickle, nose smart.

She was here because of Nuala Greene.

Because of everything Nuala Greene had taken from her.

'I'm here for *Emma*,' Maggie said under her breath, eyes shut. 'I can do this for her.'

She took a small map out of her bag, unfolded it, used her finger to trace the line from the station to the top of Nuala's road.

Eyes closed, she pictured the route she would take, the road signs she would see. It was just one more train ride away.

She reached into her bag and pulled out the only thing left: the prize.

The letter to James that Nuala had left in the guest room. She knew Pale had never searched it himself, suspected the SOCOs of only giving the guest room a cursory glance, having found enough 'evidence' in Emma's bedroom.

She tried to muster the same sense of relief she'd felt last night, the hallelujah of finding the envelope wedged between the bedside table and the mattress, James and Nuala's address on show. It felt like a sign from up above, from Tom, from Emma, that she was doing the right thing, that it would all go to plan.

She held the letter in her hand, the edges digging into her fleshy palm.

Nuala must have thought Emma had written this letter to James, that Emma had been trying to lure James home, back to her. Nuala's jealousy, her mania, must have driven her over the edge.

Maggie couldn't bring herself to look at it, to look at that writing again.

She would know Emma's handwriting anywhere.

She'd seen it every day for seven years, had recognised it on the photocopied suicide note that DS Pale had pushed across the card table.

Emma hadn't written this letter.

And Maggie knew who had.

Maggie wanted to shout, curse the name, but her voice was a pathetic whisper, lost to the clack of the trains. 'Lois Lunglow.'

Nuala had said that Lois told her that Emma had written the letters.

Why did Lois lie?

Maggie pondered the letter, thinking how desperately Lois must have longed for her son to return, how devastated she must have been to find out he would never come back.

Lois must have lied to Nuala as some kind of sick revenge, to make her angry, make her jealous, perhaps unaware that she was pushing a woman who had already lost her husband, her parents, to the edge. Why had she done it? Was it to get back at Nuala for marrying James, perhaps thinking it was Nuala who kept him away from the village? Or was it punishment for not telling her James was dead sooner, petty comeuppance for cremating him without her, as if her lie could reverse time and change that?

Or worse. Could Lois have told Nuala the lie suspecting, perhaps even knowing, how Nuala would react? What she was likely to do to Emma, the woman Lois had blamed all along for James's absence, probably blamed too for the fire that destroyed her house?

When had Lois started writing the letters? After the fire, after her house was burned down? When her life unravelled even further, when the only man who offered to help her was the one who had raped her as a girl, fathered her child then attacked her again, years later? That's when she'd started writing, Maggie knew it, felt it. That's when she would have tracked James down, begged him to come back, because she felt no one else would help her.

Not her neighbours, not her family, not Maggie who had failed her so long ago with her silence.

Did Nuala know about everything Lois had been through?

Maggie opened her fist, the letter turned to pulp.

A reminder of how strong she was, what her thick-fingered,

powerful hands could do. She pictured them wrapped around a gas canister, changing the barrels at home, her weight and the bulk of her arms adding to their force.

Nuala Greene was one more train ride away.

She dropped the pulped letter, closed the bag, her train at last approaching.

She knew what she was going to do, what she was prepared to do.

Nuala

Tuesday, 12th December, 2017

If only she hadn't left that last letter behind, in the pub. How could she have been so short-sighted?

Every day she checked online, waiting for the date of the inquest, wanting it to be over, the case closed, forgotten.

But one person, she knew, would never forget.

And that person was everywhere she looked. Today she was even behind her in the queue for the cashpoint, a fat woman with grey hair.

But no, that wasn't Maggie.

But the reflection of an old woman in the nearby shop window, was that her?

No; it was just a reflection. Only light on glass.

Her own reflection had changed. Thinner than ever, pimples across her hairline and back, hair lank and thinning from stress.

She reached the cashpoint; took out her bank card, entered the PIN, withdrew the daily maximum limit. Half she would add to a pre-pay debit card. The other she would keep as cash. She had a few thousand gathered so far, but that wasn't enough, not nearly enough, to get out of this city, run away before anyone discovered the truth.

The old woman behind urged her on with a cough.

She took her money, slid it inside her purse and moved off without meeting the old woman's eye, fearing she'd see a scarred cheek after all.

Maggie.

She was everywhere, driving every car that passed on the road, serving behind shop counters, walking through garden gates, selling the *Big Issue* in a bundle of thick coats. Even men, walking with a roll and hair growing over their collars, looked like Maggie did from behind.

Money in her purse, she stopped at a crossing.

But there, look there, who was that in the shop window?

Who was that riding the top deck on that bus?

She turned her back on the road, the cars, buses, people. She needed to get back, to get home, needed her heart rate to slow, to calm down.

She would come back later, to add the cash to her pre-pay card. It would give her something to do, focus on. It would help fill her long, empty day.

The pavement was slippery beneath her leather boots, the breeze ripping through her thin coat. She pulled her scarf over the bottom of her face, her hands deep in her pockets. Head down, hat pulled low, she walked on past the clothes shops and cafes, avoiding people, their gaze, their curiosity.

She could feel eyes on her back but didn't turn round.

The streets were getting quieter now, more residential as she neared the park.

She could sense a car slowing beside her; she ignored it.

The money in her bag burned hot at her side.

She had to get home, add it to the rest, plan her impending escape.

She couldn't go on like this, not forever, couldn't pretend to live the life of an innocent, scared that anyone looking her way was a detective off duty, would recognise the guilty look in her eye.

She had to start afresh, somewhere new, put on weight, dye her hair, melt into the obscurity of the normal.

Nearly home. Nearly there.

Soon she would be able to lock the door, turn out the lights, close the curtains, keep the outside world, the police and all the Maggies, at bay.

It was somehow worse that the police weren't interested in her, all her excuses and alibis gone to waste. No one talked to her; not one person had knocked on her door, the phone hadn't rung save for sales calls.

She'd cleaned the house, three times, from top to bottom.

There was someone there, at the top of her road, who was that?

No one, just another old woman in an oilskin with grey curling hair.

Her nerves were getting too much to bear. Only inside the house was she at peace, able to plan her escape with calm logic.

She felt in her pocket for the bunch of steel keys, cold, hard, sharp in her hand.

The grey-haired woman was speeding up now, her walk familiar.

Was that the trace of a scar on her cheek?

No, no.

It couldn't be.

She looked down at the keys, found the right one as she walked up the path to the house.

Her feet skidded on the stones as she reached the front door.

She heard a rasp of breath from the old woman jogging past on the street.

She placed the keys in the lock, heard the same breath behind her, getting closer, the old woman's reflection closing in on the door.

She twisted the key, pushed the door open. She had to get in.

Too late.

She felt the hands reach for her, her feet losing purchase on the stones.

She grabbed the keys, still stuck in the lock, but couldn't wrench them free before Maggie had her.

The old woman's hands wrapped around her neck, but the scarf saved her, tangled between Maggie's fingers and stopped her from squeezing.

Eyes wide with panic, she cried out, but no one was there, no one heard her.

She tried to scratch, lash out with her flailing arms, but too late again.

A push to her back and she fell through the doorway, her handbag thudding hard on the floor, a picture frame falling from the wall.

The old woman was grunting, face red, that angry scar pulsing, hair dishevelled by the wind.

Maggie stood above her as she scrabbled on the floor, tried to stand. She looked up at Maggie, her eyes pleading, her face covered, muffled, by the scarf.

Maggie came closer, hands outstretched and strong, ready to hold her by the neck and squeeze tight.

But she shuffled back along the floor, pulled the hat off her head, flung it away.

Maggie paused, hands mid-air, fingers twitching.

She moved backwards on the Persian rug again, increased the space between her and Maggie, took the scarf and pulled that down, too.

She stared at Maggie, the older woman looming over her, cheeks losing their angry colour, eyes moving from hatred to horror.

She pulled the scarf off, and looked up, showed Maggie the full view of her face.

Maggie

Tuesday, 12th December, 2017

Without taking her eyes off the woman on the floor, Maggie stumbled backwards against the door.

She couldn't look at the woman's face; only her hands. The hands she'd seen hundreds of times ringing the bell in the pub, drying pint glasses, stirring tea.

But whilst her heart filled with hope, Maggie's head still screamed, *no, no, no!*

A glimmer of light refracted off a piece of broken glass on the floor, caught her eye. A picture frame. James was hidden by the splintered wooden casing but Nuala was there, looking, smiling, taunting Maggie with the face of the woman she'd expected to see.

She shut her eyes, rubbed her face.

She was dead. Maggie had buried the girl herself, thrown soil on the chipboard lid.

This woman was a ghost, a phantom, a terrible lie. She wasn't real, she couldn't possibly be.

But this woman coughed and rubbed her neck, looked up with wide, blue eyes.

Maggie opened her mouth and tried to speak but she couldn't, she could barely breathe.

She forced her eyes up and finally looked, finally *saw* her. Emma.

Emma.

'I thought you were her!' She looked around her, the photo smashed on the floorboards, the Persian rug. Anything but look at her face. 'I thought you were Nuala.'

Emma pulled herself upright, stood facing Maggie.

'I could have killed you, oh, Jesus!' Maggie's hands were at her face. 'Oh, Emma, my God! I could have—' But no more words would come, replaced by a sob that squeezed her throat tight.

She could see her more clearly now, her eyes adjusting to the gloom of the hallway. Emma's skin was sallow, body thin, arms barely more than bone.

But she was alive. She was standing, breathing, living. And Maggie had almost—

What had she done? How could she? She would never have been able to live with herself if she had done to Emma what she had wanted to do to Nuala Greene.

She forced her eyes to rise above Emma's scrawny shoulders and jutting collarbone, saw her face.

She was smiling.

Her lips were smiling and tears had gathered in her eyes.

Maggie reached for her, held her head to her chest, kissed her hair, felt her skin beneath her fingertips, electrified by the very touch of her.

'You're alive.' She held her away at arm's length, marvelling at her hands, her face, her shoulder blades. Marvelling that her scent, that mixture of gardenia and bleach, was filling her senses again. 'You're alive!' she repeated and Emma laughed, nodded, held Maggie's hands in her own and squeezed.

'I don't understand. How is it that you're here? I thought . . .' Maggie looked at the photographs still on the wall, Nuala and James in monochrome, their cheeks pressed together. 'It doesn't matter what I thought.'

Emma shook her head, said, 'It was Nuala,' and tried to say more but her eyes filled with tears, her face crumpled.

'You need a drink, a cup of tea to get over the shock.' Maggie took her hand, tried to usher her down the hall, but she dug her heels in the rug, wouldn't move, forced Maggie to look at her again.

She mouthed something that Maggie couldn't hear.

Moving closer, her mouth millimetres from Maggie's ear, she tried again.

Maggie jumped back as if burnt.

'Of course I won't tell anyone, not a soul!'

The pictures on the walls looked on, Nuala smiling, James with one eyebrow raised.

Emma breathed out and nodded, slipped out of her boots, took Maggie's hand and led her to the kitchen. Maggie could feel each of Emma's knuckles, each bone and tendon on the back of her hand.

They passed the living room, the door ajar. Inside, a phone began to ring. Another started upstairs, and another in the kitchen.

Emma looked into the room and shrugged, waved her hand and let the phone ring. She continued into the kitchen, flicked on the kettle and poured herself a glass of water from a filter jug in the fridge.

Maggie leant against the butcher's block, eyebrows raised

as she contemplated the miracle before her, trying not to grin like an idiot, trying not to laugh, sing, spin Emma around and dance her across the floorboards.

'Did Nuala tell you to come here? What happened?' Maggie asked, but Emma had lifted the water to take a sip, watched Maggie over the rim of the glass.

The room was long, painted white with bleached floorboards. A wall of windows overlooked the overgrown garden. At the far end, on the opposite side of the winter-stripped hedge, Maggie could see the fields and trees of the park where James had worked.

'Lois had been writing to James, anonymously. Did you know that?' She looked at Emma. 'I think Nuala must have thought it was you.'

The phone stopped ringing and they both looked towards it. Only the grumbling boil of the kettle remained.

'I thought Nuala had come to confront you,' Maggie said, 'that she killed you for the letters and Lois for tormenting her, but clearly not. She must have killed Lois and then herself, the grief having driven her mad. I thought her unbalanced, she'd obviously been affected by James's death, Lois must have pushed Nuala beyond her limit when she started talking about you, your history with James. Maybe we'll never know why Nuala did it, what was going on inside her head.'

'Maybe not,' Emma said, placing the glass on the counter with a *ting*. 'But those letters drove her over the edge.'

A steel cook's knife rested by the kettle. She opened a drawer below it and withdrew a teaspoon. From an overhead cupboard she took a packet of chocolate digestives, throwing them over for Maggie to catch. Duchy Originals. Clearly, Nuala's tastes exceeded McVitie's.

Maggie took them and sat at the kitchen table, solid oak with eight ladderback chairs and an embroidered cloth running down its centre line. A dark stain marked the wood at the edge of the tablecloth. She lifted it with her finger, exposing smudges of browns and greys and catching a faint, sweet smell of rotten fruit.

Her stomach was churning, head light from hunger. She turned to see how Emma was getting on with the tea, waiting for her before opening the digestives. Emma's back was turned to Maggie, her fingers drumming the countertop as she waited for the kettle to boil. When she found the tea she stood, staring with a furrowed brow. Teabag in one hand, loose leaf in the other.

'Either's fine, love.' Maggie smiled but Emma didn't return it, only nodded soberly and looked down at the loose leaf in her hand.

The phone rang again, the insistent shrill repeating three-fold through the house.

Emma huffed, moved towards it. 'I'll get rid of them,' she said to Maggie and then, on answering the phone, 'Hello, yes, this is Fionnuala Greene.' She cradled the phone to her shoulder whilst Maggie tried not to look, tried not to dwell on the ease with which Emma used the dead woman's name, the ease with which she changed her West Country tones to that of the generic home counties.

Maggie looked round the room as she waited, unsure of what to do with herself.

A welsh dresser filled with fine bone china took up half of the far wall, the other half lined with thick wooden shelves holding candles, vases and a bronze-stemmed Tiffany lamp. The occasional space in between showed tell-tale scuffs and discoloration, marks on the wood where picture frames should have been.

Her mind fled back to Lois, to the bare walls in her house, to her head, resting on the kitchen table in a pool of thickening blood.

What had happened? Why was Emma here?

A click as the phone was put down.

'Here you are.'

Maggie jumped as Emma placed the mug of tea on the table, her socked feet silent on the floorboards.

Her skin was paler in the light from the window. Maggie ripped open the biscuits and dunked them, two at a time, in her tea, hoping they would make her feel better, hoping to feel the relief she had felt in the hallway, the joy of seeing Emma in the flesh.

What had happened?

The tea was hot, melting the chocolate on the biscuits.

She ran a finger around her collar, made malleable with sweat, and shrugged the oilskin from her shoulders.

'Don't!' Emma leant over, one hand on the sleeve of her coat. 'You can't stay.'

The shadows under her eyes were dark purple.

She wasn't smiling any more.

'And you can't tell anyone you've seen me.' She spoke to her half-drunk glass of water. 'I mean it.'

'I said already, I won't tell.' Maggie tried to smile. She ate another tea-dunked biscuit and carried on, 'What happened? Can you tell me that, before I go?'

Emma's eyes lifted to the white-rimmed clock on the wall above Maggie's head. 'Nuala told me about James and the letters. She'd worked out that they were from Lois, and felt bad for everything that had happened to me.' She spoke quickly, not a single breath between words. 'She was desperate, half mad. Told me she was going to walk out onto the hill and jump off, that she wanted to die in the village where James was born so everyone would remember her as *his* wife and perhaps forget he was once my boyfriend.'

She gave a short laugh then coughed, blinked hard. 'I tried to talk her out of it but she wouldn't listen. And then she gave me her bag, her keys; told me to take it, all of it, and start a new life somewhere else.'

Emma took a biscuit, picked at it. 'It was a way of saying sorry, I think, for everything James and Lois had done. She was offering me a way out, a remedy for James's cowardice.'

She looked at Maggie and shrugged. 'I took it. I took her bag, her car and came here. It wasn't until the next day that I found out what really happened.'

Emma left the biscuit alone. 'And the business with the suicide note; she didn't write her own name on it. She must have known that everyone would think she was me, must have intended to give me her identity. Don't you think?'

Maggie ate the remaining four biscuits, their debris falling into her mug. 'It sounds that way.' She looked past Emma to the park outside, a man and woman pushing a pram, collars pulled up against the cold. Her throat was dry and she could have done with another mug of tea, but Emma looked pale, her tired eyes darting, and Maggie didn't want to ask for more.

'I should have come clean, told the police, but then the postman knocked on the door and called me Mrs Greene. And a delivery arrived, food that Nuala had ordered a week before she left, and the driver called me Mrs Greene, too.'

Emma's heels were tapping a dull rhythm on the floor. She slid the glass from hand to hand across the table, her eyes flicking to the clock on the wall. 'It was as if I'd gone to sleep and woken up in her life. I kept expecting a friend or neighbour to knock on the door but no one has; I don't think she had anyone.' She shrugged again.

'What about DS Pale?'

Her eyes darkened, her gaze fixed on her glass. 'Same as everyone else; he thought I was *her*.'

'But Arthur identified you, he saw your body in the morgue!'

'Nuala had shot herself in the face! And besides, Daddy hasn't looked at me properly in seven years, anyone could have been on that table and as long as their hair was blond, he would have thought they were me.' Emma met her gaze and Maggie was struck suddenly by her resemblance to someone, who was it? The shape of her face and sharp cheekbones, who did she remind Maggie of?

'I know it's wrong of me, Maggie, I know I should have told the truth, but it's my chance to escape, to start a new life where no one knows me as the girl who got screwed at fourteen, the girl whose own father won't talk to her, still blames her for the death of both her mothers. I just wanted to get out; you have to understand that? And what options did I have, considering my money was all gone?'

Emma's face darkened with the final line, and Maggie blushed, looked down.

'Please tell me you understand?'

Maggie took Emma's hand across the table, her skin cold. 'I understand.' She waited for Emma to squeeze her hand back, but she didn't.

Maggie looked out at the garden, the grass rippling in the wind, the dead rose, and thought of the sessile oaks at home, the silver birch and sloes. 'I wish I could take you with me, though.' She laughed. 'I wish I could tell that bloody DS Pale I was right all along!'

Emma's hand shot away, 'You can't! Maggie, you can't—'

'I'm joking, it's all right.' She tried to laugh again but it stuck in her throat. Emma looked up at the clock.

'Who was it, by the way?' Maggie asked.

'Who was what?'

'On the phone?'

Emma's eyes were darting about, stopping every few seconds to look at the clock, the empty mug of tea, the phone on the wall, the knife.

'I think you should leave.' Emma pushed back her chair and stood up. 'You should go back home.'

'What is it? Who was on the phone?'

Emma wouldn't look Maggie in the eye. 'Don't tell anyone you saw me. I'll write to you, I'll find a way, but you *have to go.*'

'Who was on the phone?' Maggie hadn't meant to shout, regretted it as soon as Emma jumped, hands flying up to her face.

Emma's face caved in, eyebrows gathering in the centre like a knot. 'Why did you have to come?'

The couple walking in the park had stopped. The woman, a pretty young thing with dark, bobbed hair, was pointing to the house.

'Who was on the phone?' Maggie said again.

'The police.' Emma hugged herself, her thin fingers gripping at the bones of her upper arm. 'They know you're in

London, that you're trying to find Nuala Greene.' She looked back to the clock, 'They told me not to worry. They told me you won't be able to find me, that you don't have the address. They're going to send a car to keep an eye on the house, make sure I'm safe. One will drive by every twenty minutes until they find you. You have to go. *Now.*'

'No, it's best if I wait.' Maggie stared at the couple outside. The man had his arms around the woman's shoulders, leading her away, the woman craning her neck to see over the hedge. 'We'll wait until the first car has gone, then we'll know I have twenty minutes to reach the station and get a train back to Paddington. I'll let them find me there. It'll be OK.' She smiled, but Emma didn't smile back and the lead in Maggie's stomach grew heavier.

'I don't want you to stay. I don't want you to be here when—' Emma stopped, carried the mug and glass to the dishwasher and binned the empty biscuit packet. 'You have to leave now, within the next five minutes, or it'll be too late.'

She opened the dishwasher and put the cups inside, turned the machine on even though it wasn't half full.

'I thought you said I had twenty?'

She came back with a damp cloth and a spray bottle, wiped the table clean.

'Emma? I thought you said I had twenty minutes?'

Her hands, Maggie saw, had the scabs of bleach burns.

'*Please,* go!'

Pinned to the fridge behind Emma was an old shopping list, the black ink sun-faded to blue.

And it was suddenly all too clear, all painfully transparent. An irrelevant list of household items. *Milk, bread, teabags,* all written in Nuala's handwriting. But it made Maggie realise why her stomach felt full of lead, why her mouth wouldn't smile, why Emma wouldn't meet her eye.

Why Maggie hadn't believed a word she'd said.

Maggie

Tuesday, 12th December, 2017

'Why did you have to come?' Emma twisted the cleaning cloth between her hands, wringing out the bleach.

'The suicide letters,' Maggie whispered.

'Why couldn't you just let me be?'

'You said Nuala wrote them, but she didn't.'

'Why do you have to try and drag me back there?' Emma clawed her fingers violently through her hair. 'Every time I try to escape, you pull me back.'

'*You* wrote them; they were all in your handwriting. And she was wearing your clothes.' Maggie looked at her open-mouthed, and Emma met her eye. Her face was no longer pale but flushed, her forehead gleaming with sweat.

'For God's sake, what have you done?'

Emma turned her back, stared into the garden, fingers manically picking the scabs on her knuckles. 'Nuala was wild, raving on about how I had no right to contact her husband, that I had no claim on him. She attacked me, I had to defend myself and then I . . . I—' Emma paced the room, blood dripping in thick rivulets from the picked scabs, her socked feet catching the wood like fur. 'I knocked her out; smashed the back of her head on the flagstones by the fire, just once, but it was hard enough. Afterwards I picked up her bag and her wallet fell out. I saw the money inside, her credit cards, debit cards, everything. I saw her keys and I thought, why not? Why don't I finally run? Why don't I finally, *finally,* try and have a *life*?'

'But why kill Lois? You didn't have to do that!'

'She told me!' Emma cried.

Maggie stopped, her jaw hanging loose, saliva flooding her mouth. 'Told you what?' she asked, but she knew.

'He was my brother Maggie! My *brother*! She sat there with his Polaroid in her hands and told me who he was, said that was why she was horrified that I was pregnant. She should have just told me the truth from the start!'

Backlit against the window Maggie could see it more clearly, the resemblance Emma shared with someone. It was a similarity to her brother, to James.

'I never—' she began, but Emma cut her off.

'You never told me! You knew and you never told me!'

'I didn't know, not until recently, not until—'

'Another lie, like all the rest. Another fucking lie! I thought I could trust you, Maggie, but all you did was deceive me.'

She stopped. Maggie could see her profile, the feverish gleam in her eyes, the sheen of sweat on her forehead. 'I couldn't let Lois get away with it.' Her fingers searched out the scabs on her hands again, and a drop of blood fell to the floor. 'I couldn't leave, knowing *she* was still there, still alive, still free to do whatever the fuck she wanted.'

Maggie looked out at the park, a distant shape of deer crossing the grass. She thought of Lois, trapped in her small, cold house, the house that was owned by the man who had raped her. Thought of Emma, doorstop in hand, raising it up and forcing it down, down, down, down until Lois's face was dripping with blood, flesh, hair, brain, bone fragments and spinal fluid.

But Emma couldn't do that.

She couldn't, she must be lying again.

Her head began to ache, her ears thrumming with Emma's soft voice.

'I drove Nuala's car out of the village and left it on the hill. I ran back to the pub, dressed Nuala in some of my clothes, scrubbed bleach into her hands and the pads of her fingertips, so they'd be just as damaged as mine, and dragged her body into your car. I got my gun, Elaine's gun. I wrote the letter for Nuala. I wrote another for Lois, backdated, saying that James was dead. Then I drove to Lois's house, told her I wanted to give her the photo of James from the pub, knowing it was the only way she would ever let me in. I sat Nuala beside Lois, once Lois was dead, and shot her in the face. I left by her back garden, ran over the fields until I reached the red car.'

Emma walked to the door and flicked a switch, killing the lights. The room turned grey, the white walls and bleached floor all reflecting the colour of the dull afternoon clouds outside.

'I've tried so hard to make this work.' Emma picked up the knife beside the kettle and balanced it on the butcher's block, point end to the wood, spinning the blade. 'I've done so much. I've cleaned this whole house, top to bottom. It was disgusting, it stank of rotting food, of filth.' She faced Maggie, her eyes almost black in the dim light. 'I've read all the paperwork I could find, learned about Nuala's background.'

'What are you going to do?' Maggie couldn't take her eyes off the knife. It collected what little light filtered through the window from the winter sun, the blade decorated with spots of bright silver.

'I *was* going to move away.' Emma set the knife down. 'Sell the house, empty her account, take the money and run. But then you came. And you ruined *everything*.' The blood from the scabs had left congealed ribbons on her skin. 'Again.'

Her hand went back to the knife, clutching the hilt in her fist.

'I won't tell anyone.' Maggie looked at the knife. Her chest felt tight, the shake in her hands had returned. 'I won't say a word.' Her mouth was filling with saliva and her stomach, far from feeling comforted by the biscuits, was churning the crumbs like a mixer.

Emma dipped her head to the side. 'I don't believe you.' A tear slid down her cheek. Her grip on the knife tightened but her hand, like Maggie's, had started to shake. 'You've ruined everything, just like Lois. Just like James.'

James. The name ran through Maggie, a last opportunity to save them both.

'Think of James,' she said. 'He wouldn't want you to do this, sweetheart.'

'James?' Emma's voice was small, reminding Maggie of the child that had bounced on Maggie's knee, who had wrapped her scrawny arms around her neck.

'You loved him—'

'Is *that* what you think?' Emma's flush deepened, pillar box red across her cheeks and brow. 'That I *loved* him?' She lifted the knife and slammed it down, the point spearing the butcher's block. 'He left me! He ran and left me alone!' And again, again, again, the knife splitting the wood, the blade bending.

'I've had time and distance to reflect, to understand what he did to me; leading me on, seducing me, it was all wrong. But it went deeper than just the physical. He was manipulative, controlling, made me question my own judgement so I would trust his completely. There are few worse things that you can do to a person than making them doubt their every little action. I used to worry if I was even breathing right, if my breath was too loud, too wet, too dry for James's approval. His twisted mind made me question my very ability to survive. And once that's gone, that survival instinct, there's nothing left. You have to build yourself up from scratch. The first feeling to return, once the numbness had gone, was anger. The anger helped me survive.' Emma rubbed the tears from her eyes before they had a chance to fall. She pushed her shoulders back and stood tall, regaining control.

'Did Daddy know, too? That James was his son, my brother?' Emma's face was crestfallen, making her look so young, so damaged, that Maggie's heart ached for her, despite the knife in Emma's hand.

Maggie nodded. 'Arthur knew.'

'Why did everyone know but *me?*' Rage filled Emma's voice, her cheeks flushing dark red. 'You all thought I was too weak to handle the truth, was that why nobody told me? That I was a sorry little girl pining for the man who abandoned her?'

'I didn't know until—' *the night that you died,* Maggie nearly said, but Emma cut her off. 'I'm not that weak!'

'Do you know what I'd have done if he'd come back? Why I had been searching for him online all these years? What I had planned to do if I ever saw him again?'

Flashes of Lois filled Maggie's vision, lumps of dead meat clinging to the fur on the cast-iron doorstop.

Emma lifted the knife and held it by her side, closing in on Maggie.

All ideas of calming Emma down, of easing the tension, vanished when Maggie saw the frenzied look in her goddaughter's eyes.

Maggie knew she had to get out.

She could run out into the garden, jump over the hedge, through the park.

On cue a shot of pain ran up from her calf to her hip, aching from the earlier run, threatening cramp.

'Do you really think I'm so pathetic?' Emma said, the light from the window softening her, her eyes returning to normal, blue irises and bloodshot whites, her skin spotted and sallow.

She sat at the table, her spine curved to a slouch, top lip pulled into her mouth and Maggie remembered her at home, leaning against the kitchen door, collecting empties from the bar.

'I never thought you were pathetic.' Maggie wanted to hold her hand, to touch her. 'I want to help you, please.' But the sight of the knife warned her away, telling her to run, run, run.

'You never helped me.' Emma rubbed a stray tear from her cheek with her sleeve, the knife still gripped in her fist. 'You just stand in my way, every time. And when I finally decided to leave, to start over, what did I discover? That you pissed all my money away, that you left me with *nothing*.'

Emma was on the wrong side of the table; maybe Maggie could run to the door, into the street before Emma could catch her up. She could flag down the police car, run back to the station.

Another shot of pain ran up her leg.

Maggie had to keep her talking, had to give herself time to think up a plan. Her head was foggy, stomach cramping against the sweetness of the biscuits, too many too fast.

'I tried to do the best for you, invest your money so it would grow. I didn't know the pub would fail.'

Emma looked down at her hands, scraping away the dried blood, licking her finger and wiping the scab clean. 'You put the pub before me, Maggie. You used my money to help yourself, not me.'

She turned her scabbed hand over on the table, palm up, her other hand bringing the knife down. The blade cut into her palm, thick, black blood rising up on her skin.

Maggie gasped, cramp shooting up through her thigh, into her buttock. She tried to flex her ankle under the table to clear the pain, but couldn't. She couldn't do anything but stare at Emma's hand, blood dribbling down her wrist.

'You didn't even ask me, just used your power as trustee to take it all, spend it on that fucking shit-hole pub, ruined my chances of paying for university, or for a deposit on a flat outside of that fucking village.' Emma cut herself again with the tip of the knife, pressing it in and flicking it upwards, a spray of blood scattering her jumper, a few drops landing on her chin. She didn't flinch.

'What are you doing?' Maggie's legs had stopped hurting, her left buttock tingling lightly. She could run, she should run, but she couldn't take her eyes off the knife.

'Defensive wounds,' Emma said, cutting one more time across the bulge of her thumb joint. 'The police have to think you attacked me.'

Maggie jolted, looked up at the girl with the knife in her hand but couldn't see a murderer, a desperate killer. Maggie could only see the Emma she knew, the girl who, as a four-year-old, had wrapped her arms around Maggie's shoulders and said, 'There, there, there,' as Maggie cried at the wake following Tom's funeral.

'You don't have to do this, Emma. You can let me go.' Maggie reached for her across the table, begging Emma to drop the knife and touch her. 'I won't tell anyone.'

Emma shook her head, her eyes filling with tears, the tears giving Maggie hope.

'I'll go, I'll go now and no one needs to know.' Maggie's head felt dizzy, eyes spotting with black, dancing shapes. 'Please, sweetheart. Please.'

Emma put the knife on the table, out of Maggie's reach. She balled her injured hand into a fist, a drop of blood squeezing out and landing on the blade.

'I don't want you to get into trouble. I'll leave, I won't tell anyone.'

Emma looked up at the clock on the wall, then sighed, shook her head, blinked. 'I never wanted to do this.' Another tear sprung from her right eye and she rubbed it away, smearing blood across her face. 'Not to *you*.'

'The police haven't turned up yet, it's not too late.' Maggie leant further forward, managed to tap the edge of the knife. It spun round, slid across the table and fell.

She braced herself to run, waiting for Emma to dart for the knife, waiting for the lapse in her attention to escape.

Emma didn't stir.

The knife lay, untouched, on the floor by her feet.

And Maggie couldn't move her legs.

'I didn't want to do this.' Emma turned her eyes to her godmother. 'But you made me.'

Maggie put her hands on the table and pushed against it, but she couldn't stand.

'What have you done?' She tried again, failed again, her throat and chest tight.

She dropped her arms to her sides, tried to massage life back into them but she couldn't feel a thing. 'What have you done?'

'It's too late.' Emma sat motionless. 'I couldn't let you drag me back. I couldn't let you ruin everything.'

The clouds split, the low sun sending shards of light into the room and into Maggie's face, her vision dancing with bright, flashing pricks of light. She couldn't lift her arms.

'What—' She tried again but stopped. She could feel her fingers, a light tingling in the tips, but couldn't move them. She rolled her shoulders in their sockets, tried to shake her arms to life but failed.

'It was in your tea, Maggie. Hemlock; I picked it from Nuala's garden and dried it, it was my fallback, my *just-in-case*. I left all my apple seeds at the pub.' Emma frowned, looked sympathetic. 'You're losing feeling in your limbs. Eventually, you'll become paralysed and go into respiratory failure, then cardiac arrest. It'll look just like a heart attack. Routine toxicology tests don't detect hemlock, they won't pick it up at autopsy unless they look for it specifically. And why would they?' Emma smiled, small, meek, shrugging her shoulders to the words. 'I was hoping it would happen on your way back to the station.' Her face buckled and her bottom lip trembled, her voice breaking as she said, 'I didn't want to watch.'

Jackdaws were cawing outside. Maggie's head began to throb in earnest, electric pulses of pain travelling along the back of her neck and down her spine. She tried to speak but her voice was lost, her throat tight, her lips silently mouthing her question.

'You're asking me why?' Emma leant over, grabbed the sleeve of her coat and hauled her dead arm onto the table, clasping Maggie's hand in her own. 'Because I had to. Because you would have told someone, you would have ruined everything and I had to get out, Maggie, I couldn't bear living in that place any longer.' She kissed Maggie's hand, rested her forehead on the thumb.

'At first I thought it was temporary, that I'd stay with you until I was old enough and then move on. But you didn't want me to. You trapped me, you chained me to the pub, kept me there with your self-pity and your dependence and I couldn't leave you.'

The cawing continued, the jackdaws casting shadows through the window.

Maggie mustered her strength and pulled her arm away, hearing the tap as Emma's bent head hit the table top. She pulled too hard, her strength erratic and uncontrollable, and fell sideways.

She heard the scrape of the chair sliding along the wood, but didn't feel it move.

She heard the smack of her cheekbone against the floor but didn't feel it crack.

'I'm going to wait for you to go into cardiac arrest. Then I'll call the police.' Emma sniffed and Maggie heard her stand up, pick up the knife from the floor. She heard the rustle of her clothes as she bent down, her vision filling with the dark cloth of her jeans, her white-socked feet, a drop of blood on the toe.

Maggie was aware of something being placed in her hand. The knife.

'I'm going to tell them you attacked me. That you tried to strangle me but I broke free, that I ran to the kitchen and you followed, you grabbed a knife, tried to stab me but then you fell, clutching your chest.'

Maggie could still breathe. She could still move her eyes, her tongue wasn't yet lifeless in her mouth. There was still time.

'I just couldn't let you ruin everything, not again.'

Maggie closed her eyes and arched her neck. She clenched her teeth and let bubbles of spit slide from her mouth. She could move her back a little, so she writhed on the floor as much as she could, a gurgle escaping her lips.

Emma would call the police. They would come and Maggie could tell them what she'd done, they could save her.

She concentrated on trying to move her limbs, not on the sound of Emma picking up the phone and screaming into it. She couldn't move her legs but she could slide her arms along the floor.

She dropped the knife and tried to push it away, but she couldn't focus her eyes.

She could hear Emma, crying and shouting, begging for help on the phone.

She heard the click of the receiver.

And now Emma's hands were on her, pulling their faces close as Emma knelt beside her. Emma's hands wound their way around Maggie's neck, hugging her tightly, the side of their faces pressed together.

'I'm sorry,' she whispered, 'so sorry.' Her voice in her ear. 'Please understand.'

Emma's tears turned into cries of grief, the sound genuine, tormented with loss. She hugged Maggie tighter, as though saying goodbye, the tears stopping her from saying any more.

A siren called in the distance.

Emma struggled to her feet and stumbled to the other side of the room, slid to the floor against the window, back to the glass, arms wrapped around her shins. She was still crying, still screaming, her bloody hands clawing her knees.

Maggie stopped struggling, lay still. She let her hands fall open, her feet fall away from each other. Her head dropped to the side, mouth open, eyes closed.

Noise, so much noise.

Jackdaws cawing to the wind.

Emma screaming, sobbing, screaming.

The siren, drawing closer.

Feet pounding the wooden boards, vibrations running along the floor and rocking Maggie's skull.

Her eyes opened to a slit.

A blur of dark uniform neared Emma. Her cries increased, sobs turning to wails. The uniform tried to lift her, but she couldn't stand.

Maggie longed to raise her up from the floor, hold her, tell her it would all be OK; they could go home and it could all be forgotten.

A stab of pain at the thought of home. The place Emma had tried to escape, the place that had imprisoned her. Home, for Emma, had meant the village she was trapped in, the pub she was chained to. It meant Maggie.

'*I understand,*' Emma had said to her once, when Maggie was drunk and talking about Lee.

Maggie had held on to Emma because everyone else had

left; Maggie had pushed them all away. She held on to Emma because she loved her, because she couldn't bear to be without her.

'The village has everything you need, there's no better place, no better people.' How many times had Maggie told her that lie? She had trapped her in the place that had caused her nightmares, when she should have been the one to set her free.

More sirens and more feet, their pace like thunder travelling through the floor.

Hands grasped her shoulders.

The pain spread to her jaw.

She wanted Emma to come to her, but she was still huddled on the floor, head buried in her knees, tears torrential.

'Madam, can you hear me?' Two hands, shaking her to life. 'Can you tell me your name?'

All she needed was to utter *hemlock*. One word to save her life. She parted her lips to speak but stopped.

She couldn't do it.

Terror gripped her chest and though she couldn't move her body she could still move her head, just. Her eyes opened in a final moment of life-preserving panic and she saw Emma, finally standing, her face tear-streaked.

Their eyes met, and her panic wilted.

She pictured the life Emma would have if Maggie resisted, if she uttered that simple word that would save her own life. Prison, courtrooms and chains. She pictured an alternate life, a life if she just let go, a life of Tiffany lamps and Duchy Originals. She thought of the letter she had left at home for the police, about Arthur and all he had done, relieved that at least he wouldn't be getting away with it any longer.

She wanted to smile at her but couldn't, the poison now nearing its end.

Her chest lurched and the muscles went into spasm, forcing her body to arch. Her head jerked back and she lost Emma's gaze.

Foreign hands were holding Maggie's shoulders, unfamiliar voices calling to her. Life, once more, begging her to reconsider.

She tried to see Emma, but she had lost control of her body, she couldn't turn her face.

She thought of Emma's future, without Maggie but happy, maybe marriage, children, choice.

'I understand.'

Maggie couldn't close her eyelids, couldn't shut her eyes. The room went black, fell silent.

She thought of her son, whom she'd failed but had never stopped loving, thought maybe now she could see him, watch over him, from somewhere above. She pictured Tom, her husband, whose death she had never recovered from, his eyes clear at last, their colour bright, beautiful.

Her eyes finally closed.

She let Emma go.

6 months later

The sea outside her window was blue. Not the grey glitter of the Bristol Channel but a deep, dark blue, almost navy. By tonight she would be seeing it from a different angle again, not from the porthole of a ferry cabin, but from the opposite side of the Irish Sea. And from there, who knows? She was finally running away, a clean break.

The oval mirror in front of her, hanging over the desk, had been covered with a pillowcase from the bed. So, too, had she covered the one in the small en-suite bathroom, though with a towel, not a pillowcase. Anything to save her from her own image, her own face, every feature she shared with her father.

Every feature she shared with her half-brother, too.

With James Lunglow.

Another lie, another secret kept from her by Lois, by her father, by—

She closed her eyes, rubbed the bridge of her nose, took a deep breath, forced composure.

She couldn't think of Maggie now, of the life fading from her eyes, face paling, the paramedic's muscles tense as he prepared to give CPR, as he tried and failed to save Maggie's life.

She needed to keep steady. She didn't want to make a mistake at this late stage.

The floor rumbled beneath her feet. The chair she was sitting on tilted, ever so slightly, to the side. A tannoy rang out and the voice of the captain came through, as if the walls, the very ceiling, were speaking to her. They would be leaving very soon.

The sea was calm.

The crossing should be smooth.

The captain wished her a pleasant journey.

It was now or never; by the end of the day she'd be in another country, using another passport in another name. She was going to disappear.

The house had been sold, as much money taken out in cash and added to the pre-paid card as she could without raising suspicion. It was more than enough and the accountant hadn't yet carried out his annual review, wouldn't do so for another month yet. She had a little more time before anyone got too suspicious, started asking where she was, where she'd gone to.

She would set up another account, in her new name, once she found a place she liked, a place she could settle down in. A place that didn't remind her of her father, of Maggie, lying dead on the floor, of her half-brother and all the things he had done to her, all the unspeakable things she had done with him in that barn when she was fourteen years old.

If she'd known, if someone had just told her, she wouldn't be in this position now. Wouldn't have to run, hide, squirrel money away onto a plastic card she was petrified of losing, so petrified she kept it on her at all times, inside her bra next to her skin, the plastic smelling sour from constant contact.

She had got away with it. She had the money, she had her revenge, she had freedom.

But those with a conscience would never be free. Emma would never be free. No mirror ever let her forget what she had done, the sight of every old woman, every head of grey hair, every scar no matter where on the body it was, screamed her sins, her mistakes.

Every penny she spent was blood money, every dream she endured was a terror, every dog on the street a reminder of the cast-iron doorstop, blood streaked on the etched-on fur, a reminder of the bloody flesh, hair, skull of the woman she had beaten to death, the woman who had been raped by Emma's father, her own father.

The baby Lois bore had been Arthur's son.

The man Emma had first fucked had been her half-brother.

Good God, she would never forget it.

Her own brother.

And not just the things she had done with him, her first carnal pleasures revealed as incestuous violations, but the things he had said to her, the things she had come to believe. 'You're such an idiot,' said with a sweetness that confounded her, made her question and re-examine herself. 'Stupid whore,' spat with a venom that made her think it true. No fourteen-year-old girl was a whore, she knew that *now*, she only wished she could make her younger self recognise the truth, too.

If Emma had known who he really was, then none of this would have happened. Maggie would be alive, and so would Elaine. Emma's conscience would be clear. Why hadn't someone just told her the truth?

But it wasn't Lois's fault, Emma knew that. Nor was it Maggie's or Nuala's, it wasn't even entirely James's. To a certain, lesser degree, Emma could argue it wasn't her fault, either. The original sin lay with Arthur, his crimes tainting his victims, creating his twisted son.

The worst part was, he had got away with it scot free.

The tannoy called out again, a blast of the horn announcing their departure. They were leaving, the land creeping away, unseen from where Emma was holed in the bowels of the ship. Her porthole only looked seaward, to the future, her eyes trained on the horizon, waiting for the land that would become her new home and not the coast she was running away from, or the man who still lived there.

Her hands were shaking. They were always shaking.

She knew, though, if the time ever came, if she ever saw him again, the tremble in her hands would subside. She knew her fingers, her hands, would be steady. She would be strong enough to make him pay.

She had got away with her crimes, in the eyes of the law.

But, goddamn it, so had he.

She wouldn't let him get away with it forever. One day, she'd return. One day, her eyes would be fixed back on him.

Acknowledgements

Many people have helped me transform from the nervous woman with seemingly impossible aspirations into the writer I am today.

Kate Burke, my superstar agent at Diane Bank Associates: thank you for lifting me out of the slush pile. Thank you for your advice, your help, your infinite patience and for all the pancakes at Bill's.

Diane Banks: you are a force of nature and I would be lost without you. Thank you for always being at the end of the phone or computer and for your sterling wisdom and advice.

Chloe Seager: thank you for all your help behind the scenes, and making me laugh out loud with your own incredible book.

I have counted my lucky stars ever since signing with Hodder & Stoughton; the whole team have made me feel so welcome and I still have to pinch myself to believe this has really happened.

Emily Kitchin, my incredible editor: you have made this novel better than I ever dreamed it could be. You've taught me so much and your insight is second to none. You really are bloody awesome.

Simon Hall, my mentor and my dear friend: how can I

ever thank you enough? Thank you for your kindness and your help and your unwavering friendship. I hope I've made you proud. I wouldn't be here without you.

Hazel Prior: we've been on this journey together and you've always had my back, I hope to always have yours in return. Where would I be without your emails, coffee and cake?

To Judith Heneghan and all those at the Winchester Writers' Festival: you set me on the right path, taught me many valuable lessons and helped me overcome my nerves around public speaking. It was in the halls and classrooms at Winchester that I found my writer's voice. Thank you.

I'm lucky to live in the technological age of Twitter, Facebook, Instagram and blogs. Who would have thought such genuine support and goodwill could exist through social media? So, thank you to all the book bloggers for reading, sharing and reviewing. Thank you to the network of writers I have met online; Helen Cox in particular; you've provided amazing support and advice in so many areas of life!

Thank you to those kind souls who gave up their time to help in the research of this novel. All mistakes are most definitely my own.

Kevin Chilton: your expertise in crime and policing is invaluable. You gave so much of your time and your experience, and this book is a far better one because of it. Thank you.

Leanne Godwin at Avon and Somerset Police: thank you for guiding me through the emotional world of family liaison. I have a new-found respect for all you guys do as a result.

My very kind local fireman, R.W: thank you for helping me with the fire scenes and explaining the technicalities so well.

My friend and fellow Take Thatter, Rebecca Knaresborough: thank you for sharing your experience of growing up in a pub, for reading early versions of the book and for generally being ace.

My family, whose support and understanding I am so lucky to have. Dad: you have inspired me, spurred me on, believed in me and said those magic few words, four years ago: 'Why don't you start writing again?' And I did. Thank you, so much.

I am supremely lucky in that I have two mothers. Sarah: thank you for all your advice, your help and your answers to my most peculiar of medical questions. Whereas your expertise in pathology is incredibly useful, it's your love and encouragement I couldn't do without.

And Mum: you were my very first reader and remain my most trusted reader today. Your enthusiasm for the story and my writing made me really believe I could do it.

Alex, Hannah and Alice: the best siblings one could hope for.

To all my friends and cheerleaders. Special thanks to Elie Sharratt, Lauren Cable, Nicola Harrop, Heidi West-Newman, Clare Thomas, Rebecca Fothergill and Sasha Lithgow: thank you for the boozy evenings, the millions of cups of coffee, and the patience and forgiveness you have all shown when I have forgotten to reply to messages, answer phone calls or have failed to be in any way sociable, because I was writing. I will get better, I promise.

And to Ian Jones: my very favourite grammarian, my proofreader beyond all compare, my extraordinary master of language. Thank you for your encouragement, your pride, your pedantry and making me fully appreciate that the world really is our oystery lobster. Here's to many more adventures.

Most importantly, thank you to my children, Aoife and Ruadhán. It is not easy being the child of a writer, but you two put up with it remarkably well. I may not have taken you to Disneyland yet or spent as many hours as we would have liked romping about on the hills, but hopefully, I've taught you that you can make your dreams come true if you strive, strive, strive and believe. This has all been for you, kiddoes.

Lastly, thank you to the makers of Haribo Golden Bears and Lavazza Qualita Rossa: there is no way I would have gotten through those late-night writing sessions without your wares.

And to you, reader, whoever you may be. I hope you've enjoyed reading and thank you for picking this book up and giving it, and me, a chance.